Black Sand and Gold

By ELLA LUNG MARTINSEN

"Gold! Gold in the Klondike!"

This electrifying news broke in the depression winter of 1896. It set off one of the most fabulous, exciting, and romantic quests the world has ever known—the epic Gold Rush through the frozen wilderness of Alaska into Yukon Territory.

Ed Lung, the author's father, was in the vanguard of that mighty stampede for the precious yellow metal. The on-the-spot diary of this young accountant from Tacoma, Washington, is the basis for the unique freshness and authenticity of this Gold-Rush saga.

All the wild, ruthless passions of Gold-Rush days come alive against the bleak, rugged background of the Klondike. Here are the heartbreak, the joy, and above all the greed for riches that drove men to their death on the treacherous ice—or led them to enormous wealth. And here is the lonely misery of the prospectors, the debauchery of the boom towns, the hunger, the fierce cold.

In *Black Sand and Gold,* you too will search out the secret gold hoards of the savage Tanana Indians . . . visit the once-lawless Skagway that was ruled by the dreaded "Soapy" Smith and his gang . . . meet Joaquin Miller, the famous Gold-Rush reporter and poet. And throughout you will find only real-life characters in all their picturesque individuality.

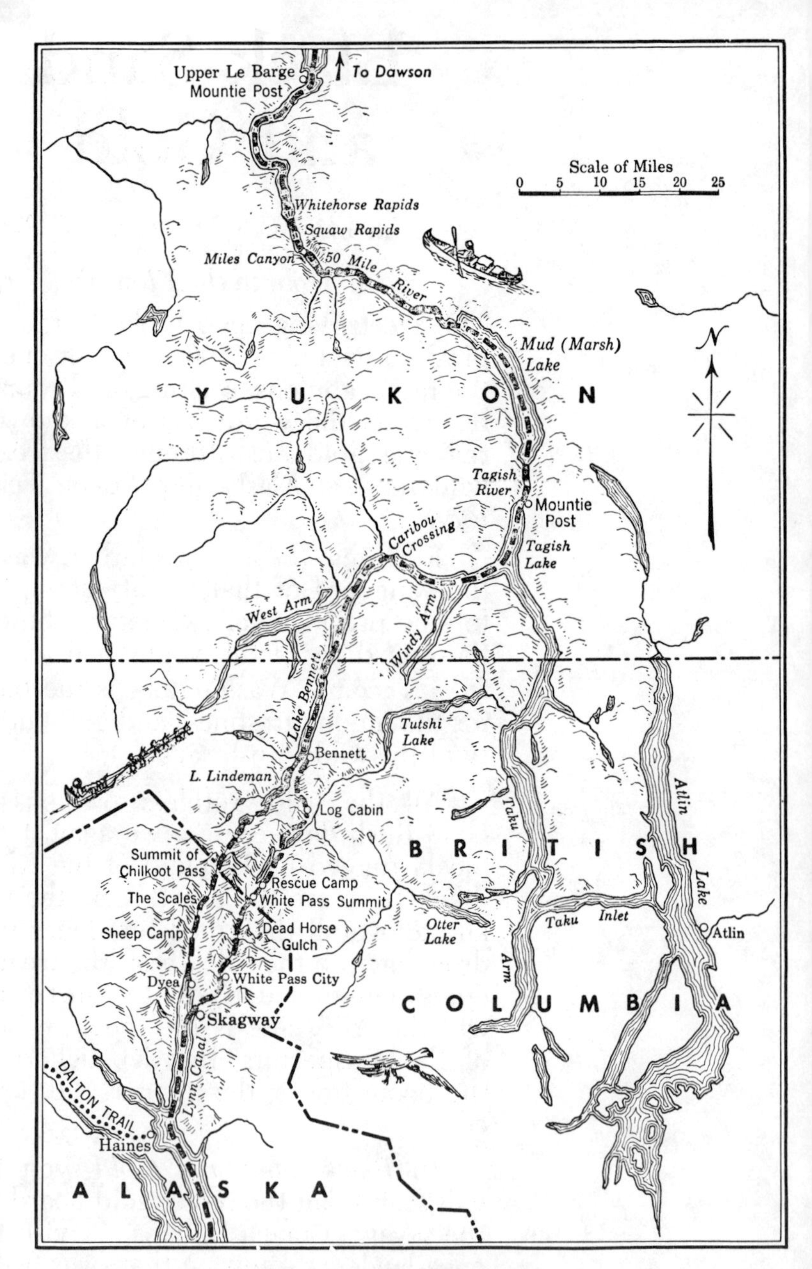

ROUTE TO DAWSON

Black Sand and Gold

TRUE ALASKA-YUKON GOLD-RUSH STORY

by

ELLA LUNG MARTINSEN

as told by her father

EDWARD B. LUNG

Binford & Mort

Thomas Binford, Publisher

2536 S.E. Eleventh • Portland, Oregon 97202

Black Sand and Gold

ISBN 0-8323-0188-4 (clothbound)
ISBN 0-8323-0189-2 (paperbound)

LIBRARY OF CONGRESS CATALOG CARD NUMBER: 56-6862

Printed in the United States of America
FOURTH EDITION 1974
SECOND PRINTING 1978

Velma D. Lung with son Clement (Clemy) and Edward B. Lung, taken in Tacoma, Washington, shortly before Gold Rush

Dedication and In Memoriam

To

Velma D. Lung, my beloved mother, and to Clement Augustus Lung, my brother, and to Joaquin Miller, gold-rush reporter, friend of my father.

And now, I rededicate my writing of this story to my beloved and intrepid father, Edward Burchall Lung, who has "mushed on" to a brighter, fairer world, somewhere near the north star. He died the 30th of January, 1956, before this book was published in a first edition.

*Chilkoot Pass**

And you, too, banged at the Chilkoot,
That rock-locked gate to the golden door!
These thunder-built steeps have words built to suit,
And whether you prayed or whether you swore
'Twere one where it seemed that an oath was a prayer—
Seemed God couldn't care,
Seemed God wasn't there!

And you, too, climbed to the Klondike
And talked as a friend, to those five-horned stars!
With mukluk shoon and with talspike
You, too, bared head to the bars,
The heaven-built bars where morning is born,
And drank with maiden morn
From Klondike's golden horn!

JOAQUIN MILLER

* This poem is used with the gracious permission of Juanita Joaquina Miller, daughter of its author.

Foreword

Perhaps I should mention here that Bob Henderson, a Canadian, is given credit by some for the discovery of gold in the Klondike—rather than George Carmack, the accepted discoverer.

The truth seems to be that George Carmack, with his Indian companions, encountered Henderson in a wilderness part of the country, in a range of mountains not far from the Klondike River. Henderson advised Carmack to go into the Klondike region and look for gold, believing it could be found there. George Carmack followed his friend's advice and struck gold on the Bonanza.

When my father met Bob Henderson in Dawson in 1897, Bob told my father that he felt he should have been given credit for the discovery of gold. He was almost broke, thoroughly disheartened, and had nothing to show for his years of exploration. My dad tried to console Henderson, but the Canadian was bitter. Later, Henderson left the Klondike for Ottawa where he was pensioned by the Canadian Government for his part in the discovery.

A word should be said here about the use of the term, "Klondike." It originated during the stampedes. Klondike is the name for the Klondike River region around Dawson, and on back into the Gold Fields.

A Cheechako is a newcomer to the North (less than a year).

A Sourdough is a seasoned miner who has lived at least a year in the North.

E. L. M.

P.S. If the reader, at times, encounters slight repetitions, it is because *Black Sand and Gold* was first published in serial form.

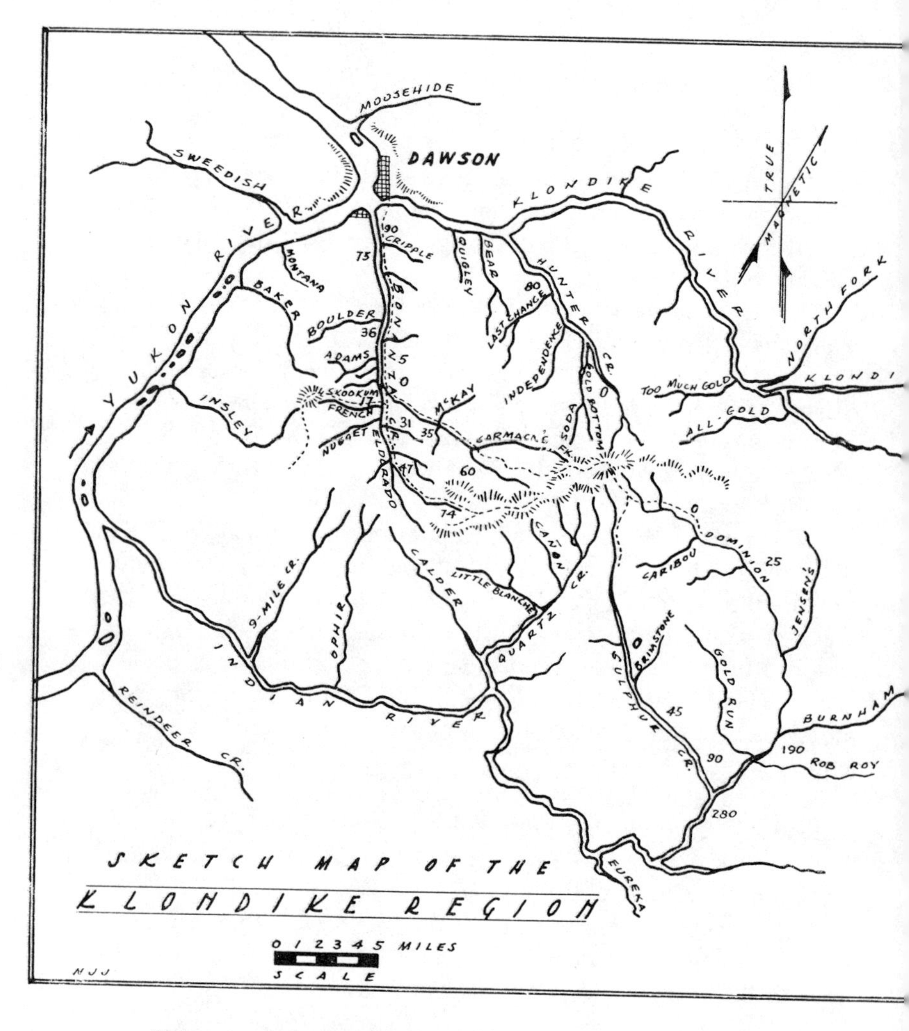

This map of the Klondike shows the various hills and creeks which produced $100,000,000 between 1898 and 1905, within a fifteen-mile radius. By the spring of 1899, all the creeks of any importance in the Klondike area had been staked.

Preface

I believe that as the years roll by, the dramatic, true stories of the fabulous Gold Rush to the Klondike and Alaska will become more and more valuable. Many years have passed since 1897 when the first cry of "Gold in the Klondike" was echoed around the world.

In the last three or four decades many fictional stories of the stampedes have been published. Also, through the years, some exciting, true gold-rush stories have been recorded, but most of them have been told verbally. With the passing of the years and the death of the narrators, many of their stories have been lost to posterity forever.

To me it seems sad that this material, of such historic value should die. Every Sourdough who headed North with pick and shovel, going into that rugged, frozen Land of Gold, was making history . . . leaving his imprint with the others in a collective way on the sands of time.

I have marveled, as I've studied my father's diaries of 1897 and '98, that he had the tenacity and stamina to keep them up so religiously from day to day during those trying, hazardous times—often on the trail while facing unbelievable hardships, often when his fingers were so cold he could scarcely hold a pencil. Perhaps he had a faint idea he was recording events which would some day be more precious than the gold he sought.

While he was in the North it was his good fortune to have met many famous and well-known people like Joaquin Miller, gold-rush reporter; Livernash, also a reporter who later became a Congressman; William Ogilvie, surveyor of the Canadian-American line, and others.

It has been brought to my attention that many old Sourdoughs, as they reminisce, argue and contradict each other on certain points. This has been confusing and often puzzling. For example, not long ago two Sourdoughs were talking about the Chilkoot Pass in 1898. One old-timer declared vehemently that there were scrub trees growing at timberline near the mountain trail, which could be used for firewood. The other Sourdough fiercely declared that when he went north, there wasn't a stick of wood to be had within miles! Come to find out, they were both right. In the spring of 1898 thousands of stampeders, swarming over the Pass like locusts, were able, in only a few short months, to cut down sparsely wooded areas for miles in order to build shelters and fires to warm themselves and cook their meals.

Naturally, this story is very close to my heart. I am proud I was born in a little log cabin on Dominion Creek, fifty miles from Dawson. As long as I can remember I have heard gold-rush stories from my father and mother. Somehow, I feel a great part of the gold-rush era.

Years ago my beloved mother began writing her memoirs of the north. Shortly before she died, in 1948, she begged me to write my father's 1897 and '98 story of the gold rush (before she went North). She said, "Ella, it is up to you. Please do this, as you know your father is unable to write, owing to the severe stroke he has so recently suffered."

Mr. Emery F. Tobin, the editor of The Alaska Sportsman Magazine, until 1958, published each chapter of the story as it was finished—beginning in February, 1951 and ending in June, 1954. Perhaps Mr. Tobin's keen interest stemmed from the fact that his father also went North during the big stampedes of 1898 to Wiseman in the Koyukuk-River-country, Alaska Territory.

So then in my acknowledgments, first of all, I gratefully thank the former editor, Emery F. Tobin and his associate editor, Ethel Dassow. Also, I wish to thank Mr. John Dines, former Mining Recorder of Dawson (now of Ottawa) for his expert advice, and then, too, Tom Hebert, wonderful old sourdough, Northwest Mounted Policeman and guide in present-day Dawson. Also, I wish to acknowledge the late Mary Vogel of Tacoma, Washington, good friend of the family, early resident of Dawson, for the help she gave me.

In Santa Barbara, I wish to acknowledge the late Allen Rogers, who provided me with some rare old documents left by his father, Eugene Rogers. He was one of the first merchants to go down the Yukon to Dawson with a barge-load of potatoes for hungry Dawson in the spring of 1898.

Grateful acknowledgments are due the late Archie McLean Hawks, chief engineer of the Chilkoot Pass Tramway Company, for his devoted interest and help while I was writing this story.

Acknowledgments are also due The Strollers Club of Santa Barbara, of which I am a member. This group of artistic people was the first to hear these gold-rush stories and offer enthusiastic encouragement.

In Seattle, I wish to thank my friend, Miss Lulu Fairbanks, former editor of the Alaska Weekly for her valuable help; and then, too, The International Sourdough Club of which I am a member. Also, I owe a big acknowledgment to the late Nathan Kresge, old sourdough and co-discoverer of Gold Hill.

I give acknowledgments for old photographs to the University of Alaska, Fairbanks; to the University of Washington Library, Seattle; to the State Historical Society of Tacoma, Washington; and to the Fleischmann Library, Museum of Natural History, Santa Barbara.

And I give loving acknowledgment to my sister, Helen Laurent, for her keen interest and faithful help, and to my husband, Perry Martinsen, whose own father, Ole Martinsen, went North with others from Santa Barbara in the great rush of '98. As a little boy, my husband went down to the dock to see his father off and still remembers the tremendous excitement.

For her encouragement and interest, I also give special acknowledgments to Juanita Miller, daughter of Joaquin Miller, who still lives at "The Heights" in Oakland, her famous father's estate where he wrote so much about the Northwest frontier and Yukon Territory.

And now, last but not least, I give heartfelt acknowledgments to the Yukon's most famous and beloved poet, the late Robert W. Service for his many letters of encouragement, urging me to complete this story while I was writing it in serial-form for The Alaska Sportsman Magazine. In one of his letters to me, he commented: "The story is vivid and spirited—one of the best descriptions of the Trail that I have come across." In another letter: "Mrs. Martinsen, you may use my photograph and poem, 'Goodbye Little Cabin' in your second book."

And one more comment before closing this preface. Apparently, in 1897 there was another man in the Klondike by the name of "Lung." Edward Burchall Lung, my father, was not the man referred to in "Klondike Diary," a small, privately published edition by Robert B. Medill.

Mr. Medill and his brother surely were among the lucky ones who had enough food to remain in the Klondike during that tragic fall and winter of 1897.

My father was without provisions, as the trading companies were closed and so he found it necessary to flee from the Klondike in September of that year with a party of seven men along with hundreds of others to escape the frightening food famine. With them was Joaquin Miller, the famous poet and gold-rush reporter, sent in to Dawson by William Randolph Hearst, owner-publisher of the San Francisco Examiner. These men got as far down the Yukon as Circle City where they became frozen in for the winter.

Black Sand and Gold is a historical, documented account, a true eye-witness story based on my father's vivid recollections and wonderful diaries of 1897 and '98, and other rare records. Actually, this story could have been called, "Alaska-Klondike Gold-Rush Diary."

Contents

List of Illustrations

Chapter I

The North Star

It was in early winter of 1896 that the first cry of "Gold! Gold in the Klondike!" reached Tacoma, Washington. By the spring of '97 the exciting news had increased in tempo and volume and reached a high fever pitch when the newsboys shouted: "A shipload of gold bound for the States! A shipload of gold bound for the States!"

Men stopped their work and rushed to the streets, bought papers, gathered in groups and talked eagerly of going North. It seemed only natural that I, too, should be caught up in that tremendous gold fever. Great excitement reigned. Neighbors and friends left hurriedly for the North.

And so, on that momentous day of May 24th, 1897, I left Tacoma with a lively, hopeful group of men. Our boat was the S. S. *Mexico* and she was loaded almost to capacity with men, animals and supplies.

It was early morning when the *Mexico* pulled away from the docks of Tacoma. Crowds of relatives and friends were there to see us off and wish us luck. As our boat steamed away, it was with a lump in my throat and tears concealed in my eyes that I waved a long farewell to my wife and my little son, Clemy.

Our boat got under way and we traveled along Puget Sound, past Brown's Point and Vashon Island. When I saw familiar scenery disappearing, my heart had a sinking feeling as I realized more forcibly that I was leaving my beloved home and family and going to the far North, where I would be almost cut off from civilization.

I wasn't the only man who felt that way, for there was a seriousness and quietness among the men for a while. However, it was a bright spring day and soon we were singing, laughing and talking jovially, swapping tales of glittering gold-rush stories which we had heard of the fabulous gold strikes along the Bonanza and Eldorado rivers of the Klondike. Yes, each one of us was on his way to make a fortune! But most of us were city bred and ill prepared for the grueling hardships which we so lightheartedly faced as our boat plowed its way merrily along through Puget Sound, drawing us toward the ordeal which would test the strength and spirit of each one of us.

At Seattle we stopped just long enough to pick up more passengers and baggage; then, with shouts of *"Bon Voyage!"* ringing in our ears, we left the docks of Seattle and continued on up Puget Sound. The scenery along the Sound was a wonderful beginning to our trip of high adventure.

The next day we reached Vancouver Island and made a short stop at Victoria, B.C., where they loaded cattle on our already overcrowded boat. Then we continued our trip on up the Inside Passage. We passed high mountains and misty waterfalls which cascaded over jagged cliffs; saw green forests stretching high on the mountain slopes and reaching down to the water's edge. There were dozens of tiny, wooded islands which seemed to float on the blue-green waters. All these added enchantment to the scene. In the distance, Mount Baker stood out clearly against the azure sky and glistened white in the sun.

Farther up the Inside Passage, our boat passed close to shining glaciers and beckoning fjords which fingered their way between high mountains to the inland sea. Each fjord was an alluring waterway pointing to a mysterious, unknown country of adventure.

In my stateroom, that first night, I opened my diary to write and found this parting message from my wife, already written in my little red book: "It seems, precious dear, we are to be parted for a time, so we may know Him better. Let the Peace of God, which passeth all understanding, keep our hearts and minds through Jesus Christ—Velma."

That night I didn't join the men for a while. I wrote a long letter to post at our next stop. Then I went out on deck and looked for the Big Dipper and the North Star, for I had promised to watch for that star every night and think of home.

A few days later, we docked at Juneau, the capital of Alaska Territory. It gave us an opportunity to complete our outfits, and I bought a whipsaw to take into the Klondike. Several hours later, we changed boats to the *Rustler*, a narrow, unseaworthy-looking vessel which was much smaller than the *Mexico*. It was loaded to the guards; so crowded that men had to sleep on boxes, tables, supplies and all over the decks. However, none of us expected to sleep much that night, anyway. All evening we had been hilariously singing, making patriotic speeches, celebrating the favorable Spanish-American-War news which we had just heard at Juneau.

Suddenly, about midnight, a terrific wind and rainstorm swept down Lynn Canal. The *Rustler* shuddered under the impact of the waves, pitched and rolled dangerously, then began to ship water.

The captain called frantically for all men to help bail, as the pumps weren't adequate against the onrushing storm. We grabbed buckets and pails, working like mad from the hold up, bailing as fast as we could and passing the buckets along the line from man to man to be emptied at the top into the sea. Like galley slaves we worked.

The storm increased in fury. The waves dashed higher. Great torrents of rain and sea water poured over our boat. In alarm, the captain called, "Bail faster! It's our only hope of staying afloat!"

Wet to the skin, standing in water knee-deep in the hold, we bailed for our very lives! After many hours, toward morning the storm subsided. However, we faced a dismal scene on board. Almost everything we owned was soggy and wet. Needless to say, we were cold and discouraged as we steamed our way up the narrowing passage of Lynn Canal.

Although it had been a terrible night, now the weather was clearing. Our immediate destination was the Dyea Indian village at the head of Lynn Canal. Soon, we would be there . . . a thousand miles from Tacoma!

As it grew lighter, all of us watched the coast line. The storm clouds gradually parted and we gazed in wonder and awe at the splendor of breath-taking, snow-capped mountains which rose majestically on every side.

All at once, we saw the Indian village directly ahead of us. Dyea was huddled in the inlet with high mountains in the background. It appeared to be made up of huts and tents, built almost to the water's edge. Figures of Indians moved about the beach, busy with their tasks. A river flowed from the mountains, emptying into Lynn Canal and dividing the beach in half.

Now our eyes took in the entire scene. Again we turned our gaze up to the mountains. We wondered which was the high and treacherous pass known as Chilkoot. We shivered when we looked at those giant mountains, for we knew we would have to transport our outfits across this part of the coast range in order to get into the Klondike.

It was said that, before the stampede of '97, Chilkoot Pass was an old Indian trail, almost unknown to white men. It was used by the Chilkat and Chilkoot Indians to reach the interior. For many years, the Indians had toiled over these mountains, carrying blubber, wild-goat skins, blankets, baskets and other things to trade with the Tagish and "Stick" Indians. This route was known as the "High Grease Trail."

The Taiya Indians (called "Dyea" by white man) had many superstitions about Chilkoot. They always watched the summit for signs of a peculiar, mist-like cloud. If it appeared, and the wind was blowing a certain way, the Indians would not venture to the top under any circumstances, for fear of sudden blizzards and terrifying avalanches. No one knew how many human sacrifices Chilkoot had already taken.

Our boat headed toward shallow water and a scow came out to meet us to take us ashore. Our supplies were unceremoniously dumped onto the oozing beach amid the confusion of hundreds of other boxes of cargo. We jumped ashore and there was a mad scramble to grab our supplies and be on our way.

Other boats had landed ahead of us, and more were arriving. In the wild confusion, all consideration and manners seemed to have vanished. Already, the gold craze was affecting the behavior of the stampeders. No doubt, we must have looked like a wild-eyed, disheveled invasion to the Indians.

On the boat I had met Bill Stacey, an ex-policeman from Tacoma. He was a tall, husky man, and I judged him to be in his early thirties, perhaps three or four years my senior. We seemed to hit it off pretty well together, so decided to travel into the Klondike as partners. We made camp on the white man's side of the river, spread out our water-soaked things to dry and took inventory of our supplies. To my consternation, I discovered that my slab of bacon and butter had become rancid en route from Tacoma. They had been stored too near the boiler!

Toward evening, Stacey and I crossed the river and walked over to the Indian village. We had noticed a large, hand-carved, brightly painted dugout canoe pulled high on the beach near by. We decided to find its owner to see if we could get transportation and a guide to take us up the river through the canyon to the foot of Chilkoot.

The Indians were having some kind of powwow. They paid little attention to us. When they did, the looks we received were anything but friendly. Undaunted, we kept asking, "Who is the owner of that big canoe?" But they shook their heads and glared at us. Some of them looked very fierce with their grotesque headdresses carved in wood depicting weird faces of animals and birds.

"Say, Ed, what do you think's wrong with those Indians?" asked Stacey. "Seems they don't like us. At Juneau we were told they were friendly."

"I can't make it out," I said. "We'd better go easy. I've heard these Indians are a very proud people. At one time, they were terribly savage and very warlike and made slaves of their captives."

"Maybe we'd better be going!" said Stacey.

Suddenly, we saw several Indian girls. Their faces were smeared in streaks with horrible black paint. They looked hideous! Several eyed us from a distance. Finally, one especially ugly girl walked by. I stopped her and inquired about the canoe. She seemed quite agitated and answered me in broken English: "Go away! Indian girl can't talk to white man."

Looking closer, I discovered that the girl wasn't really ugly. It was only the black paint which made her appear so. The Indian girl hurried away, then stopped, turned and came back.

"Canoe belong to my brother—Indian Joe Whiskers,"

she said in a low tone. "Maybe he come help you." Then she was gone.

"That's the last we'll ever see of her," said Stacey in disgust.

"Let's wait here, anyway," I said.

To our surprise, the girl returned with her brother, a tall, powerfully built young man.

"This, my brother, Indian Joe Whiskers," she said.

"Yes, me Indian Joe Whiskers," proudly echoed the Indian.

Stacey and I jumped to our feet from the fallen log on which we had been resting and acknowledged the introduction.

"Indian Joe," I said, "we are very pleased to make your acquaintance. My partner and I like your fine, big canoe. Did you make it?"

"Me make!" answered the Indian proudly.

"Then," I said, "my partner and I will pay you well if you will take us and our outfits up the river through the canyon tomorrow morning."

For answer, Indian Joe shook his head. He stood with great dignity, his arms folded across his powerful chest, his piercing black eyes surveying us. There was a long, deep silence. Then, he spoke. "White man's money not good. Indian don't like!"

While he was speaking, I noticed his eyes fastened on my watch chain, from which dangled my elk's-tooth watch fob tipped with gold. Suddenly, I got an idea. Quickly, I unclasped the elk's tooth, stepped forward and held it out to him.

The Indian made no move to accept, his haughty expression remained fixed, but I saw a flash of interest in his dark eyes.

I took several steps closer, holding out the elk's tooth, and said, "Take this, Indian Joe Whiskers, as a special gift from me. This tooth came from the elk which roam the plains far to the south in our great country."

There was another silence, then slowly the Indian unfolded his arms, stepped forward and with grave dignity accepted the watch fob. I could see real pleasure in his black eyes as he tightly clasped the elk's tooth in his brown hand. Then, he spoke: "Indian Joe likes gift. Will take white man up river in canoe tomorrow. But now, white man must go!"

Before I could answer, the Indian turned and, swiftly, he was gone. It wasn't until then that I noticed the Indian girl had disappeared too.

As Stacey and I walked back toward camp he said, "Ed, you sure knew how to handle that Indian. It was lucky you had that elk's tooth, but I wonder why he asked us to leave so abruptly."

Before we reached camp we met a stampeder who asked curiously, "Have you fellows been to the Indian village?"

"Yes," we answered. "Why?"

"Jumpin' Jupiter!" exclaimed the stampeder, "don't you know the Indians are hostile toward us? And for good reason! Some of the stampeders have recently raised hell in the village, forcing their attentions on the Indian girls. The Indians are savagely furious! None of us have dared to go to their village lately. That's why the girls have blackened their faces. And now the Indians are refusing to help us get up the canyon and over the pass. It's working a devil of a hardship on all of us!"

"Great Scott!" I exclaimed. "That's the reason the Indians were so hostile! But Indian Joe Whiskers has promised to take us up the canyon tomorrow morning!"

"Well, I wouldn't count on it too damned much," replied the miner dubiously.

"That remains to be seen," I said. "Tomorrow will tell!"

Back on the white man's side of the river, we strolled around that night and saw several heavy gambling games in progress. Stacey and I met Bill McPhee and Ben Everett. They were getting up a party of men to travel with them over Chilkoot and acting as guides. They said they knew the Klondike country well. Stacey and I talked of joining up with them, but backed out when we learned that they were charging an exorbitant fee. (Later, we met them in Dawson. McPhee owned a saloon and Ben Everett was operating the roulette wheel.)

That same night we also saw Dawson Pete, the well-known gambler. He lost $400 that evening, but seemed unconcerned. Wasn't he going back to the Klondike where there was gold galore?

The next morning, much to the surprise of all the stampeders, Indian Joe Whiskers brought his canoe around in front of our camp and helped us pack our supplies. Then we started up the rushing Taiya River.

As the canyon narrowed down and the water became swifter, the Indian and Stacey got out and walked along the bank, pulling with long ropes, while I stood up in the canoe and pushed and guided the craft with a long pole. The Indian wore a curious harness around his head and shoulders called a "tump line." With this contraption, he pulled with great strength.

Halfway up the canyon, we passed several men who had been deserted by the Indian packers. They certainly were in bad straits! Now we realized more fully just how fortunate we were. Dozens of men were going up the canyon as best they could and had to pack and relay all their goods on the rugged, stony trail which followed along the river.

It was nine miles from Dyea to Canoe Landing at the head of the canyon and it took us nearly two days to reach that point. Once, we tipped over in the rapids, but it happened near shore, luckily. Quickly, we grabbed our supplies and righted the canoe. Fortunately, nothing got wet, as we had carefully packed everything in watertight oilskin bags.

At Canoe Landing, we thanked the Indian for his faithful service, and as we paid him, we said, "You've been a wonderful help, Indian Joe, and we shall never forget you!"

The Indian took the money gratefully and said, "Indian Joe like white man. Now white man must hurry." Then, pointing warningly toward Chilkoot, he continued, "Sometime avalanche come down Chilkoot. On other side . . . high cliffs. Must go over ice of Long Lake. No other way for white man to find trail, unless he wait many weeks. Ice melts fast in lake. White man must hurry!"

We thanked Indian Joe for his advice and noticed how glad he was to receive the silver money. Later, we heard that a few dishonest stampeders had paid the Indians in worthless Confederate paper money.

After the Indian had left us, Stacey and I viewed our hundreds of pounds of supplies with much concern, especially when we saw the steep, slippery trail leading from the river up the canyon. We knew we would have to make a number of back-breaking relay trips to establish our first cache. Quickly, we began dividing our supplies, making about sixy-five- to seventy-pound packs for each. Then we started. The trail immediately crooked up, narrow and slippery. As we climbed, we threw our weight toward the inside of the trail, hugging the precipitous walls. The fact that we must make several trips over this trail for the rest of our supplies was hard to bear.

After two days of hard packing, we succeeded in relaying all of our goods to the rim of the canyon. Yet miles stretched ahead up the mountain. It was only the first lap of our journey! On up the steep trail of Chilkoot we trudged through the snow; winding, zigzagging toward Sheep Camp, a small plateau in the lap of the mountain, six miles above the rim of the canyon where we could camp and rest in the shadow of Chilkoot Peak.

At a certain point, when we reached Sheep Camp, we caught our first unobstructed, detailed view of the pass, almost three miles straight up. Chilkoot Peak stood high and forbidding like a mighty sentinel guarding the treasures of the North, challenging every one of us who would dare to pass in search of gold.

From a distance, high up on the trail, silhouetted against the snow, the stampeders looked like hundreds of black ants carrying loads almost as big as themselves as they relentlessly pushed on up the cold, hostile mountain. On our last relay trip to Sheep Camp, Stacey exclaimed as we stopped to catch our breath, "Just look at that trail! It goes straight up and disappears through that high, narrow gap. And Ed, look at that jagged peak to the left, high above the pass . . . and its glacier of blue ice. It's staggering to see where we have to climb!"

"Let's not stay here too long," I said, "if we're to get a load to the summit and come back to Sheep Camp before dark. Besides, our muscles will become stiff if we rest too long here! Come on, let's get started!"

Minutes later, Stacey and I joined that sweating, straining procession trudging up the trail. We must have looked like a column of hard-driven slaves carrying tremendous burdens to lay at the feet of some heartless potentate. Yes; slaves—every one of us! Our taskmaster—gold! Our lash—the scorpion sting of the north wind and the mad urge to get there first!

On and on we climbed. It was an arduous, dangerous trail all the way to the top. From the last thousand feet at a place called "The Scales," it was almost perpendicular. The Indian packers had chiseled out steps in the frozen snow, which helped a little, but it was dangerous and slippery, testing the stamina and grit of every one of us. It was like climbing an icy stairway to hell!

Our tremendous loads cut into our backs and weighed heavy against our straining muscles. My seven-foot whipsaw was the most awkward to carry; but the heaviest and most unwieldy was my large Yukon sled. Stacey and I each had one, and it was necessary to carry them on our backs to scale that last thousand feet up the mountain.

Some of the fellows couldn't take it and slid back down the mountain to The Scales, a place where the Indian packers weighed freight. Some even fainted and died on the trail, but most of us pressed on with unbelievable, almost superhuman strength. It seemed our every pulsing heartbeat was: "On to the gold fields!"

Stacey and I made two cold, weary trips each day to the summit, always planning to return to Sheep Camp at night to sleep. We were almost a week getting our supplies up to the summit.

My diary contains the following entry, written at Stone House, above Sheep Camp:

June 13, 1897

Stone House is a huge rock which toppled down the mountain and stuck on the rim. At a distance, it resembles a house.

Packed our load to the summit. We climbed in snow all the way. The summit is a "corker"! Almost 90-degree angle. I have not the heart to see what the other side looks like! The scenery is something grand and inspiring!

On my last trip I became violently ill and could hardly make it to the top. It was late when I reached the summit and found our cache of supplies. I looked for Stacey, but he had already gone back down the mountain. I knew I was too ill to return to Sheep Camp, so I huddled behind a huge rock and wrapped myself in a white canvas to keep from freezing.

Crowds of men streamed over the pass and headed for the other side, many of whom I had known on the trail. They saw me but took no heed nor cared about me, a sick man. I would only hinder them. Their one driving thought was to hurry over the mountain and get across the lakes before the ice would melt.

The skies grew dim and cold. The men stopped coming. I huddled closer under the canvas, so sick that I thought I would die. I knew it was from the sour beans I had eaten for lunch at Sheep Camp.

Sorrowfully, I thought of home and wondered what my family would do when they heard that I had died on Chilkoot of ptomaine poisoning. Then I prayed, "Oh, God . . . save me! Don't let me die up here!"

Soon I lost consciousness. It was a relief from the terrible pain in my stomach. I floated off into a dream of home and heard dear Velma's voice calling, "Edward, wake up! Wake up!"

Gradually, I opened my eyes. It was almost dark. I was completely alone on the pass . . . and the pain in my stomach was excruciating! Suddenly, I heard . . . crunch . . . crunch . . . in the snow. Someone was coming up the trail from the other side of the Pass. I staggered to my feet and called: "For God's sake, help me. Please help me!"

It was an Indian packer coming up the trail. I must have looked like a ghost standing there in the dim light, all wrapped up in the white canvas. The Indian didn't answer, but turned and ran back down the trail with me calling frantically after him to come back.

"He's gone," I gasped, "I will die here!"

But in a little while I heard cautious steps in the snow and an Indian's voice calling through the darkness, "Me come back. Me listen. What you want?"

"Please go to Sheep Camp and find Bill Stacey. Tell

him to come up and bring a bottle of pain killer. Hurry!" I implored. "I'm very sick! Remember that name, Bill Stacey—camping near the little store . . . at Sheep Camp!"

"Me go," answered the Indian, and then . . . crunch . . . crunch . . . crunch . . . down the trail toward Sheep Camp . . . and I was alone again on the pass.

I wondered, "Did the Indian understand me? Would he find Stacey?" I could only wait and hope.

I became hot and feverish, yet I shivered. A biting wind blew across Chilkoot and loose snow swirled down from the glacial peak. I groaned and lay back on the snow, delirious with chills and fever.

No, I wasn't on Chilkoot. Now I was on that crowded boat, the *Rustler*, laughing, talking, singing patriotic songs and making speeches. There was a cry: "Bail for your lives!" And I was sinking . . . sinking. Oh, why was it so dark? Why was it . . .? Where were the Big Dipper and the North Star? I lost consciousness. Nature was being kind to me, keeping me from feeling that terrible pain.

After a long time, I dreamed again. This time it was of Stacey.

"Ed, wake up! Wake up!"

"No, I can't," I groaned. "I'm dead!"

"No, you aren't!" he said roughly.

I felt someone pull me to a sitting position and something being forced between my teeth. I choked and gasped. It was pain killer!

"Come on, Ed," said Stacey, "it's too dangerous for you to stay up here any longer on this beastly mountain. Lucky, the Indian found me at Sheep Camp. He says it's avalanche weather. Says the ice is melting fast on Long Lake. We've gotta get across it before the breakup . . . or turn back now! What shall we do, Ed?"

"Let's go on," I groaned.

"All right," said Stacey. He pulled me to my feet and got my sled out onto the trail. It was already packed with my supplies. His sled was loaded, too. Everything was tied down with heavy ropes.

"Then we'll slide down on the other side of the mountain tonight . . . and take a chance on hitting Crater Lake," said Stacey. "The Indian packer says it can be done if we find the slide and point our sleds northeast. Says the slope isn't quite so steep on the other side. Sometimes the stampeders slide down in the daytime if they're in a hurry and don't want to take the trail. Of course, going down at night will be taking a hell of a chance . . . but we've got to take that chance."

In a daze I waited while Stacey dragged our sleds to the edge of Chilkoot. Then he came back to help me.

"Ed, I think I've located the slide the Indian told me about. We're riding down on canvas. It's the only way we can go down the mountain and make it in one trip with our heavily loaded sleds."

Stacey lashed the two sleds together side by side; then he took the big canvas and tied it securely to the backs of them. He helped me onto the canvas in back of my sled and wrapped the outer edge around me. Then he got onto his side of the canvas in back of his own sled. We both lay face down, holding on to the back runners of our sleds.

Now, we were ready to go. I peered anxiously down the mountain, trying to see; but it was almost pitch dark below.

"All right . . . let's go!" yelled Stacey as he shoved off. "Hang on, Ed!"

"Goodbye, world!" I said weakly as we left the top.

With astonishing speed, our sleds shot down the mountainside faster and faster. Loose snow tore at our faces and wind whistled and cut our breath as we plunged and dropped headlong into the dark abyss . . . not knowing where we would land.

After what seemed an eternity, we hit bottom with a jolt and shot out onto smooth ice.

"It's Crater Lake!" yelled Stacey. "I hope the ice holds! Dig your toes!"

Gradually our sleds came to a slow stop somewhere on the frozen lake.

"We made it, Ed!" shouted Stacey in relief. "Man! what a ride!"

He pulled me up onto my feet. I staggered to the rim of Crater Lake, followed by Stacey with the sleds.

Gray dawn was just breaking as Stacey made a fire from wood we carried in our packs. Soon he had a pot of coffee boiling and offered me some.

"Just look at that drop!" exclaimed Stacey when it grew lighter. "It's at least a thousand feet from the summit . . . straight down to Crater Lake. Man alive! Who said it wasn't as steep on this side of the mountain?

"Well, Ed, some day you can tell your grandchildren!" He laughed.

"Right now," I groaned, all doubled up, "I'm not interested in my grandchildren. The pain in my stomach hurts like Hades. Must've scraped over some rocks coming down!"

Stacey hurriedly dug out the bottle of pain killer and I swallowed an extra large dose, then crawled into my fur-lined sleeping bag. The trip, "belly-flop" down the mountain, had been too hard on me. However, the pain killer was wonderful stuff. It did all they claimed. I think it contained about seventy-five per cent alcohol and a small per cent of sedative. Soon I had the feeling of dopey well-being in spite of the grinding ptomaine in my stomach.

Stacey allowed me to sleep, or pass out, for about an hour, then he wakened me.

"Ed, do you think you can possibly travel now?" he asked anxiously. "Is the pain gone, old fellow?"

"Oh, no!" I groaned, "just let me sleep. Better go on without me."

"No, I can't do that," said Stacey roughly. "We'll just have to wait here until you're better, then . . ." I didn't hear the rest. I dozed off while he was still talking.

In a little while he wakened me again. "Ed," he said, "if you can't travel today, I'm going back over the pass to Sheep Camp. I didn't tell you, but I left a box of supplies cached away when the Indian came after me last night. It's a helluva trip . . . but I can sure use those things in the Klondike."

"Yeah, it's a helluva trip," I groaned drowsily. "But, Stacey, watch your step . . ." Then I dropped off again.

For several hours I slept fitfully . . . Our camp was practically on the trail by the side of the lake, and, at intervals, I was vaguely conscious of being stared at.

I heard muffled voices curiously discussing me: "Who is he?" "Is he dead?" "Naw, he's drunk!" "No, I think he's sick." "Looks like Stacey's partner. Remember, we saw them at Sheep Camp. Guess Stacey'll look after him." Then the voices died away.

About noon, I awakened and saw several sturdy, muscular-looking men approaching. One was packing a large bellows and the others were carrying very heavy loads. I recognized them as a party of men I had met at Dyea and again at Sheep Camp.

"Hello, Ed," called one of the men. "How're you feeling? Saw Stacey . . . says you're pretty sick. Well, now, that's tough luck! We'd stop, but our loads are getting awful heavy. We're hurrying to catch up with some fellows who've promised to give us a lift with their sleds. If we can get this damn blacksmith equipment into the Klondike, we'll make a fortune!"

"See you in Dawson!" they called hopefully as they staggered down the trail under their heavy loads of bellows, hammers and anvils.

Other miners passed. All had the same worried, tired, strained look. None stopped at Crater Lake. All were hurrying to get over the ice of Long Lake.

Early in the afternoon, a party of men came hastily across Crater Lake and stopped a minute to rest and talk. They were the Wisconsin crowd . . . and there were seven of them.

"Man alive!" said one of the men as they came up. "You fellows took an awful chance last night. Guess you're one of the few who ever came down Chilkoot on a sled after dark! Yes, we met Stacey and he told us about your wild ride."

"Sure wish we could do something for you, Ed," said another, "but we're not stopping here. Everybody's rushing like mad. The ice won't wait! I know you understand, Ed. Good luck!"

"See you at Linderman!"* they called back as they hurried down the trail.

---

*The oldest spelling for this lake is "Linderman." Some, however, in '97, spelled it "Lindeman."

After they had gone, I finished the bottle of pain killer, but it did not completely drown the pain this time. And their words, "The ice won't wait!" kept tormenting me. Now I realized only too well that it was every man for himself in this stampede.

In the early afternoon, the Seattle Ryan party of five reached our camp. They had just come down the steep trail from the summit. I had met them at Sheep Camp and they were a friendly group.

When they saw me, Mrs. Ryan exclaimed, "Oh, Mr. Lung, it's a pity you're so ill. We must help you!" And she made her crowd wait while she fixed me a hot drink. She did all she could to make me comfortable, then gave me several cigars as a parting gift, which I gratefully accepted.

"Look," she said, "I found this box of cigars near the rim of the lake. I wonder who could have dropped them? No doubt, some poor fellow is bemoaning his loss, unless . . . unless something has happened to him!"

I saw Mrs. Ryan shudder at the thought and almost throw the box of cigars away. Then she changed her mind, tucked the box under her arm and said, "Mr. Lung, there are so many stampeders losing their lives up here, it frightens me. I can already see that, to survive in the North, one has to constantly battle the elements. Anyway, there is something grand and glorious about being up here. It is truly God's country!"

"What a kindhearted, plucky little woman!" I thought as I saw Mrs. Ryan and her party disappearing down the trail. "She is one person who will certainly succeed in the Klondike . . . a true pioneer!"

Intermittently, I slept and looked at the magnificent scenery. Crater Lake seemed cradled in the side of Chilkoot and was about a mile across. To get my mind off my unfortunate illness I tried to picture how it must have looked millions of years ago. No doubt, it had been a fiery, active volcano; then it had become dormant and gradually filled with water. I had heard that Crater Lake was the real headwaters of the Yukon. The idea intrigued me. Here I was at the source, the very beginning of the great Yukon. I could visualize volumes of water pouring from this lake later in the spring, rushing down the mountainside to unite

(Courtesy of State Historical Society, Tacoma, Washington)

Gold seekers leaving for the North from Seattle, Washington, in 1897

(Photographed by E. A. Hegg)

Chilkoot Pass, the last dreaded stretch to the top from "The Scales," a place where professional packers stopped to weigh freight

Lake Linderman, where stampeders camped, built boats, and waited for the ice to melt – when they could head for Dawson

Dawson-bound stampeders launch a boat to cross Lake Linderman

with other lakes and streams ultimately to become lost in one big river, the mighty Yukon.

My eyes traveled down the mountain, across canyons, snow fields and glaciers. Somewhere, about nine miles below, was Long Lake . . . and farther on, in the mountains—Lake Linderman. Desperately, I wondered if we could reach Long Lake and get across before the ice would crack up. If not, must we go back over Chilkoot to find another route into the Klondike? This might delay us months!

I had heard vague reports of an old Indian summer trail which, it was said, started somewhere near Sheep Camp. Even the Indians disliked this trail because, they said, it went up along a ledge, under an overhanging glacier, then led down through a maze of gorges and valleys. To go that way, a white man would certainly have to have an Indian guide.

I had also heard of two other Indian trails. One was the trail the Chilkat Indians used from their village on Chilkat Inlet, or Pyramid Harbor. It was on the north side of Lynn Canal. This trail headed farther into the interior and was supposed to come out on the Yukon River somewhere in the vicinity of old Fort Selkirk. It was unmapped and practically unknown. Only two white men had ever gone over the Chilkat Trail successfully. One was Jack Dalton, a trader. Now the stampeders were referring to it as the "Dalton Trail," but, as yet, the miners were afraid to risk this route until more was known about it.

There was persistent rumor of a third mountain pass being explored by the Canadian Government and some of the stampeders. It ran almost parallel to the southeast of Chilkoot, only ten miles from Chilkoot. As yet, no real trail had been cut through. (However, seven weeks after Stacey and I had crossed over Chilkoot, the White Pass route was opened up, and it followed pretty much an old trail which the Indians had tried to keep secret for years. In order to open up the White Pass more quickly, two thousand stampeders went up and worked on the trail with picks and shovels, each miner donating five days of his valuable time. The White Pass proved to be a better trail for the stampeders because it could be used both winter and summer.)

Now, as I lay there by the lake thinking and half-dozing, suddenly I felt the earth tremble and shake, accompanied by a low, deep roar. Alarmed, I scrambled to my feet, anxiously looking toward the peak. There was no sign of trouble up there, but it was certain that somewhere there had been a terrific disturbance, perhaps huge, falling rocks or an avalanche.

Anxiously, I watched the summit for Stacey. In a little while, I saw a black dot poised at the edge of Chilkoot. Suddenly, it shot down with breakneck speed. I held my breath. Yes, it was Stacey! . . . and he was riding down on canvas in back of his sled. He shot out onto Crater Lake and I saw him dig the toes of his boots into the ice. When he reached camp, he was puffing and his face was red from exertion and excitement.

"Say, it's the last time I'll ever come down that devilish mountain!" he gasped. "Lord, what a ride! And did you hear that rumbling? I thought for a minute the whole peak was going to pile down on top of me! Must have been a big slide somewhere!"

We shivered as we gazed at the summit. Chilkoot stood cold and serene above us. But, slowly, a peculiar, mist-like mantle was forming over the peak. The Indians were right. Chilkoot was treacherous. In deep, ominous tones . . . it had spoken!

"I'll be glad to get away from this damn mountain," said Stacey, white-faced. "If we don't get started soon, it may be too late, Ed."

"I think I'll be able to travel tomorrow," I said. "If not, Stacey, you go on anyway."

"I'm not going on without you, ol' man," he said.

The next morning, Stacey packed our sleds while I tried my legs. They wobbled. However, my will was strong and I was determined to travel. We started slowly down the mountain trail. I staggered from weakness and fever, but doggedly forced myself along. For me, there was no turning back. We stopped often to rest. At times, Stacey came to my rescue, although his sled was very heavy with part of my load.

"Ed," said Stacey as we trudged along, "seems like I hear running water some place."

"I hear it, too," I replied. "Sounds like it's under us.

We must be on a glacier. They say there are hundreds of them in the North."

In a little while, our straining eyes caught the glister of ice far below, held between high walls of a rugged canyon.

"It's Long Lake!" cried Stacey. "And there's ice!"

We pushed faster down the mountain. The trail was easy to follow. It showed evidence of hundreds of stampeders having recently passed that way. The snow was ground to a dirty, coffee color and the sun was melting it rapidly. Already, the trail was mushy, with little rivulets forming.

"What are those black dots ahead?" asked Stacey as we hurried along.

"Why, they're people," I said as we drew near. "Look, there's about a dozen of them and they appear to be camping on the trail. Something must've happened."

Stacey and I hurried faster. When we came within earshot, we called, "Hello! Are you people in trouble?"

"Plenty of trouble!" a man's voice answered.

To our surprise, we recognized our friends—the Ryans and the Wisconsin crowd.

"What's happened?" we asked as we drew up.

"There's a deep crevasse just ahead and we can't get across," said one of the men. Stacey and I hurried forward to see.

"Look at that crevasse," yelled Stacey, "and the water rushing under it!"

"Yes, and look at the man's hat caught way down there on the ledge," wailed Mrs. Ryan. "We're afraid there's a stampeder under the glacier. See, the trail leads to the edge and drops off!"

I shivered as I peered over the edge into the deep, icy gap. "Well, I'm sure it's too late to help him now," I said. "Our main worry is to get over to the other side of the crevasse. If only there were trees up here. But we are a long way above timber line!"

I sat down on my sled to rest. Had we come all this distance only to be defeated? I looked down on Long Lake, now only about a scant quarter mile away, yet the distance seemed insurmountable. Suddenly, I got an idea.

"Friends," I said, "let's make a bridge of sleds. The crevasse is only about ten feet across. With Stacey's and my sled, plus the one you have, I think we can span the gap. Stacey and I will unload our sleds. Get out all the rope you have. We haven't a moment to lose!"

"You bet we'll try it," they all said. Quickly, they began pulling their packs apart to get all the extra pieces of rope. Feverishly, we worked with the ropes, lashing our sleds together end to end. In the meantime, some of the men were throwing their lighter supplies across the crevasse. The heavier things we would have to carry over.

When all was in readiness, we shoved the sled bridge carefully over the crevasse, all the while hanging onto ropes which were fastened to the first sled.

When the runners touched the other side, Mrs. Ryan said, "Please let me be the first to cross over. I'm the lightest of the crowd . . . and I'm not really afraid. When I get over there, I can hold the sled for one of you."

"No! No!" we all said in chorus.

"Please let me do this," she replied. "I'm not afraid. You can tie a rope around my waist and then I'll be safe."

Mrs. Ryan was a little woman, but her determination was mighty. In a few minutes she was making her way slowly and cautiously over the crevasse. We held the sled bridge firmly in place and watched her anxiously, while her husband and several others braced themselves and held on to the rope which was tied about her waist.

At last, she reached the opposite side and turned and smiled reassuringly, then knelt on the ice and held the runners of the sled while her husband cautiously crept across to her. The joints of the improvised bridge wobbled and swayed under the strain of his weight and the slender boards of the sleds bent, but the bridge held.

Now we knew it was reasonably safe for us to cross over, one at a time. However, it meant several trips each, in order to get our supplies over. Needless to say, it was a very nerve-racking and dangerous process. Chunks of melting ice from the sides of the crevasse kept cracking off and splashing into the angry-looking waters thirty feet below, rushing under the glacier. It was especially dangerous for the last man to cross because there was no one to hold the shaky bridge for him on that side of the crevasse.

At last, we were all safely over with the last load of supplies. With great sighs of relief, we pulled our bridge after us and repacked our sleds. Then we hurried toward our next ordeal.

In a short time we reached Long Lake. It was completely deserted. The light-coffee-colored trail pointed out across the ice. But already the surface along the edges of the lake looked soft and porous. To test the ice, several of us crept out cautiously onto the surface near shore. The ice creaked and groaned a little. Gingerly, we made our way back to shore and held a hurried consultation.

"What shall we do?" someone asked.

"We'd better camp here and wait for the ice and snow to melt, just as we were advised by that old-timer at Sheep Camp," said one of the men. "With the snow gone, maybe we can find our way around the cliffs and hit the summer trail he told us about."

"And waste precious time camping here?" asked Stacey impatiently. "Oh, no! Why, it might mean a whole month of hanging around here! Think of the people already ahead of us; and think of a month's provisions that would be gone for nothing!"

"Yes, and after that, think of portaging all of our stuff on our backs . . . which might add another two weeks before we could reach the next lake, Lake Linderman," chimed in someone else.

"We'd better try to cross the ice now," I said.

"But, Ed, it's too dangerous! Let's try to find that Indian trail now, in spite of the snow. It must be somewhere in the vicinity."

"Well, you can count me out!" I said. "Why, for a white man to go wandering off into these mountains without an Indian guide might mean certain death. I, for one, am going to try to cross over the ice of Long Lake now! The surface looks more solid in the middle . . . and I believe it'll hold."

"I'm with you, Ed," said Stacey.

Solemnly, Mr. and Mrs. Ryan looked at each other, and

the rest exchanged glances. There was a dead silence.

Finally, Mrs. Ryan said, "Let's go!"

The others asked, "Well, what are we waiting for?"

"All right," I said, "let's go! We must space out at least a hundred feet apart and keep going, no matter what happens. Let's draw straws for the man to take the lead."

"No," said Stacey, "I'll take the lead. Remember, I'm a policeman. I have a sixth sense for trouble. Ed, you follow me, and the others can come as they wish. You bet I'll holler if I run into trouble!"

I watched Stacey as he quickly adjusted the ropes to his sled, turned and walked cautiously out onto the ice, pulling his sled after him. None of us spoke. We all watched him tensely. He had now gone at least a hundred feet. The ice was holding.

"Come on, Ed," he called. "Follow in my path."

"I'm coming!" I shouted and stepped out carefully onto the ice. Several times it creaked, but I moved on.

"Change your course!" yelled Stacey, scarcely looking back over his shoulder. "The ice is weak at this spot!"

I quickly changed my course and continued. A little later, I looked back. By this time, the Ryans and the Wisconsians were all out onto the ice following, walking Indian file, about a hundred feet apart.

I looked ahead. It was at least a mile more to the end of Long Lake. I glanced up at the dark, unfriendly cliffs and my heart sank a little. What if the ice should break? We could all be drowned like rats out here in this deep mountain lake. Then I thought of the Bible story I had learned as a child. In a sense, we, too, were walking by faith. The ice must hold us! It must!

Now we were about two thirds of the way across the lake. All at once, the section of ice on which I was walking swayed a little and moved. My heart sank and skipped a dozen beats. I stopped short, stood perfectly still and waited, scarcely breathing. Perhaps I had just imagined the movement of the ice. Cautiously, I took another step forward. Suddenly the ice cracked and broke beneath me.

"This is it!" screamed a voice within me. I expected instantly to be plunged into icy waters. Engulfed with terror, a thousand thoughts raced through my mind. But, to my amazement, nothing more happened. I glanced down. Only my footing had dropped. Now I was standing more than ankle deep in a mass of slushly, rotten ice. Thank God! There was a second layer of firm ice beneath me! But who could tell how strong the second layer would be? Shuddering at the thought, I stepped cautiously away. I knew that the slightest extra vibration might start the chain of ice particles breaking which held the whole surface together.

"Mr. Lung," cried out Mrs. Ryan in alarm, "are you all right?"

"Yes," I answered, "but turn to the left. Don't come this way. The ice is very dangerous here!"

I looked back. The others had heard my warning and were changing their course. I knew they had been watching me anxiously.

"What a devilish walk!" exclaimed Stacey as he grasped my hand when I stepped off the ice. "Ed, ol' man, I was afraid you wouldn't make it!"

"I was afraid I wouldn't too, there for a minute," I said. "Stacey, we're just barely getting over in time. In a very few hours, that ice will break up. It's terribly rotten. You know, I had a mighty close call!"

"You bet!" said Stacey. "And you'd better not wait too long to get those wet shoes and socks off."

We anxiously watched the rest of the caravan. Mrs. Ryan was ahead of the others and her husband came next. We called encouraging words to her. In a little while she stepped ashore.

"Mr. Lung, I could never do that again!" she said. "I'm not brave enough!" She was trembling and was very pale and shaky.

"Thank God, we're safe!" exclaimed her husband as he threw his arms around his wife.

"Thank God!" she echoed fervently.

The scene was one of great rejoicing and thankfulness when all were safely off the ice.

Being very tired, we decided to camp at the edge of the lake for the night. Our good fortune called for a real celebration, but we were too exhausted to talk much. I hated to admit it, but I was ready to collapse. In no time we had a hot fire and warm food and my wet shoes and socks were drying out close to the flames.

Before closing my eyes that night, I looked for the Big Dipper and then the North Star. It seemed to reach down and touch me.

"Velma, I'm safe," I whispered as I dropped off to sleep. . . .

The next day, we followed the well-beaten stampeders' trail into a tunnel-like gorge and up over a low mountain, from where wc gained our first view of Lake Linderman. It was a beautiful lake surrounded by snow-peaked mountains and dark-green forests. What a haven it appeared to be! Here, perhaps, I could recuperate and gain back a little of my lost weight. The ptomaine poisoning had reduced me to a shadow of my former self. I had had to tighten my belt again and again, and still my clothes hung on me.

Gradually, we made our way to the lake and approached the side where hundreds of stampeders had set up tents and were building their boats, waiting for the ice to go out so they could go down the Yukon to Dawson.

As we drew nearer, we saw an angry mob and heard violent shouts of: "Send him back! Send him back!"

Coming closer and peering over the shoulders of several of the men, I saw a cowering fellow in the midst of the crowd. He was being held between two stampeders and they had his arms pinned back. Everybody was glaring at the man in the center.

"No one steals from us and gets away with it! Not when we've packed it on our backs twenty-eight miles over Chilkoot!" shouted several men in the crowd.

"Send him back! . . . The dirty thief!" yelled the mob.

There was a big fellow they called Kelly who seemed to be acting as judge and jury. He raised his hands for silence.

"All right, men, he goes back . . . and if he gets there safely . . . he'll be damned lucky! At least, we're giving him that chance. I'm sure this isn't the first time he's stolen from us!

"Now, get going, you despicable thief!" yelled Kelly

as he kicked the prisoner. "Did you hear? You're goin' back where ya came from!"

I turned away, feeling ill and sick at heart. It was very evident that there was no mercy in the hearts of these tired, gold-crazed men. Later, I heard that we were the last ones to cross over the ice of Long Lake that spring!

While Stacey and I looked for a camping place, I kept thinking of the scene we had just witnessed and I asked myself, "Did the punishment fit the crime?"

(Now I think of a brutal happening a year later, which was described to me by Archie McLean Hawks, civil engineer of the tramway on Chilkoot Pass, a friend of mine, who was an eyewitness and took photographs of the episode. It was during the big stampede of '98, a year later, that three thieves were caught stealing from caches along the trail near Sheep Camp. On the spot, the furious miners called a meeting and said, "These men have stolen from us. They're worse than horse thieves! We could easily perish for lack of the supplies which they have taken from us. Therefore, they are potential murderers. We demand that they be lashed unmercifully on their bare backs with the cat-o'-nine-tails—fifteen lashes!" The thieves begged for mercy, but there was no pardon from the stampeders. The three men were tied to tramway construction posts and lashed by the men from whom they had stolen. One of the thieves got off with a light whipping, but the other two were flogged until their backs were cut and bleeding and their blood dripped to the snow. At last, the miners were going to let the thieves go when an unidentified man in the crowd yelled, "That isn't enough!" And he drew his revolver and shot one of the thieves and killed him.

Pandemonium broke loose. Someone yelled with vengeance, "Let's hang the others! That's what they do with horse thieves where I come from!" Terrified, one of the two remaining thieves grabbed a gun and turned it on himself, committing suicide. The third man was seized and a sign fastened to his back which proclaimed in big letters, "I AM A CAMP ROBBER." The last that was ever seen of him, he was running as fast as he could down the trail toward the canyon. His hands had been tied in such a way that he couldn't free himself of the sign. No one ever saw him again. News of this terrible happening spread along the trail and, in a short time, reached the "outside" and was reported in the San Francisco *Examiner.*)

Yes, that first day at Lake Linderman, I could see that life was going to be very savage and cruel as we pushed deeper into the great North country. Sending that thief back was almost like a death sentence!

Stacey and I found a good camping place near the edge of the lake, not far from the forest, and set up our tent and stove. Hundreds of stampeders worked near us building boats. Their tremendous, driving energy seemed to charge the very atmosphere. The whine of the whipsaws, the metallic pounding of hammer on nails, the smell of fresh lumber and pitch permeated the air. All of this for one mighty, concentrated purpose . . . gold!

At noon the next day while I was working in camp, Stacey came back from the hills with a load of wood and said, "Some Indian packers are coming over the summer trail; I saw them through the forest. They're coming around the lake now. Why, there are dozens of them!"

"Listen, Stacey," I said. "I've got some exciting news! While you were gone, a young fellow came by camp. He was thin and ragged, and half starved, but you should have seen the gold he was packing! His pockets bulged with nuggets, some as big as walnuts, and he carried pokes of fine and coarse gold! I gave him hot coffee and food, and while he ate, he told me he had been nearly three months traveling over the ice of the Yukon to get out of the Klondike. He was there soon after the big gold discovery was made. Said he picked nuggets out of the 'pay dirt' of the Bonanza with just his bare hands. Says it's gold! . . . gold! . . . everywhere you look! It's on the surface and deep in the ground. Man, you should have seen that gold! Stacey, we've got to have our boat ready to take off the minute the ice goes out!"

"Nuggets as big as walnuts! Man, oh, man!" shouted Stacey, his eyes popping. "You bet we'll be ready, Ed, give me that saw and hammer!"

Chapter II

The Stampeders of 1897

More exciting news of fabulous gold strikes in the Klondike kept reaching us as we waited impatiently, Stacey and I, watching the ice of Lake Linderman, all the time working like slaves, building our boat to be ready to leave the minute the ice would clear enough in the lake.

Spring in the upper reaches of the Yukon is a delayed season. It is nearly always a whole month late, even though the lower Yukon region is usually cleared of its ice by the first of June. Lake Linderman, being in the high mountainous headwaters of the great Yukon Valley, would be perhaps the last lake to give up its ice.

When Stacey and I arrived at Lake Linderman, it was about the middle of June. Already the melting process had begun on the lake but the nights were still cold enough to freeze over the top surface of slushy, porous ice which the Klondikers called "anchor ice." This ice sometimes reached a thickness of two or three feet, and even though it was porous for weeks, still, at times, it could be crossed safely, especially early in the morning following a freezing cold night.

But now the hot sun beat down on the ice, melting it rapidly. Only a few scattered snowbanks still remained in the shadows of the forests. The earliest spring flowers were already pushing their way through the warming earth along the hills. Little pools formed in the hollows and from these hordes of tiger-like mosquitoes flew out in humming black clouds to torment us. To keep them away, we built smudge fires and our lungs filled with choking black smoke while we worked and slept. However, we were becoming more weathered each day; more rugged and better able to cope with the hardships at hand.

In spite of the heat of the sun, the rotten ice of Lake Linderman clung stubbornly. If Stacey and I could have reached the lake about six weeks earlier, we probably could have gone all the way to Dawson over the ice.

The Land of Gold seemed very far away.

One morning, about a week after Stacey and I had arrived at the lake, we were terrified to see an unknown man venturing out onto the ice. He had gone perhaps a hundred yards before our attention was called to him. The man was carrying a pack on his back and apparently was going to attempt to cross the anchor ice to the other side of the lake. We all yelled at him to come back, but it was too late. He staggered, screamed, clutched wildly at the air, then suddenly disappeared through the ice. None of us dared go out to try to rescue him. All we could do was look in horror where the man had been.

With a low, weird, rumbling noise, the ice was breaking and moving a little all over the lake. This man's death was like a signal. There was a great commotion and stir among the stampeders, as all along the lake they rushed to the shore line to watch the movement of the ice.

"A man has gone through the ice!" they cried. "But look, the ice is breaking! The ice is breaking!" The echo was picked up and amplified joyfully around the lake.

Everyone knew it wouldn't be long now before we could all launch our crazy-looking boats and be on our frenzied way to that glittering Bonanza country of beckoning gold. But what about the poor devil who had just lost his life? Well, perhaps his family might hear of his tragic death, or they might never know. In that freezing, icy water, the lakes in the North rarely give up their dead. The unknown man would be just another casualty who had been swallowed up in the icy jaws of the North.

Stacey and I struggled faster with our boat. Neither one of us had ever built a boat before and we were among the greenest of greenhorns. We weren't the only ones. There were hundreds of others like us! "Build strong!" we had been told. "Your very lives will depend on it!" We had few tools to work with and only a limited supply of nails. Between Stacey and me, we had a whipsaw, a small handsaw, a hammer, an axe, and a chisel. We had also brought a small supply of oakum and a calking iron.

And now we were fitting and pounding the roughly hewn boards together with our meager supply of nails. Each hour our boat was slowly and painfully taking shape.

Our friends, the Ryans and the Wisconsians, camped near us. We worked feverishly side by side, often joking about our queer-looking boats and wondering which outfit would be the first to reach Dawson and who among us would be the first to strike it rich.

And now, at last, our boat was nearly ready. Only the seams and cracks had to be sealed. Stacey and I spent long hours dipping the stringy, fiber-like oakum into the pot of boiling, sticky, yellow pitch and carefully forcing it into the seams of the boat with the chisel and calking iron; using the hammer to pound and wedge it in more solidly, then ending the process by heating the calking iron and running it along the entire surface of the cracks to be sure the pitch filled every crevice.

We saw many of the boys from Tacoma camped along the lake and someone introduced to us two stampeders named Jourgensen and Crawford. No one called them by their first names. The men were looking for passage to Dawson and offered to pay us $60 apiece and also furnish their own grub. The money appealed to Stacey and me, so we contracted to take them along, reminding them that they would be riding at their own risk.

After a few days of anxiously watching the ice jams break, move a little, then pile up and lock, then break loose again, we could see that the ice was slowly moving out of Lake Linderman, moving through a canyon which was the outlet of Lake Linderman and which flowed into Lake Bennett just beyond. The breaking and moving of the ice was a fairly rapid process now, once it had begun. Nature seemed to be pushing with terrific, unseen force to clear the lake and make way for a short summer.

One momentous morning, about ten days after we had arrived at Lake Linderman, an exultant shout went up along the lake. "The ice is clear enough to start!"

"Let's go!" we cried as Stacey and I and our two passengers hurriedly piled our supplies into our crude, twenty-foot, flat-bottomed boat and all jumped in and shoved off. In no time, scores of fellow stampeders dotted the lake in boats and barges. All bows pointed in one magnetic direction—the Klondike!

"Goodbye," we called, and "Good luck," they sang out as we sailed down the lake. Our friends, the Ryans, the Wisconsians, the Nelson brothers whom we had met on the trail, and the Canadians, the Swedes, the Kellys and

Hydes whom we had met at Lake Linderman, sailed close behind us. We were all very gay and hilarious, for wasn't the land of gold nearly ours? Hadn't we successfully scaled Chilkoot and passed over a hundred other dangers? True, there would be ordeals ahead, but we felt strong and adequate to meet them.

Heading down the six miles of Lake Linderman toward the canyon outlet of the lake, we saw large blocks of anchor ice piled against the left shore. It had been blown there by the heavy winds. Occasionally we dodged in and out among a few scattered ice floes still floating in the lake. However, nothing could dampen our lighthearted spirits. We waved and shouted to the parties ahead of us and behind us and all around us. But after several miles of exuberant travel, we began to settle down to visit amongst ourselves.

"Say, Ed," said Jourgensen, one of our new traveling companions, "when will we reach the Yukon River?"

"Look," I said as I smoothed out the creases of a crude little map, "this is a sketch of the North country which Bill McPhee, the well-known Klondiker, drew for me when I met him at Dyea Indian village the night before Stacey and I started over Chilkoot Pass. It will be invaluable to us. He says this country is very wild and rugged and mostly unexplored, but if we stay on the water route we ought to reach Dawson safely. Says we'll see a few scattered Indian villages along the way, and occasionally a few miners and trappers."

"Has he marked distances on the map?" asked Crawford anxiously.

"No," I said, "only lines and names. At the beginning, there's Chilkoot Pass marked here with a number of lines which resemble a claw; then directly below Chilkoot is Crater Lake, Long Lake, then a chain of lakes with Lake Linderman at the head. From Lake Linderman there's a little straight line representing the connecting river leading into Lake Bennett. From there, are several winding lines curving northeast, marked Carcross, Caribou Crossing; then the line goes into another lake marked Tagish, with a straight connecting line heading north to another lake called Marsh Lake, which looks quite large. From there, a long curving line swings northeast and there there are three names underscored as 'dangerous.' They are Miles Canyon, Squaw Rapids and White Horse Rapids. After those comes another straight line heading north which is called the Lewis River. This flows into a very large-looking lake marked Lake LaBarge and from there the heavy river line continues for some distance with the names of Five Fingers and Rink Rapids marked on the map as 'quite dangerous.'

"A little farther on, McPhee has drawn from the northeast a rather long line marked the Pelly River. It comes into the Lewis River and joins it. At this point, he has marked the river as the Yukon. Here, also, he has a marking called 'Fort Selkirk.' From Fort Selkirk the Yukon veers to the northwest, then turns and heads almost due north. And there is Dawson, marked in big letters!"

"How long do you think it will take us to reach Dawson?" asked Jourgensen.

"McPhee says it's around five hundred miles and he thought we could make it in about two weeks," I said. "But look, we're coming to the canyon!"

Our boat was now racing along in the company of dozens of other boats. The current was very swift as it boiled and poured between low cliffs and we had to be very much on the alert for rocks and tumbling chunks of ice. There were several dangerous places, but we shot through the last quarter mile of rapids in good shape.

"We're coming into Lake Bennett now," said Stacey. "Just look at the boats ahead! There are hundreds of them, all strung out from end to end of the lake!"

Stacey was right. It was a sight long to be remembered. Hundreds of white sails moved like ducks across the broad expanse of the lake. Many of the boats had been built at Lake Linderman, but scores of them had been built at Lake Bennett, which was the larger of the two lakes. We all wondered if there could possibly be enough gold in the Klondike for such an armada of stampeders.

For a long time we watched the impressive sight. Lake Bennett stretched ahead for a distance of at least twenty-six miles. The huge lake was hemmed in on both sides with snow-capped mountains and I judged the lake to be about a mile across. From both shores the mountains rose abruptly from the bottom of the lake. It looked as though, once we started down that huge expanse of water, there would be very few places to land until we reached the lower end of the lake.

Now only occasionally we caught glimpses of our friends the Ryans, the Wisconsians, the Nelson Brothers, the Canadians on their raft, the Swedes, the Kellys and Hydes, but gradually we lost track of them all in the confusing maze of sails.

I kept a sharp lookout for Bill McPhee and his large party of men. I hadn't seen him or any of his men at Lake Linderman, so decided he must have gone directly to Bennett to build his boat. I looked at my little hand-sketched map again and thought how lucky I was to have met McPhee. So many of the stampeders had nothing to guide them, only hearsay . . . and that, sometimes, was very sketchy and indefinite.

I thought of Bill McPhee at Dyea. He had been kind enough to tell me a great deal about the Klondike.

McPhee had said, "Ed, you'll find Dawson a rough, rip-snorting, typical mining camp. Dawson grew overnight. It happened last summer when that fellow from California, George Carmack, and his Tagish Indian wife and two of their Indian companions made that rich discovery on the Bonanza Creek. I was at Circle City at the time; owned some mining property and ran a saloon.

"One day in late August a fellow came poling down the river yelling like a maniac. 'There's gold on the Bonanza! There's gold on the Bonanza . . . barrels of it!' My saloon was full of fellows at the time.

"Man alive! you should have seen that stampede from Circle City! The fellows tore out of there like crazy men, grabbed anything that would float and started poling up the river like mad toward the Klondike. Some of them didn't have enough food or supplies to last a week. That didn't stop them. Three hundred miles is a long way to pole against the current of the Yukon, but that didn't discourage them. Of course, pretty soon the gold-fever struck me, too. Besides, Circle was practically deserted and I hadn't any more customers, so I closed my saloon, joined the stampeders and got myself a good claim on Bonanza. Then I sent back

Lake Bennett, below Lake Linderman, connected by canyon. At this lower lake thousands of stampeders built boats to take them to the Yukon River

Stampeders rush boats to completion on the shores of Lake Bennett

(Courtesy of Canadian National Railways)

Stampeders daring fate, going through Miles Canyon—sometimes called "Dead Man's Canyon"

A large scow with men and supplies fighting to get through frightening Whitehorse Rapids

to Circle for my supplies. In a few weeks I had set myself up in business in a tent; after that, in a shack . . . and now I'm building a good log house which should be finished this summer."

McPhee continued, "Early this spring I came out over the ice and went to San Francisco to get a large stock of supplies and I'm sending them in by boat . . . around by Bering Sea to St. Michael at the mouth of the Yukon. That shipment of liquor and tobacco is worth its weight in gold! I'll be roaring mad if it gets lost or damaged, or if the boat gets stuck on a sand bar some place down the river!" Then, with a twinkle in his eye and a laugh, McPhee added, "I can only dilute the whisky just so much with water . . . When the whisky runs out, I can't serve just plain water!"

I remembered McPhee had paused in his story of the gold rush to say cordially, "Ed, come and see me when you get to Dawson. You may need a friend. Even though my place is a saloon, you'll find that it's a place of business, also. We have excellent gold scales and can tell you what your gold is worth. We give friendly advice, too, about the gold strikes, and on cold winter nights, when the thermometer hits fifty below, my place is always open and is cozy and warm. Many come there to just get thawed out!" He laughed.

In parting, McPhee had slapped me on the back and said, "Goodbye, Ed, will be seeing you in Dawson."

I had promised I would look him up. I rather liked this tall, broad-shouldered Scotchman with the frank, jovial manner and hearty laugh, but I was not in the habit of going to saloons and did not drink and I began to wonder just how I would fit into that rugged life of the North, being the son of a Baptist minister. Still, I would need friends. I already knew several in McPhee's party, including Ben Everett from Tacoma.

Now I turned my attention to our twenty-foot boat and my companions riding along with me on Lake Bennett. For the first time since we had started, I had a real opportunity to study our two passengers, Crawford and Jourgensen. Crawford seemed to be a mild, soft-spoken fellow, quite refined and apparently well educated. I decided he would be an agreeable companion for our long trip ahead. I liked Jourgensen, too. He was the rugged, out-spoken type, perhaps not as well educated, but he had a natural intelligence of his own.

We had been keeping a straight, even course down the middle of the lake, but in the early afternoon we felt what had been a pleasant breeze turn cold at our backs. It grew blustery and blew hard from the west across the stern of our boat. From over the mountains, dark clouds were gathering and the sky and lake looked threatening and ominous. Soon, heavy squalls struck the water, chopping and making it writhe to an ugly, grayish yellow, causing uneven, jagged waves to roll across the lake.

Our boat was so heavily loaded that we watched the approaching storm with much concern and apprehension. By leaps and bounds the wind increased in strength, piling the waves high. Whitecaps curled on the rollers as the wind hurled them furiously across the lake, pounding us and everything in their path. The situation began to look very serious for us. Gradually, the other boats were disappearing from the lake, or perhaps they were merely concealed by the huge size of the waves.

With great difficulty, I stood up in our boat, bracing myself against the heavy wind, and took down the sail. Suddenly, a large wave struck us and threw me off balance. I would have pitched headlong into the lake if Crawford had not grabbed me by the seat of my pants, and I sprawled back in the bottom of the boat. I saw Stacey bailing furiously as water from the whitecaps came hissing over the sides of our boat. Jourgensen was at the oars, fighting hard to steady the boat.

"The pitch is coming loose from the seams of our boat!" yelled Crawford. "I'm trying to stop them up. Water is seeping in very fast." Now we knew we were in for real trouble!

Desperately, we looked for a place to land, but there were only the steep, unfriendly cliffs for as far as we could see on both sides of the lake.

"We must keep fighting the storm!" I shouted. "We can't give up! If we could only reach the lower end of the lake we'd be safe!"

Suddenly, the wind shifted to the northeast. It came roaring across the lake with almost hurricane velocity. Like a thousand furies, it struck the water! It tore at our boat and our supplies and ripped at the canvas and we were wet and cold and afraid, for we knew that if we capsized in that deep, icy water, there would be no hope for any of us. In spite of all our frantic efforts, we were being rapidly pushed and driven toward the left-hand side of the lake where the water dashed itself high against the cliff and fell back, writhing and foaming into the angry lake.

"Help, Help!" we heard frantic muffled cries coming over the waves in the distance.

"Help! Help! Help!" more heart-rending cries reached us from another direction.

We looked hurriedly over the lake and spotted several boatloads of stampeders splashing and churning through the mountainous waves and we knew they were in great trouble and distress. The discordant howl of the high-pitched wind and the furious undertone of the thunderous pounding of the waves on the nearby cliffs seemed to be calling out our doom!

All at once, I saw a break in the cliffs where a tiny finger of rocks jutted out a little into the lake. It was ahead . . . just about five hundred yards, and I surmised there must be a ledge or perhaps a tiny cove behind it. Ordinarily, the place would have looked too rocky and too hazardous to land, but now we were in great danger. It was our only chance.

"Pull, men . . . pull for your lives to that rocky cove!" I shouted. "If we're caught here in the trough of the waves we'll be swamped; and if we're knocked against those cliffs, we'll be dashed to pieces!"

With frenzied energy, Jourgensen and I gripped and pulled on the oars while Stacey and Crawford bailed like madmen. Somehow, with the mighty strength which fear alone can summon, we forced our heavy boat away from the terrifying shoreline and fought our way through the storm toward the break in the cliffs, which proved to be a very small, rocky cove.

As the waves flung us up on a narrow, tiny beach behind the small, protecting finger of rock, we threw back our heads and sent up loud, jubilant shouts of relief. We were safe!

"Just barely in time!" we all said as joyously we leaped ashore and pulled our heavy, water-soaked boat up to safety. "We just barely made it in time! We couldn't have stayed afloat much longer!"

"By all the Fates, we should now be at the bottom of the lake," said Stacey shakily. "It was a close call! I'm wondering if gold is really worth it! I don't mind admitting I was afraid!"

"Just look at the scow in the middle of the lake!" exclaimed Jourgensen. "It's bobbing like a cork!"

"And look at the raft out there," said Crawford. "They're throwing cargo over. See how desperate they are. Poor devils!"

"I'm afraid it's the Swedes," I said as we stood helplessly watching the men struggle for their lives. We tried calling and waving to them . . . but apparently they never saw or heard us. The storm swept their raft by . . . and soon we lost sight of them completely.

Then it was that our thoughts turned to our other friends, the Ryans, the Wisconsians, the Nelson brothers, the Canadians, the Kellys and Hydes, and McPhee and his party, for we knew that their boats were built like ours—made out of green lumber and sealed with pitch. Our friends were nowhere in sight, and we began wondering if the cries for help could have been any of theirs. We all felt sick at the thought.

But, miraculously, we were safe, perched on a ledge, crammed up against the frowning cliff with only a narrow beach line to escape the storm. No doubt many centuries of such pounding, dashing waves had carved this tiny, protecting place, which now sheltered us from the lashing, dragon-like fury of the lake. Suddenly we realized we were miserable and cold, so we built a fire of driftwood and dried out. Our next step was to get some heavy pitch to calk the seams of our boat. Fortunately, we discovered a few scrubby pines growing in among the rocks along the cliff, so Jourgensen and Crawford took their hatchets and crawled up and began slashing them down while Stacey and I emptied the boat and turned it over for a thorough overhauling and pitching.

All afternoon, intermittently, we worked and watched the progress of the storm. Toward evening, the wind slowly died. The waves quieted and subsided, and out over the lake and beyond the ridges of the mountains, the grayish sky slowly changed. A peculiar sunset glowed across the heavens, tinting the clouds to a weird, unearthly color. A dull red shone malignantly on the waters, reflecting deep into the cruel lake which had now calmed to a gentle ripple. A few, pitiful, tattered sails floated on the waters.

"Ed," said Stacey, "our boat is repaired. Hereafter, let's carry a can of pitch for safety."

"Yes, we must carry a can of pitch," I answered dully as I stood watching the lake, wondering how many stampeders had vanished in the icy waters of Lake Bennett and would never sail to the land of glittering gold! Was human life so cheap as to be risked here and a hundred times again for a handful of yellow nuggets?

Chapter III

Racing Down the Yukon Trail

The furious and devastating storm on Lake Bennett the day we left for Dawson had been a terrible blow to all of us. It had delayed us hours. But now our boat was repaired and made more seaworthy for our long journey ahead and we felt a tremendous urge to hurry. In our vivid imaginations we could already picture the stampeders ahead of us striking it rich, their pockets bulging with thick pokes of yellow gold.

That morning, July 3, 1897, at 3:30 A.M. we packed our boat and shoved off from the protecting ledge which had sheltered us the day before. Lake Bennett was calm and placid now. Only a few scattered sails appeared on the horizon; however, we never caught up to see whose they were.

Approaching the end of Lake Bennett, we saw Indians fishing near shore. "This must be Caribou Crossing," I said as I consulted the little map McPhee had drawn for me.

"He said we would see Indians here. Also, he said there would be more at Lake Tagish, as the Indians have a village there and several communal houses for use during the cold winter. Says they hold their famous Potlatches and ceremonials at Lake Tagish."

"I've heard that the caribou cross here by the thousands during the migrating season," said Crawford.

"If it wasn't for gold, I'd like to stay here and hunt," said Stacey, who was an expert hunter. "Just think of the thrill of getting a caribou!" he remarked enthusiastically.

Now we were sailing and rowing as fast as we could through the outlet of Lake Bennett. The Indians along shore watched us curiously from a distance. The outlet of Lake Bennett was a connecting river of about a quarter of a mile. Nearing the end of this channel, we could see that we were fast coming into another body of water.

"What a large lake and rugged country!" said Jourgensen. "Look at those high cliffs to the east. It must be Lake Tagish."

Jourgensen was right—the cliffs on the east side of the lake were breathtakingly high—sheer precipices towering several thousand feet skyward and rising directly from the water's edge. At their tops, these massive cliffs had formations resembling medieval fortresses with impregnable battlements and looked as though they had been carved by the mighty hand of Nature in a wild, combative, warlike mood.

The whole atmosphere was still. There wasn't a sound on the lake or a stir among the cliffs. There was only the creaking of our heavy oars and their rhythmical dip and splash in the water to break the stillness, with an occasional far-off mournful cry of a bird or the sudden splash of a fish. Only these marred the glass-like stillness of the dark lake which mirrored the shadows of the cliffs, for it was yet early morning.

"Where could Indians live in such a country?" asked Stacey. "It's so desolate and barren, it looks as though the wrath of God had visited this lonely place!"

"Still, it's very beautiful," said Crawford enthusiastically, for he had from the start shown a quick eye for beauty.

I'll be glad to get across this lake," I said uneasily. "McPhee warned us about Tagish. Said to look out for

Windy Arm. Many have been caught unawares and drowned here. He said that sudden winds often come howling down the canyon along the water and sweep across Lake Tagish. They think these hurricane winds are caused by the heat of the sun beating on the cliffs and waters, generating hot drafts of air."

With considerable dread, we watched the lake and cliffs. There was no wind at all and our sail hung limply. Two of us worked hard at the oars. I judged we had gone perhaps a third of the way along the lake when, suddenly, the cliffs to the east parted and there we gazed down the sinister gap of Windy Arm, which appeared to be at least five hundred feet wide for as far as we could see, extending up into the mountains. The water in this arm of the lake was quiet and calm and sparkled in the sun. Hurriedly, we bent on the oars to get across the entrance, for the sun was quite warm and, at any time, those sudden winds could start. Luck was with us, however. The Arm remained gentle and placid and we crossed safely and continued down the lake.

Later in the day, we began approaching the end of Lake Tagish. The cliffs had rolled back, forming low foothills. Black pines were appearing near the water's edge.

"I wonder where those Tagish Indians are?" said Stacey anxiously.

"I've heard a lot about these Thlingets," said Crawford. "They are said to be closely related to the Chilkat and Chilkoots living along Lynn Canal. Everyone knows that, in the past, they were a very fierce tribe of Indians. Even the Russians couldn't cope with them when they owned Alaska, and it is said that, secretly, these Indians continue some of their ancient ceremonials even though the American and Canadian Governments have banned them by law."

"Yes," said Stacey, "I've heard they still have what they call their 'Cannibal Secret Society.' They say Indians, to be initiated, are supposed to eat the flesh of a corpse! And that isn't all! Underneath the pillars holding up their communal houses, often they buried their slaves captured in war. It is said they buried them alive and then dropped the heavy foundation posts and timbers onto the poor, luckless captives. They usually took snips of hair before the ceremony to be used on dance sticks afterwards as proof of the superior quality of their tribal house. This all was to prove the greatness of the tribe and to raise the prestige of their chiefs!"

"Great Scott!" said Jourgensen. "Let's not stop at this lake!"

"Oh, we're safe," I said. "These Indians are reported friendly to white men."

Lake Tagish was narrowing down rapidly now. At this point, it was a river-like channel of several hundred feet across and the current was quite sluggish. Lake Marsh would be just beyond.

Suddenly, we saw Indians along the left bank. Simultaneously, they saw us and began shouting and running along the beach. We got the general impression that they wanted us to land, but Jourgensen and Stacey had another idea. They were at the oars and began rowing as fast as they could. When the Indians saw we were ignoring their shouts, several canoes filled with whooping Indians put out swiftly from shore. They paddled rapidly toward us, yelling wildly and motioning for us to stop.

Stacey and Jourgensen braced their feet against the footboards and pulled with frantic strength on the oars and we plowed faster through the water, but not fast enough.

"By George!" gasped Stacey. "I don't like their looks! Those Indians are up to no good. Their canoes are lighter than ours. Look how they're gaining on us!"

It was true, the Indians were rapidly overtaking us. It was foolish to think that our heavily loaded boat could outstrip those fast-moving canoes. Then what? Even though we'd heard these Indians were friendly, still, one could never really be sure. Great Scott! Would they take us prisoners? Many unpleasant thoughts raced through my mind. Yes, a boatload of men could easily disappear in this vast territory and no one would ever know what had happened. After all, this country had once been all theirs. Mightn't they resent our coming, just as the Indians in our own country had done? These thoughts made my scalp creep.

Quickly, I glanced back along the lake, hoping to see signs of other white men, but there wasn't a stampeder in sight. The Indians were getting closer and closer now, and I could see they were greatly excited. I measured the distance with my eyes. Three hundrd feet, two hundred feet . . .

"Shall I shoot?" shouted Stacey, who had suddenly put down his oars and was reaching for his gun.

"No," I said, "let me handle them. Let's see what they want."

Suddenly, the Indians put down their paddles and sat perfectly still while their canoes skimmed over the water towards us. There was a dead silence.

"Now, what?" said Stacey in alarm.

All at once each Indian reached down into the canoe and held up something. By this time the canoes were just a few feet away.

"It's fish, it's fish!" I laughed in relief. "Look, fellows, those Indians have fish to sell and some of it's dried. See, they're holding it up for us to buy!"

"Trade fish! Trade fish! . . . Money and tobacco!" the Indians chanted in peculiar, broken English, all speaking at once.

"Well, I'll be goldarned!" said Stacey. "I'll gladly buy some fish and part with a plug of tobacco!"

A little later, seated around a campfire on the beach of Lake Tagish, we broiled pieces of fresh fish, which tasted rather good for our supper. We had landed because of a very insistent invitation from the Indians which we couldn't very well disregard, and while we ate, about thirty curious Indians watched us and hovered near.

They were too close for comfort, and the smell of drying fish on huge racks nearby and the odor of perspiring Indians was almost overpowering and nearly took our breath and appetites away. Some of the Indians sat nearby, gleefully smoking some of the tobacco they had newly acquired and some were trying to chew the plug that Stacey had given them.

One young Indian boy of perhaps eighteen was very talkative and, in his broken English, told us a little about himself and his people. It seemed that, many years ago, his tribe had had a very terrible battle with an invading tribe of Indians called the Sticks. I gathered they had come a great distance from the interior, and the Tagish Indians, aided by the Chilkats, had defeated the Sticks and had killed many warriors and had taken many slaves. The boy spoke with great pride of the victory of Tagish house. He said some white missionaries had been there for a short time and had tried to convert his people. He thought maybe they were a "little converted," but he wasn't sure just how much. Seemed that the white missionaries had taught him some useful ways and how to talk English. The boy pointed out two of their communal houses about a quarter of a mile back on the slope of a foothill near by and said, "See, missionaries bring us windows."

In the fading light, we thought we caught the reflection of window glass, but we weren't going up there to investigate. We took his word for it.

"Now we've had our supper," we told the gaping Indians, "and we must be on our way. We can still make many miles before dark."

"Too many white men in too much hurry," said their chief philosophically.

Bidding the Indians goodbye, we pushed our boat off and, with great relief, continued down the river-like outlet of Lake Tagish. The Indian squaws and children waved, the dogs barked and the men held up their spears in a last salute. It was goodbye to Lake Tagish and on to Lake Marsh!

After the Indians had faded out of the picture, I drew out my little diary and wrote this account of the day, for I had decided to keep a record of each day, no matter what!

> July 4, 1897 (Between Lake Tagish & Marsh Lake)
>
> Got up at 3 A.M. at Lake Bennett. Made good time across Windy Arm! A dangerous place when wind is blowing. Wind was light, had to row part of time. Wonder what dear folks are doing at home? Some Indians were camped. Wanted 50c per dried fish. Do not know what name of fish is, but the flesh is color of salmon when cooked, was rather tasteless, but it's good for a change. Took supper near Tagish house, where Indians have their Potlatch every year. Here, a war was fought between the Stick and Chilkat Indians and Tagish Indians.

That night we camped at Lake Marsh. It was a large, rather marshy lake about twenty miles long, and some of the stampeders called it "Mud Lake"; but, altogether, it presented a pleasing, restful place to stay, as we were very tired from our long day and encounter with the Indians and welcomed this place to camp.

The following morning I wrote some good news in my diary, for we had sighted some of our friends and a number of other stampeders.

> July 5, 1897 (Lake Marsh)
>
> Camped here last night. Mosquitoes were terribly thick. Hyde's scow passed before we were up, but we caught up with them 5 miles down. Made an extra sail out of a sheet & now are scooting along, passing all the boats. The Swedes we just passed. They had a hard time on Lake Bennett and Tagish.

"Well, thank God, the Hydes and Swedes are safe," I said, "and we've caught up with part of the crowd."

"But how about the others?" asked Stacey.

"We must keep inquiring about them," I said. "Surely someone has seen them! They may be ahead of us—who knows?"

"But those cries for help during the storm on Lake Bennett," said Crawford.

"Yes, I know," I replied, "they still haunt me! If only we could have gone to their rescue!"

"Pretty soon let's land and hunt for game," said Stacey, abruptly changing the subject. "I'm getting awfully tired of fish! We've had fish for breakfast, lunch and dinner ever since we met those Indians! This is moose and caribou country. I've heard that they feed on the tender buds of willows and marshy grass along the rivers, and this river is lined with willows."

"Fresh meat would taste mighty good," agreed Jourgensen, who was already checking his rifle making ready for the hunt. "Besides, fresh meat will help stretch our provisions."

We were drifting slowly along now close to shore, watching the muddy beach for a likely place to land. Stacey hungrily scanned the shore for signs of animals. "Think I see bear tracks. Let's pull in here," he urged.

"Thought you wanted a moose?" laughed Jourgensen.

"Say, I'm so hungry for fresh meat," said Stacey, "I'd settle for a tough bear, or most anything!"

By this time, we had nosed our boat up onto a narrow beach. At this particular spot, the bank rose about ten feet up from the beach line. The bank seemed to be of clay and looked damp and slippery.

Stacey and Jourgensen grabbed their rifles, scrambled up the bank and disappeared among the willows while Crawford and I waited in the boat, which was half floating in the water, being anchored to a large rock on shore. We waited and listened for some time, but there wasn't a sound from our hunters. Finally, Crawford and I dozed, for we had lost much sleep the night before fighting those beastly mosquitoes at beautiful Lake Marsh.

Suddenly, our peaceful cat nap was disturbed by the sharp, staccato reports of rifles and almost simultaneously we heard the thundering beat of hoofs. Crawford and I lunged crazily to our feet and, almost before we could gain our balance, there was a crash in the willows and a huge moose came leaping over the bank, flying through the air straight at us. We were too petrified to move; besides, we didn't have time. For a hundredth of a split second, we had the horrifying picture of a mammoth body, blazing eyes and huge antlers descending on us. But somehow, in mid-air, the beast seemed to veer off to the right, just barely clearing our boat by a few feet. Landing in the water, it sent up a tremendous splash, then, kicking and snorting, it righted itself and swam wildly towards the opposite shore. In rapid, quick succession, two other moose leaped the bank, and landing in the water near by, they struck out after their leader. Reaching the other shore, they all disappeared quickly among the trees.

It all happened so fast and was so unexpected that Crawford and I could have sworn we'd been dreaming, had we not been soaking wet from the splashes.

"Well, I'll be jiggered!" sputtered Crawford, shaking the water from his clothes. "It's the first time I ever saw a moose and it came near being my last!"

All at once the bushes parted on the bank and there stood our two hunters, looking very disgruntled.

"Why didn't you shoot?" they yelled. "The whole herd got away!"

"Come on down," I laughed, "we still have some dried fish for supper and we can make some flapjacks."

"I'm going to take off these wet clothes first," said Crawford. "A good bath, even in icy water, will be better than food right now!"

"Me, too," I said as I began peeling off my wet shirt. "When have any of us had baths?"

"It's been a long time!" laughed Crawford as we both splashed into the cold water. "You know, Ed, I was beginning to think I smelled those Tagish Indians around here," laughed Crawford again as he looked up significantly at our two disappointed hunters who were perspiring freely, looking obviously displeased with us. But, in a few minutes, Jourgensen and Stacey had good-naturedly taken the hint and joined us in a rousing community bath.

"Well, I'll still get a moose," chattered Stacey in the cold water. "I never want to leave the North without getting one moose to my credit!"

Crawford and I kicked and splashed cold water over our hunters and threw back our heads and gave them the "horselaugh." "A whole herd of moose," we taunted, "but only fish for supper!"

Later in the day, much cleaner and in better spirits, we traveled down the fifty miles of the Lewis River. The bath must have done us a lot of good, for we were struck with the enchantment and beauty of the river. It looked as though a man-made canal had been put through here by a marvelous landscape gardener and that the trees and shrubs had been planted there just to add to the beauty. The water was so crystal clear that the reflections were like fresh murals at each bend of the river. A more picturesque stretch of country could scarcely be imagined.

Very later in the day we camped, and the next morning I was in joyous spirits when I wrote in my diary. We had met some of our friends and they had camped overnight with us.

July 6, 1897 (Lewis River)

Last night, Hydes and Kellys and several other parties caught up with us. This morning we were the first off! Had to go back for stovepipe, which I forgot at camp.

Just seeing these men again was like a tonic and was good for us. It made it seem more like a real stampede. The race was on again! We were headed for the glittering sands of the Yukon with added zest, new energy and hardening muscles. It was forward down the river, faster and faster. Who would get there first?

"See you later," we called to the Hydes and Kellys and the others as we finally shoved off from the beach and hoisted our double sail, one of which we had made out of an old sheet in my pack.

"Look for jade along the river," called one of the men. "The Indians find it up here. It's valuable."

"Now who wants jade?" called Stacey in disgust. "It's only gold we're after!"

There was a good wind that morning and our boat went sailing along at a fast clip. The added sail helped carry us miles ahead of our friends.

Suddenly, we noticed the contour of the river, which was about two hundred feet wide, begin to narrow and we could feel a heavy pull on the boat. Hurriedly, we lowered the double sail and made for the right bank, hugging the shore, where the current was less strong. The wide valley had now closed in and the rocks were of glistening basalt formation of dark-grayish color.

"Look," said Stacey, "there's a sign posted on the bank. It says, 'WARNING! WATCH FOR CANYON!' in big letters."

Hardly had he spoken when our ears caught a low, muffled roar.

"It's Miles Canyon!" yelled Crawford.

Quickly, I consulted my map. Somehow, I had miscalculated the distance to this dreaded stretch of water.

"What shall we do when we reach the canyon?" asked Crawford nervously. "Ed, I'm worried. You know I'm not a good sailor and have had no experience until this trip."

"Don't worry," said Jourgensen, "I'm a sailor and have spent half my life on the salt water. It'll be a cinch after that storm on Lake Bennett."

"Oh, yeah?" sneered Stacey. "Not this stretch of water! I've heard tell of it all the way to Tacoma. Nope, it ain't going to be easy!" he concluded as he spat a juicy wad of tobacco into the river and watched it quickly disappear in the current. "I tell you fellows, I want to reach the Klondike —not rest in peace somewhere in the river!"

"Look," said Jourgensen, "there are some men on the bank motioning us to come ashore."

"Guess we'd better land," I said as I steered the boat toward the right bank.

"Say, fellows," the men called, "Miles Canyon is just around that bend, and the Squaw and Whitehorse Rapids are beyond that. You'll have a tough time getting through. It's a hell hole!"

"Yes," said one of the men, "a boatload of stampeders was drowned in the canyon only this morning, and yesterday a scow was smashed to pieces against the big rock. The water below the rapids is full of wrecks. Now, we'd hate to see that happen to you fellows and we are offering to take you through the canyon and Whitehorse for one hundred dollars. It's cheap at that, because if the canyon doesn't get you, the Whitehorse Rapids may. We know all the dangers!"

"It sounds pretty bad," I said, "but we'll have to talk this thing over. A hundred dollars is a lot of money. Can we see the canyon from above?"

"Yep," they said, "just follow the trail. It takes you along the rim. You can see the Whitehorse Rapids from there. It's a long way below the canyon, about three and a half miles."

In double-quick time the four of us hiked up the trail. By this time, the roar of the river was getting so loud we had to shout to be heard. Crawford had bolted on ahead of us. Suddenly, he stopped and pointed.

"Just look down there," he yelled. "It's a hundred feet below! Ed, you can count me out. I'm walking around the canyon. It's a hell hole!"

"Great Scott!" I exclaimed as I caught up with Crawford and peered over the cliff. "It's worse than I thought. Look at the current and the suction of the water!"

I glanced at Stacey—he had turned a bilious green. Then I looked at Jourgensen—he had thrown himself down on his stomach and was cautiously peering over the brink at the thrashing waters below.

"Suff'rin' cats! What a water inferno!" he yelled. "Look at the swiftness of the current and look down the canyon at those two big whirlpools licking against the cliffs. See, there's a big stump being sucked down in the center of one of them."

Suddenly, as we watched, a boatload of stampeders came hurtling crazily through the canyon. They seemed to be entirely at the mercy of the tornado-like water and they were going at tremendous speed. Gaping, fascinated, we watched, fully expecting at any moment to see their boat dashed to pieces against the canyon walls or sucked under by the terrific undertow of the whirlpools; but, somehow, the men slipped through the middle unharmed and disappeared behind a column-like bend in the canyon.

"Jumpin' Jupiter!" yelled Jourgensen, "what a thrill! They shot the canyon in just about a minute and a half. That's as fast as a locomotive! If they can make it, we can too. All we have to do is to stay in the middle of the canyon and row like demons and bail like hell! Ed, let's go back and tell those fellows we're shooting the canyon without them!"

"O.K.,"* I said, a little startled, "I'm with you."

"Me, too," said Stacey.

Crawford was dead silent as we walked back down the trail. His footsteps lagged. At the landing, the three men were waiting for us.

"Listen, fellows," I said, "we've decided to shoot the canyon and rapids by ourselves."

"You fellows must be crazy!" said one of the men. "But why don't you play it safe and portage your boat and goods around the canyon and below the Whitehorse. There's a trail back in the woods."

---

*The term "O.K.," was used in 1897, especially by accountants and business people.

"How far is it to below the Whitehorse?" we asked.

"About five miles," they replied.

We all looked at each other in dismay—four outfits, comprising hundreds and hundreds of pounds, not to mention our heavy boat!

Then I asked, "Are there any places to land on down that stretch of water where we can get out and portage if we shoot the canyon and want to change our minds about the Whitehorse?"

"Yes," they replied. "The first place to land is just below Miles Canyon, to the right bank. A natural eddy swings you in if you're quick enough. The other place is about two and a half miles down, below Squaw Rapids on the left, just before you hit Whitehorse Rapids. . . . But, brother! take our advice and don't try to shoot the Whitehorse with your heavily loaded boat unless you are flirting with death! Nearly everyone pulls in there and portages around from there by trail. It will take you a day extra, but it's worth it!"

"I'm walking around the Canyon and Whitehorse," announced Crawford.

"It's O.K.," we said. "We'll wait for you and pick you up below the rapids. We'll be there in only a few minutes."

Hurriedly, we redistributed our cargo and covered everything with canvas. Then we were ready to start.

"Jourgensen," I said. "I'll steer the boat. You man the oars. Stacey can bail and have calking material ready in case we get into trouble. If all's ready, let's shove off."

"Hey, fellows, wait a minute," yelled Crawford. "I'm going, too. You need another man to row, don't you?"

"Sure," we said, "jump in and let's go!"

"Good luck," called the men. "You'll need it!"

"Thanks," we called. "Thanks for your advice."

With a few strokes of the double oars, Crawford and Jourgensen swung the boat out into midstream. With sudden fury, the current gripped our boat and, in a few split seconds, we were being funneled into a mad torrent of rushing waters, forced between high, perpendicular cliffs against which the raging waters boiled and roared. At terrifying speed we shot along, passing unfriendly cliffs and jagged rocks against the walls.

Quickly, I glanced at the dark cliffs of glistening rock,

which appeared polished and slippery, and I caught a blurry vision of hundreds of marble-like colonnades rising out of the river from thirty to seventy-five feet, crowded in bas-relief against the canyon walls. They looked like hundreds of tombstones. I knew we could find no refuge here if we were thrown out into these furious caldron waters. No wonder this canyon was sometimes called Dead Man's Rapids!

With lightning speed, we swept through the upper part of the canyon and came to the place in the river where the canyon opened wider into a circular, cliff-bound chamber, and my eyes shot ahead to where the whirlpools on either side leered at us, their ugly lips moving irregularly toward the middle of the river and then back again toward the cliffs, showing a deep maw in the center.

Suddenly, I realized that the whirlpool to the left was reaching up the river with fiendish, unseen fingers, sucking us rapidly and hungrily toward its ugly center.

"Quick, Jourgensen, Crawford," I yelled. "Pull to the middle! We're headed for the whirlpool!"

The men shot quick, frightened glances over their shoulders then laid hard on the oars. I gripped my oar and tried to steer, but already the suction of the whirlpool had caught us and we began swinging to the left, then whirled around and around, drawing closer to the throat of the pool. My eyes fastened in horror on the center, where down we would go once we reached the middle. The men and I fought the current, bending every last atom of strength against the demonic waters.

Battling our way toward midstream, somehow we miraculously escaped its clutches. But here the overpowering strength of the mad current caught our boat, sending us careening and hurtling through the canyon, hitting the combers which came bouncing and crashing back from the canyon walls.

Our boat almost leaped out of the water as a huge comber hit us with such force that we were knocked sideways, then another and another struck us; immediately, Stacey went into action, bailing like a madman and shouting, "We're going under! We're going under!"

Stacey's voice was almost drowned in the maddening roar of the river and we seemed to be engulfed in a deluge of water. I grabbed a pail and bailed frantically.

"I can't control the boat!" yelled Jourgensen.

Now I glanced up to see that we were headed for the right wall of the canyon. There seemed no escape. We would surely hit it. I grabbed my oar and tried to steer . . . but suddenly a comber from that side hit us with crashing force, sending us tipping and careening, literally spewing us out of the canyon into open river.

"I'm pulling to the right bank," shouted Jourgensen.

Reaching shore, we leaped onto dry land with trembling, shaking knees. We were very much unnerved. Pulling our boat up onto a low bank, we finished bailing, then inspected her for damage but found none.

"She took a terrible beating," said Stacey. "The last few seconds . . . I thought we were goners! Ed, she's a good boat after all!"

We decided to hike up along the hill and scout the river from there, looking down on Squaw Rapids. Had we had enough of the river? Should we pack our boat and goods from this point? It would be at least four miles over a rough trail to below the Whitehorse Rapids.

No, we decided, we'd risk Squaw Rapids. But we certainly wouldn't attempt the Whitehorse; at least, not with our heavily loaded boat. On that we were unanimously agreed.

While we were getting ready to shove off, other boatloads of stampeders came shooting out of the canyon and made frantically for the right shore. Their faces were white and drawn and we knew the strain they'd been under! They said they had had enough and were going to undertake the back-breaking job of portaging everything, including their boat, around both the Squaw Rapids and Whitehorse.

"Well, we're off," we said as we shoved away into midstream and were soon greeted by the icy spray of Squaw Rapids. Now we found ourselves shooting along between low canyon walls, racing at breakneck speed. Squaw Rapids rushed us through a foaming gauntlet of hissing waves and huge black rocks. Farther down we caught sight of pieces of broken boats wedged in among the rocks and openings in the low, twenty-foot cliffs. All the while, the threatening river muttered ominously, then, suddenly, the voice of

Squaw Rapids rose to a high pitch and shrieked of death straight ahead!

"My God!" said Stacey as we shot around a bend in the river. "It's the Whitehorse!"

Looking downstream, we caught a lightning glimpse of more terrifying waters ahead.

"Pull! Pull to the left shore!" we all yelled at each other.

The current clutched at our boat, but we hit the side eddy and swung into the left shore, landing safely.

Here we were at the head of the mighty Whitehorse, the wildest of all Yukon waters, ready to pack our supplies and, if need be, our boat around the rapids.

At this point I sat down on a rock, resting just long enough to scribble this entry:

> July 7, 1897
>
> Reached Canyon 10 A.M. Devilish hole, ⅝ mile long. Current swift & full of combers. Stacey, Jourgensen, Crawford & I shot the canyon, then down to head of Whitehorse Rapids, 2½ miles, & made it in 8 minutes. The Whitehorse Rapids are a terror! Camped at this point. Mosquitoes horrible!

After making a hasty camp, we walked along the Whitehorse for a little distance. The mighty flood was now being forced between low basalt banks perhaps sixty-five feet across from bank to bank. Here the river seemed to rush at land, sky, and again at water . . . kicking, spouting, spraying into the air ten and fifteen feet, furiously defying anything that got into its path.

As we stood there watching, a large boat, half-covered with canvas, came plunging through the Whitehorse. We could hear the men calling frantically to each other, then their voices were drowned by the roar of the river as, momentarily, their boat was hidden from sight behind a spray of water; then we saw them emerge again farther down the river, plunging on and on into the chaotic waters ahead.

Spellbound, we watched until they were out of sight.

"Great Scott!" I said. "What a villainous stretch of water! Our heavily loaded boat could never make it. Let's get started packing around the rapids and be ready to take off tomorrow if we decide to shoot the Whitehorse."

Quickly, we sorted our goods, loading ourselves down like pack horses with seventy-five- to hundred-pound packs each. It was easy to find the trail, which went up a hill and then followed along the Whitehorse at a little distance parallel with the river, and it was evident that hundreds of other feet had plodded over this narrow, dusty trail, portaging their goods. Tiger-like mosquitoes lay in wait in the woods, attacking us from all directions.

At last, we struggled to the end of the first weary mile below the Whitehorse, where the portage ended. Here the trail pointed down to the river's edge. There we cached our first load and returned to camp for another and another load. Moving hundreds of pounds of supplies was both a heart- and back-breaking job. We only allowed ourselves a few hours of rest that night; then we were up again early, repeating the toil of the evening before.

Several parties of men, who had landed ahead of us and had already finished portaging their supplies, were now going to let their boats down through the rapids from along shore with ropes. To help them, and also to gain a little experience, we walked along shore for a short distance, giving them a helping hand with ropes and poles to steady the boats. We discovered, however, that getting a boat through the rapids like this was no easy matter and amounted to a tug of war with the river. We had to jump over rocks, climb over fallen logs, pulling and straining with the ropes against the current, while the boats bounced and leaped in the rapids like bucking broncos.

Up until now, Stacey, Jourgensen, Crawford and I had talked seriously of portaging our boat up over the trail on skids or taking it through the rapids with ropes, but now just going this short distance along shore made us change our minds.

"Let's go back and shoot the Whitehorse," I said, "and get it over with in a hurry!"

"But what about that last load of dried beans and the Klondike stove?" asked Jourgensen.

"Say, I wouldn't go back into those woods again for all of the beans in the Klondike," said Stacey. "Look at me—

I'm just covered with mosquito bites and I've got blisters all over my feet!"

"Then, fellows," I said, "let's pile the stove and beans back into the boat and take off. They no doubt will make good ballast!"

In no time, we had set the stove and fifty-pound sacks of beans back in the middle of the boat; then, quickly, we stretched some canvas across the bow of the boat and tacked it down. Now we were ready to go. As in Miles Canyon, again Jourgensen and Crawford were at the oars, Stacey had the bailing can and I took the steering oar.

"Whitehorse, here we come!" we yelled defiantly as we shoved off and braced ourselves for the tremendous ordeal ahead.

Looking anxiously downstream as we shot around a bend in the river, we caught a forbidding perspective of what lay ahead. But there was no stopping now, no turning back . . . no matter how much we regretted our decision!

With a mighty roar, the Whitehorse seemed to rush out to meet us, tossing wildly, frothing, furiously white, charging and racing; it caught our boat with terrific force and sent us crashing through the rapids, knocking us sideways, forward, diagonally and, it seemed, in every direction, spraying us, racing and galloping beneath us and carrying us to what seemed certain destruction. All we could do was to hang on desperately and try to steer, but it seemed of little use. We were almost completely at the mercy of the Whitehorse.

With dashing speed, we passed the fellows who were letting their boats down with ropes along the bank and heard them all yell at us. In the wild confusion of water, we barely missed large rocks, scraped over half-concealed ledges, and poured through low cascades of boiling water. In this leaping torrent, we seemed lost! However, each moment we managed to stay afloat was in our favor.

Then, at last, about a mile down the rapids, the mighty Whitehorse, as though thwarted, kicked us high on a tossing wave, then, snorting and shaking with white rage, threw us violently out of the rapids into open river, where we floundered and shivered for several hundred yards before we could catch our breath and get our boat to shore.

"My God," said Stacey, "look at the wrecks in the river! We could have been one of them!"

Looking downstream, we had a sweeping view of this stretch below the rapids, and there we saw, caught in the eddies and washed against the rocky shore, dozens of wrecked boats and splintered timbers. Anxiously, we looked for the boats of our friends—the Ryans, Wisconsians, Nelson brothers, Canadians, Swedes, Kellys and Hydes—but it would have been almost impossible to have identified these boats, as all of them were badly damaged and some of them were actually broken in half.

Along the shore, a few stampeders were drying out their outfits and repairing their boats, but we saw no one we knew. Needless to say, we were thankful to be ashore and, as we worked to repair a top board which had come loose in the Whitehorse and collected our outfits, we glanced at the river, looking with fear at each new wreck which came tumbling down and watching with excited interest each new boat which made it safely.

Little did we dream that we were almost on the present site of the town of Whitehorse.

Chapter IV

Riches on the Yukon

Now it was "Hi-ho for Lake LaBarge!" Stacey, Jourgensen, Crawford and I were in high spirits as we raced faster and faster toward the beckoning Klondike, meeting more and more stampeders after we had pulled away from the great bottleneck of the Yukon—Miles Canyon and the mighty Whitehorse Rapids. We were now about a fourth of the way to Dawson along the Yukon Trail!

Skimming down the Lewis River, the swift current carried us past scarped banks of white silt a hundred feet high, and, in places, we steered away from triangular-shaped sand and gravel bars which emerged from out of the river. To the west, the hills changed into rugged mountains and seemed to be composed almost entirely of granite. Soon we passed the turbid waters of the Tahk-heena River, which poured in from the west, cutting through those jagged granite mountains. Here again we saw Indians, for the distant headwaters of the Tahk-heena were said to be only about fifty miles away from Lynn Canal. We judged the Indians to be Chilkats, but didn't stop to find out.

The Tahk-heena was little known in 1897. The reports were that there were almost insurmountable mountain barriers between the source of this river and the sea, and there was only an indefinite Indian trail, which made it almost impossible for a white man to get through with supplies.

Now the Lewis River was carrying us almost due north. Somehow, we felt better when we were going in that direction.

As the four of us glided swiftly along in our twenty-foot boat, I put down my oars to rest a minute and began writing in my diary.

"What are you writing now?" asked Stacey curiously. (It was my habit to try to write a few lines, if possible, each morning while in the boat, but often I didn't complete the diary until late in the evening, perhaps while sipping my coffee sitting on a rock or log by the fire, or sprawled on my sleeping bag.)

"Here is what I've just written," I said as I handed Stacey my little red diary book.

> July 8, 1897 (Lewis River, below Whitehorse—Warm.)
> Got up and got breakfast. We fixed our boat. She is now O.K. Added an extra top board. Lost my ½ inch rope. We started off at 12:15 P.M. Shot out into current below the Whitehouse Rapids. Fairly flew along and made 3 miles in 8 minutes! . . .

After reading it aloud, Stacey handed back the diary and remarked, "Ed, I don't know how you manage to keep these up from day to day. Just getting into the Klondike is enough effort for me!"

"Well," I said, "writing diaries happens to be a hobby of mine. I've written them since I was a boy. Guess it sort of runs in our family. You see, my father was a war correspondent as well as a chaplain in the Civil War, and he kept diaries and sent back dramatic and vivid front-line battle descriptions telling how he even had to help with amputations in the improvised hospital tents. It just makes your blood run cold! Although he has been dead these ten years, my family still have and cherish his writings."

"Now I understand why you're so faithful with these diaries," sighed Stacey. "Some day, after we strike it rich, I'd like to read them all again. Can't you just picture us back in Tacoma talking about adventures during the gold rush!"

"I hope I can be with you then," said Crawford.

"Me, too," said Jourgensen. "And, by that time, I hope to have my own yacht and a home on Puget Sound."

Gradually, we noticed the river was widening and flowing through a broader valley. The current was less swift and the banks had taken on a sandy, stratified appearance of reddish, iron-stained color. To the east, a mountain range of limestone partly covered with snow and ice glistened in the light of the July sun. We continued through the afternoon and early evening, passing an ever-changing panorama of river, mountains and valleys, with occasional mountain reflections of breath-taking beauty. In places, large, mossy cushions like green-colored velvet touched and dragged in the water. Wild Flowers of every hue and color nodded in the warm northern breeze and added their enchantment to the scenery along the lower banks of the river.

About nine o'clock in the evening, we shot out of the river into a large lake of great beauty. The sun was riding low on the horizon but we could still see for miles and miles along the lake. To the northwest, across the water, a very large island of dark rock sparsely covered with spruce trees seemed to command and dominate the lake. This huge, ocean-like body of water was completely surrounded by mountains; the highest seemed to be at the upper end of the lake where we now were.

"It's Lake LaBarge!" shouted Stacey. "Look at the size of it and see the boats in the distance! We've caught up with the crowd of stampeders!"

All at once, we noticed a boat coming from down the lake with two men in it, and they were rowing rapidly in our direction. As they came closer, the sun caught the brilliance of bright-red jackets and we could see that the men wore broad-brimmed hats.

"Holy mackerel!" exclaimed Jourgensen, "they're mounted police and headed in our direction!"

"Good," said Stacey, "I've wanted to meet those boys ever since we crossed Chilkoot into Yukon Territory."

"Say, men," called the Red Coats, "we want to ask you a few questions. Where are you from?"

"Tacoma," I volunteered.

"How far have you come today?" they asked.

"We left Whitehorse Rapids this morning," we answered.

"Did you happen to see two men poling up the Lewis River in an Indian canoe?" they asked. "One fellow was very dark and the other of lighter complexion."

"No," I said, "the men we saw were all coming down river, headed towards the Klondike."

"Well," said one of Mounties, "the two we're looking for robbed and killed a stampeder on down the Yukon."

"Perhaps they're hiding somewhere right here at the lake," suggested Stacey, glancing significantly at the dark island and mountains beyond.

"They could be," said one of the police, "but we think they're fleeing up the river towards American territory."

"Are you having much trouble with the stampeders?" asked Stacey anxiously.

"No," replied the mounted police, "most of 'em are honest fellows, but now and then a bad egg slips into the country. Perhaps he hasn't brought in enough supplies or provisions and begins stealing, then ends up killing. The Canadian Government at Ottawa may have to pass a law requiring each stampeder to bring in a thousand pounds of provisions and have at least five hundred dollars before he can enter Yukon Territory. They are going to put a checking station at the summit of Chilkoot Pass and one at Lake Tagish, and will probably have stations at intervals on down the Yukon. In this way, the Canadian Government can keep a close tab on those who come into the country."

"Guess none of us could get by such drastic regulations if they were in effect now," I said, thinking of my 500 pounds of supplies and the $300 I had in my pocket.

"Well, if you're lucky, you'll survive," said one of the police, "but if you're not, the North can be pretty ruthless. Supplies are too slow coming up here and prices are sky-rocket high in Dawson!"

"Hope you catch your men," said Stacey. "I'm an ex-policeman from Tacoma. Darned if I wouldn't like to join you in the hunt!"

"Thanks, fellow policeman," said one of the Red Coats. "But you go on, search for gold, and we'll find our men. We'll catch them. We always do!"

"Good luck, then," we called as the Mounties pulled away and headed south.

"Just think of coming all the way up here only to get robbed and killed!" said Stacey, checking his gun carefully. "Poor devil, whoever he was. Tough luck!"

On the horizon, the late summer sun was dropping lower and lower. Swinging our boat toward the right bank, we looked for a camping place for the night. The shore line was quite irregular here, with high banks and terraces above sweeping back from the lake. A little farther down the lake, we spotted a more level place to land and saw blue smoke curling up from the trees and caught the glint of dozens of campfires. Pulling in, we landed and, to our amazement, found the Swedes and Canadians among the crowd. They were about to have a late supper.

They greeted us warmly with much back-slapping and hearty hand-shaking, and one of the Swedes said, "Vell, vell, just to tink of meeting you vellows here! Ve tought maybe vot you got lost in de big Vitehorse. Ve had a tough trouble dere!"

It was jolly being with the Swedes and Canadians and we felt like old friends.

"Where are the others?" we asked. "The Ryans, Wisconsians, Nelson brothers, Kellys and Hydes?"

"Oh, the Kellys and Hydes are here somewhere at Lake LaBarge," said one of the Canadians, "but we haven't seen the others for several days, and no one has seen the Ryans or Wisconsin parties since the storm on Lake Bennett."

That evening, we sat up very late. It was chilly, the altitude of the lake being over 2000 feet. We watched the changing degrees of twilight on the water and over the mountains and sat smoking around the campfire, telling stories and occasionally singing old songs we had known back home. It was the first time we had relaxed and really enjoyed ourselves since coming into the North country. Somehow, the gentle lapping of the water on the pebbly beach and the soft wind among the trees seemed to bring peace to our fevered souls and hurried spirits bent only on reaching the land of gold these last six weeks.

Before turning in for the night, I knocked the ashes from my pipe, leaned far back and searched the heavens to locate the Big Dipper and then the North Star. It was only a pinpoint in the summer night, but I gazed at it for a long time. My thoughts were very far away with my dear Velma and our little son in Tacoma when I rolled up in my sleeping bag and finally went off to sleep.

Although we hadn't planned to travel with the Swedes, the following afternoon they overtook us and we continued on down the lake together. During the day, we had seen a number of stampeders camping on shore and others in their boats hurrying down the lake, and we had caught sight of the Kellys and Hydes anchored off shore.

The northern end of Lake LaBarge narrowed down and we could see two valleys branching out. One veered off to the northwest, which, we learned, was the Ogilvie Valley, and the other, a much smaller valley, pointed out to the northeast. Through this valley we could see the outlet of Lake LaBarge flowing as a narrow ribbon of water, then it disappeared behind high hills and mountains.

I glanced at my map and saw that Lake LaBarge was the last of the river-connected chain of lakes over which we had been traveling.

"Tomorrow we will be going through the outlet and will reach Thirty Mile River," I said.

About eight miles from the end of the lake we made an early camp with the Swedes and I wrote again in my diary.

July 9, 1897. (Lake LaBarge)

"Had breakfast at 4 A.M. Cold last night. Had fair

wind for 3 hours. Took left side of island. Passed Hydes and Kellys. . . . Rowed all day. Water like millpond. Some very beautiful landings. The Swedes caught up with us. Took supper at 6 P.M. and rowed across to left bank, where we found Canadians camped. Got tin cup I left at head of lake. The mosquitoes almost ate us up in the night. Had to make a smudge; finally slept fairly well."

That first day, we had made good time rowing across Lake LaBarge, considering there was no wind to use our sails. On the second morning, July 10th, 1897, at 4:00 A.M. we rolled out of our sleeping bags and shoved off, leaving the Swedes still sleeping in camp. There was a fair wind that morning and we sailed towards the outlet.

Looking back along the lake, we judged it to be over thirty miles long and perhaps five miles across at the upper, or southern end. The large rocky island seemed lonely and dark as it stood a little off center in the lake. We had learned that the miners called this island Richtofen Rocks. Far to the west, the early morning sun was spotlighting the mountain peaks which stood out against the clear northern sky. These mountains bore the significant name of Miners' Range. A more magnificent setting could hardly be imagined.

"I wonder how our Mountie friends are faring?" I remarked. "In this vast wilderness, there would be many places to hide."

"Look," said Stacey, "there's quite a large boat coming down the lake in double-quick time. I wonder who they could be?"

Soon a very fast, almost elegant-looking sailboat overtook us and, as it came within hailing distance, we recognized the four men in the boat as the Nash party from Lake Linderman, some men we had seen while building our boat.

"Hello, fellows," we hailed.

"Hello," they answered.

"What kind of a trip have you had?" we asked.

"Damned exciting!" they replied. "Met some Mounties above the lake going up the river. They questioned us. Were looking for two men in an Indian canoe. We told them we hadn't seen the criminals. Think the Mounties are coming back to Lake LaBarge to hunt this entire area."

"Yes, those Mounties stopped and questioned us, too. We'd all better be on the alert!" I said. Then I asked, "Say, have you men seen the Ryans, Wisconsians or Nelson brothers?"

"Only the Ryans," they called. "Saw them way back at Lake Tagish near Windy Arm. They were having a devil of a struggle with their boat. Never saw them after that. Don't know what happened."

"Hope they are O.K.," called Nash as his boat came closer. "Never saw so many wrecked boats in all my life. Lord, what a lot below the Whitehorse Rapids! Over a hundred have been reported drowned already, and there will be a lot more before the gold stampede is over. Well, guess that's a chance we all have to take," he concluded. "But we're in a big hurry now, fellows. Will see you later in Dawson," he added as the wind caught his tall, white sail and his light, slender boat picked up speed and shot ahead of us.

"Goodbye," we waved as we watched them skim over the water.

"Nash has the fastest boat of all," said Crawford enviously. "He must be a professional boat builder to have constructed a boat such as that. Look how she takes the wind and rides the water! They'll be in Dawson long before any of us!"

"Never can tell about these boats," said Jourgensen. "We might beat them yet."

We reached the outlet and took one last look, bidding adieu to Lake LaBarge, then jubilantly headed out of the lake into the fast-moving river.

Now we were tearing along a narrow, crooked river between high hills of pale-gray limestone. We could see large jagged rocks just under the surface of the water and huge boulders rising out of the river ahead of us. The slant of the river bed was visibly downward and the heavy overflow waters from Lake LaBarge were pouring and rushing through this narrow slit in the valley.

"It's Thirty Mile River," I said as I held the rudder oar firmly and steered hard as we dodged in and out among the rocks. We've heard many warnings about this stretch. Many brave fellows think it's as bad in places as Squaw and Whitehorse Rapids."

None of us dared relax our vigilance while going through Thirty Mile, but the fact that the river was high helped us over the worst places. Later, we learned a large boatload of stampeders had been wrecked in this river and all that was ever found to identify them was a carpenter's chest of tools marked "Black Diamond C" on the lid. The chest also contained a black vest, a key made of a German coin and a Waltham watch. These were the only things ever found of the ill-fated stampeders who were racing to the "land of too much gold."

At last we were out of the dangers of Thirty Mile River. We passed with flying speed a very large stream coming in from the east. It was known to us, the stampeders, as the Hootalinqua, but it was sometimes called the "Teslintoo." This river poured millions of gallons into the Lewis River and its headwaters were from Lake Teslin, a very large body of water high up in the mountains. The Tagish Indians called this lake the greatest of them all. It was reported to be over a hundred miles long, almost like an inland ocean.

Still traveling down the Lewis River later in the day, we passed many sand bars and a few miners panning for gold along an especially large, gravelly bar.

"Getting any gold?" we asked excitedly.

"A little, but it's not like it used to be!" they answered.

Later we learned this was the celebrated Cassiar Bar, discovered by a couple of miners over ten years before the big Klondike gold rush. The Cassiar Bar we had just passed was so named because of the gold which was washed down the river from some unknown source, possibly from Lake Teslin, where there had been some gold discoveries. This exciting discovery at Carriar Bar was, to the early miners, like finding an enormous sluice box with rich deposits of gold caught in the huge riffles. It reminded the old miners of the very rich sand bars yielding coarse and fine gold on the Stikine River, 300 miles to the south in the famous Cassiar District, where millions had been taken out, beginning around the year 1874.

Pulling into shore a few miles below Cassiar Bar, we

made a hasty camp. We had come perhaps fifty miles from Lake LaBarge, a good day's run. The following morning, it was up and away: journeying down the river, passing more streams coming in from the east, including the Big and Little Salmon rivers, where we sighted more stampeders and several Indian camps.

Here, again, the scarped banks and cliffs were about a hundred feet high, showing a strata of white deposit. To the east, the greenish-colored Seminow Mountains came into view and stayed with us for many miles, and the banks of the river showed a discolored volcanic rock with occasional outcroppings of a coal-black stratum running along the river banks.

Traveling at a good clip on July 11, 1897, late into the evening (for the sun was up until about 10:30 P.M.) we finally pulled into a good landing place on the left shore of the river. We had seen a cabin through the trees. On landing, we discovered three deserted cabins. No one was around, so we selected the best-looking one and began making ourselves comfortable.

Stacey and Jourgensen went searching for firewood and, in a few minutes, returned with large chunks of shiny black rock.

"Look here," exclaimed Stacey. "See what we've found."

"Why, it's coal!" I said in surprise.

"Yep," said Jourgensen, "and we found it near the river. Real Yukon coal!"

In no time we had a roaring fire in the old Klondike stove. "Boy, we'll have hot baths tonight!" we all exclaimed.

Suddenly, there was a knock on the door. Opening it, we saw an old Indian standing there. "What do you want?" I inquired in surprise.

"Me, caretaker for George Carmack," said the Indian. "This, his trading post. Carmack go to Klondike. Find much gold. He stay. Me watch trading post for white brother. Some day he come back."

"My partners and I wish to stay here tonight," I said.

"White man stay in cabin tonight," answered the Indian, "but white man pay with . . ."

"Tobacco?" I suggested.

"Tobacco," answered the Indian with a pleased grin.

In a few minutes, Stacey had parted with another much-cherished plug of his chewing tobacco, just as he had done at Lake Tagish.

"Hmph!" grunted Stacey after the Indian had closed the door. "Hope we don't meet any more of those tobacco-chewing Indians, or I'll run out of it before we reach Dawson!"

Quickly, we cooked and ate our supper, then threw our sleeping bags onto the bunks and stripped for our wash-pan baths. All at once, we were startled by a great red light blazing through the whisky-bottled window. Fearful, thinking it meant a sudden forest fire, we dashed out into the open, looking in all directions for the fire; but to our intense relief, we discovered it was only a very brilliant, flame-colored sunset lighting up the sky, mountains, forests and river into a terrific blaze of reddish color. Spellbound, fascinated, we watched as the sunset flamed and glowed, then smoldered below the horizon, seeming reluctant to let the shades of twilight settle over the Northland.

When this wondrous display of vivid color had faded, shivering, we all returned to the warmth of the cabin and finished our baths, then turned in for the night. Who could have predicted that, in only a few hours, there would be a drastic change in the weather!

Before snuggling down into my sleeping bag that night, I scribbled this entry of the happenings of the day.

July 11, 1897 (Lewis River—Warm)

Made about 20 miles; the river is very swift & we just shot along, taking our breath away. Nobody passed us today. We were ahead of entire party. We camp at Carmack's Trading Post, where are three cabins; one had a stove on which we cooked. Washed ourselves. Beautiful sunset. It looked as if an immense fire was just below the horizon!

Early the next morning, we were awakened by a heavy rain. At first it was a pleasant sound, but then the heavens opened and it just poured cats and dogs!

"We can't push on in this pouring rain," I said. "Might

as well relax and be thankful we're under cover and sleep a while longer."

At first, the heavy patter of rain on the cabin roof seemed like music to our ears, and being snug and warm in our sleeping bags was a great luxury to us. It was the first morning we had not gotten up at four o'clock since landing at the Dyea Indian village five weeks before.

At last, late in the morning, the storm abated. By that time, the four of us were up, had breakfast, and were eager to be on our way again. Although it was still drizzling, we shoved off and started down the river, hoping the storm had passed. But this was not the case. We spent a miserable day on the river. However, we were determined to travel on.

Wrapped in canvas and with cold fingers, I huddled in the boat and managed to scrawl this brief account:

> July 12, 1897 (Lewis River)
>
> Woke up 4 A.M. Raining hard. So far, have been fortunate. Have lost nothing. (Everything was covered with canvas.)

Traveling in a strange land on an unknown river, and soaking wet, does not add to a man's spirits. "Stacey," I said, scanning the river. "I'm worried. I hope we run out of this bad weather soon."

"Hope so too, Ed," he replied. "Rain makes it hard to see, not to mention bailing the boat!"

"I think we should be coming to the Five Fingers soon," I announced, consulting my little map.

"Going through the Five Fingers will be a cinch!" exclaimed Jourgensen.

"Sure it will," agreed Crawford. "Nothing could be as bad as Miles Canyon and the Whitehorse!"

"But some people think it very dangerous," I said. "We must be alert and ready for trouble. The river is high and angry and the current very swift. Besides, the visibility is bad."

After we traveled for a while, the rain softened and became a fine drizzle, but a misty, foggy veil hung over the river, blotting out most of the shore line. Only occasionally could we see the high cliffs which loomed ghost-like out of the fog. We traveled cautiously in this eerie, uncertain atmosphere and had just rounded a bend in the river when, all at once, straight ahead, about three hundred feet, loomed four triangular-shaped, huge, precipitous rocks, almost blocking the path of the river. They looked like enormous battleships plowing upstream in abreast formation with water splashing across their sharp bows.

"Great guns!" shouted Stacey, who was sitting as a lookout in the bow of the boat. "Quick, Ed, row for the right-hand channel. Hug the cliffs. It's the safest!"

"Jourgensen," I yelled, "grab the other oars. Both of us will have to manage the boat. The ride through will be quick but dangerous!"

We whipped our boat to the right channel against the defying cross-currents of the four other rushing channels. With steel-like muscles, we pulled and reached the entrance, then clung to the oars and boat as it struck the battling waters. We held our breath as we suddenly took a deep plunge into a white, frothy cascade of wild, tumbling waters which leaped and poured over a sudden, uneven drop in the river bed of about three or four feet. Our boat jumped and plunged, plunged and jumped again; then we came up and hit the smoother surface of the river and rushed on through the channel. In a few seconds we were out of the minature canyon of about 65 feet high and 200 feet long, flying along in open river, leaving the Five Fingers behind.

"What a thrill!" exclaimed Jourgensen. "Just like the Whitehorse and Miles Canyon while it lasted!"

"And we took in only about a bucketful," said Stacey, scooping the water out with a can.

"What a relief!" sighed Crawford. "Glad that's over!"

"Yes," I agreed, "but Rink Rapids are six miles ahead. I've heard there's nothing much to worry about. They are reported very mild."

Thirty-five minutes later I drew out my diary and added these significant words:

> Ran the Five Fingers and Rink Rapids. . . . 5:15 to 5:50 P.M. All is O.K.

The river beyond headed northward, the sun was breaking through and our spirits lifted. Below the Five Fingers, we passed numerous small wooded islands and saw many sand bars and inviting channels, but we kept to the middle of the ever-widening river. High, beetling mountains and broadening valleys came into view, but the character of the main river valley was gradually opening out onto a high plateau with occasional mountainous volcanic outcroppings.

I had set up my stove in the boat way back at Whitehorse, so we cooked and ate as we traveled along. Being the most versatile cook of the party, the lot seemed to fall to me and I was learning to throw together some very original and weird concoctions!

Stacey was so hungry for fresh meat that, at times, he was a little out of sorts . . . and so were we all! No doubt, if we could have spent more time on shore, Stacey and Jourgensen would have gone hunting and we could have had fresh moose or caribou steak, for we were in big-game country. As it was, we had to be content with a few scrawny blackbirds which Stacey and Jourgensen shot from the boat and several stray fish which I managed to hook onto as we traveled along. However, Stacey kept his gun polished and ready for immediate action, always hoping for an opportunity of spotting a moose.

Now and then we saw Indians, but we continued rapidly down the river, whoop-along-bang, greatly intent on minding our own business and reaching the Klondike. Several times we got stuck on sand bars and had trouble shoving off.

Early in the afternoon on the 13th of July, the day after we had left the Five Fingers, we approached the junction of the Lewis and Pelly rivers.

"Look!" said Crawford, pointing with much excitement. "I believe we've reached the Yukon River at last!"

Hurriedly, I consulted the little map McPhee had given me. "Yes, it's marked the beginning of the Yukon at the junction of the Lewis and Pelly."

The main river abruptly widened to about 2000 feet at this point, and, coming into the river through a deep valley from the northeast, was the Pelly River. It was pouring volumes of murky water into the clear, blue waters of the Yukon.

"Hurrah for the Yukon! . . . And a salute to Fort Selkirk!" cried Stacey with a sudden burst of wild enthusiasm, and, grabbing his rifle, he fired a volley of shots into the air.

"Hurrah for the Yukon? . . . And a salute to Fort Selkirk!" we all echoed as Jourgensen shot another volley into the air.

"But where is Fort Selkirk?" asked Crawford, watching the shore closely.

"Look," I said. "There's a large log cabin and some shacks about a quarter of a mile down the river on the left bank. Let's land and find out."

Immediately, we made for a small float anchored near shore and were just tying up when a rather short, elderly-looking man came down to meet us.

"Welcome to Fort Selkirk and Harper's Trading Post," he greeted cheerily. "It's good to have you men stop here. Come on up and see the trading post."

"Where's the fort?" asked Jourgensen eagerly.

"There isn't a fort here now," answered the trader, "but we're almost on the site of it."

"But this place is marked Fort Selkirk on the map," I said.

"Yes, I know," answered the trader, "and although there is no longer a fort here, this place will probably always be called Fort Selkirk, but the fort was burned about eighteen fifty-two by some of those devilish Chilkat Indians. The ruins are nearby. However, there are only a few bricks left hidden among the trees."

"What kind of Indians are these?" asked Stacey, for, as we walked toward the trading post, we saw Indian children playing nearby and several old Indian women in squatting positions leaning against the logs of the cabin pretending to be asleep. Several times I saw them peek out from under their leathery eyelids, but, otherwise, they never budged from their drowsing positions in the warm July sun. The trader opened the door for us and we entered.

Closing the heavy door behind us, our friend explained,

"These are Knife and Wood Indians. They live around here and have for years and years been friendly with the white people."

While the trader was talking, our eyes quickly took in the interior of the trading post. It was a good-sized room and the logs were peeled and chinked with moss. A large stove stood in the corner with a high chimney extending to the ceiling. Miscellaneous supplies and canned goods were piled up on shelves. There was the acrid, salty odor of dried pelts of various furs stacked up on a table and the smell of dried fish greeted our nostrils.

"You say the Indians have for years and years been friendly with the white people up here?" I asked.

"Oh, yes," answered the trader. "But it was because of this friendship with the white people that the Hudson Bay Company lost Fort Selkirk in eighteen fifty-two, the year it was built.

"It was like this," he continued. "For many years before the white man came into this territory, the Chilkat Indians from faraway Lynn Canal made regular trips over the Chilkat Trail to this area to trade with the Knife and Wood Indians and to get their valuable furs, including mink, fox, beaver and muskrat. But the Hudson Bay Company moved in, built the fort and took away the fur trade from the Chilkats. Naturally, those warlike Chilkat Indians were furious."

"What happened then?" I asked with interest.

"Well," continued our friend, "one day the Chilkats, in overpowering numbers, swooped down on the Knife and Wood Indians, simultaneously attacking the fort. There was a bloody battle and, of course, the fierce Chilkats won. They pillaged and burned the fort, but the Canadian soldiers escaped into the woods. It was the beginning of winter and the little band of soldiers fled across country through Canada toward the east coast. They were led by a very brave man, Robert Campbell, who was an official of the Hudson Bay Company. The remarkable thing about that trip was that they traveled on snowshoes, three thousand miles over the worst kind of country in the dead of winter, finally reaching the company's headquarters on Hudson Bay early the next spring. Of course, these men never could have made it without the aid of several friendly Indians. Robert Campbell urged the Hudson Bay Company to rebuild the fort. He even traveled to England to see the company's highest officials in London, but they decided against it!"

"Then how did Arthur Harper happen to build this trading post?"* I asked.

"Well, Arthur Harper came into Yukon Territory about eighteen seventy-two as a prospector and trader. He had a way with the Indians and they liked and trusted him. Before he came up the Yukon to this area, he had been prospecting on the Stewart and at Sixty Mile River. Then he went into partnership with Jack McQuesten and Alfred Mayo, starting a trading post at Forty Mile. That was about eighteen eighty-six. Forty Mile, which is down the Yukon from Dawson, at that time was the most promising gold field of the Yukon. The miners were getting quantities of fine and coarse gold. There were about a hundred and fifty men prospecting along the river at that time.

"Just as there has been great tragedy and loss of life connected with this big Klondike gold rush, so was there tragedy and loss of life in the Forty Mile stampede. It seems that gold has always taken its toll! Soon after the gold strike at Forty Mile, we were saddened by the news of the death of a fellow miner named Williams who had made his fortune and started up the river toward the 'Outside' with the exciting news of gold. He got as far as Chilkoot Pass and there he was caught in a terrific blizzard. His body was found by the Indians weeks later. And clutched in his frozen hands were several pokes of yellow gold. Poor devil! He never lived to tell the tale!

"But, to get back to my friend Arthur Harper. After staying at Forty Mile for nearly a year, Harper became restless and traveled up the Yukon in search of more gold . . . and found the ruins of old Fort Selkirk. While prospecting

---

* The original fort and trading post was built in June, 1848, at the confluence of the Lewis and Pelly rivers on the point of land between the two rivers. It was because this point of land was subject to bad floods during the spring breakup of ice, that the fort was finally moved to the left bank, across the river from the mouth of the Pelly River.

here, he became very friendly with these Indians and won their confidence. Among us old-timers, it is a well-known fact that Harper became a peacemaker between the Knife and Wood Indians and the hostile Chilkats, for he finally got them to bury the hatchet. He saw that this would be a good location for another trading post and would benefit the Indians and serve the prospectors and traders coming down the Lewis and Pelly rivers, and also those coming up the Yukon. So he went back to Forty Mile and persuaded McQuesten and Mayo and, also, Joseph Ladue, another well-known Yukoner who had started a sawmill at Forty Mile, to come up to Fort Selkirk with him and establish this trading post, which has been here ever since."

"What a wonderful place for a trading post!" I said. "After traveling hundreds of miles through such wild country, we can certainly appreciate it!"

"I've been wanting to ask you," said Stacey, addressing the trader, "what kind of bones are those standing against the walls of the trading post?"

"Those are the remains of mastodon," answered the trader. "They are found all through the North, and especially in the gravel around Fort Selkirk. Occasionally, we even find tusks of prehistoric mammoth."

"Jumpin' Jupiter!" exclaimed Stacey. "Look at the size of those teeth and jaws!"

"Holy mackerel!" said Jourgensen. "How would you like to hunt one of those critters!"

"Well, it's a good thing those animals are extinct now," laughed our friend. "They tell us that, at one time, the North was tropical; and great herds of those prehistoric animals roamed this country."

"What is that white, chalky streak along the banks of the Lewis River which we've been noticing for the last two hundred and fifty miles?" asked Stacey curiously. "We noticed it in the scarped banks just below Whitehorse Rapids? Is it volcanic rock?"

"That is a stratum of pumice stone which, they tell us in recent times, was caused by a very great eruption, perhaps four or five hundred years ago. There is a legend among the Indians up here telling of a rain of 'hot snow' caused by a burning mountain. The legend goes on to tell of how hot ashes covered the earth for a radius of hundreds of miles around here and how the Indians had to hide in caves. They have lost track of how long ago this happened and they don't know how many days the ashes fell, but it must have lasted many days. The ashes are thickest here at Fort Selkirk, as the stratum is two and three feet in depth.

"Now, among us old-timers," continued the trader, "there is a great deal of speculation about this legend and the burning mountain. There is a small extinct volcano fifteen miles back from the river across from here, which you can see if you walk back on the hills; also, there is another smaller, extinct volcano near the mouth of the Pelly River, which we call 'Split Mountain.' However, some of the scientists think that Mount Wrangell or Mount Logan may have showered the ashes. It's my guess that they all may have erupted at once."

"With Indians, mastodons, trading posts and volcanoes, Fort Selkirk is a mighty interesting place! But what about gold?" I asked eagerly.

"Ah!" exclaimed the trader. "All of you stampeders ask me that! Well, there's gold up here, plenty of it! I've been in this country many years and I ought to know. I was at Forty Mile when they discovered gold and I prospected along Sixty Mile and the Stewart River and at the Big and Little Salmon. I watched them pan for gold at the famous Cassiar Bar and then I went to Circle City on the big stampede there in eighteen ninety-four when gold was discovered. My friend Arthur Harper had a lot to do with that stampede, for he staked two miners who struck it rich on Mastodon Creek near Circle City."

"Where is Arthur Harper now?" I asked. "I certainly would like to meet him!"

"He is very ill with consumption," answered the trader sorrowfully. "He went down river and we think he has gone 'Outside.' He's greatly beloved by all of his friends and the Indians simply worship him. Many of them have named their children 'Arthur' and 'Harper.' Constantly they wait for news of him. We are all hoping that he can go to Arizona to be in the warm desert sunshine where he may get well, but we are afraid he waited too long."

(It was reported in Dawson, months later, that Arthur Harper had died at Yuma, Arizona, during the winter of 1897.)

"Well, to get back to gold," sighed the trader. "I guess you already know that George Carmack and his Tagish Indian wife, together with Skookum Jim and Tagish Charlie, made the biggest gold strike in the history of the North. Last summer they hit the jackpot of the Yukon near Dawson! It's a funny thing, too, because they were all set to mine coal up the Lewis River at Tantelus Butte. They had found a good supply of bituminous coal there and they planned to supply the whole Yukon! Now, I understand, they've forgotten the project and are going on a 'gold spree,' as they are worth millions! They say Carmack is planning a trip 'Outside' with his Indian wife and they may even go to England to see the King and Queen!

"Although Carmack struck a rich vein of gold, many of us old-timers believe the 'Mother Lode' is yet to be discovered in the Klondike. It may be hidden near the Bonanza, where Carmack made his initial gold strike, or it may be miles from there. One of you Cheechakos might even discover it! Ah, your eyes are shining." He laughed.

"Fellows, always remember this, gold is very illusive! It's where you find it, and it's often in the most unexpected places. Remember, too, that the great masses of ice that once covered this country buried many ancient river beds under tons of rock and gravel. Some of these streams are now redigging their channels in the auriferous gravels and black sands of the Klondike and Alaska.

"In Dawson you'll see all kinds of gold," he continued. "Light yellow, dark yellow, greenish color, and there are even nuggets as black as cats, but it's all gold just the same. For example, let me show you."

The trader reached up high on a shelf and brought down some small cans and began pouring out a little of the contents from each one onto separate sheets of paper. One large, blackish-colored nugget rolled out.

"Look," he said, "here is a black nugget. It's from Bear Gulch. Bear Gulch has the distinction of having two bedrocks three feet apart. On the lower bedrock, they find these amazing black nuggets; but on the upper stratum, three feet above, they find gold as bright and yellow as you ever saw. Here are other specimens. There's coarse and fine gold and also some gold dust."

The trader kept pouring more of the yellow metal out onto the paper. We watched with spellbound interest; then he continued: "Show an old-timer this gold and he can just about tell you on which creek it was found. Gold bears a signature to one who knows!"

"About how much gold do you think you have there?" asked Stacey, his eyes bugging out with excitement.

"Perhaps five or six thousand," he said.

"By George!" breathed Stacey. "Let's get going to Dawson. I want to start digging!"

"Men, if you'll only wait a little while, an Indian hunter may come in with fresh moose and caribou!" announced the trader as he carefully put away his gold into the tin containers.

"No thanks," said Stacey. "I'm hungry as hell for fresh meat, but we mustn't wait. We still have two hundred miles yet to go to reach Dawson!"

"By the way," I said as we prepared to leave, "have the Ryans, the Wisconsin crowd, Nelson brothers or the Swedes traveling on a raft been here?"

"No," replied the trader. "I haven't seen 'em."

"Well, then, how about a party of Canadians and the Kellys and Hydes? And have you seen a fast sailing boat with the Nash party of four aboard?"

"No," replied the trader again, "there have been many stampeders stopping here, but I don't recall any you mentioned."

"Well, I wonder if McPhee and his crowd are ahead of us?" I said.

"Why, yes," answered the trader. "About a week ago, McPhee and his party stopped. McPhee was in a big hurry, though. Was anxious to get to Dawson for the opening of his new saloon."

"McPhee asked me to look him up in Dawson," I said. "Stacey and I met him at the Dyea Indian village below Chilkoot."

"Better do that," advised the trader. "Bill McPhee certainly knows the Klondike!"

A few minutes later, we waved goodbye to the old trader, who came down to the river to see us off. We had lost an hour at old Fort Selkirk, but it was well worth it!

"Good luck, boys! I hope you strike it rich, and, on your way out, don't forget to stop off at Harper's Trading Post!" called the trader.

"Thanks! We'll be sure to," we called back.

"He's a grand old man," I said as we saw his figure fading in the distance. "But what a lonely life he must lead up here among the Indians. Did you notice how he seemed to thoroughly enjoy talking to us, telling us about the early days and the riches on the Yukon?"

Later, I drew out my little diary and wrote:

July 13, 1897 (Yukon River)

Reached Pelly Post, which is Harper's Trading Post at junction of Pelly and Lewis rivers. The Yukon proper begins here. Got stuck on a sand bar just below post. We sailed very fast. Got stuck on another sand bar before dinner. Am gaining weight. Must have gone down to 135 pounds while I was sick (on Chilkoot).

Just below Fort Selkirk, the Yukon wended its way between high rampart cliffs and palisades, and, as we looked ahead the ever-widening river, we were more and more aware that we were traveling on a colossal water highway of the great North!

Now we were on the last lap of our journey. Lightheartedly, we whistled and sang; the wind blowing down the mighty river caught our double sails; the Yukon waters surged reassuringly beneath us. We traveled speedily toward Dawson, our hopes high, our spirits jubilant!

Late in the afternoon, we saw thunderclouds hovering over the mountains, and the next morning I described it in my diary:

July 14, 1897 (Yukon River—Thundershowers)

Camped last night on beach to get rid of mosquitoes. Got up at 5 A.M. Stopped at small creek; found good colors. Made about 80 miles yesterday. Best time yet! Passed White River, which comes in from west. Powerful current and milky in appearance. (Probably gets milky color from stratum of white pumice stone.) Lots of driftwood. Valley to west open and wide. Passed Stewart River. Camped at Sixty Mile Post. No one there. Some Indians camped just above. Had two thundershowers!

"Tomorrow, we should be in Dawson," I said as we all leaned back comfortably in the boat and let the double sail and current of the Yukon rapidly propel us along. We had made eighty miles the day before and there was no need for rowing now that the wind and current were in our favor!

Now we had the luxury of resting and watching the ever-changing panorama of marvelous scenery, and it was only natural that I should begin to think of home and of my wife and little son Clemy. It was nearly two months since I had left them in Tacoma and now I was nearly two thousand miles away from home. Suddenly I felt very homesick and wondered desperately if it would be possible to get a letter to them before the ice closed in in the fall!

My mind traveled back over the vast territory through which we had recently come. Could anyone be persuaded to carry mail into Dawson over this hazardous route? Then I thought of the other route . . . by ocean steamer from Tacoma, up around the Alaskan peninsula to St. Michael on Bering Sea and on up the Yukon to Dawson by river boat, a distance altogether of nearly 4,500 miles! This route, too, was long and hazardous, and the boats uncertain.

I knew my loved ones would be waiting anxiously for news of me and I resolved to get a letter off at the first opportunity, either by a stampeder returning "outside" over the route we had come, or going down the Yukon by way of St. Michael.

Gradually, my thoughts returned to my companions and our stampeder friends—the Ryans, Wisconsians, the Nelson brothers, Canadians, Swedes, Kellys and Hydes, and the Nash party who had passed us on Lake LaBarge. Where were all of these people on this huge river? Would they reach Dawson safely?

"It's been a hard but exciting trip," I thought, "one I shall never forget. How fortunate I have been to travel with such fine men!" Mentally, I took my hat off to each one in our party. Never once had we had a serious quarrel. True, there had been small irritations under stress of hardships, but there had been no feelings of strong antagonism . . . such as wanting to saw the boat in half, which we had heard some stampeders actually had done in their extreme anger!

I wondered what lay in store for us—for Stacey, the ex-policeman; Jourgensen, the sailor; Crawford, the gentleman; and for me, the expert accountant. Would our ways part in Dawson, or would fate throw us together again? What would be our reward after traveling 1,800 miles, over 500 of which had been in an open boat? Would we strike it rich?

The next day, July 15th at 1:00 P.M., we swung around the big bend in the Yukon and there, to our boundless joy . . . was Dawson—built on a low flat with high hills in the background.

"Hurrah! Hurrah for Dawson!" we shouted to the miners camped along the sand bar.

"Hello, Cheechakos!" they called. "Welcome to the Klondike!"

At last, yes, at last we had reached the land of glittering gold!

Chapter V

Nothing Marked This Spot!

Now Stacey, Jourgensen, Crawford and I were at the end of our long, hazardous journey into the Klondike and on the very threshold of our exciting quest for gold! From our boat we looked with intense, fascinated interest at Dawson, which was rapidly looming up on the right bank of the Yukon as we approached closer and closer.

To us this place looked more inviting, more wondrous, than any spot we had ever seen before. We had heard that it was the most unusual and promised to be the largest settlement in the Northern wilderness.

Eagerly, our eyes shot ahead and took in every detail of Dawson. The gold camp sprawled in unruly fashion along the right bank of the Yukon for perhaps a mile, then straggled back among a scattering of low, stunted trees towards the high hills, which rose back of the town only a short distance of perhaps a half mile from the river's edge. Dawson seemed to be made up of hundreds of tents, shacks and log cabins, many of which were in the frenzied process of being erected. Along the curve of the river, the open front street was black and teeming with men. Hundreds of boats were tied up or anchored at the river line.

Quickly, we turned our boat toward the right-hand shore so as not to overshoot Dawson, as here the pull of the current was very strong. Suddenly, from the east, we came upon the mouth of a river about two hundred feet wide pouring volumes into the Yukon. It cut through the high hills which had been following on both sides of the Yukon for many miles. These hills extended back of Dawson, continuing northward for as far as we could see. On a low, swampy sand bar on the south side of the mouth of this river, dozens of stampeders had set up tents. Later, we learned this was called "Louse Town" by the stampeders.

"Look!" I said excitedly as I pointed to the east. "It's the Klondike River coming into the Yukon! And fellows, somewhere up there about fifteen miles are the gold fields . . . the richest in the world!"

"Oh, brother! I can hardly wait to get my hands on some of that gold!" said Stacey, fired with new enthusiasm as he pulled hard on the oars to get across to the mouth of the river and make a landing at Dawson.

"Yes, it's great to be here!" exclaimed Jourgensen. "How I can use some of that gold!"

"Let's hurry and land!" urged Crawford earnestly.

Quickly, we found an opening in among the boats near the confluence of the Yukon and Klondike rivers and nosed our boat to shore. As we were tying up, we were surprised to see several red-coated mounted policemen and discovered that we had landed near their barracks.

"It's a good place to land," laughed Stacey. "Now our supplies and boat will be perfectly safe."

"Better cover everything, anyway," advised a nearby

stampeder. "Yesterday, we had a heavy rainstorm, and, judging from those clouds, we'll have more tonight!"

Thanking the friendly stampeder, we took his advice and covered everything with canvas, then hurriedly rushed up into Dawson, which began just a stone's throw away from the river's edge. Eagerly mingling with the crowd, we pushed our way to the post office, which was only about a block from the police barracks and around a corner.

"No, no mail!" was the curt reply to our anxious inquiries. "You're in Yukon Territory now. Can't expect a letter this soon! Some miners wait five or six months, even a year!"

Naturally, we turned away feeling very disappointed. However, our first day in Dawson could not be blighted by homesickness, so quickly we pushed our way back onto the street and mixed with the crowd. Gaping and breathless, we listened to all of their conversation and, at the same time, looked for familiar faces. Wedging ourselves in among groups of old sourdoughs and Cheechakos, we were able to catch snatches of big talk of unbelievable amounts of gold on the Bonanza, the Eldorado, Hunker, Gold Bottom, Nugget Gulch and Bear Gulch, and Too Much Gold; exciting accounts of new discoveries on Sixty Mile River, Indian River, the Stewart River, the McQuesten, and of gold found near a place called "Ogilvie;" also, very promising reports of a recently staked creek called "Dominion."

It all sounded glowing but a little bewildering to Cheechakos like us. It sounded as if all we needed to do was choose the creek, go there, stake a claim and get rich. (What we failed to hear that first hour in Dawson was how many miles we would have to tramp to reach the farthest creeks; how much food it would take to keep us alive through 50-below-zero weather; how many tools it would take to gouge the frozen, hard-as-flint earth; how many backaches, how many heartbreaks, might be in store for the less fortunate stampeders.)

As convincing proof of all of the glowing tales we heard, gold appeared everywhere! It shone in nuggety splendor suspended from heavy watch chains across the chests of obviously wealthy Bonanza and Eldorado Kings who strutted down the main street, pockets bulging with gold

Dawson at the earliest period, 1897. The view is from Moosehide Mountain, looking up the Yukon

(Photographed by E. A. Hegg)

Interior of a store in Dawson, 1897, with gold scales on counter

Waterfront at Dawson where stampeders set up their temporary business projects

Post of the North West Mounted Police at the mouth of Stewart River. Boats going downriver were required to stop here to be checked

dust. It appeared in all of the stores as the only medium of exchange for goods, and shimmered on gold scales with delicate weights and measures. It shone in the small display windows, under glass, of the two biggest trading companies, The Alaska Commercial and The North American Trading Companies, which were both in log houses with adjoining warehouses halfway down the waterfront. We were allowed to look at fascinating nuggets of all sizes at the Gold Commissioner's, which was next door to the Mounted Police barracks. The largest nugget was a pear-shaped mass of almost pure gold and was the center of extreme interest to us wide-eyed newcomers. It was said that this particular nugget was from a fabulous mine up on the Eldorado.

Even the muddy town of Dawson was a Bonanza. The men at the land office, which was owned by Ladue and Harper, told us that less than a year ago there had been nothing on the site of Dawson and the ground was then considered practically valueless. But at the first whisper of gold . . . Ladue and Harper had received an exclusive land grant from the Canadian Government and they had named the place "Dawson."

The first week, business lots sold for $5; now, they were selling for $5,000, with extravagant promises of doubling or tripling in less than another year!

Joseph Ladue's sawmill at the northern end of town worked overtime and kept up a steady whine as the old machinery chugged, chewed and sawed the logs for anxious cabin-builders. This sawmill had been hurriedly moved down from Sixty Mile to Dawson, which was hourly mushrooming into the most amazing gold camp the world had ever seen. The town bustled with activity. Men selling logs and cabins, selling mines and equipment, selling wood and water from the hills, and the hotels and restaurants, did a rushing business, though prices were almost beyond the reach of nearly all of the newly arrived Cheechakos.

A piece of pie cost 75c; a dish of canned tomatoes, $1.25; a bowl of mush and coffee, $1; a steak was $3; etc. All food, and, in fact, everything was sold by weight and was a dollar a pound—even tents, stoves, shovels and all other equipment. At first glance these prices seemed unreasonable; but when we considered the great distance of wilderness over which every item had come to reach Dawson, especially during the spring and winter of '96 and '97, no one could really complain. It meant that nearly everything we saw in Dawson, except the wood, furs, etc., had been hauled in over torturous Chilkoot Pass and then brought over the ice of the river by dog team, or carried in on the backs of many stampeders during those exciting, hectic months following the first discovery of gold in the Klondike.

To us stampeders, teeming Dawson seemed to vibrate to the footsteps of eager, determined men, and to our eyes, the very atmosphere seemed to scintillate with a golden, dusty glow. The colossal drive, energy and supreme test of stamina and sacrifice which had built Dawson was amazing beyond words to all of us, for when we reached there, very little freight had come up the Yukon from St. Michael and Bering Sea even by middle summer.

Stacey, Jourgensen, Crawford and I rapidly took in the town. It was good to have haircuts and shaves from fellows who had set themselves up in business by the river. And the taste of a variety of civilization's canned foods was an added luxury. After six weeks of steady wilderness travel, it was exciting to be in this amazing place which held out promises of sudden wealth to all of us.

We had only been in Dawson an hour when we discovered that the numerous saloons and dance halls were doing a thriving business, and it was evident that they were the high spots around which all Dawson seemed to revolve and swing. There was a prolonged holiday spirit. Ordinary prejudices of the "Outside" were obviously thrown to the high, cold winds. It was evident that these places were the only spots where a fellow could get in out of the weather and sit in a comfortable chair.

"The game never ends!" were the carnival-like words slung across the tent flap of a newly opened gambling place. "Come in and let us help you make a fortune!" was the arresting bid for attention on another place.

"Where is there a lawyer?" someone asked a miner.

"Oh, there's one down at Kerry's saloon," was the astonishing answer. "He meets his clients there at the first table."

"Quick! Where is there a doctor?" was an agonizing inquiry.

"Oh, you'll find one at the saloon next door," was the matter-of-fact reply.

Mixing with the crowds, we continued along the street until we came to a place where there was a sign which read: "The Sky Is the Limit!" Our curiosity got the best of us here, so we ventured inside. It was quite a large hall, packed with fellows all talking and drinking at once, and the air was filled with tobacco smoke. Incessant music greeted our ears . . . caused by a piano-thumper who played on an old loose-keyed piano which obviously had seen better days. Baritone and bass voices burst into snatches of unsteady song as the musician improvised from one familiar tune to another. At intervals, a tired-faced violinist played on a melancholy, whiny-sounding violin.

Stacey, Jourgensen, Crawford and I stood inside near the door and took in the situation. A man at a gold scale sat at the entrance by the bar; across from the bar, on the right hand side of the room, was a stage with curtains drawn. At the end of the long hall were the gambling tables, where dozens of miners were playing faro, roulette, and black jack amidst clouds of cigar smoke while a few dance-hall girls looked on. Up near the front of the hall were more tables, where several flashily dressed girls drank and chinned with the men. In the middle of the hall was a cleared space for dancing. Behind the long bar stood several bartenders, looking more city-like and dressed up than anyone else in the room.

"Come on in and make yourselves at home," invited the man at the gold scales.

"Want something to drink?" asked a bartender.

"Not now," I said. "My party and I just got in town and are getting our bearings."

"Well, this is a good place to get them," laughed the bartender. "And if you need any help, just ask the girls," he added as he poured out some more liquor for three grizzly old miners who carelessly threw their thick pokes of gold onto the counter. The four of us watched as the man at the gold scales took the sacks and weighed out the desired amount of gold dust while the miners drank and paid not the slightest attention.

"Guess those fellows trust each other," I remarked to Stacey.

One of the old miners must have overheard, for he spoke up: "Cheechako, we men of the Klondike do trust each other. Why, I'd leave my gold with that fellow and bet my last dollar that it would all be there when I called for it! But look who's coming!" he added as he pointed to two unusual characters who had just entered the saloon. They were Indians dressed in white men's clothes. They wore red plaid shirts, loud ties and black trousers tucked into heavy brown shoes. Both Indians wore black hats with red hatbands, and across their chests dangled heavy watch chains with double rows of yellow nuggets.

"It's Skookum Jim and Tagish Charlie, the wealthiest Indians in the North," said the miner closest me.

"They should be," said another miner. "They're relatives of George Carmack's, one of the Bonanza Kings, and they call themselves 'King George's Men.' They were with him when he discovered gold . . . and they own several of the richest claims on the Bonanza."

"Both Indians drink too much," said another miner, "and they spend a lot of time in 'Skookum House,' which, jokingly, they are beginning to call the jail over at the Mounted Police barracks. They're a real worry to Carmack, as Tagish Charlie is his brother-in-law."

"All right, now, let's all have drink," yelled Skookum Jim as he strode to the bar and threw down a thick sack of gold. "Come on, let's everyone drink to our King George! We're his men. Drink to King George!"

"Now, my turn," shouted Tagish Charlie as he strode to the bar and threw down his sack of gold, and a second round of drinks was quickly swallowed up.

Then there was a pause. "Now, all sing George Carmack song," shouted Tagish Charley as he raised his voice in peculiar nasal tones and began leading a song which everyone seemed to know and which repeated praises of Carmack's discovery of gold on the Bonanza over and over again in a sort of continuous round. Each stanza seemed to begin with, "I wonder why, I wonder why . . ." It told of how Carmack wandered over the North from Chilkoot to St. Michael and of the long, cold winters, and at last the song came to the point, telling that George Carmack found gold in spite of the fact that "the willows the wrong way did bend," and it finished by announcing Carmack was worth a million and that the old-timers "they were broke." Then the song repeated the chorus, "I wonder why, I wonder why . . ." with the miners nearly raising the roof.

All at once, the door flew open and in strode a rather tall, black-whiskered man. He was very well built and had fine features. Taking each Indian firmly by the shoulders, he escorted them quickly out of the saloon and marched them away.

"It's George Carmack!" gasped one of the miners. "And he'll try to get them to go up on the Bonanza or send them back up the river toward their own villages. But these two Indians are privileged characters and are special Canadian subjects. They are privileged to enter saloons and that's why they like to hang around Dawson. No doubt, they'll end up in Skookum House again!"

While we were talking, the piano-violin orchestra struck up a familiar tune and the curtain on the stage slowly rolled up. The miners were all attention. A few seconds more of music, then out danced six rather pretty girls clad in bright-colored, satiny costumes trimmed in ostrich feathers. The girls all wore dangly, flashy jewelry and flung their arms and gayly tossed their heads as they danced in a lively manner across the stage. Kicking highly into the air, they gave the boys quick, breath-taking glimpses of forbidden charms covered with silken tights and partly enshrouded in underlace petticoats, ribbons and fluffy stuff.

After the girls had gone through this eye-opening routine, they stopped and sang, with the audience joining in lustily. To finish the act, the girls repeated part of the dance again, and that was a signal for the gold to start flying. Nuggets and small sacks of gold rained through the air. Obviously, they were thrown by the more wealthy, or the most foolish, of the miners. The entire crowd watched with much pleasure as the girls scrambled to pick up the gold. Before the curtain rolled down, the dancers, with flashing smiles, blew lavish kisses to their generous admirers.

Then the violin and piano struck up a lively tune and a voice called: "Grab your partners and git ready for a cow-tillion!"

This was the signal for a mad scramble. The boys outnumbered the girls more than a dozen to one and the miners fought in a free-for-all to "git" a partner. Soon the dance began in earnest with a wild, mad whirl. Heavy, muddy boots accentuated and pounded the beat of the music on the rough board floor.

Suddenly, the music stopped and the voice called: "All promenade to the bar . . . and those who haven't partners, git one there!"

"Look," said Stacey. "It's the same old game. The girl gets a percentage on every drink she sells."

"I can't see how these dance-hall girls drink so much," I said.

"They don't," answered Stacey. "Watch and you'll see how cleverly they dispose of their liquor. Perhaps they only take one swallow. Used to see them in the dance halls in Old Town in Tacoma."

"Let's get out of here!" I said as I spied a girl headed in our direction with a golden glint in her eyes. "Just remembered we promised to look up Bill McPhee."

"You bet! If we don't, we might lose our shirts in here!" laughed Stacey. Quickly, we elbowed our way out into the fresh air. As we walked along the river on Front Street toward McPhee's, all at once we realized that Jourgensen and Crawford weren't with us. Somehow we had lost them in the mad shuffle.

"Well, guess they can take care of themselves," I remarked to Stacey. "After all, Jourgensen and Crawford are on their own now."

"They're darned good fellows," said Stacey.

"The very best!" I replied.

"Just remembered, Ed," said Stacey. "Jourgensen and Crawford said they're going to look for quarters at the low log house up the street. Said it would be a luxury to sleep in a bunk and it would give us more room in the boat for our sleeping bags."

Stacey and I found McPhee's down on Front Street, not far from the Gold Commissioner's. His place appeared to be one of the finest of log structures. However, it was still in the last finishing stages of construction. Extra-heavy logs were being fitted against the sturdy foundations to withstand any flooding from the river. Directly behind this structure, a small log cabin for McPhee's living quarters was being finished. In spite of all of this activity, McPhee was open for business.

"Hello, hello!" he boomed as we entered. "Ed and Stacey, welcome to Dawson. It's good to see you!"

The saloon was crowded with men. A fellow with a gold scale perched in front of him sat in a cage-like affair near the door. The bar ran along the right-hand side of the almost square room. In the center of the saloon there was a large stove, around which were groups of small tables. Against the back wall were the roulette and faro tables.

At one of the gambling tables we saw Ben Everett of Tacoma running the faro game. He never moved or looked up. Over his eyes he wore a green shade which cast a sickly reflection onto his features. Somehow, he looked tired and ill, not as he had appeared when we had last seen him at Dyea, the Indian village below Chilkoot Pass.

McPhee introduced us to Mr. Ruby, the bartender, and told him to pour us a drink "on the house." "Mostly water," he laughed. "But, oh, yes, Ed doesn't drink," he reminded himself. "Well, then, here's a cigar. It's one of my very best!"

Thanking McPhee for the expensive cigar, I lit it, leaned back contentedly, puffed and watched the miners who crowded the place. Obviously, they were all in a carefree mood. Gold seemed the keynote and very atmosphere of the place. It was the persistent theme behind all conversation.

"Ed, what are you and Stacey planning to do now that you are here in Dawson?" asked McPhee.

"What are chances of staking on the Eldorado or Bonanza?" I asked.

"Hate to disappoint you fellows, but there're absolutely no claims left on those streams. All were staked months ago. The only ones now where a fellow can stake are out on the creeks fifty to a hundred miles away. Gold strikes on these small, unexplored creeks are often just rumors and sometimes they are in very wild country where there are practically no trails. Some even run into mountainous country where white man has never been, like in the Rockies, only seventy-five miles to the east. It would be sheer folly to rush off up there half-cocked. But Ed, and Stacey, it's possible you might get a good 'lay,' or lease, on one of the rich claims on the Eldorado or Bonanza. This would entitle you to fifty per cent of the gold you take out."

Then McPhee lowered his voice and leaned closer. "But if you fellows want to go on a stampede, wait around Dawson for several days. I may be able to help you. In my business, I hear constant rumors. If I tip you off—go like hell! Don't tell anyone, because the stampeders are like a pack of wolves on the scent of blood! Hundreds hang around Dawson, just waiting for a chance to stampede. Nine out of ten of these rumors prove to be false alarms and the miners return thoroughly disgusted. But occasionally, an astonishing strike will be made. That is what happened up on Hunker last winter. Hunker turned out to be almost as rich as the famous Eldorado. They're pulling out nuggets up there that far outclass those on the Bonanza. A discovery of that kind is beyond the Cheechako's imagination!"

"Sounds thrilling!" said Stacey.

"You bet it is!" answered McPhee. "And the fastest runner with the lightest pack on his back will often get the choicest strip of pay dirt. But I must warn you . . . it's the Canadian law that a fellow can stake only one claim on a creek. Naturally, everyone tries his level best to get a rich one. Last year it was very different when the Klondike discovery claim was made by Carmack. There was no town of Dawson then. There were no mining laws here for this particular district. Fellows from Circle City and Forty Mile rushed in here like grasping madmen . . . staked everything in sight for themselves and even for their friends, who perhaps weren't in the North. Fifteen miles of solid Bonanza claims were taken first, then the miners tore up to the Eldorado and staked that stream, and then they went up above and staked Hunker. And so it continued until every tributary, creek and gulch was bristling with prospectors' stakes in this area, now called the 'gold fields.' "

"How do they stake claims?" asked Stacey.

"They drive four-foot stakes two hundred and fifty feet apart along a river bank with the name and number of the miner on each stake," answered McPhee. "In barren country, rocks piled up on the four corners of a claim mark the spot. Most of these claims run back five hundred feet from a river or creek."

"Is there anyone in authority over mine boundaries?" I asked.

"Why, yes," said McPhee, "Major William Ogilvie, Canada's official surveyor from Forty Mile. He's out on Dominion now. Probabaly there's no one in the country who knows the territory like Ogilvie. He's the famous surveyor who explored and made the Canadian and American boundary line a reality. Started surveying it about ten years ago when the big dispute arose as to its exact location. Now he's here with his surveyors straightening out the tangle of claims. After the first few weeks of Klondike gold rush, Ogilvie came up here and worked long hours measuring the exact footage of already staked claims. Sometimes the miners would be caught short of ground because of under- or over-staking. So Ogilvie, in order not to throw off the measurement of miles and miles of claims, decided that a few miners would have to be short of ground. Naturally, this created terrific discord, especially if that ground proved very rich. Occasionally, free ground or fractions would show up between the claims. These fractions were a great bone of contention also, and created many violent quarrels, but sometimes a new miner could slip in and grab one. On very auriferous pay dirt, a strip of ten or twelve feet might yield a small fortune."

"No wonder there was discontent among the miners!" remarked Stacey. "But everything seems orderly now. Those Mounties sure look like stern, capable men!"

"You bet they are!" laughed McPhee. "The miners don't dare break the law. But before the Mounties came, Ogilvie had a devil of a time, as he had no police authority. Finally he got Captain Constantine to come from Fort Cudahy. Order was quickly established. Then came Thomas Fawcett, the new Gold Commissioner, with hastily drawn up regulations from Ottawa for this new district, which they called 'Throndike's Division of Yukon Mining.'* The discontent and temper of the miners was openly exhibited against Fawcett because of the ten and twenty per cent royalty demanded by the new mining laws. Some Americans, thoroughly disgusted, left and went down the Yukon to Circle City, which is on American territory. None of the disgruntled miners who left the Klondike that soon dreamed of the gigantic discoveries which were yet to be made during those early winter months of ninety-six, as the miners dug deeper and deeper in the gold fields."

While Stacey and I leaned back, relaxed and listened intently, McPhee continued: "Not even the old-timers like Ladue, Harper, McQuesten, Mayo, Ogilvie, and no, not even I, grasped the full significance of the overwhelming amounts of gold that began pouring from the ground after those first few months. Five to six dollars to the gold pan was average on the Bonanza. Then came the unheard-of findings of a hundred dollars to the pan on the new 'river of gold,' the fabulous Eldorado! Think of it! . . . a handful of dirt would pay the daily wages of a miner! . . . and the mine owners were getting five thousand dollars to the box length! It was then we all realized that this was a very unusual country of enormous and astonishing wealth!"

"Say, have you told them about the new kind of golddiggers we have up here?" asked a miner who had sauntered over to our table and was listening to the conversation. Obviously, he had been drinking too much and and he was eager to butt in.

"No? . . . Well, we have 'em up here," he remarked. "About a dozen of the hardest-digging kind you ever did see! I ought to know, 'cause I've been 'dug'! Those Bloomer Girls sure know how to get the gold dug out of a feller!"

"Now what are the 'Bloomer Girls'?" asked Stacey half amused. "They're a new species, aren't they?"

"Sure thing," laughed the miner sarcastically.

"Well, I'll have to explain," said McPhee, snatching the conversation away from his customer. "You see, the Bloomer Girls are the 'gay' girls who climbed Chilkoot and came down the Yukon last fall with the sole intent of digging

* Throndike was the Indian name for Klondike.

gold from the miners. They wore bloomers with such good results coming into the country that they flaunted them publicly on the streets of Dawson—that is, until Inspector Constantine ordered them to put on long skirts or keep off the streets. But these intrepid, wild women, in open defiance to the Mounted Police, continued to parade their bloomers. Finally, the police threatened to send them out of the country. So now the Bloomer Girls wear very abbreviated, short skirts . . . which equally irritates and shocks Captain Constantine."

"Yep," interrupted the miner sourly. "Even the Bloomer Girls' company seems more valuable than his gold when a feller gits lonesome and down in the mouth! It just ain't natural to be up here in the North with only fellers for company," he added dolefully as he staggered to the bar for another drink.

"Yes, but there are a few good women in town, too," said McPhee, picking up the conversation again. "And there're several up in the gold fields. A few miners have their wives with them and they're the envy of the Klondike. But it's really too hard on women to live in the North. This is really a man's country!"

McPhee left our table for a little to greet some new customers who had just come in.

"Say, I've been listening to what that fellow told about the Bloomer Girls," said a nearby miner as he sat down at our table for a few minutes. "A fellow does get lonely for the company of a woman up here. Dance-hall girls and even Bloomer Girls have their good points. They've been known to save the lives of some of the miners. I ought to know!" he added wistfully. "One saved my life last winter! But let me tell you about several of the very high type of women up here," he said hurriedly. "There are only fifty women altogether in the Klondike.

"In Dawson, there's a very beautiful woman, Mrs. Eli Gage, wife of the North American Trading Company's auditor. She is the daughter-in-law of Lyman Gage, secretary of the United States Treasury. She seems very much out of place up here, though, more the type one would expect to see at a fashionable, exclusive tea in Boston.

"In contrast, there's Miss Belinda Mulroony, a rugged

pioneer type of woman. She has a log hotel up at the Forks of the Bonanza and Eldorado and is much respected by the miners. Serves good home-cooked food and has good clean bunks for the men. She's a remarkable woman. Came over Chilkoot Pass and has staked herself a few good claims.

"And then, there's another wonderful woman, Mrs. Clarence Berry, wife of one of the Berry brothers who owns the fabulous mines up on the Eldorado. Mrs. Berry and her husband are the 'bride and groom' of the Klondike. It was less than a year ago that they came down over the ice of the Yukon by dog team. They only had a few dollars left and were out of food when they reached Forty Mile. There they joined Frank Berry, a brother who worked for the trading company. A few weeks later, the big news of the gold strike hit Forty Mile. They rushed up there, got No. 40 on Bonanza and then staked No. 4 on Eldorado and built themselves a little log cabin. All winter Mrs. Berry worked with her husband. This spring they took out one hundred and thirty thousand dollars in just thirty box lengths. Once they struck a pocket of nuggets worth ten thousand dollars alone. One weighed thirty ounces! They left this spring for Fresno, California, after they had bought up several claims on the Bonanza. They say Berry is going to buy his wife a diamond ring and the ranch she has been dreaming of ever since their marriage."

In a few minutes, McPhee came back to our table, leaned over and whispered: "Ed and Stacey, at the next table are two very well-known men. The good-looking, big Scotchman is Alexander McDonald, the Klondike King. He is the richest man in the North and maybe the entire world. Owns fabulously rich mines up on the Bonanza and Eldorado. He holds about three solid miles of Bonanza claims. This year he will no doubt get over a million in gold! Sitting next to McDonald is Pat Galvin. He's very wealthy, too. They have holdings together and are often in Dawson."

(Little did any of us dream that day—and certainly not Alex McDonald, the Klondike King—that fourteen years later he would die almost a pauper on Sleugh Creek, quite far away from the rich claims of the Klondike.)

In a moment, McPhee was called from our table again

and Stacey and I strained our ears to hear what the two men were saying.

"No, sir, there's never been such a tremendous gold field in all history! It beats anything I've ever seen! And the gold isn't running out either, as some of the old-timers from Circle City and Forty Mile predicted. It's actually increasing in richness! There's nothing like it in the world and I wouldn't be surprised if two hundred tons of gold aren't taken out this year!" sat Pat Galvin.

"Yes, I know," said Alex McDonald, "but I'm concerned about the miners."

"Fifteen dollars a day are good wages," said Galvin, "and should keep them going. It's better wages than in the States. A fellow works for that for a whole week at home."

"Yes, I know," agreed McDonald, "but everything is damned high up here. When the miners get sick, it's over a hundred dollars to get a doctor to walk out to the creeks . . . at least a thirty-mile round trip. A lot of the men are tired out after the hardships of coming into the country. Most of them are disappointed and homesick. Hardly any take time to cook properly. Their diet is usually the same: flapjacks, beans and coffee. A lot of them are getting the scurvy. Most of my men only work for me because they haven't found gold for themselves. It must be galling for the better educated. I have several miners who are professors, and even a lawyer, working on one of my claims up on the Bonanza. I even suspect I have a preacher, as he's always quoting the Bible and won't allow the fellows to cuss."

"It's true," said Pat Galvin, "there are a lot of fine men who've had bad luck. There just aren't enough claims for everyone! But . . . there's something else which worries me far more. We've got to do something about this typhoid epidemic. Already several have died. It's getting very serious!"

"I'm worried, too," answered McDonald. "Some of the water is polluted and the miners won't take time to boil it. I've heard the Catholic Mission has sent word 'Outside' for at least a dozen Sisters to come as soon as possible to care for the sick. They're coming by way of St. Michael, but you know how uncertain the boats have been. And the boats that have arrived and were supposed to bring food . . . have brought other supplies instead. Dawson only has enough food to last the rest of the summer and they are expecting an early winter. Every day dozens of stampeders are arriving. Most of them only have a few weeks' supply of food!"

"Sounds alarming," answered McDonald. "I'll have to talk to the commercial companies."

"I already have," said Galvin. "They say the boats should be in any time now and there's no real need to worry, unless . . ."

Suddenly our eavesdropping was interrupted by a familiar voice. Turning our chairs, we recognized two fellows from Tacoma—Linc Davis and a man by the name of Cotswell. They greeted us warmly and sat down at our table and we began exchanging news. Linc Davis was one of the fellows who had come over Chilkoot Pass and into the Klondike with McPhee.

"We've been expecting you," said Cotswell. "Linc said you and Stacey were coming. Say, but is there anyone left in Tacoma?" He laughed. "We heard that two thousand of Tacoma's best citizens are heading North, not to mention Judge Osbourne of Seattle, Brigadier General M. E. Carr and, most amazing of all, ex-Governer McGraw, who's been running for the Senate!"

"They must have started after we left," I said. "But it's true about Tacoma. You never saw a town in such a wild bedlam of excitement. The whole population has gone crazy about the gold rush . . . and everybody and his uncle and cousin wants to come North!"

"Well, there are quite a number from Tacoma here already," laughed Cotswell. "There's ex-Councilman Coates; Captain Ellis, ex-chief of police; and H. H. Hebb; Patton; Clark, a lawyer; a fellow named Breeze and a lot of others. Half of them are camping up on the Bonanza and the other half are up on the Eldorado. But, say, have you heard about Euly Gaisford, the barber? He got a claim eight months ago up on No. 7 Bonanza which is now worth at least a hundred thousand dollars!"

"A hundred thousand dollars!" exclaimed Stacey. "Holy mackerel! Guess he won't have to cut hair any more!"

"But he's the same good Euly Gaisford," said Cotswell. "Still cuts your hair if you need him."

"How about Coates and Captain Ellis?" asked Stacey.

"Ex-Councilman Coates is a lucky devil!" said Cotswell. "Happens to be the uncle of the Berry brothers and has a lay on their rich claim No. 4 on Eldorado. He's washing out seventy-five dollars a day in each clean-up. Coates is trying to get a good lay for Captain Ellis, too."

"Say, are there any more of those rich lays up there?" asked Stacey excitedly.

"Don't think so," answered Cotswell. "I've been here for a while now, and I haven't located any yet. Guess I've just had hard luck. Seems that even up here a fellow can have too little or too much gold, but we always live in hopes of the big strike and sudden wealth."

"Isn't there a creek in the Klondike called 'Too Much Gold'?" I questioned with great interest.

"Yea," answered Cotswell, "but it's a long way from here—about fifty miles. Rises way up there near King Dome. But 'Too Much Gold' isn't as exciting as it sounds. They say it got its name from the Indians after the big strike on the Bonanza. The Indians said: 'There's much gold on the Bonanza, more gold on Hunker, and too much gold in another stream way up in the mountains!'

"Seems the Indians had gone a little way up this unknown creek and, looking down into the clear waters, they saw thousands of glinty, golden particles. Thinking it was real gold, they called this stream 'Too Much Gold.' Actually, what they saw was only mica! But a little later, gold was really discovered up this river closer to the Dome."

"Is Too Much Gold all staked?" I asked with hopeful interest.

"Yes, every bit," said our friend, "but this stream has yielded a surprising amount of gold, in spite of the fun originally poked at it by old-timers."

While we were talking, an old miner by the name of Johnson joined us. He seemed to know Cotswell and Linc Davis and was anxious to sit at our table. It developed in talking to him that he was a sourdough, originally from Forty Mile. Now he owned a fairly good claim up on the Bonanza, which he was working part-time.

"Yes," he said, eagerly entering the conversation, "there are a lot of you fellows from Tacoma up here, but there are others from all parts of the country, too. There're perhaps nine or ten thousand in the Klondike now. Many have struck it rich. Some have gone "outside," never to come back. Others will return next spring to work their claims.

"One of the wealthiest to leave is F. W. Cobb, the man who discovered gold on the Eldorado and named the stream. He and his partner, Frank Phiscator, own two of the richest claims on the Eldorado. Each took 'Outside' nearly a hundred thousand dollars for a 'home stake'!

"Two other rich Cheechakos to leave Dawson this spring are William Stanley and Gage Worden. They own claims adjoining the fabulous Cobb Mine on Eldorado. These men were utter greenhorns and knew nothing of mining when they came North, but fate tossed a fortune into their laps!

"Yep," added Johnson, "the Klondike is an awfully rich country and I'm going to stay here until I make my stake. But the problem is to get the gold out of the frozen muck and ground, which is as hard as flint both winter and summer. But man, oh, man, it's the thrill of your life to see those yellow, nuggety babies smiling up at you once you bring them to the light of day!"

"It's hard to believe," said Linc Davis, enthusiastically entering the conversation, "but I've actually seen gallon oil cans just filled with nuggets up there on the Bonanza and Eldorado! And I've seen pack trains of dogs just loaded down with boxes and bags of gold dust that would stagger your imagination! They carry the gold back to Dawson to the trading companies for storage and shipment."

"Just think!" said Stacey. "A pack train of gold! It's like a tale from the Arabian Nights!"

"Yeah," added Johnson, "and that isn't all. We've heard the safes are bulging with gold in Dawson and there's a lot of it lying around in old valises, boxes and even tomato cans which the miners are holding back until a boat comes in."

Our gang from Tacoma stayed late at McPhee's, sitting around the table, talking about the Klondike gold, mostly. McPhee joined us when he had a moment from his customers and seemed especially interested in our group. Linc Davis, I learned, was going to help McPhee in his spare time. He had lay No. 6 up on the Bonanza. One of the lucky ones!

"Come up to the Bonanza in the morning with us and you can meet the boys and see the gold fields," Cottswell invited us as we pushed our chairs back and prepared to leave McPhee's.

"You bet!" we promised as we bid them all a friendly good night. "It was great to meet you fellows here!"

Leaving McPhee's it was only a matter of a few minutes' walk back to our boat where Stacey and I would spread our sleeping bags for the night. As we strode along, dazzling thoughts of sudden wealth pranced through our minds.

"Stacey," I said, "I wonder what lies ahead of us in this astonishing country of too much gold?"

"Whatever it is," said Stacey with great exultation, "I intend to be very rich when I leave the North. I'll be a Klondike King!"

It was still twilight when I pulled out my worn little diary to write on its weathered page this momentous account:

> July 15, 1897 (Dawson—Yukon River)
>
> Arrived at Dawson City 1:00 P.M. City can be seen ½ mile before reaching, after swinging around a sharp bend in river. Dawson is a marvelous place! One year ago nothing marked the spot! . . .

I put down my pencil a moment and looked across the Yukon toward the high hills which rose sharply out of the river, blotting out the vast wilderness of unexplored mountains beyond, far to the west, and on to the Northern sea.

"Just think, Stacey," I said. "A year ago nothing marked this spot!"

"Yeah, I know," replied Stacey. "But Ed, I think I felt a drop of rain. Let's put the tent up over the boat; looks like a heavy storm brewing. Hope those fellows, Jourgensen and Crawford, located a good bed tonight!" Then Stacey added, "Hope this storm doesn't last long. We've got to be up early, Ed. Tomorrow, we go to the gold fields!"

"You bet!" I said with enthusiasm, repeating a slang phrase which originated during the gold rush.

Chapter VI

We Hit Bedrock!

Where was the midnight sun, and where were those northern lights we had heard so much about?

The skies opened, and all night it poured torrents on Stacey and me and on all of the hundreds of other stampeders camped at Dawson and along the Yukon. We had slept little and, in the early morning, climbed wearily out of our soggy sleeping bags. The date was July 16, 1897, and a useless, dreary day seemed in prospect for us!

Huddling under the canvas tent stretched across our boat, we tried to cook breakfast on our little Klondike stove set up in the center of the boat. Scores of other fellows in nearby boats and barges were struggling with sticky sourdough pancakes. Gray smoke smudged up from sputtery stoves all along the river front.

"What a tough break!" bitterly complained Stacey between gulps of hot coffee brewed from muddy Yukon water. "Look at it rain! And this was the day we were going to the gold fields!"

"We'd better remain in Dawson another day if this storm persists and if we value our health!" I cautioned Stacey. "Hiking fifteen or twenty miles up to the Bonanza and Eldorado carrying a seventy-five-pound pack in this kind of weather isn't my idea of seeing the diggings or hunting for gold!"

At first, Stacey seemed resigned to wait, but a little later in the morning when the storm had let up somewhat, he became restless; so, throwing a pack together, he prepared to leave, saying he was going up to McPhee's first to meet the boys and from there he would go to the gold fields, rain or shine! Even a storm couldn't stop him!

I didn't argue much with Stacey. I could see it was useless. However, I did remind him of the hazards of becoming ill in the North, nearly two thousand miles away from home.

But he was unimpressed. Wasn't he in the best of health? He simply couldn't wait another hour. Besides, he had dreamed so much of gold, coming down the Yukon, and had waited so long that nothing could prevent him from going now that he was so near his goal. Why, he might be lucky enough to locate himself a good 'lay,' he told me, and an hour's delay might make all the difference between poverty and riches. No, nothing could stop him—rain, winds, hell or high water! He delivered this ultimatum with great determination as he fastened his pack strap and stalked away, soon disappearing down Front Street toward McPhee's.

Stacey's arguments seemed very convincing, but my better judgment told me to wait in Dawson, all the same. Besides, the storm had dampened my enthusiasm for gold. Somehow, I felt a strange lethargy and a gnawing ache creeping into my bones. My ankles felt sore and my muscles hurt terribly. Could it be a cold or a touch of the scurvy? I reached for the citrus extract, a miners' remedy. If I continued this treatment, I had been told, I could be rid of the symptoms in a few days; but let the disease persist, and I might be laid up for weeks. Some miners had even died of the scurvy. In the beginning, they told me, the sufferer would often have what he thought was a cold, then sore muscles and aching bones would follow. Later, the gums would become very red and swollen and the teeth would loosen and fall out. In the very last stages, the flesh and bones would turn black in spots and the flesh would decay . . . and that would be the end! I had been told that the dreaded disease was caused from lack of fresh foods and it was aggravated by the steady diet of sourdough pancakes and rancid bacon, with that telltale yellow streak running through it, which the miners sardonically referred to as the "pay streak"!

Well, I had eaten plenty of bacon with that yellow "pay streak" while coming down the Yukon as my slab of bacon had become rancid even before I reached Chilkoot Pass.

Digging a grave in the North was a hard and grim task. Cotswell and I had worked intermittently all day between heavy showers, chiseling out a hole long and deep enough in the frozen, icy ground to take the coffin. Our picks and shovels had struck flint-like, unyielding ground just a little under the top layer of spongy moss.

"How contradictory!" I thought. "Summer rains beating against eternally frozen earth! How many centuries has it been like this?" I stopped digging and rested. (Cotswell and I were working on the slant of the hill back of Dawson, about 300 feet from the nearest cabin in the south end of town, and about a half mile from the river. The grave had to be completed for the following day.) I leaned heavily against the handle of my shovel. The touch of scurvy had taken a toll on my vitality, but I gritted my teeth. I wouldn't give in. I must finish the job I had started. Surely, this was a job I had never anticipated!

I glanced down wearily over the town of Dawson. What a gloomy, dreary place it appeared now in the cold gray light! The whole scene was so utterly melancholy, not as I had first seen it from the river when the gold camp had seemed to be a beckoning, glittering, enchanted city of promise. This back view of Dawson was anything but glamorous. The town sprawled along the now very much riled Yukon. How boxed in and ugly the area now appeared! To the north and south, and across the river, high, somber hills seemed to press in, giving me a cramped, morbid feeling. And how still the air was! There was hardly a soul in sight. Dawson seemed so remote and cut off from civilization. I thought of those long, weary, hazardous miles back up the Yukon, then over the lakes and over the back-breaking Chilkoot Pass, and then the long steamer voyage of a thousand miles from Dyea to Tacoma. Suddenly, I felt very homesick and ill!

I listened intently. Every sound carried along the river and echoed back in this natural amphitheater. All at once, my ears caught the staccato sound of hammers pounding nails on wood. It was coming from the north end of town, from Ladue's sawmill. Soon, that roughly hewn coffin would be finished. I shivered! Life! Death! Gold! How futile it all seemed here on the fringe of eternity! I thought of Stacey . . .

"Cotswell," I said, "how much deeper must we dig? This job is really getting me down! That last bunch of miners coming in over the hill trail from the gold fields gave us the horselaugh. Thought we were digging for gold!"

"Oh, don't mind them," consoled Cotswell. "Perhaps we should have selected a spot farther from the trail. You see, Ed, they've had several stampedes up toward the big slide, but they were all false alarms. It's a big joke in Dawson, how the new Cheechakos will dig most any place, even on a hill!" Then he added rather thoughtfully, "But wouldn't it be funny if someday a Cheechako would strike it rich on a hill!"

"Well, I hardly expect to find gold while digging a grave," I said. "But how deep do you suppose we should dig?"

"The usual six feet, I guess, but I don't see how we're going to go down that far," answered Cotswell. "We're coming to large rocks now and bedrock can't be too far under. If it weren't for this blasted damp weather," he complained, "we could try building fires to thaw the muck and rocks like the miners do when they're sinking a shaft for gold!"

Cotswell and I worked strenuously, making slow progress, and as we worked, naturally we talked of Stacey.

"Gold isn't worth all of the risks!" I told Cotswell.

"No, it isn't, Ed," he agreed. "I tried to tell Stacey and the boys that, but they wouldn't listen. Stacey, Jourgensen, Crawford and some of the Tacoma fellows left Dawson in that storm! I even went a few miles with them. We crossed this hill, went down to the Klondike River, crossed on the little raft pulling ourselves over by cables and reached the mouth of the Bonanza when the storm broke loose in all its fury! Thunder, lightning, hail and high winds! Lord, how it rained! The streams were swollen and running high. It amounted to almost a cloudburst; mud and water nearly knee-deep in places near the rivers. Everybody was soaking wet. Some of the fellows turned back to Dawson, but not Stacey! He and a few others were determined to go on. Well, Ed, I've discovered since I've been up here you just can't talk reason with fellows when they're terribly smitten with the gold fever!" concluded Cotswell as he bent over and pulled up a heavy rock and heaved it out of the grave.

I stopped digging and rested a moment, wiping the

sweat from my forehead and shaking the raindrops from my hat and raincoat. It had been drizzling most of the day, but now a thick fog blotted out Dawson and a misty vapor swirled about us and hung low over the ground like a shroud.

Cotswell and I had only gone down about three feet! I shivered. . . . That touch of scurvy was certainly making me jumpy and I had a weak, eerie feeling. . . .

Huge sparks flew from Cotswell's dulled pick as he struck the rocks furiously, working like a demon. He was making a mighty effort to split some large boulders which blocked his way. Shooting flashes of green and purple lights darted from his pick off into space like lightning out of purgatory. I watched, almost expecting to see the devil himself appear in a flash and emerge from the rocky grave.

Suddenly, I heard a strange, faraway, muffled voice calling, "Who's there? Who's digging?"

"Cotswell," I said, "listen!" Cotswell put down his pick and we both stood motionless, listening.

"It sounded a little like Stacey's voice," I said dubiously, "but surely it couldn't be!"

"No, it's hardly possible," agreed Cotswell.

"Well, perhaps it only sounded like him," I said as I picked up my shovel and was about to resume digging, when, all at once, we saw the shadowy form of a man coming toward us through the mist. The face showed up very white and ill-looking, and dark, bluish circles hung low under his sunken eyes.

"My God! It looks like Stacey!" I heard Cotswell gasp.

I dropped my shovel and called, "Stacey, is it you?"

"Yeah, it's me all right, and I had a hellish time getting back!" said Stacey as he leaned heavily against the trunk of a nearby tree and spoke in a weak, raspy voice. "You see, I heard you digging. I got lost from the trail up on the hill in the fog. Lucky for me you were here. I've been walking for hours. Left the Bonanza early this morning. . . . Say, why are you fellows digging up here on the hill?" he asked curiously in a hot, feverish voice. He took several hasty steps forward and leaned over, peering down at us. "Getting any gold?" he asked eagerly.

"It's the same question they've all been asking!" said

Cotswell with a grin. "You bet we're getting gold!" he added with a forced, malicious little laugh. "Look here, Stacey!" And Cotswell yanked a tiny sack of gold from his hip pocket and held it up for Stacey's benefit. "Look, I've got an ounce already and I'll get at least another ounce tomorrow, and so will Ed."

"Jumpin' Jupiter!" exclaimed Stacey with eyes glistening. "You've hit pay dirt! But don't you realize you're foolish to be prospecting so near the trail? And what a funny-shaped hole you've dug! Have you fellows staked this spot yet?"

"No," I answered, keeping a straight face and lowering my voice. "Stacey, we've got to bury a fellow up here first."

"My God!" yelled Stacey recoiling back from the opening. "Then it's a grave you're digging!" Stacey shot us both quick, frightened glances and asked cautiously. "Ed, you and Cotswell haven't gotten into any trouble, have you? Do the Mounted Police know about this?"

"Sure," answered Cotswell with a sly little grin, "and they heartily approve of burying a corpse, don't they, Ed?"

"Oh, come now, Ed, give me the dope fast," implored Stacey, suddenly looking very ill and upset. "Can't you see I'm about played out! And I still have about a half mile to reach camp!"

I looked at Stacey in alarm. It was very evident at first glance that he was half sick. I could see he had lost pounds, as his clothes hung like muddy sacks and his boots were all caked and heavy with muck.

"All right, Stacey," I said quickly, "I'll make it snappy; then you make tracks for camp. "Well, it was like this: There was an accident in McPhee's mine and a poor workman or miner was suffocated to death. When it came to digging a grave, McPhee found that the miners were all too superstitious to take the job. McPhee was desperate, so he talked Cotswell and me into digging the grave at fifteen dollars a day, to be paid in gold dust. Neither of us cared much to take the job, but we took it as a special favor to McPhee. Of course, two ounces of gold isn't to be sneezed at! But, since we started the grave, the miners, who know what we are doing, avoid this spot. It's been a devilish, unpleasant task and I keep thinking of that dead man lying down there among the whisky bottles in McPhee's storeroom. It just makes me shiver to think of burying him tomorrow!"

"Say, Stacey," interrupted Cotswell, "you sure look terrible and as white as a ghost!"

"It makes me shudder to suddenly realize what can happen to a fellow up here!" exclaimed Stacey in awe as he clutched at his throat, buttoning his mackinaw tighter and staring down into the grave. "I saw lots of gold up there in the gold fields coming from the deep, frozen earth, but I'd forgotten that a fellow could die up here!"

"Oh, come now, Stacey," said Cotswell lightly. "Snap out of it! You evidently had a tough trip up there."

"Yeah," admitted Stacey, "It was a devil of a trip and we were like drowned rats most of the way, but I admit it was a thrill when we finally made it. Why, it was the most exciting moment of my life, seeing those rivers literally pouring gold into the sluice boxes. Euly Gaisford, the Tacoma barber, let me pan a little for myself. Man, oh, man! You should have seen those big yellow nuggets come rolling out of just one shovelful of pay dirt!" cried Stacey, warming up to his subject, again flushed with the gold fever. "And while I was at Euly's cabin, ex-councilman Coates from Tacoma and Captain Ellis dropped by. Gave me a rousing welcome to the Klondike. The captain said he was trying to get a good 'lay' on Berry's No. 4 claim. Says it should be a rich one. Ellis said he might even take me in as a partner. Ed, he's a darned good fellow. Used to be chief of police in Tacoma when I was on the force there."

"And, Ed," continued Stacey, "if I get this chance to go in with Captain Ellis, it will be a lucky break! It will mean fifty per cent of the gold! I'll count my trip up there in the storm well worth the risks!" concluded Stacey with jubilant enthusiasm.

Very late in the day, back in the boat, Stacey, all wrapped up in a warm blanket with feet soaking in hot water, doctoring himself for a cold, watched me thoughtfully while I wrote a few lines in my diary. Although I was very tired, true to my custom I recorded the unusual happening of this particular day.

July 16, 1897 (Dawson—Showers)

Stacey got back at 5:30 P.M. He was all tired out. Says trail is holy terror! McPhee wanted us to dig grave for man who was suffocated in his mine. Cotswell and I took job at $15 per day (gold dust). Broke both of our picks and dulled the third. Ground frozen hard as flint.

"Yes," I told Stacey as I put down my pencil, "it was a hard, grim job, digging that grave, and I'm afraid McPhee will be displeased if we don't go deeper. Tomorrow morning early, Cotswell and I are going to try to dig deeper in order to give the poor fellow a decent burial."

"Poor devil," sighed Stacey. "After all of the terrific hardships of coming into this country, it doesn't seem fair a fellow should die like that!"

Then, between fits of sneezing and coughing, Stacey talked feverishly about gold and, although I was dead tired, I listened to him for a long time.

"I tell you, Ed, it's all they say about the Klondike! There's no doubt these gold fields are the richest in the world! You should see the amounts of gold those mine owners are getting. It's almost unbelievable! Those two streams, the Bonanza and Eldorado, are like rivers of gold! No wonder the miners who came into the Klondike first went out this spring with untold wealth. They say that the steamers *Portland* and *Excelsior* were loaded to the guards —like treasure ships! But there is real concern among the miners too, that the gold they're shipping out might be captured by Spanish warships after it leaves St. Michael by ocean steamer. They say that the Spanish-American War is really beginning in earnest now, and anything could happen!"

Stacey slept fitfully, wakening several times during the night and continued: "Why, Ed, there's so much gold up there . . . would you believe it? The miners are actually afraid the yellow stuff may become too common and lose its present value. Many of the fellows are rushing 'Outside' with their gold to invest or spend before that could happen!"

"If I could only lay my hands on just a little of that so-called common yellow stuff," I told Stacey, "I'd be satisfied for the rest of my life. Why, I'd return home happy as a king! And so would about five thousand other poor, homesick fellows!

"Listen, Stacey," I continued, "in contrast to what you tell me, since you've been gone I've seen hundreds of miserably discouraged men hauling water, cutting wood, waiting on tables and even taking the disgusting job of emptying dirty spittoon cans just in order to get a square meal. And most of these men are too proud to write home and say they haven't struck it rich! It makes me think!

"Seeing all of this has been a startling lesson, Stacey. So, to be on the safe side, I've applied at the Alaska Commercial Company for an accountant's job in case Dame Fortune does not smile immediately. They told me they'd put me on the list, though there are dozens ahead of me."

I went on to tell Stacey how alarmingly fast my funds had dwindled in just the few days we had been in Dawson. "Prices are terrific! Why, Stacey, even an ordinary sewing needle costs fifty cents. 'It isn't the weight of the needle that counts in this case,' the merchant assured me. 'It's the importance it has up here.' And so it is true, Stacey. How very important even a little needle may become in this isolated country, especially if a fellow needs to mend a tent, a sock, or a pair of moccasins! Then the little needle may become more valuable than a nugget!"

As I talked to Stacey, it was quite apparent he wasn't listening. Besides having a cold, I could see there was something else wrong with him. I questioned him closely.

"Oh, it's just a bloody flux and probably a touch of the blasted scurvy," he said evasively. "Nearly everyone gets a touch of it up here!"

The following morning very early, I climbed wearily out of my sleeping bag, had a cold breakfast, being very careful not to awaken Stacey, and, taking my pick and shovel, I stepped quietly out of the boat and trudged the half mile to the hillside. I found Cotswell ahead of me, working like a Trojan. He had bailed the water out of the grave, for it had rained in the night, and he was wielding his pick with all of his strength, chipping out pieces of rock. While he rested, I cleared the rocks away, and we took turns, reversing the procedure.

At last, at 9:00 A.M., Cotswell announced: "Ed, it's no use! We've struck bedrock! It's impossible to go deeper. McPhee will just have to be satisfied. Although we've only gone down a little over three feet, I'm sure it'll take the coffin."

As we had anticipated, McPhee was displeased, but seeing it was impossible to go deeper and too late to dig a new grave, he ordered the funeral to proceed as planned. The coffin was brought from Ladue's and a crude cart drawn by a team of huskies waited in front of McPhee's warehouse to haul the box and its sorrowful contents to the hillside.

Just as the funeral procession was about to leave, suddenly, off in the distance, the mournful, blood-chilling howl of a lone dog reached our ears, and immediately it was taken up and chorused by the whole team of malemutes and at least a dozen other dogs in different parts of Dawson. We all stood glued to the spot, the cold chills running up and down our spines as the wild, unearthly sounds echoed back and forth across the river and through the hills!

"The dogs always seem to know!" exclaimed McPhee. "It's almost uncanny!"

Then, as suddenly and mysteriously as it had started, all was silent again. It seemed that a great hush had settled over Dawson as we moved slowly up the hill.

Only a few brief words were spoken at the shallow grave by a fellow miner while the others stood with bowed heads, and then Cotswell and I shoveled the damp, gravelly earth over the pitiful, crude pine box. The opening was just barely deep enough. And by mounding the earth a little, we managed to cover the coffin adequately. McPhee then drove a small wooden slab at the head of the grave to mark the spot.

And so we buried one of the first miners to die in the Klondike gold fields in 1897. And although the grave was in full sight of Dawson, somehow it seemed like a pitifully lonely spot! As we followed the funeral party back to

Dawson, we heard one miner say to another, "Yes, it was a tough break, the way that dump caved in on the miner and suffocated the poor fellow. But in a few weeks—if it's any consolation—his body will be frozen stiff as a board and probably will stay that way for centuries!"

(Many times later, during the years I was in the Klondike, I passed this shallow grave and saw it was being gradually lost to the forest. The wooden stake rotted and dropped away and eventually the place was forgotten, as the grave was not in a real cemetery.)

How sad and true, the old Bible saying: "As for man, his days are as grass: as a flower of the field, so he flourisheth. For the wind passeth over it, and it is gone; and the place thereof shall know it no more."*

During the several days which followed the funeral of the miner, I watched anxiously for Stacey to recover from his "temporary illness," as he called it, and for the weather to clear. At that time, quite a few other miners were sick and complaining and there was much scurvy, dysentery and pneumonia due to bad diet and the damp weather conditions.

However, I myself began to feel in better health. (I had taken quantities of citrus extract.) But now I began to realize that valuable time was running out for me. During Stacey's illness, he had spoken often of his hopes of going into partnership with Captain Ellis on the Berry claim. The more I thought of it, the more probable it seemed that Stacey would get this marvelous opportunity.

"Well, a fellow can't stand in the way of another's good fortune," I said to myself. "I guess it's every man for himself up here. And although we did come into the Klondike as partners, after all there was no real agreement that we should remain so."

But here I had been in Dawson for nearly a week, and still not even a glimpse of those marvelous gold fields!

---

* In the Dawson of today there are at least six cemeteries, four of which date back to the year 1898, the year of the greatest gold rush to the Klondike. In these old cemeteries there are hundreds of unidentified and unmarked graves of the stampeders, some of whom died in the epidemic of typhoid fever which ran rampant in the year 1898.

Those fifteen miles up to the diggings, which a day or so previously had seemed like an impossible fifteen hundred, now took on their proper proportion, and I resolved to get up to the Bonanza in all haste before many more hours should elapse!

That certain strange inertia and deadly fatigue, no doubt caused by the touch of scurvy, plus the hardships of the trip into the country and the forced exertion of digging the grave, had all vanished. Now I stood as a new man—ready and eager for the great adventure of licking the North!

Chapter VII

Rivers of Gold!

The weather had cleared!

I took a deep breath, filling my lungs with the sweet, soft air blowing down the Yukon. It was truly the smell of late spring in the North, although it was now way past the middle of July. In this country it seemed that the seasons crowded each other. Blueberries, wild raspberries, currants and salmonberries were ready to pick on the hills, and soon wild cranberries would be ripe in the gulches. Spring flowers still bloomed along the Yukon and back of Dawson. Bluebells, buttercups, wild heather and, in places, a deep pink haze from millions of blossoms of fireweed shone on the hillsides.

What a great and marvelous country it truly was! I began to feel like a vital part of it all!

"Stacey," I said, "I'm going to the gold fields today. Will you be able to make the trip?"

"Ed, I wish I could, but you'll have to go alone. This blasted sickness has certainly laid me out! But I'll be all right in a couple of days. I know it'll be a great experience, Ed, going up there for the first time to the diggings. Please don't worry about me. I think Captain Ellis is coming to town. He'll look me up."

Stacey flopped back on his sleeping bag and was snoring almost before he hit the pillow. I stood looking down at him for a few minutes. It was evident his vitality had hit rock bottom! He needed complete rest. Hurriedly, I put food near him and laid out the citrus extract; then I penciled a quick note and laid it near his pillow. I gathered up a few supplies, rolled them hastily into a bundle and fastened it to my back, then stepped quietly out of the boat which was anchored to the bank near the Mounted Police barracks at Dawson. I knew if Stacey needed any help he was within easy call of the Mounted Police and dozens of stampeders close by.

Before leaving for the gold fields, I stopped at the post office, scarcely expecting a letter, but, glory be! hallelujah! there, was a letter from home! It was food for a hungry soul! My wife and little son Clemy were waiting eagerly to hear of my success. They prayed it would come soon. Times were still very hard back there in the States. They were still living with her mother, but how my beloved Velma longed for my return and to have a little home of her own! It could be just a cozy, simple little white cottage with flowers and a low picket fence. Never again would she care to live in a mansion like the one her once wealthy father, Horatio Clement, had provided for the family when he was living. But how she hated the box-like roominghouse her mother had been forced to run since the death of her husband and the immediate loss of the Clement fortune, including the loss of a large tract of South Tacoma and one of the leading hotels in Tacoma, The Abbott! Almost penniless overnight! That is what had happened to her family during the Panic of the Nineties!

Yes, my dear Velma had always been used to luxuries, and since our marriage of a few years, I had never been able to provide them for her. I had barely made a living as an accountant during the Depression working for Reese, Crandall & Redman, Wholesale Grocery Co., in Tacoma.

With a lump in my throat, I read and reread her letter. She mentioned watching for the North Star every night. She said, "Although I know that perhaps it is too light for you to see it always, way up there near the Arctic Circle on these light summer nights, still, I know the star is overhead. It is our star. May it guide you and bring you home safely to us very soon—that is the most important thing, even more so than gold!"

The letter contained words of intimate endearment. I

folded the treasured bit of paper and put it in my pocket for a dozen other readings, then set my face resolutely towards the gold fields with new determination. I would succeed! I must! A little white cottage with flowers and a picket fence moved ahead of me like a beckoning mirage.

As I approached the Klondike River, I met Patton, a man from Tacoma. "Hello, Ed. Going to the gold fields?" he asked jovially.

"You bet!" I answered.

"Well, then, let's hoof it together. I'm packing supplies to upper Bonanza and to # 4 Eldorado, Berry's claim. The Tacoma bunch is there and will be mighty glad to see us."

"Which way are you going?" I asked.

"Well, there're three trails," explained Patton. "One takes you over the hill back of Dawson a distance of about two miles. It drops down to the Klondike River, where there's a small raft and a cable stretched across the river to hang onto to pull yourself over to the opposite bank. At this point, the Bonanza cuts into the Klondike and, from there on, just follow the Bonanza up to the gold fields. You can't miss it. You'll see the diggings all the way for about fifteen miles."

"I've a very good reason to know a little about the hill trail back of Dawson," I told Patton. "You see, Cotswell and I dug a grave up there a few days ago. It was sad about that miner!"

"Yes," said Patton. "It must have been a tough job! Too bad you did a job like that your second day in Dawson. It's time that you see the gold fields and get your bearings. Now, the second trail to the Bonanza begins at the mouth of the Klondike River. You follow the river until you hit the Bonanza. But this so-called trail is more or less on swampy ground all of the way and is made up of hundreds of those damned niggerheads, which seem to grow several feet apart. They are big, round, mop-like bunches of grass, slippery as eels and as tipsy as drunken sailors! When you step on one, unless you hit the middle, over you go, and many's the time I've landed in the mud or been dunked in the river. Man, oh, man! You have to be an acrobat to take that trail. But it's a shortcut to the gold fields, if you're in that much of a hurry.

"But the third trail is a fairly good one. It's used often

and I'm taking it this trip," continued Patton. "Starts from across the mouth of the Klondike River, at Louse Town, and takes you over the hill, cutting a little across country to the southeast until it hits into a ridge which follows along in the same direction as the Bonanza and runs about a half a mile back, parallel with the river. If you follow this trail to its very end, you will land in the back country, past King and Queen Domes, way over there in that rugged, partly unexplored territory somewhere near Quartz Creek and the upper part of Indian River. However, there's a cut-off which drops you down near the Forks of the Bonanza and Eldorado—our destination."

"Let's get started!" I said eagerly. "I'm rarin' to go!"

In a few minutes, Patton and I reached the mouth of the Klondike River, where a scow ferried us groaningly across the swift current. There was a crowd of miners from Dawson aboard, and we could look up the Yukon and see scores of new stampeders swinging their boats around the big bend of the river, heading swiftly for Dawson.

"Just look at the new stampeders coming!" said one miner in amazement. "I only hope they've brought enough supplies! Hundreds have swarmed in here just the last few days, they seem to be traveling light, not bothering to bring the things they really need for a long winter. It's bad, a damned shame!"

"Yeah," said his companion, "and there'll be more like 'em when that new trail over White Pass is completed. It's supposed to be finished the end of this month. They tell me there're several thousand stampeders waiting at the base of White Pass, on Lynn Canal. They're beginning to call the new town, 'Skagway.' Someone says it's the Indian name for north wind. . . ."

"Say, do you suppose they'll use Chilkoot Pass any more?" asked one of the miners who was listening intently.

"They certainly will," volunteered a miner. "Why, there's even a rumor afoot right now that an aerial tramway company will begin working this fall and will stretch a long cable from Canyon Camp clear to the summit of Chilkoot Pass to carry huge freight buckets for the stampeders who land at Dyea Indian village. Of course, they say passengers won't be allowed to ride. These buckets will travel high in

Claim in foreground, #2 Above Discovery. Bonanza was staked by Skookum Jim. George Carmack took the Discovery claim at mouth of Little Skookum Gulch. Tagish Charlie staked #2 Below Discovery

Testing the pay dirt in a miner's cabin. Note the gold pan

Claim #16 Eldorado. This rich claim, showing miners underground, was owned by Thomas Lippy, several times a millionaire

Skookum Jim's claim, No. II, above Bonanza. He was with George Carmack and Tagish Charlie when they made the big discovery on Rabbit Creek (later called Bonanza)

the air suspended from moving cables, probably seventy-five to a hundred feet above the ground. They say it should be finished by the summer of ninety-eight, and that Archie McLean Hawks, civil engineer of Tacoma, is on his way now to start the seven-hundred-thousand-dollar project. They say it will be financed by S. S. Bush, a millionaire of Louisville, Kentucky. I understand he is in San Francisco now making final arrangements with the company which will furnish the materials for a power house at Canyon Camp and another smaller one, possibly at Sheep Camp."

"Yes, and they say the buckets will be large enough to carry hundreds of pounds of freight and could even carry a small boat to the summit!" added another miner.

"Man, oh, man! What a break for the new stampeders once they get their goods up from Dyea to Sheep Camp!" exclaimed someone in the crowd. "Brother, I can still feel the weight of those heavy packs, and I still have the scars where the leather straps cut my back!"

"Yes," said another fellow, "it certainly will be progress, all right, and you can bet your boots this country will be overrun next year. They tell me the newspapers all over the world are running sensational stories of the gold we're finding up here. No doubt, stampeders will be coming from all parts of the globe! They should tone the news down a little!"

"But what percentage of these fellows do you think will ever strike it rich?" I asked eagerly.

"Oh, very few, just a small percentage, young man," the miner answered gruffly, looking at me closely and spotting me as a new Cheechako; "unless, of course, many new discoveries are made . . . which is quite possible!"

In a few minutes, the scow reached the opposite shore of the Klondike River. Louse Town swarmed with a motley crowd of stampeders, Indians, half-breeds and many dogs—some malemutes, huskies and mixtures. There was hardly a place to step on the muddy, soggy path, for Louse Town had been built on a low, swampy sand bar facing the Yukon at the confluence of the two rivers.

We wasted no time here. The trail led almost grudgingly across the low, damp flat among the greasy tents and a few shacks and immediately straggled up the steep, uneven hill.

Hundreds of fellows wallowed along the slippery, narrow trail, most of them carrying heavy packs like ours.

It was in the middle of the afternoon. The sun beat down bright and hot, and we perspired mightily under our heavy loads as we hiked through the steaming woods of low spruce, evergreens and aspens. Often we stopped to rest our aching backs and blistering feet and to catch our breath. Many times we stepped aside to let the other fellows, who were both going and coming from the gold fields, pass us on the narrow trail. Sometimes we paused long enough to carry on brief conversations or to hear other fellows talking near us.

"My two shovels were stolen this morning," one man vehemently proclaimed to another.

"And, say, I had a shirt stolen right out of my cabin!" a miner by the name of Shaw volunteered angrily.

"These newcomers are a thieving lot!" the third miner joined in hotly. "Why, just this morning I had a cake of tar soap stolen right out of my wash pan, almost under my nose. And the big Swede had a whole slab of bacon stolen right out of his cache last week!"

"Those boats scheduled to bring in grub haven't arrived yet," said the first miner, "and Chute of the H. T. Company says the food situation is getting critical. Some of the men are very worried, as they are short on supplies."

"Well, we can always eat Yukon salmon," laughed a young fellow who had just come up and had thrown himself down to rest in the shade of a tree. "The fish are running in the Yukon now. Only yesterday, a fellow brought some salmon to the Bonanza. Sold it for a dollar a pound."

"Yeah, I know," his companion answered, "but the river will be frozen over in September and then no more fish until next summer! And, anyway," he added disgustedly, "who wants to eat fish all winter?"

"Well, there're still caribou and moose back there in the mountains," said one miner hopefully, pointing toward the Rocky Mountains.

"Now who wants to chase all over the North hunting moose and caribou and probably get lost? That's an Indian's job, anyway!" said the first miner sarcastically. "Besides, a whole tribe of Indians starved to death up there near the Arctic Circle last winter. And they had had their hunters out for days. It was a mighty queer thing how those herds of moose and caribou knew enough to disappear."

"Oh, hell!" broke in another miner. "I came up here to mine gold, not to worry about grub!"

Hearing these conversations, naturally, made me begin to feel a little concern. During my week in Dawson, I had overheard snatches of similar conversation, and while I was at the A.C.C. company applying for a job, I had heard a clerk saying to a customer, "This year, the boats coming from St. Michael up the Yukon have been very slow and disappointing. Only a couple of the smaller boats have reached Dawson and they brought mostly whisky and barroom fixtures."

As Patton and I walked along toward the Bonanza, mentally I began to take stock of my own supplies. By being very careful, I decided, I could make my food stuffs last through the summer and into the fall, but after that I would be out. . . . Well, I wouldn't worry . . . yet!

"Ah, look who's coming down the trail with his gang of miners!" suddenly exclaimed Patton.

"Who?" I asked, looking up the trail with interest.

"Why, it's Swiftwater Bill Gates himself, the notorious gambler of Dawson! Has a rich claim up on the Eldorado and is also associated with Big Alex McDonald, the Klondike King. He's probably headed for Dawson to gamble away another fortune!"

Even if he hadn't been in the lead, it would have been easy to have spotted this unusual character. I stared with interest at the gambler as he quickly approached us, swinging along the trial. Swiftwater Bill presented almost a comical picture. He was a man perhaps five feet eight inches tall and he tripped along in a laughable, bowlegged fashion. On his head he wore a derby tipped jauntily over one eye, and he puffed on a long cigar, leaving a cloud of smoke trailing behind him. His complexion was swarthy; his eyes and hair were brown; and he had a thick beard of the same color. A loud-colored vest glorified his thick chest, and a businessman's suit of striped material covered his rather uneven figure. His pants were tucked into high, mud-covered boots, miner's style.

As he approached closer, I could see that he was literally covered with big yellow nuggets; nuggets on his stick pin, large nuggets glistened on his watch chain, and he wore several large, nuggety rings. A gold buckle studded with nuggets adorned his waistline. As Swiftwater Bill came abreast of us, we stepped aside to let him pass. His peculiar walk slowed to a swagger.

"Hurry, fellows! Keep coming with that gold! We've got to make Dawson for that big game at Kerry's Saloon!" he called back loudly to his miners for our benefit as he brushed by us.

"Well, I'll be darned!" I said after they had passed on down the trail. "So that's Swiftwater Bill! But where did he get that name?"

"Oh, it's a big joke in Dawson about his nickname," laughed Patton. "He boasts that he stayed for a time at Miles Canyon helping pilot some of the stampeders through those dangerous waters. But the fact of the matter is, he's scared to death of swift water! Yep, Swiftwater Bill is quite a character around Dawson!" Then he added musingly, "And he's quite a ladies' man, too! Looks up all of the pretty show girls who come to town. Right now, he's courting a new one. . . ."

(I heard later that he married two of the Drummond girls, and his third unsuccessful venture in the field of matrimony followed later when he married one of their cousins, who nearly cleaned him out of his fortune. Also, I heard that, on one of his trips out to Seattle, he made the headlines of newspapers all over the country by standing in a Seattle hotel window and tossing bills of various denominations to the crowds of amazed and gaping people who delightedly scrambled to pick up the bills which rained down from Swiftwater's hotel window! Occasionally, he would wave a bill tantalizingly in the air, then he would shock his audience by nonchalantly lighting his cigar with it! All through these escapades, they said, he wore a very conspicuous parka and was adorned with his traditional number of Klondike nuggets. It was rumored many times that he was hooked up with a large London mining syndicate and that he had made millions for them—and, no doubt, for himself, too! In Dawson, I was to see him many times gambling away fortunes which would have made the hearts of many a poor fellow glad!)

"Ed, do you realize what time it is?" asked Patton as we stopped to rest our weary feet a little later after passing Swiftwater Bill.

"No," I answered, "because I no longer possess a watch. You see, Patton, I lost my watch nearly two months ago coming into the country. It was in a terrific storm on Lake Bennett. I happened to be standing up in the boat adjusting the sail when I was nearly pitched overboard. A tremendous wave hit our boat and my watch flew out into the water. To my consternation, I saw it disappear in the lake before I could grab it!"

"Tough luck!" sympathized Patton, "but for your information, Ed, it is now almost midnight, and we've been walking about seven hours."

"Seems more like seventeen!" I laughed wearily.

"Well, I figure we'll hit down into the Bonanza around one A.M. Then, brother! If we keep going like this, we'll get something hot to eat at Euly Gaisford's claim, then roll into one of their bunks and catch a little sleep before going up to the Eldorado, where half of the Tacoma boys are camping at # 4, Berry's claim. Ed, when we reach the Bonanza you'll see most of the miners still up working. They hardly take time to sleep in the summer. Many of them work all night long because it's cooler. They sleep during the day when the sun is hottest."

Patton and I continued to hike along the trail, meeting groups of miners headed toward Dawson. Traveling light, and in places where the trail was smooth, these miners made very good time, stepping along in lively fashion; some, even double-tripping it (dog trotting).

As we trudged along the ridge, we watched the sun drop slowly down behind the mountains to the west. Then, quite a little past midnight, the sunlight softened and glowed in very light, pale pastel shades. A little later, it became even more subdued, having the same quality as the light in late afternoon when the sun temporarily goes behind a cloud.

The night was perhaps at its darkest when we came to the worst stretch of the whole trail. It was becoming very rocky. Naturally, I was growing very tired under my heavy load, as we had been walking since early afternoon and had only rested at brief intervals. Also, I began to realize that I had definitely overestimated my strength.

"The trail is very rough," I said as I leaned against a scrub tree to catch my breath.

"Yes, it is, Ed," answered Patton. "You see, this was originally an old caribou trail leading into the back country toward the Rocky Mountains, and later it was used by the Indians. No one up here ever takes the time to improve any of these trails, so they remain pretty much as they were."

Fifteen miles at a stretch, to one who is not accustomed to it, is a long way, especially if he has been ill and has grown soft from riding in a boat for several weeks. My muscles sagged and my feet seemed to lose their elasticity. . . . Then, suddenly, it happened!

My foot caught on a sharp rock in the middle of the trail and I pitched headlong, twisting my ankle terribly. I writhed in pain, immediately thinking I had broken it, as my ankle had taken the brunt of my fall. A thousand thoughts rushed through my mind as I lay there helpless for a few minutes, my supplies spilling over the trail. Curse the luck! Here I was up on the ridge with a broken ankle!

Patton rushed to my assistance and helped me to a sitting position, pulling off my boot. "Ed, it isn't broken, after all, I'm sure," he said, examining it closely. "Lucky for you! But it is badly bruised and will probably swell. It's a mighty good thing we're not far from the cut-off leading down to the Forks!" Patton bound his handkerchief tightly around my ankle and, painfully, we started out again.

It was about 1:15 A.M. when Patton and I finally reached a high vantage point overlooking the Bonanza. I stood there looking with excited interest and leaning heavily against an improvised crutch I had made from a stout branch of a scrub tree.

Up the valley less than a quarter of a mile, we could see the Forks, the junction where the famous Eldorado came into the Bonanza and flowed as one river down the valley. Both streams were much smaller than I had pictured them, and the valley, in places, was only three or four hundred feet wide with high hills on both sides.

The rivers wound in and out like tortured things, running the gauntlet of miles and miles of sluice boxes which speared out from the many claims.

Gravel dumps and tailings mounded the valley and many tents and a few shacks dotted the outer edges of the claims. A few tents were stuck in among the dumps, looking like dirty toadstools sprung up overnight.

Hundreds of men worked at the shafts near the dumps and sluice boxes. Even from where we stood on the hill in the still, clear night air, we could faintly hear the scrapings of shovels on gravel. Every foot of the valley, for as far as we could see, was taken!

This was my first glimpse and impression of the fabulous rivers of gold! And I looked in wonderment and awe. But where in this valley was there even a fraction of "pay dirt" left for a new Cheechako like me! I knotted my fists and shoved them hard into my pockets. One hand came into contact with the tiny poke of gold—the two ounces which McPhee had paid me for digging the grave.

"I must get more of this gold dust—lots more of this wonderful metal—only I would acquire it in a different sort of way. Yes, it would be from the ground, all right, but it would be from good 'pay dirt' and from my own claim down there somewhere in that valley! I would tear the gold out with my bare hands if need be!" I thought savagely.

I gritted my teeth. My foot was hurting me terribly. I would succeed! I must find gold! My wife was going to have that little white cottage and many other things she and my small son needed. Besides, I must pay back those hundreds of dollars I had borrowed to get myself into the Klondike!

It seemed that Patton must have sensed my thoughts, for I heard him saying, "I know, Ed, it does look mighty discouraging sometimes, but don't give up. Too many fellows have left the Klondike, beaten, without giving it a real try.

"Of course," he added, "we all know the North can be pretty tough! But there is yet undiscovered gold up here, I feel sure. It is for fellows like you and me to discover it. And when we do, boy! I'm sure we'll appreciate it and hang onto it! A lot of these very wealthy miners squander their money on liquor and lightheaded dance-hall girls."

Patton and I rested a little, and while we were up there, high on the hill, he pointed down to the Bonanza and continued, "Look, Ed, down the valley and across to the side hill. See that little log cabin over there? Well, that's Euly Gaisford's, the little barber from Tacoma. It's # 7 Bonanza. That's where we're headed first. Euly Gaisford is a lucky devil! You should see those huge nuggets he gets! At first, he wasn't even interested in the other kinds of gold—just picked out those big nuggets, not even bothering to look for the fine and coarse gold. Yes, he's lucky, all right! The 'pay streak' runs clear across the valley where his claim is! The richest part of the Bonanza! You see, it's only a short distance from where the fabulous Eldorado comes into the Bonanza.

"See how the Bonanza bends up there near the Forks? Well, right there to the right is Big Skookum Gulch and just about a thousand feet this side of the Forks is Little Skookum Gulch. At the very entrance to Little Skookum Gulch is the famous Big Discovery claim found by George Carmack; the two claims, one on either side, are owned by his two Indian friends, Skookum Jim and Tagish Charlie."

"Who would ever guess?" I said, looking down in awe, remembering that I had seen all three of these famous men with their thick pokes of gold on my first day in Dawson. Anyone a year ago could have gone right by this place and never have suspected the richness in those gravels!

"Brother! and if you think this stream is rich, just let your eyes travel up there beyond the Forks to the Eldorado. Man, oh, man! Now you're really looking at a river of gold, almost four solid miles of it! Why, Ed, only recently Alexander McDonald took out ninety-four thousand dollars from the surface of claim number thirty. He has only worked a forty-foot stretch of it and he's gone down just two feet! Think of what he'll get when he reaches bedrock! And this is just one of the many claims he owns on the two rivers. As you've probably heard, he is the richest man in the Klondike!

"But talk about luck!" continued Patton. "Why, there's one fellow in the Klondike who sure has a lucky star! Charlie Anderson, the 'Lucky Swede,' they call him. No man could be more fortunate than he. Charlie Anderson owns number twenty-nine Eldorado, just one claim below Alex McDonald's. It's a funny thing—he was practically forced into taking it. It was like this: In the fall of ninety-six Charlie Anderson came to Dawson from Forty Mile, and two miners got him to buy their claim while he was dead drunk. They got six hundred dollars out of him . . . all he had! When he sobered up, he was as mad as a hornet. He even tried to get the miners to refund his money, but they flatly refused, being awfully glad to get rid of what they thought was a blank and worthless claim. Well, to make a long story short, the Swede went to the Mounted Police and complained bitterly that he had been gyped. The Mountie he talked to was a French Canadian, and, becoming very much out of patience with the Swede, said angrily, 'Why for you get drunk? Now get out of here and go up there to that Eldorado claim and work eet. I no more want to hear about eet!'

"The Swede was very angry and left town with his pick and shovel. Grudgingly, he went to work on his newly acquired claim. Cursing the two miners who had sold it to him, he began digging deeper in the same shaft where they had left off. A few days later, he was jubilantly celebrating in Dawson. Charlie Anderson had only gone down two feet when he struck a pocket of almost pure gold . . . a hundred and fifty thousand dollars' worth! The 'Lucky Swede,' they called him, and he was the talk of Dawson. Now the mining experts say he has a two-million-dollar claim!"

"Great Scott, Patton!" I said, straining my eyes to see as far as possible up the Eldorado. "Can you see the Lucky Swede's claim from here?"

"No," answered Patton. "It's up there about three miles around that bend in the valley."

"It's a funny thing, Ed, about the pay streak," continued Patton. "It seems to begin up there on the Eldorado around claim number forty, and runs amazingly rich all the way down to the Forks. There's four solid miles of it, you might say, with the pay streak at least two hundred feet wide! From the Forks, the Bonanza runs very rich for quite a long way, then runs a little less rich for several miles until finally it seems to peter out somewhat near the mouth of the Bonanza where it empties into the Klondike River. There are about one hundred claims on the Bonanza, and seventy on the Eldorado."

"Where do you think all of this gold originally came from?" I asked excitedly. "In other words, where do you think the Mother Lode possibly could be located?"

"Well, that's a great matter of speculation among the miners up here," answered Patton. "Whoever could find the Mother Lode, no doubt would be the richest man in the world! William Ogilvie, the official government surveyor, says it can't be too far from this area. And the reason he says so is, because the nuggets in these creeks are all very rough and unpolished, which shows that they have not been washed down these streams for any great distance!"

"Look at this mining map by Ogilvie," said Patton, producing a small map from his hip pocket. "See how all of these rivers of the Klondike region flow like the spokes of an enormous wheel, with the King and Queen Domes up there, about fifteen miles to the east, forming the hub, or gigantic center, of this tremendous gold field."

Patton held the little map closer for me to inspect. Suddenly, as I looked, I could see what he meant. The wheel leaped out at me! All of the well-known and lesser-known creeks, except the Klondike and Indian rivers, were like immense spokes of a wheel—a wheel stretching out, covering a wide area of perhaps a hundred and fifty miles. Most amazing of all, these streams all seemed to rise in the general vicinity of King and Queen Domes!

I studied the map more closely and noticed that, beginning this gigantic wheel from the location where we now stood, first, there was the fabulous Eldorado; second, the north branch of the Bonanza; then came rich Hunker to the left, around the wheel, with its famous tributary, called Gold Bottom, where Robert Henderson had first discovered tiny particles of gold in early summer of 1896. The intriguing-sounding stream, Too Much Gold, came next on the wheel; and on around King Dome, a little to the north, All Gold showed up clearly; then came Dominion Creek, a very long and lesser-known stream, a little to the northeast; on around the colossal wheel, almost to the south, rose Sulphur and Quartz creeks, also not very well-known streams, both rising high between the King and Queen Domes. There were many little creeks and gulches of auriferous sands filling in the gaps between the spokes, all pointing to the same source and in the same general direction—towards the peaks.

"Maybe the King and Queen are sitting on thrones of solid gold!" I said musingly to Patton. "Maybe their treasure is buried deep under their feet."

"Could be," answered Patton thoughtfully, folding up his little map and putting it carefully away. "But, Ed, others in the Klondike have had the same idea and have searched up there on the Domes, but they haven't yet found the Mother Lode. It's a long hike to reach the Domes, but on a clear day it's well worth the effort. The view you get of this country is magnificent! And when you see those big Canadian Rockies to the east, you'll understand why that country a hundred and fifty miles away is still unexplored."

As I limped slowly down the rough trail to the Bonanza, leaning heavily on my improvised crutch, my mind was aflame with wild speculations and exciting thoughts, and, temporarily, I forgot my injured foot. I must climb over the foothills to stand high on those two peaks, the King and Queen Domes, and see for myself this wonderful territory.

Perhaps even I might be lucky enough to locate a fabulous treasure!

Chapter VIII

Glittering Fortunes and Empty Pokes

It was July 21, 1897, my first exciting day in the Klondike gold fields!

In spellbound, open-eyed amazement, I looked at the miles and miles of rich diggings as Patton and I walked along passing the mines. It seemed there was gold, gold everywhere! It glistened in gravel dumps, in sluice boxes, in rockers and in deep, open shafts. It spun around mixed with black sand in battered old test pans, as grizzled, seasoned miners, or eager young ones climbed out of their gopher-like holes to take a quick look at the "pay dirt" to see how much the gold was running to the pan.

Fifty cents to the pan was disappointing. A dollar to the pay was still something to grumble about! Whereas, they told us, up on the Eldorado, not far away, some of the miners were getting from $100 to $200 to the single pan!

Patton and I had stayed at # 7 Below, on Bonanza, where we had caught a few hours' sleep at Euly Gaisford's claim, and were now headed toward the Grand Forks, the confluence of the Bonanza and Eldorado. Although my injured foot and ankle bothered me greatly, still I was able to hobble along, aided by an improvised crutch. I was determined to continue on up to Berry's fabulous # 4 Eldorado claim with Patton.

At times we paused to talk to rich mine owners who almost lovingly watched the wealth literally pour from the earth and accumulate. In many cabins, we caught glimpses of gold standing around in rusty tomato cans, in oil cans and in bottles placed on rough shelves in open view of strangers as casually as though the metal stuff were to be stirred hastily into some kind of magic sourdough batter!

All along the valley, millions in gold were being torn from the frozen earth and there were yet untold millions to be brought to the light of day. Number 6 Below, on the Bonanza, seemed to be the banner claim, with the very rich "pay" running from rim to rim, about 300 feet across the valley . . . and 20 feet deep!

Heading up the Bonanza, Patton and I passed the big Discovery claims # 1, # 2 and # 2* at the entrance to Little Skookum Gulch (owned by George Carmack, Tagish Charlie and Skookum Jim). Just a short distance beyond these claims we reached the Forks, the momentous place where the fabulous Eldorado poured into the Bonanza River. On the left side of the Bonanza, against the hills,

*# 1, Discovery; # 2, Below Discovery; # 2, Above Discovery.

stood a roadhouse and several log cabins. Looking across the Forks to the Eldorado side, there were a few cabins also against the hills. This area of ground, known as the Grand Forks, was a rather wide space of gravelly ground of about five acres, triangular shaped, on the floor of the valley where the high hills opened up three ways. Here we could look up the Bonanza, up the Eldorado, and back down the Bonanza for a short distance. And yes, at a certain spot to the right, one could look up another opening in the hills into Big Skookum Gulch.

"Ed, you are now standing on the richest and most extensive gold-mining district in the world!" said Patton. "These claims you see from here are making mining history. But the ones up the Eldorado are the most amazing of all! They are the envy of the whole country!"

Then Patton began pointing out the different Eldorado claims as we started slowly up the Eldorado Trail. He told me the first mine belonged to a Mr. Whipple; the second and third belonged to Frank Phiscator, Cobbs and Clemens; the fourth one, of course, belonged to the Berry brothers; of the fifth claim, Frank Kellar was the lucky owner; the sixth belonged, half interest, to Antone Standard and Clarence Berry; and the seventh one was owned by Louis Empkins.

"Yes, Louis Empkins has a marvelous claim, too!" said Patton. "This spring, with the help of only one man, he took out thirty-five thousand dollars in a single month!"

(It is interesting to note that, in the following spring in 1898, Louis Empkins took out over $300,000 and then he seemed to lose the "pay streak." Later, he sold to Billy Chappel, who in turn sold to the Chittick brothers who spent a small fortune searching for the "pay streak." The Chittick brothers were the first to introduce the hydraulic system of mining in the Klondike. However, they, too, finally gave up the claim, as they never located that illusive "pay streak"!)

"Ed, I don't suppose you've ever heard of Emil Gay and George Lamarre," continued Patton. "No? Well, no one else had either—that is, not until recently, since the gold has been literally pouring into their laps! They're the lucky owners of claim number thirteen! Ed, their claim is simply amazing and proves that the hoodoo of number thirteen is all bunk! Both fellows were poor when they staked that claim. A lot of the first miners had passed it by. Why, Emil Gay could now buy a whole business block in San Francisco, and George Lamarre one equally as good in Montreal. Just think, before coming to the Klondike, Emil Gay sold waffles on the streets of San Francisco to make a living!"

"Great Scott! What a lucky break for them!" I exclaimed. "I'd be satisfied if I could get just enough gold in the Klondike to buy a little home for my wife and son and have enough to start a small business in Tacoma!"

"I think I would too, Ed," said Patton. "But it's a funny thing about gold. When a fellow starts getting it, he wants more and more and is never satisfied!"

"Guess you're right," I agreed. "It's just human nature! But, Patton, can we see from here the famous number sixteen, Lippy's Eldorado claim I've heard so much about?" I asked straining my eyes, looking longingly up the river of gold.

"No, Ed, you'll have to walk up to see that one," answered Patton. "It's a world beater—a marvelous claim! And they are getting five thousand dollars to the box length, just like Berry's enormously rich number four. But not only does Thomas Lippy own number sixteen mine, he also owns very rich ground on the Bonanza, which makes him a millionaire several times over! Perhaps you've heard he went out with Clarence Berry on the *Excelsior* to San Francisco this spring. Why, that boat was loaded to the guards with Klondike Kings and their gold! It was a real treasure ship! And Thomas Lippy owned a big share of it. They say he plans to return in the spring of ninety-eight, and plans to build a big scow at one of the lakes and load it with food and supplies and shoot Miles Canyon and White Horse Rapids!"

"If he tries that, he's a mighty brave man!" I said. "We had a terrifying experience just bringing our twenty-foot boat through the Canyon and White Horse, and I don't think I'd like to do it again!"

(But little did I dream at that time that I would be going through Miles Canyon and White Horse again in '98, and would witness the wrecking of Lippy's immense, ill-fated scow!)*

"Patton, tell me," I said, changing the subject abruptly, "who would you say is the richest of all of these hundreds of wealthy mine owners represented in this valley?"

"Ah . . . Alexander McDonald, of course! He is the acknowledged Klondike King . . . the King of the North!" exclaimed Patton in eloquent, almost reverent awe. "Besides owning the fabulous number thirty, it's reported he holds large shares in many of the other Eldorado claims, beginning with number nineteen, and even extending up as far as number forty-six. He bought these upper claims and is sure they will yield vast riches too, even though many think they may be blanks. Ed, from the very beginning, he's been lucky! His first claim was Eldorado number twenty-seven which he bought for only four hundred dollars back in the fall of ninety-six. It took nearly all the money he had. With the gold from that claim, he began buying other claims on the various creeks. Of course, at that time a lot of these mines were not known to be rich and he got them dirt cheap . . . some for as little as one hundred dollars apiece! Just think of that!

"Not only does he own dozens of claims," continued Patton, "but he is buying up whole blocks of real estate in Dawson and plans to build business houses and a hotel. Yes, he's a big man, all right . . . with luck that has been simply phenomenal . . . and a bank account that is staggering! It seems he can't lose, and is putting all of his bets on Dawson and the Klondike gold fields! And to think that he came in here from Forty Mile less than a year ago, a poor miner from Juneau . . . originally, from the silver mines of Colorado. Yes, his luck has been amazing this past year. It seems everything he touches turns to gold . . . just like King Midas of the legends of old! No, McDonald will never never have to worry about money for the rest of his life. Pretty nice, eh?"

(But little did the people of the Klondike dream that in a few years after the turn of the century the great wheel of

---

* Lippy died in San Francisco, a poor man. His friends had to bury him.

fortune would spin again, only this time in reverse, turning up all black, losing numbers for some of the Klondike's richest men; and that Alexander McDonald would suffer great reverses, while Dawson and the whole world would look on in startled amazement, seeing the great Klondike King's enormous fortune topple and fall, then vanish completely away, leaving only a legend of his glittering Empire of Gold!)

("His deeds were good," they tell you in Dawson today. "He was the big-hearted Scotchman who never let a friend down and gave fifty thousand dollars in gold dust to build the first real hospital in Dawson.")

"Hello . . . hello, Ed and Patton," called many cheery voices as we turned off the Eldorado trail at # 4, Berry brothers' claim. Walking in among the miners, sluice boxes and dumps, Patton and I saw quite a number of the Tacoma boys there, as ex-councilman Coates of Tacoma had a "lay," being the Berry brothers' uncle. Naturally, this fact had attracted many of the other fellows who hoped in some way to get in on this fabulous claim. We talked awhile with the men, then continued making the rounds of the claim, as I was all eyes and eager to see everything.

"Why, Ed Lung, it's you!" called a friendly, familiar voice, and to my surprise, out rushed the Nelson brothers from a tent partly concealed behind a huge dump of gravel. Naturally, there was a grand commotion and a jolly exchange of salutations and news. I learned they had been on the Berry claim several days. We asked many questions back and forth.

Where was the plucky Ryan crowd? What had become of the Wisconsin party, the Swedes, the Canadians, Kellys and Hydes? And had anyone seen Nash and his party in their fast sailing boat?

"The Ryans are safe in Dawson," one of the Nelsons assured me. "Got there just the other day and are buying a lot and they've put up a tent already. It seems they had a tough time at Windy Arm, and a helluvuh trip down the Yukon in their leaky boat! As for the Swedes, there is rumor of a bunch of them down on middle Bonanza, but there are lots of Swedes in this country! Not sure they're the ones. And as for the Canadians, well . . . the woods are full of them. After all, this is Canadian territory! No one has seen Nash and his party, but he could be most any place!"

The Nelson brothers missed seeing Stacey at my side. They also inquired about Jourgensen and Crawford.

"Well, fellows," I told them, "Stacey is recovering from a temporary illness in Dawson. As for Jourgensen and Crawford, I don't know where they are. I'm afraid they rushed off with only a few provisions up the Bonanza, possibly heading toward King Dome and Dominion Creek, but no one seems to really know. Naturally, I'm anxious about them. They're fine fellows! Hope they strike it rich!"

"Now, ain't that just the trouble with these new Cheechakos!" exclaimed an old miner piping in, leaning on his shovel and spitting a big wad of chewing tobacco over a sluice box. "Some of these new fellows come up here, take a quick look at the Bonanza and Eldorado, see it all staked, then rush off pell-mell into that big country beyond, where there is more square miles than there is square meals! First thing you know, they git lost 'cause there ain't many trails over there! And I want to tell you fellows right here and now, there is big b'ars over there, the big grizzly kind! And there's the big brown kind, too, that can rip the belly right out of a fellow, or bite his head clean off! 'Course, there's gold over there all right, but those big b'ars can be mighty mean about it!"

"Well, say . . ." called a miner who had been listening from a distance. "You forgot to mention that we have bears down here, too! How about the bear who chased a fellow out of his cabin the other day and another fellow out of his tent! And how about the Frenchman who had a whole ham stolen just yesterday!"

"Yeah, but them warn't big brown b'ars or grizzlies! Just the common kind," replied the first miner in disgust. "Them fellows was just chicken for runnin'!"

"Ed, you're limping," observed one of the Nelsons, abruptly changing the subject as I hobbled over and sat down on an empty sluice box.

"Yes," I said, "I very clumsily tripped over a rock coming along the ridge trail with Patton last night, and darned if I didn't sprain my ankle, or strain the ligament badly, and bruise my foot! I suppose it will give me trouble for a few days."

"Tough luck!" sympathized one of the Nelsons. "But if it's a sprain, it'll take more than a few days. Ed, you should really keep off that foot!"

"That is going to be pretty hard to do," I said.

That evening we sat around a large bonfire smoking our pipes, talking and occasionally singing. It was good to be with these jolly fellows from Tacoma, the group of old sourdoughs and the Nelson brothers. The real purpose of the fire was to thaw the muck to start a new shaft to bedrock. It was apparent the miners made it a social occasion while accomplishing work which had to be done. We sat around in a semicircle enjoying the heat of the fire, for even on summer nights toward the end of July there creeps into the northern air a strong hint of frost.

"Just think," said one of the Cheechakos, "of all the gold in this valley! Where do you suppose it all originally came from? I mean, of course, in the very beginning, before the glaciers and rivers began pushing it around?"

"Don't you know?" laughed an old-timer playfully. "It dropped from the moon, of course!"

"Of course not!" chimed in another old-timer. "Haven't you heard? It dropped from the tail of Halley's Comet and rained gold over the North!"

"You're both wrong, fellows!" said another old sourdough with a knowing grin. It dropped from the 'Lode Star,' some call it the North Star."

"Yes," said the old-timer, "and they say the North Star points to the mysterious magnetic pole. And who knows what is buried there?"

"Look!" he said, pointing dramatically to the North Star, which showed faintly in the pale summer night. "Just draw an imaginary line from the North Star straight down to earth, and there, you will probably find the Mother Lode of all this gold!"

During the long, eloquent silence which followed, each man, with head tilted back, was secretly drawing his own imaginary line. . . . And mine seemed to touch the region around King Dome, the hub of the Klondike!

The fire was kept burning bright and hot, and it was evident that the dirt was thawing, for the earth around the fire began to grow soft and mushy, and now and then a miner would drive his pick into the earth to test it.

"Look out, fellow!" cautioned someone. "You might be hitting one of those big nuggets like they're pulling out of number thirty-six Eldorado, up there on Knutson's! That last one, I'll swear, weighed at least thirty-four ounces! If I'm right, it's worth about six hundred dollars!"

"Just think of it!" I said suddenly. "According to the gold they are getting to the box length on this claim, we're sitting over a fabulous treasure right here!" Then I leaned back and chanted, making up the words as I went along . . .

> "Where, oh, where could a fellow like me
> Stake a claim that is rich and free?
> Where, oh, where could one inch be?
> Oh, fabulous treasure, please come to me!"

"A fabulous treasure!" chuckled one of the old sourdoughs. "Well, Ed, how about a nice little claim right here on the Eldorado?"

"On the Eldorado! What wouldn't I give for some rich pay dirt here. But don't tantalize me, fellow, I'll bet there isn't one inch unstaked for a Cheechako like me!"

"No, I guess not," laughed the old miner. "I think Three Inch Jim is the last one who succeeded in prying a few inches loose!"

"Do you mean he prayed?"

"No, I mean he pried—p-r-i-e-d!" laughed the miner.

"Now who is Three Inch Jim?" I asked, my curiosity mounting. "And what's the big joke?"

"Well," said the old sourdough, knocking the ashes from his pipe, "Jim White is a fellow just like hundreds of others who arrived too late to get a good claim, but he wasn't one to be thwarted, so he began snooping and prying around the claims. It was very apparent he had his eyes on number thirty-six and number thirty-seven. He kept measuring the ground, telling the owners their boundaries were very much out of kilter. He boasted that he had great pull in Ottawa and could have the mine boundaries adjusted to their satisfaction if they would let him have a 'fraction.' Otherwise, he told them, they might wake up and find themselves minus a great part of their claims. At last, the threats of Jim became unbearable. The mine owners sent for William Ogilvie, the government surveyor, to come up and settle the dispute."

"How did it turn out?" I asked.

"Well," drawled the miner, obviously enjoying his story, "Ogilvie sure kept that vulture waiting! He took his time surveying . . . and even the owners were getting pretty uneasy. Ogilvie went down in the hollow and set a stake. Then he rested awhile before measuring up the valley toward number thirty-six and number thirty-seven until it seemed his audience would go mad with suspense. By this time quite a crowd had gathered! Well, to make a long story short, Ogilvie finally reached the boundary lines. There he measured the ground slowly and carefully, and deliberately sat down on a rock to rest again before writing something on a stake. Then he drove the stake slowly into the ground. Jim White rushed in the for kill . . . for it is the Canadian law that a man not having a staked claim on a desired creek, may grab a 'fraction' if one actually shows up in the surveying. And guess what it said on that stake?" asked the miner, pausing and looking at me with a twinkle in his eyes.

"What?" I asked curiously.

"Three Inches . . . Jim White! And 'Three Inch Jim' they've called him ever since!"

"But how can a fellow prospect three inches?" someone asked with a roar of laughter.

"You may be sure those mine owners would never let him try it!" someone else said.

Unusual and wild speculations flew thick and fast around the campfire as to how only three inches of rich pay dirt could be prospected.

"A fellow could hang from a balloon and use a long trowel!" was one of the wildest of observations.

"Well, I guess that settles it!" I said when the hilarity had quieted down. "There's nothing left in this valley!

"No, Cheechako, there ain't," replied another old sourdough, grabbing the conversation. "There ain't even one inch left in these valleys now, unless, of course, you go up there on top of them hills. But everyone knows there ain't gold up there!"

Exciting talk of gold continued far into the night, occasionally interrupted by outbursts of lively songs, such as: "There'll Be a Hot Time in the Old Town Tonight!" and "The Pirates' Chorus," "Matrimonial Sweets" and "Nothing Else to Do!" The evening ended by singing, nostalgically, "Tender and True" and "Home Sweet Home," I, carrying a strong part of the tenor.

During the several days I spent up on the Eldorado, I hobbled in among the sluice boxes, visiting with the men, watching and learning the fascinating process and art of gold mining . . . and grew tense with excitement when yellow nuggets showed up in the riffles of the sluice boxes after the water had washed the gravel away. And in the evenings, in the cabins, I watched with keen interest, the delicate process of separating the coarse and fine gold from the black sand which had been scraped from the riffles of the sluice boxes with a large wooden paddle. This entire process was called the "clean-up." It was interesting to see the little piles of black sand, after they had been thoroughly dried on the Klondike stove in pans, and after the sand had been drawn off with a magnet and the remaining fine, black dust blown carefully away. Then, behold! there was new gold gleaming in the bottom of the pan!

Naturally, the longing for gold of my own was mounting in me, and the knowledge that I was too late to own even a tiny strip of this fabulous pay dirt was a great and bitter disappointment! Everyone advised me, as they did all of the new Cheechakos, to go over into the outlying creeks to seek fortune. But that would mean a trip of a hundred to a hundred and fifty miles (round trip) over rough, mountainous country and into an almost unexplored wilderness! How could I possibly walk that far with an injured foot, build a cabin and prepare for the winter?

While I was with the men on the Eldorado, I tried to make myself useful, helping to keep their shaft fires burning and also helping with their tedious cooking, even baking a batch of sourdough bread. On the third day, I packed up my belongings and told the fellows goodbye, including Patton. Said I was going back to Dawson . . . would see them all later.

I headed down the trail past the Grand Forks to # 7 Below, on Bonanza, where I had stayed the first night. An acquaintance of mine from Tacoma, Captain Breeze, held a "lay" on Euly Gaisford's rich claim. Breeze was a fine fellow, a tall giant of a man, fair complexioned and with light, wavy hair—looked like a Viking! They said he had been captain on one of the Puget Sound boats before the gold rush. He was perhaps ten years my senior.

"Ed, let me give you a little tip," said Breeze after I had told him that I was quite discouraged at the prospects for myself. "Look up there about two hundred feet just above us on that hill. There you'll see some free ground. Ed, why don't you climb up there and sink a hole, and if it proves to be anything, stake it. It's certainly worth a try!"

I looked up at the rocky hillside above us, then back into Breeze's eyes. Surely, he was joking! But no . . . he was really serious. Suddenly, I could see myself with Cotswell back on the hill facing Dawson digging a grave. Again, I could hear the horselaughs and jeers of the miners, "Cheechakos digging for gold on a hill! Ha! Ha! Ha!"

I found myself answering, "No, Breeze, if I should stake up there on the hill, my chances would be ruined for staking any other claim if a really good opportunity should ever present itself in this section."

"But, Ed, there's nothing left in these valleys, I tell you. What could you possibly lose by staking that ground?"

"No, I've decided to return to Dawson and get Stacey. If he's well enough, we'll try to go over beyond the Domes, possibly to Dominion or Sulphur Creek. Surely there's free ground over there!"

Breeze looked at me in alarm. But, Ed, you've got a bad leg and Stacey has been sick. How'll you two ever make it? Why, you'll have trouble even getting back to Dawson as it is! Fifteen miles is a long way to walk with a leg like yours!"

The next morning, against Breeze's friendly advice, I started hobbling down the Bonanza Valley Trail, a different route from the one on which I had come over from Dawson.

All of the way down the Bonanza, I followed the seemingly never ending trail of gold, but to me it became a trail of torture. It had rained a little in the night, making the walking doubly hard. The ground in places was boggy and there were many of those slippery niggerheads to hurdle over, as along the Klondike River.

"You sure look played out!" said a miner sitting in the doorway of his cabin sorting over big, yellow nuggets. "Come on in, stranger, and put your leg up on a chair and rest awhile."

"Yep," said the miner showing me his gold proudly while I rested, "this is number seventeen Lower Bonanza, and one of the last claims where you'll see nuggets as big as these! On down the creek, they come much smaller. And below number twenty-nine, there's mostly gold dust."

After leaving # 17 and seeing all those big nuggets, I felt more discouraged than ever and my leg began raising particular H——! Finally, reaching the lower end of Bonanza, I felt I couldn't go farther when a friendly miner invited me to stop and have hot coffee and sourdough pancakes with him.

As we ate, he talked. "Yes, sir! I've been up here almost a year now and haven't struck a goldarned thing! Look at those damned empty holes, and hardly a color shows up! And right next to me up the creek, those fellows are hitting it rich! Getting gold galore! Looks like my claim is just a blank! Sure makes a fellow sick! And down the creek they're getting plenty of gold, too. Seems the pay streak swings along in this part of the valley like a damned wiggly snake! And up above me about a quarter of a mile, there's another blank claim . . . owned by two fellows who've worked like slaves!

"Yes," continued the miner, looking dolefully at his hardened, callused hands, "and this creek, they boast, is the great and famous Bonanza, supposed to make its owners independent for the rest of their lives!"

As I was leaving, I thanked the miner for his kindness and told him about the two miners I had heard of up near # 46 Eldorado, who were just about ready to give up after sinking three holes. However, on the fourth one, they really struck it rich! I wished him better luck next time and hobbled on my way. The rest had refreshed me and, I hoped, given my host a new interest in his mine.

At last, I reached the mouth of the Bonanza. Not caring to tackle the niggerhead trail along the shore of the Klondike to Dawson, which would have been a shorter route, I chose the trail leading to Dawson across the hills. I found the raft Patton had told me about and got across the Klondike River without any trouble, pulling myself by cable, hand over hand, until I reached the opposite shore. I knew I had to go about two and a half miles yet to reach Dawson. Before starting over the hill, I took off my boot and examined my foot carefully. It was badly swollen, but I forced the boot back on. That foot just had to carry me to Dawson . . . no matter what!

A well-defined trail led up the hill. At last, I gained the top and threw myself down to rest. Several miners came along and stopped. I asked them many questions. Most of all, I wanted to know if any steamers had come in with food and supplies.

"No," said one of the miners, "no steamers yet! And it's beginning to look mighty serious with those damned stampeders coming in by the hundreds expecting to buy food and other supplies in Dawson!"

"We just can't understand what's holding the boats up," said his companion in disgust. "Why, we even had difficulty buying a quarter of a sack of flour today."

"But seems like there's plenty of whisky in Dawson though, at forty dollars and fifty dollars a quart!" said the first miner sarcastically. "But you can't live on whisky, no matter how much some fellows try! In this country, it's lots of food a fellow needs to keep alive and working during the cold winter months. I want to tell you, last winter on Glacier Creek it wasn't funny watching the bacon grease sizzle away in the pan and staring at the bottom of the flour sack. That was the month we were caught in an early freeze and snowed in with the wind and wolves howling outside our cabin door!"

In a few minutes the miners had disappeared over the hill toward the gold fields, leaving me to ponder the situation. Slowly, I picked my way down the steep trail, thinking the matter over seriously. What were the prospects for me for the coming winter? I was certain that I would need, before many days, flour, bacon and canned milk. And I certainly needed dried fruits, especially dried prunes, at least five pounds. I felt in my pocket for the tiny poke of gold dust, my pay for digging the grave. The gold felt cold, crunchy and hard . . . two ounces of it! Why keep the stuff any longer? I needed food and had better buy it now, as soon as I would reach Dawson. But with prices so exorbitant, it would probably take all the gold dust I had to get just small quantities of provisions. Then my poke would be empty! But who cared? It might even bring me luck!

What was all of this alarming talk about the boats? Why, there were at least four weeks left before the Yukon would begin to freeze over. Surely, by tomorrow, or the next day, a boat would come in. Then, when good old Stacey was well, and my foot was well enough, too, we would start out for that beckoning country around the Domes to seek our fortune. Might even find that exciting, illusive Mother Lode! Stacey and I would hunt for it until we were blue in the face! You bet we would!

The trail leading down the hill toward Dawson was still a little damp and slippery from the night before, and I had to pick my way along carefully, leaning on my walking stick. Coming to the more gradual slope lower down, suddenly I reached the spot where a fresh grave showed plainly just a short distance from the trail. Yes, it was the one Cotswell and I had dug over a week ago. I took a few steps off the trail and stood looking down at the freshly mounded earth. Already, a thin veil of green was showing on the grave. In just a few weeks there would be a thick, velvety covering of green moss. Poor fellow!

I found myself sitting on a rock near by. How peaceful it was up here—no rush, no worry, no scramble for gold! I looked down over the hectic town of Dawson. How rapidly it was changing! Certainly, it appeared much bigger now than when I had seen it only a few days before. I shaded my eyes, looking up the Yukon. At least a dozen stampede boats were coming down the river towards Dawson. Then my eyes followed the wide ribbon of river to the north just beyond Dawson, where the current seemed to slacken and flow more lazily toward the horizon of dark-blue mountains. I strained my eyes in that direction, too, but there were no river boats coming from the north.

Arriving in Dawson about an hour later, I stopped at the Alaska Commercial Company. After much persuasion, I was able to buy the supplies I had set my heart on, even getting the five pounds of dried prunes. As I hunted through the store, I couldn't help but notice that the shelves were showing glaring bare spots.

"Please keep this box of supplies for me," I requested the clerk, who was an acquaintance of mine, as he completely emptied my sack of gold dust on the scales for payment. "I'll call for it tomorrow."

"Sure will, Ed, I'll try to keep an eye on the box for you, but don't leave it here long. Someone might just grab it and make off. As you can see, Ed," he said, lowering his voice, "food is getting awfully scarce, and there isn't much to replace it in the warehouse! We're puzzled to know why the boats haven't come in yet. If they don't arrive before the ice closes in, it'll be a tragic situation for Dawson this winter!"

Then he added, "But perhaps we are a little too apprehensive. The picture could change overnight."

As I trudged along the riverfront, hurrying as fast as I could toward our boat (which was anchored in front of the Mounted Police barracks a good ten minutes' walk from the A.C.C. Company), I watched new stampeders landing along the shore and was forcibly struck by the small amounts of supplies they were bringing in. It was evident they expected to buy the bulk of their winter supplies in Dawson!

When I finally reached our boat, I found to my surprise it was empty and Stacey was gone. Then I noticed my tent pitched on the bank near by and found Stacey resting comfortably inside. He still looked pale, but said he guessed he was over the worst of his disgusting illness. He truly seemed glad to see me. Said some of the fellows had helped move our supplies out of the boat and set up camp.

While I soaked my neglected aching foot and ankle in hot water, Stacey got up and tried to fix a little supper. While he struggled with the food, we had a hurried visit and I told him of my eventful trip to the Bonanza and Eldorado.

Then Stacey announced jubilantly, before I could tell him my wonderful plans for the two of us, that Captain Ellis had been there and stayed while I was away. Stacey had accepted partnership with Captain Ellis on a "lay" near # 4, Berry's Eldorado claim.

"It should be a very rich one, too, Ed, and I know I'm lucky!" added Stacey with high color mounting in his pale cheeks. "And just as soon as I'm able, we'll set out for the Eldorado to work it. Yes, we've decided, the captain and I, to pool our resources. It seems he's out of certain supplies which I have. And Ed, isn't it funny," laughed Stacey, "the captain has discovered we both wear the same size shoes. We never noticed it before when he was chief of police and I was on the force in Tacoma. Why, he's borrowed my best boots and is wearing them right now and is probably walking all over Dawson!"

I laughed with Stacey, but my mirth was a little forced. I had to confess to myself that I was disappointed. Secretly, I guess, these last few days, I had hoped the deal between Stacey and Captain Ellis would fall through. Now, it seemed, I was without a partner. I was fond of Stacey. He had saved my life on Chilkoot and we had faced a thousand dangers together while coming down the Yukon.

During the few days which followed in Dawson, new and pressing events crowded each moment. First of all, I went after my small box of food at the trading company. Stacey happened to be out at the time when I arrived back in camp and didn't see me cache it away in my corner of the tent. Little did I dream then, that the five pounds of prunes in that box would almost cost me a valued friendship!

"Ed, how about giving us a few days' work?" asked Jack Currie, foreman of the A.C.C. Company, when I met him while there picking up my supplies. "Ben Everett and Charlie Debney have recommended you as an accountant; however, that job isn't open right now. This one will be hard work, but we'll pay you ten dollars a day in Canadian money."

"I'll take the job," I answered. "What is it?"

"Carrying logs for the extension of our building," was the reply.

Carrying and lifting heavy logs, even with the help of several husky fellows, is a muscle-tearing, backbreaking job, especially to one who is of slender build and unaccustomed to such grueling work. My injured foot was still giving me lots of trouble. But the $10 a day looked too good to resist.

In the meantime, Stacey was rapidly recovering and Captain Ellis was a steady visitor, seeming to greatly appreciate the "slumgullion" meals I threw together. The main topic seemed to always center around their plans for working their "lay" on the Eldorado. They usually ended up by asking me to go up there with them when they made the trip. Then Captain Breeze tried to persuade me further when he came to camp and stayed a day with us. But I wouldn't commit myself. Somehow, I couldn't get the idea of that beckoning country around the King and Queen Domes out of my thoughts. I was determined to go there and hunt for gold, even if I had to go alone. And there was no one among the Cheechakos I had met who appealed to me as a partner.

On one of the few days I was working for the A.C.C. Company, I heard someone calling, "Ed, is it you?" Turning around, I was very pleased to see the Lake Linderman group of Canadians, en masse, smiling at me. Naturally, as before with the Nelson brothers, I reminisced with this group about our thrilling race down the Yukon and ended up asking about each stampede group and their whereabouts.

"Don't tell me, Ed," finally exclaimed one of the Canadians, "that you're going to keep on with this heavy work!"

"Great Scott, no!" I replied. "But I can certainly use the ten dollars a day! You'll discover, fellows, that money goes pretty fast up here!"

"Money sure does!" agreed one of the Canadians. "We've only been here two days and they tell us flour has gone up to fifty dollars a sack! And they tell us it might even go higher if the boats don't come in. Surely wish we'd had the foresight to've brought more flour!"

"Guess we'd all better tighten our belts until we know

just how we're coming out on this food situation!" I advised.

"I've been as hungry as a bear since I landed here!" said one of the Canadians, "and I don't like wrinkles in my stomach, but I guess it's good advice, Ed!"

"Yeah," said one of his companions, "we'll have to begin by cutting down on the size of those sourdough pancakes! And we'll tell all the other fellows to do the same!"

The Alaska Commercial Company, where I was working, was on Front Street about a half mile from the confluence of the Klondike and Yukon rivers. It was housed in an oblong-shaped log structure. We were adding about a 50-foot extension on one end of the building. It was evident that the A.C.C. Company was preparing for further growth by enlarging their building.

One day during the latter part of July while I was at work lifting logs, a wild cry went up along the river. We fellows who were working on the store listened, then dropped our logs and rushed to the river front.

"A boat's coming!" the cry went up. "A boat's coming up the river . . . from St. Michael!"

In a few minutes, it seemed that all Dawson was at the waterfront excitedly watching the puffs of smoke showing above the hills along the horizon. Then the boat rounded the bend. It was a stern-wheel river boat.

"Listen to it puff!" shouted someone in the crowd. "Just listen to it puff! It's like music to our ears!"

As the boat drew closer, someone else shouted, "It's the *Weaver!* And look at the crowd she's bringing!"

Eagerly, we all watched as the whistle blew in shrill salute to Dawson. The stern-wheeler's paddles whirled frantically against the stiff current as the boat plowed upstream to a point a little above Dawson. Then, turning, she pointed her prow rapidly towards shore, the current carrying her swiftly to a landing right in front of the A.C.C. Company!

Her decks were crowded with men, all straining to see Dawson and waving to us fellows on shore. The gangplank was pushed to the bank and the passengers, with grips and bundles in hand, hurriedly came ashore.

After the first hilarious greetings, the crowd grew silent, tensely watching and waiting while the freight was being unloaded. Then, suddenly, a miner in the crowd shouted. "Where's the food? Where's the food?"

"This ain't food!" sang out a deck hand as he rolled a barrel ashore. "Just nails! No food in this cargo! Just hardware stuff! And we've got a lot of crates of glass and window casings in the hold. Dawson sure must be booming!"

"Oh, yeah," added the deck hand, his face lighting up, "I did see a big box down there in the hold marked . . . 'Spices'!"

Two days later when the *Weaver* pulled out, she was loaded to the guards with the lucky fellows heading home by way of St. Michael, their pokes bulging with Klondike gold! But, on shore, there were hundreds of fellows like me with empty pokes and tightened belts who stood wistfully watching as the *Weaver* disappeared around the bend down the Yukon!

Chapter IX

Uncertain Destiny

Disconcerting, foreboding, frenzied rumors ran through Dawson like wildfire after the *Weaver* pulled out! "The Yukon is lowest in history!" . . . "Probably no more river boats can reach Dawson this summer!" . . . "Already several stern-wheelers disabled, stuck on sand bars, hundreds of miles down river!" . . . "Hordes of stampeders streaming over newly opened White Pass, heading north to Dawson, traveling light!" . . . "Trading companies very low on supplies!" . . . "If no relief, food may soon have to be confiscated and redistributed!" . . . "Thousands may be forced to leave the Klondike to escape starvation!"

Time was certainly running short for us stampeders. The high hills along the Yukon and around Dawson seemed to lean back on their rocky heels and laugh mockingly at us. Wherever we dipped our pans, there was usually the tiny glint of gold dust in tantalizing, infinitesimal amounts—along the Yukon, in front of Dawson, at the mouth of the Klondike River, and even in the very gravels of the town itself. Illusive, scattered, maddening glimpses, these! Whereas up on the Bonanza and the Eldorado gold stared at us coldly in large, unobtainable quantities from very rich ground which had already been staked months before!

An eclipse of the sun on July 29th of that summer, 1897, had seemed to cast an ominous shadow over the Yukon as the sun dropped slowly down towards the hills to the west and hung low as though suspended, and was almost completely blotted out by the moon. Most everyone, including the dance-hall girls, climbed the hills back of Dawson to get a better view of this remarkable phenomenon. The air was tinged with a faint veil of smoke from distant forest fires, causing the sun to cast a baleful, bloodshot eye on all of us stampeders. And all Dawson shivered while the mournful wails of the malemutes and the distant cries of wolves added to our feeling of utter desolation and forlornness in this far, isolated country!

After the eclipse of the sun, growing tension mounted at the thought of being cut off from civilization. And the old-timers were saying that, in about three weeks, the icy blasts of the North would start whipping down the Yukon, and in no time the river and lakes would begin to freeze over.

Now the streets of Dawson were pack-jammed with miners who had rushed in from the creeks to buy anything in the way of food. Many had come from remote creeks fifty to seventy miles over rugged country. The three trading companies, the A.C., the N.A.C. and another called Healey's, were literally jammed to the doors with excited miners, all arguing and shouting their great need for any food yet available. Long lines of fellows waited their turn to get inside. But before all had a chance at the rationed goods, the doors were suddenly closed. Great consternation swept through the crowds. It is impossible to exaggerate the unspoken fear in each man's eyes as he stared at the heavy, locked doors. Men who had faced a thousand dangers getting into the Klondike, blanched at the thought of empty knapsacks!

With such a large, high-strung crowd milling about

town, naturally many wild sprees followed, taking place in tents, cabins and saloons, for, strangely enough, there was plenty of liquor in Dawson and everyone seemed anxious to forget the situation temporarily.

The Mounted Police were unusually tolerant, only arresting those who were completely out of hand, for their barracks were very small and inadequate to accommodate a horde of wrongdoers. And, besides, it took food to feed prisoners!

Across the Klondike River at Louse Town, it seemed many of the fellows had congregated, perhaps because there was the whole width of the river between themselves and the Mounted Police barracks.

It was now the second of August and, in our tent, Stacey and I anxiously began checking over our rapidly diminishing foodstuff and other supplies.

"By Jiminy! We're wasting valuable time here in Dawson!" Stacey said impatiently. "Just think of all the gold Captain Ellis and I could have been getting up there on that 'lay' of ours. Boat or no boat, we're going to leave here by the fourth of August! I think, with all the food stuffs I have and with what Captain Ellis has already on the Eldorado, I have enough to last me till the middle of winter."

"Well, I'm afraid mine won't last that long," I said uneasily, looking at my smaller portions of bacon, beans, flour and dried fruits in a box on my side of the tent. "I figure I've got just about a two months' supply, and then I'm completely out!"

"Aw, come on, Ed," said Stacey with forced optimism. "It may not be as grim as it all sounds. Mostly, I'm worried about you, Ed. I hate to see you go it alone this winter. I'd feel a lot better if you had some good pay dirt to work somewhere near Captain Ellis and me. Ed, I've been thinking—why don't you grab that Bonanza hillside up there above Euly Gaisford's? It's just possible, old fellow, there might be gold there, like Captain Breeze suggests."

"Stacey," I said, "don't you think it's pure folly spending valuable time hunting for gold on a hill? Think of the tremendous task it would be to sink a shaft on a hillside and the loss of time it would involve. Remember how we've talked to the old-timers and how they have pooh-poohed the idea? Just look up there at the big slide at the north end of Dawson. Remember hearing about that exciting stampede almost the first day we arrived? Well, what did they actually find up there? Someone found a few flecks of gold, but it was rumored it had been planted by a practical joker! But what they actually did find was a white, porous-looking stuff which someone claims is asbestos!"

"Golly, that sure must have been a surprise, finding asbestos," said Stacey; "but, after all, who wants to bother with it? And as for those few flecks of gold, I admit they may have been planted. But, Ed," he persisted, "I still think you should try that Bonanza hillside. If you should make a strike, I'm sure it would be the real thing. I'm sure no one will bother to plant gold on the hills.

"Say, Ed," continued Stacey thoughtfully, "I'm just beginning to wonder a little. . . . Do you suppose there's a chance that those are false rumors about no boats coming and starvation facing us? It could be just to scare us newcomers out of the Klondike."

"But, Stacey," I said, "if these rumors are true, and I believe they are, the very thought of being trapped here in this God-forsaken, frozen wilderness in the dead of winter without adequate food is enough to frighten anyone and make a fellow shiver in his boots! Just think, Stacey, how far we are from home! Is it any wonder we all worry at the prospect of winter? I've heard that already quite a number of fellows have started back to the 'Outside'! I wish I could see into the future . . . there's so much at stake! If these rumors are true, it's a desperate situation for all of us!"

"But, Ed, if they're not true, it's a dirty, scurvy trick to play on us!" said Stacey grimly. "But let's not worry yet!" Then with a sudden flash of lighthearted humor, he added, "Right now, I've got a mighty important job!" He yanked from his corner of the tent a large canvas sack stuffed with grimy clothes and began dragging it to the river's edge about fifteen feet away. "Come to think of it," he laughed again, "those clothes haven't had a wash since I fell into the river a month ago. They could just about walk away by now! And clothes are mighty scarce, and may be even scarcer this winter!"

In a few minutes, Stacey was energetically dunking and splashing his washing up and down in the river in front of our camp, furiously stirring up a muddy lather.

"Hey," said a miner who had sauntered over to our camp, "there isn't much food in Dawson, but they say we fellows needn't freeze to death this winter, if that's any consolation! Know why? Well, the trading companies have overstocked on long red-flannel underwear and woolen socks. And I thought you'd like to know this, too, fellows—they have a big supply of nice, brown derby hats—the kind the gamblers wear when they're skunking us out of our gold! And I'll tell you another one, fellows—this is good—they have dozens of nice, thick whiskbrooms. Yep, just think of it, we're going to be mighty ritzy this winter!"

"Yeah," exclaimed another stampeder in disgust, "can't you just picture us hungry fellows this winter sporting sassy brown derby hats, all dressed up in pretty red-flannel underwear and brushing the mud off our socks with nice, expensive whiskbrooms?"

"Yep, and maybe eatin' nothin' much else but sugar and spices all winter," said the first miner sarcastically. "Yep, that's about all I saw down there at the trading companies today."

"But the trading companies should have foreseen this crisis!" broke in another fellow angrily. "Haven't they been in the Yukon for years? Haven't they been supplying the Indians and miners?"

"Yeah, but Dawson is a very new town, grown by leaps and bounds . . . started less than a year ago!" spoke up one of the old-timers, partly in defense of the trading companies. "Why, the town is so new, do you know we don't even have a mayor or city council? Who was there here who could foresee the enormous growth of Dawson and the Klondike gold fields? I ask you."

But no one had an answer to that one.

"Well, I guess about all we can do is to hope for the best," said another fellow grimly, "but I'll tell you one thing, I'm not going too far from Dawson, not on any far, wild-goose stampede. If a boat comes in, believe me, I want to be here Johnny-on-the-spot!"

A little later, the crowd of stampeders had dispersed

from our camp and Stacey's muddy-looking laundry flapped in the breezes, strung out haphazardly on an improvised line. The Yukon looked a lot muddier too, as several of us fellows, including Stacey, had taken a quick plunge in the river, cooling off our irate spirits and having much needed baths!

About an hour later, rain unexpectedly swept down the Yukon. Stacey was delighted with the help Nature was giving him in the way of an extra rinse job! Happily, he saluted the storm and left his muddy-looking laundry slapping crazily in the rain while we both ran to shelter in one of the near-by log houses, where it said over the door in big letters: "THE GAME NEVER ENDS HERE!"

The place was packed with gamblers and fellows who just wanted to get in out of the rain. Several poker games were in progress and, of course, there was more than the usual drinking. At one table there were five fellows with sheets of notepaper spread out before them on which they placed their bets in little mounds of gold dust. There were no chips—just pure gold in evidence, which made the game doubly exciting!

The play was on! At the beginning of the game, it was first agreed that ten ounces would be the limit; but it seemed none of the fellows were satisfied, so they raised it to fifteen ounces. They were loaded with gold! The game was opened and the fellows called for cards from the dealer. The fellow they called "Sandy" McLeod, the ex-mounted policeman, reached down under the table and drew out a good-sized handful of nuggets from his sack, adding it to his pile of gold dust. He had a pleased look on his face as he placed his bet of nuggets in the center pile, then ran through his cards and said jubilantly, "I raise you a handful!" The other four fellows immediately followed suit in turn with their handfuls of gold. This raising continued for several rounds while the players kept tense faces, their eyes never leaving the game, following the lead of Sandy, matching him equally and raising his bets each time in nuggets and gold dust. At last, the betting got too much for the Swede and he threw his cards face down and dropped out! The dealer looked long at his hand and at the large piles of gold heaped in the center of the table, then he, too, reluctantly put down his cards. Now there were just three men playing—Sandy, Johnson and Hollingshead. It was the opener's turn, and he raised the bet another handful of gold. Then he sat back and waited. Sandy hesitated a second, then nearly knocked his audience cold when he pulled from his knapsack a two-quart jar of nuggets and said, "I raise you this whole jar!"

Hollingshead smiled smugly with glistening eyes. He also pulled from his knapsack, an oil can full of gold—equally as big! And so did Johnson, the third fellow, do likewise. Then a showdown was demanded! The crucial moment had come! You could have heard a pin drop!

Sandy had three aces, a queen and a jack; Johnson had three queens, a jack and a ten; but Joe Hollingshead had four kings and an ace!

As Joe Hollingshead triumphantly gathered up the quarts of nuggets and gold dust, Sandy said dolefully, "Well, Joe, I'm flat broke! Guess I won't be going 'Outside' this year!"

After the big game, Swiftwater Bill, the notorious gambler, came swaggering into the saloon with a fellow named Pierce. Both men seemed very drunk. There was a pool table at the end of the room and, while a crowd gathered around them, they began playing. The two men at first bet $10 a game; the next game they loudly raised to $50; then upped it to $200 for several games more; and at the end of the afternoon, they raised the final game to $500 while we all pressed closer, watching with interest.

Swiftwater Bill was dressed almost as I had first seen him on the Bonanza trail a week before—in his striped business suit, with pants tucked into muddy boots, loud vest and a brown derby hat perched ludicrously on his head. He puffed incessantly on a long, expensive cigar, blowing thick clouds of smoke over the billiard table into the faces of his eager audience.

He had a bottle of whisky, from which he kept taking nips all afternoon. And he was finally so drunk that he could hardly hold his cue and many of his aims went amiss, the balls shooting off into the crowd. His stickpin, rings and chains of yellow gold nuggets glowed mockingly at us under the artificial light. Obviously, Swiftwater Bill enjoyed flashing his gold and being in the limelight, and

Red-light district or "White Chapel"—"A group of hard workers

The Yukon River steamer *Hannah* belonged to the Alaska Commercial Company

At Bonanza in 1897, Mrs. G. I. Lowe told fortunes to supplement her laundry business. Note the stampeders' tents in the background

The Grand Forks of Bonanza and Eldorado, 1898

played for the benefit of us gaping stampeders. There was no doubt . . . he was a born showman! Swiftwater won the $10 game, but lost all the rest. At the end of the final game, he staggered to the bar and downed several more glasses of liquor, cheering Pierce loudly as the winner, then challenging him to take him on again. But Pierce was wary. It was plain to see he was through for the day. Hadn't he won a small fortune in just one afternoon?

"Aw, that's nothin'! A thousand dollars in one afternoon is nothin' for Swiftwater Bill to lose!" said one of the bystanders. "He'll win it all back and more too, tonight in poker. Just wait and see! Trouble with Swiftwater this afternoon, he didn't have his lady love along! She seemes to bring him luck. Boy, you should see her! She's a dazzler! And you should see the gold he showers her with. Five hundred dollars at a crack! No one knows how many five hundreds she's collected! But, man, oh, man! the miners say it's plenty . . . and they oughta know! Yep, she's a five-hundred-dollar-baby, if you know what I mean!"

"Fellow, be sure to come back tonight to see her and the big game," volunteered another miner. "I hear Swiftwater is gonna play Joe Hollingshead for that two hundred forty thousand dollars he just won this afternoon. I'll wager he'll get a big hunk of it, too! Boy, it'll be a show! When Swiftwater wins, he always treats the crowd. What does he care if it costs three hundred dollars a round? That's just peanuts to him! Yep, fellow, it'll be the show of your life!"

"But doesn't it seem silly, after all," I remarked, "for these fellows to get such foolish pleasure out of gambling and squandering so much gold?"

"Perhaps," replied the miner, "but the main attraction in every gold camp are always gamblin' and wimmin!"

In our tent that evening, on the bank of the Yukon, only a short distance from where the dozens of big gambling games were going on, Stacey and I rolled wearily into our sleeping bags, not caring to take part in any more of the high life of Dawson. Besides, we had seen Swiftwater Bill in action several evenings before at the faro table. He had won a large fortune in gold dust, with his well-known voluptuous $500 baby looking on with calculating approval in all of her brittle, scintillating splendor! Somehow, Stacey and I were extremely low in spirits that night. I was particularly discouraged for the future; and besides, I was running low on everything!

It must have been about midnight when, suddenly, I was awakened by wild, piercing screams which sent icy chills running through my spine. I jumped from my sleeping bag and sprang to the opening of the tent, pulled back the flap and looked anxiously up and down the river. At first, I thought someone must be drowning. (Directions of sounds are hard to trace in Dawson, due to the natural echoes of the place.) But I saw nothing on the river, no boat upturned or body struggling in the current. Stacey, too, had jumped up and stood shivering beside me. Again, those horrible, incoherent, agonized cries pierced the air, bloodcurdling, gruesome . . . sounding almost inhuman and brutish, like a wounded, caged animal at bay!

Then the voice shrieked frantically, "For God's sake, help me! Save me!" Then it lapsed into hysterical sobbing, moaning horribly, finally trailing away in a suppressed, agonized wail.

"Good Lord, Stacey!" I cried, grabbing my clothes and pulling them on hurriedly. "Come on, we've got to find him and help that fellow. He must be in great agony!"

"Ed, I'm sorry, but you can't help that man. Nobody can!" cried Stacey, clutching my arm and holding me back. "I know that voice. Poor devil! He's a dope fiend! Every night, Ed, while you were away on the Eldorado, he cursed like hell and screamed bloody murder for morphine. All Dawson heard him! The fellows have been just pouring him full of whisky trying to keep him quiet, but it's useless! Lord help him now! Guess the effects of even liquor have worn off. None of us will get any sleep tonight."

"There he starts again!" I shuddered. "Poor fellow, he must be suffering the torments of hell! And he's so far from civilization!"

"Well, he'll never, never get 'Outside,' that's sure!" said Stacey, shivering. "Poor devil! He's certainly done for and he's from a good family."

Hourly, Stacey and I watched the swelling numbers of

newly arrived stampeders swarming into Dawson, hard bitten with the gold fever. We could pick them out easily by their gawky stares and excited enthusiasm. How well we knew their every emotion, for hadn't we, too, landed just as they? And hadn't we stared in fascinated wonder at the glittering city of fortune? Of course, they would strike it rich! Weren't their dreams like ours? Wouldn't they return home as rich as Klondike Kings? But—would they?

"Say, fellow," called a newcomer, "where is that fabulous mine we've heard so much about, the one where they say William Ogilvie found five hundred and ninety-five dollars' worth of nuggets in just two shovelfuls of pay dirt! We overheard some men talking on a streetcar in San Francisco. Heard 'em say Ogilvie just poked around in the dirt a little and filled a small bucketful and in just a few minutes he had panned out five hundred and ninety-five dollars' worth of pure gold. Believe me, when I heard that, I packed my things and hustled up here. Why, five hundred and ninety-five dollars is half a year's wages for me! Golly Moses, I want to see that claim! Where is it?"

"Well, fellow," I said, "it's probably # 4, Berry's claim on the Eldorado sixteen miles away. . . . Just take the trail leading over the hill from Dawson, but don't get your hopes up too high. Those valleys of gold are all staked—and I don't mean maybe!"

It was now the third day of August. Stacey kept urging me to go with him and Captain Ellis to their lay on the Eldorado and have another look around. I finally acquiesced. I had one more day to kill in Dawson, so decided I'd make another check on the boats for any news. Also, I decided to try again for the job of working on the logs for the new extension of the A.C. Co., as I could certainly use the ten dollars they paid.

As it turned out, I was too late for the job—several husky fellows were ahead of me. As I stood watching and talking to the men, I could easily spot the heavy logs I had helped to heave into place only a few days previously. These new fellows were working like slaves, too. Soon the roof would be ready to put on.

"The company certainly hasn't much grub to put into the

new annex!" suddenly volunteered a clerk who stopped to watch the progress of the work. "But next year, of course, we'll be ready for a big trade. The officials are predicting a great future for Dawson in ninety-eight, as you can see from their preparations!"

"But what about us this year?" grumbled one of the workers.

"Well, your guess is as good as mine," the clerk answered with a shrug. "No one knows yet what the rest of the season will bring. But my advice to you is make your food last as long as you can. A lot of trouble is that, in past years, freight has been shipped up the Yukon from St. Michael in small, flat-bottomed boats in order to get over the many sand bars and shallow places that usually appear at this time of year. But this particular year, because of the enormous demand due to the gold rush, larger boats of the round-bottom type, with drafts too deep, have been very foolishly put on the Yukon. And, it is true, some of them are stuck on sand bars hundreds of miles down the river. They were headed for St. Michael to pick up cargo from the States. If any boats make it now to Dawson, they will be of the smallest type. This is bad news for Dawson, of course, as we need tons of food!"

In a worried, apprehensive mood, I began walking along the riverfront toward the north end of town where the high hill seemed to rise directly out of the Yukon, forming the big bend of the river. Here, Dawson ended abruptly. I looked longingly up toward the high ridge. From there, I might be able to see a boat if it were coming up the river from St. Michael. I knew that the Indians had once used this high point as a lookout.

Reaching the north end of Dawson on the last slope of the town, I found a small log building which proved to be a little Catholic mission. It seemed to stand apart, aloof from the gambling and many sins of the gold camp. However, I thought it was in a rather precarious spot itself, as it was at the base of part of the big slide. Some thought this peculiar-looking slide resembled a moose hide from a distance, and so it got its name. It could be seen plainly from almost any spot in town, and loomed up tremendously big from the riverfront. However, as I approached it closer, somehow it lost its strange appearance and became just a gouged-out, ugly slide of volcanic-looking rocks, shale and gravel.

At the base of the slide, behind the mission, I found the crystal-clear spring I had heard so much about from many of the fellows who had gone down to get pure drinking water. How really good it tasted after all that gritty, boiled Yukon water I had been drinking the past week! As I was poking about at the base of the slide examining the rocks and gravels, I discovered a small trail which led up the mountainside to the right of the slide. Eagerly, I began climbing and found that it led almost straight up for about 1,500 feet, then turned abruptly to the left toward the center of this enormous, concave-shaped slide. Here the trail grew very narrow and, in several places, there was scarcely any footing at all. If I slipped, it was a long way down to the north end of Dawson! Toward the center of the slide, the trail suddenly broke off and disappeared. Here I was forced to stop. Naturally, I was extremely disappointed not to get up to the top of the ridge to the high lookout point, as I had been told I would be able to see for several hundreds of miles to the north. And if a boat were coming from St. Michael, it could easily be spotted at a great distance. As it was, I found my view blocked by the concave-shaped slide and the high ridge above me! But it had been a strenuous climb to this point and I was glad to rest. I dug my heels hard into the gravel to get a firmer footing, then leaned back against the slide.

On this perch, high on the mountainside, my sagging spirts began to soar a little. It was good to get out of the feverish, reckless atmosphere of Dawson, to get a new grip on myself and to get a better perspective.

What a thrilling view from here! And there was Dawson sprawling at my feet. I could see every detail of the town. The people looked like little dots moving along Front Street and on the tiny, thread-like paths in among the trees, tents and cabins. Looking beyond Dawson up the river to the south, I could see part of the vast territory through which I had recently come and the wide Yukon trailing back into the surrounding mountains, then disappearing. Looking straight across the Yukon to the west over some lower mountains, I could see ridge after ridge of dark-blue peaks marching off to far horizons of snow-capped Cordilleras.

What a dramatic panorama it was! For a moment, I felt exultant, like a king looking over his vast domain of gold! But where was my gold?

Then my eyes swept back to the trail and the slide, and I began looking more closely at the area below me. Suddenly, I saw sticking out of the gravels at crazy angles by partially caved-in drifts, several weather-beaten miners' stakes, mute evidence of a fruitless stampede and lost dreams! I wondered what had become of these stampeders. It must have been devilish hard digging in such a precarious spot . . . only to be disappointed!

Then I began wondering what the future held for me. So far, since coming into the Klondike, I had had nothing but bad luck! Would Fortune finally smile on me? I took a handful of volcanic-looking gravel and gripped it hard in my hand. Surely, somewhere in this region, there must be good pay dirt for me!

While I was up there on the slide, I asked myself many questions. When Stacey and I split up on the Eldorado the following day, what would I do? . . . Where would I go? Should I strike out for the big Dominion Creek area? Certainly, there was gold over there . . . but 50 miles was a long way! Confound the luck! Already the ligaments in my leg were sending warning twinges of pain from the strenuous climb. Should I gamble with destiny—go, anyway, with an ailing foot and in spite of the critical food shortage? Like all of the fellows in the Klondike, I thought of that illusive, undiscovered Mother Lode. Where was it? Was it to the north, south or east? It might even be to the west in that maze of mountains. The very thought of it was maddening!

But, facing reality again, I thought, "Well, there's that Bonanza hillside the fellows have been trying to get me interested in. But surely everyone knows by this time it is always low and deep in the valleys, as deep as a fellow can go into the frozen gravel and muck, that the miners are finding fabulous deposits of nuggets and gold dust." Hadn't I seen it all with my own eyes both on the Bonanza and

Eldorado? Hadn't I climbed down into the shafts and seen the gleaming gold!

As I continued pondering, watching the changing colors on the country below, I couldn't help noticing how enchanting and almost reassuringly the sun sparkled on the Yukon. Certainly, there was nothing ominous or foreboding about the river right now. How friendly it appeared from this great height! But I knew full well that, in a few short weeks, rumbling chunks of anchor ice would be flowing savagely in the river, and then the Yukon would freeze over and these mountains would lock arms to hold prisoner all unlucky fellows caught in their icy grip!

I asked myself over and over, "What will be the fate of thousands of men in the Klondike this winter if not enough food is brought in! And what will I do, if worse comes to worst? Will it be necessary to make a dash for the 'Outside' . . . after all of those terrible hardships of coming into the country?" But that angle seemed unthinkable! It would mean I would return to my wife and little son in Tacoma empty-handed! No, I couldn't disappoint them!

As I was walking slowly down the waterfront about an hour later, suddenly I met Mrs. Ryan of the Lake Linderman crowd, the plucky little woman who had so kindly helped me on Chilkoot when I was so desperately ill with ptomaine poisoning.

"Why, Ed Lung," she exclaimed, "it's wonderful to see you again. Have you found any gold yet?"

"Well, nothing to shout about," I laughed, half embarrassed, pulling out of my pocket my very flat-looking gold sack and shaking out a few specks of gold dust into the palm of my hand. "These specks of yellow stuff I found in various spots . . . several right in front of camp. But you can't stake in front of Dawson . . . and so, they're just a big aggravation! Like all eager Cheechakos, Mrs. Ryan, I'm still hoping for a big strike somewhere in the gold fields!"

"Well, Mr. Lung, I surely wish you luck," she said with enthusiasm.

I was very glad to see Mrs. Ryan and we talked for a while longer, exchanging news about our exciting voyage down the Yukon and the gold rush in general. I told her I had been very pleased to learn several days before that her party had reached the Klondike safely, in spite of their leaky boat.

"Oh, that boat." She laughed. "Well, it's a wonder we ever got here at all! Now, we are going to try our luck building a log cabin in the north end of Dawson. Heaven only knows what it'll look like! But all joking aside, Mr. Lung, I'm very worried at the prospects of being here in Dawson this winter. Reports are far from reassuring. In fact, I'm almost frightened! I'm not telling my husband how really worried I am. But if a steamer should come in tomorrow, I believe I'd be tempted to go back home and forget all about the Klondike. So you see, Mr. Lung, I am not really as good a pioneer woman now as I was when I met you on Chilkoot. Yes, the gold rush seemed a great and thrilling adventure then, but somehow, the excitement has worn off and I'm sick and tired of camp life!"

Chapter X

Broken Trails

It was now the fourth of August, and Stacey and I began packing and sorting over our supplies. Naturally, coming into the Klondike as partners, we had used many things in common. Now, at last, we were breaking camp and going to the Eldorado. Several times we had small, friendly arguments as to who owned what. While packing, I began to realize more forcibly than ever that, from now on, I would be going it alone, and I thought I noticed a peculiar, strained look in Stacey's eyes.

By the time we were all packed and ready to leave for the Eldorado, Captain Ellis came swinging briskly into camp, as usual wearing Stacey's best boots. Immediately, he took charge and command of our expedition, choosing the high Bonanza ridge trail.

Stacey and Captain Ellis were loaded down like pack mules with Stacey's things. Since all of his supplies could not be transferred in one trip, he had made arrangements to leave the rest of his things with McPhee, planning to make several relay trips. But I left nearly all of my things and carried only a light pack, as my plans were still indefinite. Perhaps it was a good thing we were leaving, as the Mounted Police had ordered all campers off the government reservation, and many of the fellows had gone down to camp on the sand bar.

Captain Ellis, Stacey and I crossed the mouth of the Klondike River by ferry to Louse Town, and then proceeded on up the ridge trail, our packs strapped to our backs in the usual miners' fashion. We had gone along the ridge perhaps five miles when, suddenly, we rounded a bend and ran into a crowd of excited miners gathered around something in the trail. Pushing into the crowd, we saw a miner sprawled full length, his upturned face stiff and ashen, his eyes staring into the sky.

Stacey, who was ahead of me, jumped back in startled alarm, "It's a miner!" he cried in a hoarse voice. "He's dead!"

"Yes, he's dead, poor fellow," exclaimed one of the men as he leaned down and unstrapped the pack from the dead man's shoulders. "It's Ed Gunderson. Just came recently from Circle City. Has a wife and child up there. Too bad! We warned him not to carry such heavy loads. Must have had a heart attack, just dropped dead in his tracks. Somehow, we'll have to get his body back to Dawson. Certainly hate to send word to his wife. Know it'll be mighty tough on her!"

Seeing we could do nothing for the poor fellow, Stacey, Ellis and I pushed on, for we had ten miles yet to go to reach the Eldorado. Naturally, we were unnerved and all we could talk about for a while was the possibility of sudden death in the North and how it would affect our families if such should happen to us. Somehow the subject seemed to weigh heavily on Stacey's mind. Reluctantly, he admitted to us that he wasn't really as well as he had led us to believe. Said he still had a touch of the "bloody flux" he had complained about two weeks earlier. In fact, he didn't have to tell us. We could see for ourselves. He was having a hard struggle to keep up with us on the trail. I insisted on carrying part of his load to make it easier for him, although I was getting lame in my right leg.

A few miles farther on, we came to another group gathered around something near the trail and we almost hated to look . . . but this time it proved to be a fine spring bubbling out of the gravel by the trail. The men had stopped to rest and make camp for the night. Mostly because of Stacey, we suddenly decided to camp with this jolly group of packers, as they turned out to be. Originally, we had planned to make the fifteen miles to the Eldorado in one day.

"The only drawback to this packing game," said a fellow, helping Stacey off with his pack, "is that a man needs to be as strong as an ox when he makes a damn, human pack horse of himself! Now, take me, for instance. Would you believe I was a lawyer before I came up here? Had never done any real physical labor in my life! . . . And here I am, working like a coolie! But I get twenty dollars a day for packing. And that's probabaly more than I would be getting scratching around for gold. And I know it's more than I'd be getting from my clients back home, too! Wouldn't they be surprised to see me now!" He laughed.

The nights were getting much longer, I had noticed, and much colder too, although the days were still very warm. But when the wind blew from the north, there was a hint of ice in its breath.

Up bright and early the next day, we hiked along with the congenial packers, as they were going our way. It was very cold and nippy that morning and a faint trace of frost showed on the ground and on the leaves of the trees. It was perhaps the first frost of the season.

As we walked along, the flesh on my heels and toes began burning from the old frostbite I had suffered on Chilkoot Pass, and it added considerably to the confounded shocks of twitching pain I suffered in my right leg. At times, I walked stifflegged to avoid them.

"Say," remarked Stacey after we had gone a few miles, "I sure wish I had a good pack horse to carry my goods!" Obviously, he was growing tired.

"Well," said one of the men, "we're the only pack horses up here. But there is a little burro in the Klondike we know of."

"Where is he?" asked Stacey eagerly.

"Oh, he's out in the hills grazing some place . . . probably getting fattened up for winter. But he's a lazy cuss!

You can't get him to do any work!" replied the packer with a laugh.

"What wouldn't I give to have him here, anyway," sighed Stacey, trying to adjust his pack strap and wiping the sweat from his brows. "I'd sure put him to work."

"Well, fellow, I don't think you'd make that burro work! They call him 'Wise Mike.' And, believe me, he is a wise, lazy cuss! You see, he got shot in the rump out in the hills last winter. Some green Cheechako took him for a moose! Poor Mike limped into Dawson and the fellows all felt so sorry for him that he became a sort of public charge. And did that wooly little burro from Colorado like it! Well, you bet he did! While he was convalescing, he enjoyed the sympathy and donations of Dawson so much, that even when he got well, he kept up a steady, rather put-on limp, hunching his back so high he looked like a camel. Well, it turned out that Wise Mike became quite a loafer and public pensioner. Systematically, he went from camp to camp last winter for food and shelter and, in so doing, formed quite a taste for liquor. At first, the miners forced him to drink whisky just for the fun of it, and then he began to like it. Soon he became an addict. Many's the time, after that, he'd butt his way into a saloon to beg a few drops of liquor from the amused miners. And many's the time the bartender and proprietor had to throw him out. But if Wise Mike would decide to stay . . . boy, it would take a dozen men to get him outside while he kicked and bucked. But the big pay off would come on cold winter nights when Wise Mike would get his two front feet into the door of the opera house, then butt his way through the crowd and make straight for the big round stove where he would stay for hours warming his rear while the show went on . . . till his steaming hide would get too much for the crowd and then poor, unsteady Mike, who'd probably had several drinks, would be fired out into the cold night!

"Yeah," laughed the miner, "Wise Mike is quite a burro and a lovable old cuss if you get to know him! When the weather gets cold, you'll probably see him back in Dawson. That is," added the packer, looking at Stacey meaningfully, "if another green Cheechako doesn't take a pot-shot at him!"

"Well," grinned Stacey, "I left my gun back in Dawson!"

We had to rest many times, and the packers were glad to rest, too. At last, we reached the hill just a short distance from the confluence of the Bonanza and Eldorado, where the trail made a cut-off from the ridge and turned down to the Bonanza. As we made the turn, which was perhaps a quarter of a mile back from the Bonanza, I looked longingly up along the ridge to the northeast where the trail pointed, leading off in the exciting direction of King and Queen Domes, Sulphur Creek, Quartz, and the Dominion and Indian rivers. Wistfully, I looked up that trail. There were many fresh footprints leading off in that direction, too.

When we reached the long hill overlooking the Bonanza and Eldorado, we paused to rest again and look down on the rivers of gold stretching out at our feet. And almost directly across the Bonanza, staring me right in the face, was that rocky hillside above Euly Gaisford's claim where the fellows had been urging me to stake.

"Ed, they're sure getting big nuggets down there on Euly Gaisford's claim," said Stacey.

"Yeah, and it's just possible a few of them are up there on that hill, too," said Captain Ellis with a tantalizing laugh.

"Ha! Ha! Ha!" laughed one of the packers. "Getting Cheechakos to dig for gold on a hill! That's sure an old sourdough trick!"

We continued with the jolly group of packers on down to the forks of the Bonanza and Eldorado, where we told them goodbye, as they were going to the upper Bonanza. I had formed quite a liking for Clark, the lawyer from Tacoma, and said I hoped we would meet again.

Stacey, Ellis and I walked on up to the Berry # 4 Eldorado claim above the forks, arriving there just in time to have lunch with the Tacoma fellows. After having a quick snack with the miners, I helped Stacey and Captain Ellis set up their camp, even starting a batch of sourdough bread as a last friendly gesture to Stacey. Naturally, I was concerned about Stacey, as I had done most of the cooking up to this time. Also, I was concerned about his state of health. How would he manage with the grueling, backbreaking work ahead of him? It was incredible how rapidly his vitality had waned since our arrival in Dawson. He had been such a tower of strength coming into the country. But his first headlong trip up to the Eldorado through the storm was the beginning of his loss of buoyant health and vitality!

I knew it would be hard, telling Stacey goodbye. He had been like an older brother to me. And there was no doubt about it . . . Stacey had saved my life on Chilkoot! Late in the afternoon, with the customary salutations and good wishes, I made the final break, wishing Stacey and Ellis much luck in their quest for gold.

Again I noticed, as in Dawson, a peculiar, strained look in Stacey's eyes, which I thought I understood. Good old Stacey—he hated to see me having to go it alone!

Chapter XI

The Stakes Were High

Great unrest seemed to vibrate through the gold fields. Miners digging along the Bonanza and Eldorado leaned on their shovels and listened, unconsciously hoping to hear the jubilant echoes of whistles from river boats reverberating through the hills, even though they knew full well Dawson was a good fifteen miles away. How desperately necessary it was for the boats to reach Dawson with supplies from the "Outside"!

It was food, food the miners craved now, almost more than gold. How utterly, digging that hard, yellow metal stuff, they depended on it! But, strangely enough, the steady stream of gold dust and nuggets seemed to pour from the earth from the very rich mines more rapidly than ever, like a gigantic horn of golden plenty—tipped high—lavishly spilling forth! But the ominous tom-toms of famine in the Klondike beat a little louder each day as the pages of late summer turned slowly, keeping us all in a vise of nerve-racking suspense.

Even in this far North country, important, vital news travels swiftly. No river boat had come in since we had left Dawson the week before. We knew it almost before we saw it printed in the lined and worried faces of gaunt miners as they trudged up from Dawson along the trails to the diggings with drooping, sagging shoulders. For days now, we stampeders had been watching the grim hand of Fate deal out the winning cards, playing the game of life and death on the Yukon against the enormous and glittering hand of gold!

The stakes were high! Thousands of stampeders looked on anxiously . . . waiting for the game to end. Again, the high hills seemed to lean back on their rocky heels and laugh mockingly at us!

Indecision is a great and terrible burden for anyone, especially so for one who has always been of a very positive, decisive nature. Here I had been in the Klondike now almost three weeks—and still no prospects in sight! And, certainly, I had not counted on being faced with the grave problem of starvation for the coming winter almost immediately upon arriving in the North. All of the way into the Klondike, the golden star of fortune had glittered bright on the horizon, smiling, beckoning, luring me on. But now . . . it seemed to glimmer very dimly!

It was already the middle of August. In desperation, I had followed the advice of others and I had staked that Bonanza hillside above Euly Gaisford's # 7. However, I didn't feel satisfied. Certainly, I knew no experienced miner wanted a hillside claim, such as the one I had staked, even though they were finding unbelievable quantities of gold in the valley just below.

After I had staked the claim, I turned my eyes to the steep, high hills running along on the opposite side of the Bonanza and there wasn't another claim in sight. (This was the picture in 1897.) Neither was there any claim on the hill where I had staked, as far as I knew; no, I saw no fellows digging for gold that high up. It was quite evident that only a green Cheechako like myself, newly arrived in the Klondike, would stake this high on a hill! But there was a great urgency now. Already, it was being rumored that, if worse came to worst, the Mounted Police would order all fellows without adequate food for the winter to leave the Klondike, and, of course, I would be among them! What if I were suddenly forced to leave the North and make a dash for the "Outside"? I certainly wouldn't want to leave without having a strip of ground registered in my name. No, not after I had battled my way through such terrific hardships to get into this country. Even a rocky hillside would be better than nothing!

But arguing the case the other way: What if I registered this claim in my name, and this emergency should pass, and then a really big, new discovery would be made some place in this district—and an exciting stampede take place —what then? Well, according to the Canadian law, my hands would be tied until I could either sell my claim or forfeit it. But it would take months to forfeit it! And who would want to buy a hillside claim, anyway? If I should find myself in this unbearable predicament, it would certainly be mighty hard to take! This had happened before to others . . . and it could happen to me. I knew that staking an unproved plot of ground was a big gamble.

The following day, after I had staked the hillside claim, I was really coming to grips with myself as I walked down the trail from the upper Bonanza toward the Grand Forks, where I had been looking over the area trying to see if there was any other possible chance anywhere of getting a foothold in the valley before I would go to Dawson to register my new hillside claim. According to the mining laws, I still had two more days to decide whether or not I wanted this claim. Of course, there proved to be absolutely nothing available. Scores of other Cheechakos were frantically doing the same kind of scouting. The trails were crowded with men, every inch of ground was taken; both valleys of the Bonanza and Eldorado, from rim to rim, bristled with hundreds of miners' stakes, even at the mouths of all the many small gulches and little pups which fingered and pushed their way down from the high hills, cutting into the rich valleys with wide open mouths, scooping up their share of the gold.

As I approached the Grand Forks where the Eldorado pours into the Bonanza, my footsteps lagged although I was not really tired. It seemed as though a hand was holding me back and I stopped often to observe the very rich mines and see the enormous amounts of gold the men were getting. Then, for some unaccountable reason, I felt the urge to cross over to the opposite side of the valley to the left limit, facing downstream, and I had a sudden impulse to climb the big sugar-loaf-shaped hill which seemed to jut out a little into the valley at this point, right at the Grand Forks.

I began climbing, trying to reach a well-worn-looking trail which I had spotted running along the side of the sugar-loaf-shaped hill about two thirds of the way up. From the Forks, it had appeared as though the trail followed closely an outcropping of rocks which ran almost parallel with the valley. To reach this trail, I had to scramble up over rocks, around scrubby trees and over thick, spongy moss, as there seemed to be no real path leading up the hill to the trail, although I could see many places where the fellows had gone up to chop wood.

When I finally reached my objective, the well-worn-looking trail, I saw to my surprise that it wasn't continuous, as it had appeared from the Forks. I discovered the trail ran along the hillside for a way, then would suddenly break off and disappear by, or under, a rock or tree, and then perhaps ten or twelve feet farther on it would suddenly reappear again, looking as well worn as ever, but always following the outcropping of rock. It continued this odd pattern for quite a distance across the hillside; then, suddenly, it vanished completely, leading absolutely nowhere . . . like a strange, phantom trail!

"How odd," I said to myself, "for a trail to be like this! It's been useless to follow it, but, nevertheless, it is very puzzling. Oh, well, I'll get to the top by picking my way up. Perhaps this path I've been breaking my neck so hard to follow is an old moose or Indian trail, long unused, very much weathered and forgotten."

When I had gained the top after another scramble over rocks, through the underbrush and up over unusually thick moss, although this wasn't the highest of the hills, I had a rewarding view of the surrounding country. Off in all directions—to the north, south, west and east—was a labyrinth of high hills and mountains, and as I had done on several occasions before, from the high ridge trail coming into the gold fields, I looked again longingly in the general direction of the far-off ridge which enthroned the King and

Queen Domes, the intriguing hub of the great Klondike gold fields.

"Someday soon, by Jiminy, I'm certainly going over there!" I said to myself with resolute determination. "So far, fate has been dead set against me, has blocked my way every single time I've planned to go. But one of these days, I'm going there, so help me, Moses!" I added, gritting my teeth and kicking at a loose rock vehemently with my good foot.

I glanced down at the Forks. There below me, about six hundred feet, was the fabulous Eldorado with all of its wealth pouring into the Bonanza, and down below the Grand Forks about a quarter of a mile was Euly Gaisford's rich claim and, of course, that hill above him which I had staked the day before! Confound that hill!

"But what a spot this truly is!" I exclaimed to myself, catching my breath, looking down with new interest and enthusiasm onto the rivers of gold. "If only in centuries past this hill could have been flattened out to get the wealth that flowed down the two rivers at the Forks. . . . What fabulous pay dirt this hill could hold!

"Those lucky, lucky mine owners down there!" I said to myself, half enviously as I observed the miles and miles of rich claims and thought of some of the fellows I knew. "Surely, Nature and Fate has conspired to make them millionaires!" I wondered if some day Captain Ellis and Stacey would be among them, too. From my perch on the hill, I could make out their tent on the left side of the Eldorado near the Berry claim. Already I could see a gopher-like hole they were digging to bedrock. It had been several days now since I had seen Stacey and Ellis, and I made up my mind to pay them a visit in a few days after I had registered my claim.

For a while I scouted the hill, walking all over the top and looking down into the gulches on either side which separated this particular hill from the others. There was French Gulch emptying into the Eldorado just above the Forks; and there was Big Skookum Gulch emptying into the Bonanza below the Forks. (Very rich claims stood at the mouths of both of these gulches.) Those lucky gulch-claim owners, too! How fortunate for them that the mouths of these gulches had been like wide-open sluice boxes catching some of the gold that had swept down the two rivers!

I stayed there on the hill for some time, musing, speculating, still arguing fiercely with myself over that Bonanza hillside I had staked. Reassuringly, I told myself, I could still give it up. I hadn't yet registered it in Dawson. I had only staked it . . . and, after all, stakes are easily pulled up! My emotions were strange, troubled and varied. They seemed to zoom from discouragement to great expectation, from doubt to intense excitement, as though I was on the threshold of something great—momentous!

Oddly stirred, it seemed I was being held to the scene and this hill as to a magnet. Visibily, there was nothing up here, just scrubby trees, rocks and deep, thick moss and, oh, yes, that peculiar, phantom-like trail. But, Lord help me! If only I could have seen what lay hidden under the thick moss, rocks, and roots of trees, I would have rushed to Dawson in great ecstasy and cried out for all the world to hear!

Several times I had the impression that I should stay up on the hill for the night and scout more thoroughly in the morning, but it was growing chilly, as it was late in the evening and I had not taken my blankets along with me on this particular scouting trip. All I had was a small hatchet fastened at my belt, a gold pan and, of course, no food. I had had lunch with Linc Davis and other Tacoma fellows I knew on the upper Bonanza, but it was a very light lunch, due to the food scarcity . . . and the pit of my stomach ached for nourishment. My friend Captain Breeze on Euly Gaisford's claim was expecting me for supper. Said we'd have moose steak. What an inducement!

Euly Gaisford was going to be there, too. Now, I thought of the gold he was going to pay me for the work I had done for him the past two days, adding more stakes on his boundary lines, making them taller for all new Cheechakos to see, so that there would be no more confusion or dispute as to ownership. This happened frequently in the gold fields, followed by fist fights and law suits. And, of course, there were the claim jumpers, the chiselers the wealthy mine owners always had to guard against. Euly's claim measured 500 feet along the Bonanza and 350 feet across the valley from rim-rock to rim-rock. It was one of the largest and richest claims on the Bonanza. Yes, Euly Gaisford, our goodhearted little barber from Tacoma, was one of the lucky ones, all right. (But how could any one of us guess that Gaisford, for all his gold, had tragedy waiting for him in Oregon a few years later when his rowboat would upset in the river and he would be drowned while on a fishing trip?)

"We fellows from Tacoma must all stick together here in the Klondike, Euly Gaisford said when he offered me the job of setting the new stakes. "And, Ed, now that you've staked that ground on the hill above me, and after you've looked around a little further to satisfy yourself and are convinced that you really want that claim, you'd better get to Dawson and register it with the Gold Commissioner. Captain Breeze and I think there's gold up there. It's true, the gold runs thin on my upper boundary line, but Captain Breeze and I have found a few very large nuggets in our pay dirt . . . and you can never tell what may be up higher above us at bedrock!

"How deep is bedrock in this part of the valley?" I had asked him anxiously.

"Well, bedrock here in the valley is, in places, from thirty to forty feet deep, and I admit it'll be a tough job to sink a shaft much deeper on a hill. But if you can do it, Ed, you might really be rewarded."

Now the shades of dusk were dropping fast and I still had that strange inertia and reluctance to leave this peculiar hill above the Forks. An icy blast cut along the ridge from the Canadian Rockies and, with a sighing cry, swept across the hill. I shook myself. Yes, I must be getting on down to Captain Breeze's, since he was expecting me for supper. I was hungry as a bear! And it would be good to get inside his nice warm cabin!

I stood up and braced myself against the wind, pulling my jacket closer about me. At last, I made up my mind positively. I would register that claim above Euly Gaisford's. I made my way slowly down that peculiar-shaped hill and . . . unknowingly away from unbelievable riches! The hill had beckoned . . . Fortune had spoken . . . but I had not understood.

The next morning, early, I was on my way back to Dawson to register my new Bonanza hillside claim and also to get my pick and shovel and some of my other supplies from McPhee's. Then I would start digging in earnest!

I started hiking along the trail with more zest than I had had for many days. Perhaps it was because I had quite a large pokeful of gold dust nudging me at my hip from Euly Gaisford's claim that I felt a new confidence and exuberance.

But later, on the trail, I began meeting the weary miners coming from town.

"How's the situation in Dawson?" I enquired anxiously.

"Well, fellow, to give you a little idea of how really serious conditions are," said one of the miners, "flour is now one hundred dollars for a fifty-pound sack—that is, if you can get it! The stores have only opened once in the last few days . . . and then for just one hour! Most of the fellows in Dawson are watching the stampeders as they come down river and are trying to buy provisions from them before they get wise to the situation. But those who are aware of it are charging plenty! Just think! One fellow paid five dollars for a single dried onion, and another paid two dollars for an orange. The miner in the camp next to me had an egg for breakfast this morning—cost him three dollars and fifty cents—just like eating gold! Bought it from a newly arrived stampeder who had brought a few in packed in sawdust. Down by the waterfront, I saw a stampeder offering to sell two live chickens and a rooster in a little wire cage for one hundred dollars. He calls it a bargain! Has a big sign on the cage. And you should see the crowd of hungry fellows gathered around, watching every move those chickens make . . . mouths drooling! There's a nostalgic gleam of fried chicken in their eyes! I wouldn't punish myself that way, so I took one look and beat it!"

Almost to Dawson, I met two fellows approaching along the trail. They both had heavy packs, and, as they came closer, I recognized Clark, the lawyer from Tacoma, the packer with whom I had camped and traveled on the trip in with Captain Ellis and Stacey. Clark and I greeted each other as old friends and he introduced me to his companion, Paul Hebb. Hebb was a tall, well-built fellow of handsome appearance, with thick dark hair and large brown eyes and a friendly manner. I liked him immediately.

We chatted for a little and Hebb told me he was taking as much food as he and Clark could carry from his log storehouse in Dawson; even though it had a thick door and heavy padlock, it might be broken into.

"Believe me, I'm not taking any chances with my food supplies," he said. "The Mounted Police look for serious trouble. When men are hungry, you know many will steal to keep alive. Frantic pleas have been sent to the 'Outside' for relief ships, but it's too late in the season now. It looks doubtful if they can ever make it. Three thousand miles by water is a long way, especially through Bering Sea, which will become a barrier of ice in several weeks. So, it may turn out, the only relief we'll get will be by dog team over the ice."

"But say, fellow," said Hebb, suddenly changing the subject, "have you got a claim yet?"

"Yes," I answered hesitatingly, looking a little sheepish. "I just staked one on the hill above Euly Gaisford's claim on the Bonanza."

Hebb looked askance with raised eyebrows, and there was an eloquent pause. . . .

"Well, Cheechako, if it doesn't pan out, come and see me on #29 Bonanza. I own that claim, and I could surely use a good man like you, especially since I've already heard that you're an expert accountant."

"Thanks," I said, "I'll remember your offer. But, frankly, Hebb, I wish to have a claim of my own."

"All right, Ed," Hebb answered, "but I'd like to see you again, and don't forget my offer."

(How could I possibly know that Fate was dealing me out a special card when, by chance, I met Paul Hebb on the trail that day? Later, he was appointed appraiser for mines for the Canadian Bank of Commerce in Dawson.)

As I trudged along my way toward Dawson after I left

the two men, I walked with uneasiness. What was ahead of me for the winter? The hills bordering the Klondike River seemed to press in and my spirits sagged.

"But," I said doggedly to myself, "come what may; I'll be the owner of a claim. Certainly, there will be satisfaction in that! The sourdoughs will probably raise their eyebrows and smile a little when they see me, the expert accountant from Tacoma, up there on that Bonanza hillside . . . digging my heart out for gold!"

Well, let them laugh! I set my jaw. I would get a footing in the gold fields, so help me! It would take $15 to register my claim in Dawson. But I had that much and more, too, in my poke . . . thanks to good old Euly Gaisford.

My hopes were up . . . and climbing! I had set my stakes high!

Chapter XII

Moosehide Stampede

Late summer's sun beat down hot and sultry. I stopped digging for a moment. How hungry, tired and thirsty I was! I reached over and dipped an old tin cup into a pail of cool water near the hole where I was digging and took a long drink, then leaned wearily against my shovel and looked down over the great valley of the Bonanza. There, in that valley, enormous quantities of gold were being sluiced from the miles of pay dirt even equal to the wealth of the Count of Monte Cristo! There, only 200 feet below me on Euly Gaisford's claim and on others I knew, a fellow could become rich in a single day . . . could have enough gold to buy a home, a business, a yacht, maybe . . . might even become wealthy enough to tour the world—England, Europe, the Orient, South America . . .

I thought of my wife and little son waiting anxiously back home in Tacoma in that ugly boardinghouse. How I longed to see them and bring them some of that gold!

From where I was standing, I could see Captain Breeze's cabin below me against the hill. What a fine fellow he truly was. He had earnestly tried to help me gain a footing in the gold fields. I could barely see the top of his blond curly head bobbing up and down in a shaft he was sinking to bedrock. He was certainly one of the lucky ones! How generously he had offered me a corner of his little cabin, which I had gratefully accepted. Why only last night, he'd helped me with my shaft fire, taking turns coming several times to this spot during the night, piling logs on the fire so as to melt the muck and gravel faster.

But in the cabin last evening, I had watched Captain Breeze with his amazing clean up after he had first helped me make a sample testing of the pay dirt from my claim. But nothing, not even a "color," had shown up in my mine! In Captain Breeze's gold pan, however, besides finding gold dust, there were several huge, gleaming nuggets which partially filled the palm of my hand when I held them. Could there possibly be gold such as this for me on this miserable hillside? The mining experts said, "No! Gold is heavier than gravel and will always sink to the lowest levels."

In spite of all this, here I was digging for gold on a hill! I could look down on "lays" below rim-rock on either side of Captain Breeze where fellows who were only working on a percentage basis were getting $80 to $100 a day! At intervals, I could hear their excited voices whoop each time they found a few nuggets. I looked across the narrow valley to the high hills. There was no one over there digging for gold; neither was there anyone on my side of the valley on the hills. I glanced at my pitifully small, rocky dump a few feet away. The first two days of hard digging, I had gone down only three feet through thick gravel and stones. Now, I had reached a stratum of heavy, frozen, unyielding muck, mixed with frozen sod. How unusual! How puzzling!

The sun was very hot. I felt a little dizzy. I wiped my brow and took another cool drink of water.

"Ed, you're wasting your time up here on this barren, rocky hill!" an acid voice spoke within me. "I tell you, you're just wasting your time up here! See . . . it's all down there in the great Bonanza Valley. And there wasn't an inch of it left for you to stake! You were just too late! Too late!"

With a jerk, resolutely, I straightened, threw the cup of riled water away, grabbed my pickax and savagely began chisling into the resisting earth. I would dig that blasted hole to bedrock if it was the last thing I ever did! I'd see if there was gold up here on this miserable hill! The heat of the bonfire last night had certainly not reached the level of ground where I was now digging! I was coming into a heavy stratum of rocks—large, flat ones mixed with frozen muck, which cemented them together. I wielded my pickax with all the strength I had. Being on the steep slant of the hill made it extremely difficult. I braced myself for a hard blow to split some frozen rocks apart in the hole I was digging, raising my pickax high overhead, poising, aiming. Suddenly, I slipped and lost my balance and footing and, at the same time, the descending blade of the pickax struck the smooth surface of the rock with a tremendous blow, glancing off and coming straight at me. For a split second, I had a horrified glimpse of flashing steel swinging into my right leg, then I felt a stunning blow and a simultaneous crash of pain . . . and down I went, out like a light!

When I came to, I was lying on the hill and Captain Breeze was kneeling beside me. He had my shoe off and was stopping the blood with his handkerchief.

"Say, ol' man, are you all right now?" he asked anxiously. "You were bleeding like a stuck pig when I found you a minute ago. Thought I'd better come up to see how you were doing. That pickax sure dug an ugly wound in your leg. Made a long, deep gash clean to the bone! And, good Lord, Ed! Isn't this the same leg you hurt before?"

I nodded painfully, still a little stunned and dazed.

"Guess, you're lucky, though, not to have shattered the bone and been crippled for life! As it is, Ed, well . . . you'll probably have to stay off your foot for a while. Looks like you hit your head an awful wallop, too, when you went down against those rocks. You've got a lump the size of an egg on the back of your head!"

All through the night in the cabin, I burned with fever and twisted with pain. A narrow board bunk is not comfortable, at best!

"Oh, curses!" I moaned. "What a foolish, awkward fellow I am! What business has an expert accountant trying to be a miner, anyway? Until I dug that grave back of Dawson, I'd never used a pickax in all my life!"

Now, in a hot, fiery blur, I was racing . . . racing away from the Klondike . . . racing back thirty-five hundred miles to Rochester, New York. Time was spinning . . . spinning backwards fourteen years. . . . I was sixteen, back in the parsonage with father, mother, George, Emma, Charles and Carrie. Solemnly, my father, Rev. Augustus Lung, was reading from the Bible: "In my Father's house are many mansions. . . . If it were not so, I would have told you. . . . I go to prepare a place for you and . . ." His voice trailed on.

Then, brief prayers, and he continued speaking: "My dear family, I'm leaving . . . a week's evangelistic tour . . . some small towns in New York. My subject will be, 'Prepare to meet thy God!' I must seriously remind people they know not the day or hour they may be called to meet their God." Father's voice trailed on fervently. . . .

Now he was addressing me, "Son, you still think you want to be a lawyer? Well, if you've made up your mind, I'll try to arrange for your further education when I return. While I'm away, take good care of your mother."

Time spun . . . seventy-two hours. . . . It's night . . . a knock at the parsonage door . . . a frightened cry . . . sobs. . . . "Oh, your father is dying, dying! . . . I must go to him! . . . See—a telegram!"

"Rev. Augustus Lung stricken with apoplexy while preaching in Jeddo. Is in a coma. Can't live. Come quickly!"

Sadly, time whirls . . . confused . . . muddled. . . .

"How old are you, young man? Sixteen? You say you must help support your mother and sisters? Well, you should be in school, but I'll give you the job of office boy. W. H. Reid Company has a fine reputation. We are importers of expensive seeds. But study hard at night, young man, learn to be an expert accountant—more opportunities!"

Faster, time whirls. . . .

"You've done well, young man. . . . Three years in the office . . . Ah, yes, a salesman. . . . You'll travel as far as St. Paul . . . good experience. . . ."

Time races. . . .

Travel . . . brief cases . . . sample seeds . . . sales . . . St. Paul . . . cheap hotels . . . homesick! . . .

An exciting letter from brother Charles: "Ed, come

West! Great opportunities! . . . Big country! . . . Tacoma booming!"

Mother is speaking: "Edward, my son, I can't hold you back any longer. You're now twenty-three. Join your brother. I'll manage now, somehow. George has Annapolis scholarship . . . Carrie is organist . . Emma, teaching school . . ."

May 6, 1890. A train ticket . . . Canadian Pacific . . . bulging satchel . . . hustle! . . . last-minute bundles . . . a big basket lunch to last across the country . . . a four-leaf clover for luck. . . . The address of Mr. Henry Achilles, President of Trader's Trust Bank, Tacoma, Washington . . .

A shrill steamwhistle . . . tears . . . goodbyes . . . blurred faces of Mother, Emma, Carrie disappearing . . . and I'm rolling West!

Cinders! . . . smoke! . . . plains! . . . lakes! . . . mountains! . . . real, live Indians—first I've ever seen! . . . Good Lord! How close they ride to the train! . . .

Cramped quarters . . . stale sandwiches . . . Canadian Rockies . . . Breath-taking scenery . . . Puget Sound!

A shrill whistle . . . Tacoma . . . eager faces . . . Charlie!

"It's good to see you, boy! . . . Great country!"

Cheap boardinghouse . . . five dollars left in pocket. . . . Ah, yes, the address of Mr. Achilles, childhood Sunday-school teacher in Rochester, now President of Trader's Trust . . . 9th and Pacific.

"Mr. Lung? Well, if Mr. Achilles recommends you, that's enough for me. . . . Glad to have you in our office as accountant. Reese, Redman and Crandell Company is one of the biggest wholesale grocers in Tacoma."

"Can you sing, young man? . . . Fine! We need tenors. . . . First Baptist choir . . . Sunday, 10:30. . . ."

"Shh! . . . Don't look now! Who is that pretty, dark-eyed girl . . . tenth row, between distinguished-looking lady and gentleman? . . . Whisper louder! . . . They can't hear us above the singing. . . . You say she's Velma Clement? . . . Hard to meet? Goes to Annie Wright Seminary? Ha! I'll meet her . . . Just see!"

Excitedly, ecstatically, time spins. . . .

"Do you, Edward, take Velma to be your lawful, wedded wife? . . ."

"I, Edward, take thee Velma, to be my lawful wedded wife for better . . ."

"I, Velma, take thee Edward . . . for better . . . for worse. . . ."

Time spins heavenward. . . .

"It's a boy! A boy, Mr. Lung! . . . Big blue eyes . . . light, curly hair—just like you!"

"Dear Edward, let's call him Clement Augustus for my father and yours. . . . A pity they didn't live! . . . Your mother, how she would have loved him, too!"

Time whirls darkly, unevenly. . . . Troubled!

Reese, Redman and Crandell are failing! . . .

"Sorry, Ed, can't hold on longer. . . . Going into bankruptcy! . . . Look hard for another job!"

Businesses closing! . . . boarded windows! . . . no work! . . . banks failing! . . . Panic of the '90's!

"Dear Edward, don't worry. . . . live at mother's . . . take in boarders . . . Somehow, get along . . . somehow. . . ."

Listen! . . . Listen to those newsboys!

"Gold in the Klondike! Gold in the Klondike! Rivers of Gold! The Bonanza! The Eldorado! Gold in the Klondike! Gold in the Klondike! . . ."

"Great Scott! What ails you, Ed? Wake up!"

I opened my eyes, groaned a little and rolled over and saw Captain Breeze standing over me, looking down with troubled, worried eyes. It was broad daylight.

"Ed, you've been thrashing around all night, feverish, talking in your sleep, whispering 'Prepare to meet Thy God!' Gosh, it scared me. I thought you were dying! Then you rambled on about imported seeds . . . whooping Indians . . . for better or worse . . . and just before I shook you, you were raving about a big discovery of gold in the Klondike. You must have had a high fever. Better keep off that leg, Ed, and rest up till you're better!"

"No, Breeze," I said, "I'll be all right. I'm not dying, by a long shot! I'm getting up. Umm! That coffee and bacon smells mighty good."

Later in the morning, with Captain Breeze's help, I hobbled up to my claim, even though my right leg was badly swollen, stiff and sore. Captain Breeze poked around in the hole where I had been digging the day before and removed several large rocks. We stood looking down into the uneven, gaping hole, which now showed a solid rock bottom.

"Well, what do you think of that!" said Breeze in puzzlement. "It's either an ancient, buried slide of heavy rock, or else real bedrock. But, so far, we know that not even a 'color' has shown up in the pay dirt. It's strange, though. There's no indication of as shallow a bedrock down there in the valley, so you've probably hit an ancient slide, all right . . . and it's pretty hard telling just how far it extends over the hill. Evidently, it slants at a steep angle down toward Euly Gaisford's claim and leaves off at rimrock. It might pay you, Ed, to try to dig around it for some distance . . . and then, again, it might be utterly useless. If you just had a good, working partner like Stacey, I'd say it'd be worth the tremendous labor to find out. But, Ed, you can't do it alone!"

Then, reluctantly, he added, "Maybe the old sourdoughs were right about hills . . . It does make more sense, after all, digging for gold in the valley and on the lowest benches."

"Well, Breeze, it just looks like I'm stuck with a lemon of a claim!" I said in extreme disgust.

Breeze nodded sympathetically. . . . Three days later found me hobbling painfully down the Bonanza Valley toward Dawson, very much disheartened. It seemed the bright star of hope had suddenly gone out!

I looked at my blistered and swollen hands. They were raw and calloused from digging, splitting and lifting rocks on that worthless claim. I was dog-tired and disgusted as I crutched along the Bonanza. Now the river of gold seemed like a shimmering, writhing snake, hissing out poisonous vapors of bitter disappointment from the mossy, steaming earth.

It was 8 P.M. when I finally reached the mouth of the Bonanza, where it pours into the swift-flowing Klondike River. It had taken me the entire day to travel those painful thirteen miles to reach this spot! But there is something in man, at times, which defies medical analysis . . . that something which, in gold rushes as well as wars, gives a man superhuman power and strength to endure pain and hardship and still go on. . . . Later, I was to see a great deal of this among the stampeders when I saw men walking on the ice with frozen, wood-like feet!

Here, at the confluence of the Bonanza and Klondike, there was quite a large encampment of miners and I knew of a spare tent set up for emergency shelter, put there by some of the Eldorado Tacoma fellows. I limped painfully to it and pulled the flap back hopefully, only to be greeted by a wild commotion and a feminine screech. Startled, hurriedly I backed out, very much embarrassed. Great guns! This was a new angle!

Fortunately, I then spied a large tent nearby marked "Hotel." It was owned by Mr. Pate, an energetic fellow who had chosen this strategic spot to set himself up in business.

Mr. Pate took one look at me and hustled me off to a place in the corner of the tent where there were a number of crude bunks set up. He asked me what on earth was the matter with me. I showed him the deep gash in my leg, which, by this time, was extremely red, swollen and angry-looking. Horrified, he quickly made compresses and used some of his first-aid equipment. Later, he brought me a large plate of moose steak. Boy! Never did any steak taste sweeter or better in all my life!

"It's about all we have for supper," said Mr. Pate apologetically. "You see, those confounded steamers haven't come into Dawson yet! Guess we are lucky, though, as Isaac, the Indian hunter and his three Siwash wives, came by yesterday. Were returning from a hunting trip in the Canadian Rockies. He says the moose are thinning out; says the herds are heading deep into the Rockies. Indian Isaac seems very worried. Says it's going to be mighty slim hunting this winter. At first, he was reluctant to sell any of his hard-earned meat, but one of his wives finally persuaded him."

"Ha! Ha! You should see that old Indian with his harem," laughed Mr. Pate's handy man from behind a pile of dishes. "He doesn't care what you think of him and his two extra wives. Says he's been reading the Bible. Says if King Solomon could have a thousand wives, guess he could have a few, too! Only, now he thinks three are all he can manage. Says it takes most of his time just settlin' their quarrels. But you should see those squaws. They follow him like devoted dogs. We call him Isaac, the Yukon Mormon. Ha! Ha! he's quite a character!"

The following morning, Mr. Pate served moose steak again. "Isn't it just my luck, having a terrible food shortage like this when I'm establishing such a good business? I'd planned to build a roadhouse here this summer. I tell you, the outside world can't realize what serious trouble we're in! Why, I may have to close up business and leave the Klondike!"

Mr. Pate was very kind and introduced me to two fellows who had a light skiff and were about ready to shove off down the Klondike River. He called their attention to my injured leg. Immediately, they offered to squeeze me into their boat, although they were already heavily loaded.

"O.K., partner," said one of the fellows as I climbed in, "glad to take you as far as Dawson. Then we're poling up the Yukon as fast as we can go. We want to get out of this God-forsaken country! Figure it'll take us nearly two months to get up the river five hundred miles against the current. It's likely, too, we'll be poling against the ice in a couple of weeks. . . . It'll be a tough trip and we're dreading it!"

"A river boat might get up the Yukon," I suggested hopefully.

"Yes, and a boat might *not* get up the Yukon. Even if one did, it would take a dozen boats to bring enough grub for the Klondike!"

In no time, our boat had whizzed the two miles to the confluence of the Yukon and Klondike rivers, where Dawson stands on the right bank. Here they pushed ashore.

"Men, you'll never know how much I appreciate the ride!" I told them. "It would have taken me several hours to hobble over the hill to Dawson, and maybe I wouldn't have made it!"

"Goodbye, partner!" they called, as hurriedly they shoved off. "Take our advice, get out of the Klondike before winter if you can!"

For several minutes, I watched the two men battling against the current, headed up the Yukon. As I walked towards McPhee's Saloon, from time to time I turned to watch the two men as their boat gradually diminished in size to a mere dot on the water, then finally disappeared around the bend of the river. But no sooner had they vanished from sight than at least a dozen stampede boats swung around the bend to take their place; second by second, they grew larger and larger as the current swept them on toward Dawson. I could almost see their gold-hungry faces and eager eyes as they came closer and closer toward the City of Fortune and Famine!

I made my way to McPhee's Saloon. The heavy, nauseating smell of liquor greeted my nostrils and the place was crowded with men, drinking and gambling as usual.

"Why, Ed Lung! Glad to see you! Where have you been?" asked McPhee in his big, booming voice. "I've been watching for you. Stacey and Captain Ellis were here just a little while ago playing faro. Seems they've struck a small pay streak. Came to town to celebrate. Having a whale of a good time!

"Now, Ed, don't look like that. Stacey didn't lose very much gold . . . perhaps an ounce or two; but I know how you feel about Stacey, and I don't like to see the fellows lose, either—especially those who haven't got it or are just barely making it. But take these rich mine owners—well, that's a different story! They've got gold galore! If they didn't gamble here, well, they'd be throwing it away some other place. Maybe in the dance halls—if you know what I mean?"

"How does Stacey look?" I inquired anxiously.

"Not too good, Ed. He has a bad color. Guess he's working too hard and not eating enough. But, anyway, who does these days! You don't look so much in the pink yourself, Ed!" Then McPhee suddenly changed the subject. "What luck are you having? . . .

"Well, Ed," said McPhee after I had told him of my mishaps, "sorry about your leg. By golly, you've sure had a tough time. And as for that claim you've staked, you're probably stuck with a worthless thing! But listen, Ed, there's been a stampede going on all day down to Moosehide Creek. It's out of the Bonanza and Eldorado district, so you'll be entitled to stake if you can find a strip of ground. Jump in your boat and go down the Yukon. It's only about three miles from here, just around the big mountain. The creek flows through the Indian village and empties into the Yukon. It'll be an easy trip. Better hurry, though . . . nearly every miner in town has been down already, or is going!"

In a few minutes I was at the river's edge, where dozens of fellows were excitedly pushing off in boats loaded with picks, shovels and gold pans. Hurriedly, I looked for Stacey's and my boat, but it was gone. While I was still standing there, a man by the name of "Wheezy," who had come into the Klondike with the Kelly crowd, hailed me:

"Hello, Ed! Come on, jump in my boat. I'm going on the Moosehide stampede and I'm alone.

"Guess we could both use a little gold," said Wheezy. "I haven't struck a goldarned thing since I hit the Klondike and guess you haven't either, Ed. And I've been as hungry as hell lately . . . haven't had a square meal for days. Nearly drives a fellow loco, waiting for those blasted boats! Dawson is in a devil of a predicament! You'd be surprised, Ed, what I've been living on. Haven't much left in my knapsack. Tried fishin' the last few days, but do you know? those slithery, slippery fish are as wary as game! Just seem to know I'm hungry . . . take those precious bits of bacon I'm sacrificing as bait and away they go—leaving me cursing, drooling and hungrier than ever!"

"Well," I laughed, "we'll probably all end up chewing our boots! But, seriously, Wheezy, has the A.C. Trading Company opened its doors the last few days?"

"Yea," said Wheezy belligerently, "but do you know how they worked it? The last three days they opened their doors for just one hour each day. Someone says they'd been combing their caches in order to do it. No one ever knows when the doors will open, and by the time the word gets around, the doors are closed again. The other day I rushed down there with a hundred other miners, but it was too late. You should have heard us howl—just like a pack of hungry malemutes! The miners threatened to break down the doors and the officials called the Mounted Police. We were in such a mad fury that John J. sent word it wasn't his fault there wasn't enough food to go around, said it wasn't his fault the boats hadn't arrived or that the home office in San Francisco hadn't sent in provisions early enough in the summer to ward off the threatened famine.

"For answer, someone threw a rock through a window, but there weren't any arrests. The police just barred the way and told us to keep our shirts on! There might still be enough food for all if relief ships could get up the river. I'm telling you, Ed," continued Wheezy, "I'm getting mighty concerned, and I don't mind saying I'm getting a little scared. I didn't bargain to come up here to die of starvation! The only glimmer of hope I can see is that they say Dalton, the trader, is going to attempt to drive a herd of cattle over the trail named after him. But they say that that Dalton Trail, even though it goes through low mountain passes, can be mighty treacherous, even in summer. They say sudden blizzards seem to whip up out o' nowhere! They say if Dalton gets through to Fort Selkirk, he plans to build a big barge, slaughter the cattle and bring the meat down the Yukon to Dawson. But Lord, that's mighty uncertain. And even if he gets through, how far will one or two barges of meat go with all of us hungry fellows in the Klondike?"

Now, for the first time, I felt real misgivings. I thought of those two fellows frantically poling up the Yukon to get away from the North and I almost wished I could have gone with them. Wheezy's hungry eyes and thin body alarmed me. I looked up at the high hills bordering the Yukon, and it seemed they were closing in on us closer and tighter! Our boat was racing faster with the current and we were both silent . . . thinking.

Now we were coming opposite the peculiar, big, white-faced slide on our right, high on the mountainside and as I looked up at it now, somehow instead of resembling a moose hide, curiously, it had taken on the pallid, ghastly face of Famine, staring at us until we rounded the big bend of the river out of sight of it and Dawson.

We found the Moosehide Indian village just beyond the bend of the river. Small huts and a few cabins were scattered over the low flat. A little creek poured into the Yukon, coming down from the mountains which stood high in the background. Dozens of stampede boats were pulled up on the sandy bar. We landed and met an old Indian repairing parts of a fish wheel.

"Is this the Moosehide Creek?" we asked.

He nodded. "But you white men come late. Hundreds

here first. Now, whole creek staked . . . all way up ten miles in mountains. . . . You go up see."

"How much are they getting to the pan?" I asked eagerly.

"Oh, about ten . . . twelve cents. It take long time for white man to make fortune like that," said the wise old Indian with a knowing grin. "Maybe five . . . ten years . . . maybe longer! You see, little Moosehide Creek not like great Bonanza or big Eldorado where Indian brothers discovered much gold. No! But little Moosehide Creek good Indian creek all same. . . . Good water! Now white man come . . . stir up water . . . water won't be good no more!" He ended sadly and turned away.

"Let's go up the creek a ways and see for ourselves," said Wheezy.

But we hadn't gone very far when we met several miners coming back who said, "You're too late, fellows, the creek is all staked for ten miles up. But it isn't worth a candle, anyway!"

As we started poling up against the current of the Yukon toward Dawson, I said to Sweezy, "This is one stampede I am not too disappointed over. It's plain the Indians resent the white man on this side of the mountain . . . and I don't blame them much!"

Chapter XIII

Big Skookum Gulch Stampede

It was now the 27th of August and I had just returned to Dawson from a very hectic stampede. I happened to spot Abe, the likable Jew whom I had met while we were both piling logs for the extension of the A.C. Company several weeks before. He was in a crowd of miners gathered in front of the A.C. Company. The Mounted Police had barred the doors. Low mutterings were running through the crowd of miners, who seemed to be in a threatening mood.

"Hello, Ed," called Abe. "No use waiting here longer.

We're just wasting our time! They've just closed the doors . . . and they never open twice in one day. Hard telling when they'll ever open again. I'm beginning to think I'll have to eat those candles yet which I brought in with me! I've got a whole caseful, you know," he added with grim humor.

The two of us pulled away from the crowd and Abe asked suddenly, "Where have you been the last week, Ed? I've missed you in Dawson."

"Man, oh, man!" I exclaimed. "Am I glad to be back here, even if I haven't much grub left. Abe, if it hadn't been for a group of miners, I might have been lying at the bottom of the Yukon! *Maybe murdered!*"

"Holy mackerel! What happened to you, Ed?" he exclaimed. "Looks like you've had a spell of sickness since last I saw you."

"Well, Abe, it was like this: After I came back from that little Moosehide stampede with Wheezy, I expected to go back to the Bonanza, but, quite by chance, I ran into a young fellow named Hank, whom Stacey and I had met at Lake Linderman while building our boat to come down to Dawson. Hank seemed like a friendly sort of a chap. Began telling me confidentially about a rich vein of quartz he'd discovered. Said it was at Coal Creek, about twenty miles down the Yukon. He talked glowingly about the fine prospects and urged me to go. Said he needed a partner. Said it would be an easy trip, too. Promised me half interest in his wonderful quartz claim if I would furnish part of the supplies and half of the grub. Naturally, I became very enthusiastic, thinking, at last this was my big opportunity! The fact that I could ride in the boat appealed to me, too, because of the injury to my leg.

"A week ago, we packed our boat late in the afternoon and took off down the Yukon—I, with my mind centered on the rich vein of quartz, at least three feet wide, which Hank had so elaborately described. But Dawson had hardly disappeared behind the bend of the Yukon when it became apparent that there was something rather puzzling about my new partner. His mind suddenly seemed centered on something else besides gold. . . . He began using his rifle to wantonly slaughter the birds that flew over our boat, and, besides, he kept taking pot shots at everything that loomed up along the banks of the river.

"That first night, we camped near an old Indian graveyard. Hank insisted on camping there . . . and he prowled most of the night, shooting in the cemetery. Said he was after grouse, but he may have been shooting up the graves!

"In the morning, Hank had taken on a wild, disheveled, queer look. Naturally, I was alarmed. He kept cocking his head at intervals and asking if I heard something. I didn't, and told him so. This seemed to irritate him. It was lonely there at the graveyard and I was anxious to get out on the river, because I didn't know what Hank would do next. Thought I could persuade him, once we were out in the boat, to turn back to Dawson. But Hank began shooting wildly at every bird in sight. He would usually knock them off, too, as he was a good shot. Many times his aims came perilously close to my head. From this, I could see he seemed to gain real pleasure. He kept watching me coldly out of the corner of his eye. I didn't make one false move, for, believe me, I didn't trust him. I sprawled as low as I could in the boat, hoping to keep out of range of his shooting."

"Good Lord! What happened then?" asked Abe breathlessly.

"Well, after many nerve-racking hours, and Hank's furious refusal to turn back, I realized with a terrific jolt that I was in the hands of a crazy man . . . a man who would as quickly shoot and dispose of me in the Yukon as if I were one of those unfortunate birds he enjoyed slaughtering. In other words, by a sudden whim, I too could be a dead duck! Yes, it was definitely clear, I was a prisoner of Hank's. He kept his gun cocked and in readiness and I never knew what minute he might decide to pop me off! I realized, too, that he had been lying to me about the distance to Coal Creek. He had said it was about twenty miles from Dawson, but we had already gone almost twice that distance when he finally admitted he didn't even know where Coal Creek was! We were in a lonely country and it was growing late on the second day. I had repeatedly asked Hank to land, but as he held the oars and had his rifle close to his knee, I had to be careful not to antagonize him. At last, toward evening, I spotted a thin curl of smoke coming up from among the trees back a little way from the river.

"Suddenly, Hank consented to land. I could see he was tiring and I felt quite sure that he had not seen the smoke. As soon as possible after making camp, I made an excuse to get away for a few minutes and, quickly, I bolted through the woods toward the smoke and discovered a party of miners eating their supper around a campfire. Hurriedly, I told them my hazardous predicament and they returned to camp with me. We found Hank in an ugly mood, cleaning his gun. During the course of the cleverly maneuvered conversation, the miners talked him into starting back up the river with their party to Dawson the following morning, reminding him of the great distance to Coal Creek, which they said was actually up past the Arctic Circle. They also talked of the great uncertainty of food and equipment for the coming winter. Tex, a former Texas cowboy, was the most persuasive in the party of miners. I think Hank was really afraid of him.

"Finally, Hank reluctantly consented to return to Dawson the following day. But all that night he prowled in the woods—shooting. The next morning, he was haggard and tired, said he'd been shooting wolves all night!

"Well, to make a long story short, we packed the boats and started back to Dawson, but I was very uneasy. I knew Hank had it in his mind to murder me, but the fact that these men were near in their boat hindered him. He kept asking me if I heard anything and became more irritated than ever when I said I didn't hear anything unusual. I saw that Tex kept his lasso coiled for action. Red hatred brooded in Hank's face as slowly we poled back up the river toward Dawson against the stiff current. Tex had told me that he would try to get Hank's rifle away from him at the first opportunity. So when Hank began lunging around in the boat in a very dangerous place in the river, Tex very cleverly lassoed his rifle out of the bow of the boat and let it drop in the Yukon. Of course, Tex made it look like an accident, but you should have seen the look on Hank's face when he saw his rifle disappear in the river! He was in such a mad fury that I thought he would overturn the boat, and

I had to threaten him with my oar. We all breathed easier when the rifle was gone and we discovered that, without his gun, Hank proved to be a real coward. . . . But it took him a long time to calm down.

"At last, we all made camp on the bank of the Yukon that night. It was agreed secretly that one man among us would stay awake to watch Hank. But he seemed to know, and slipped stealthily away during the night. In the morning, the boat, Hank and my supplies had all disappeared!"

"Great Scott, Ed! What a hair-raising experience you had! And what a loss of supplies! But I'll say you're mighty lucky to be alive!" said Abe with a low whistle.

"You bet I am mighty thankful to be alive! And even though I lost half of my equipment and supplies, I still have a little cached away at McPhee's."

"But say, Ed, did you find any gold down the Yukon?" Abe asked eagerly.

"Well, yes," I said. "On my way back with the miners, we stopped at all the little streams coming into the Yukon. Once we went three miles back, got a few 'colors,' but the miners said it wasn't enough to count."

"Hello, Ed, hello," called a fellow named Wold as Abe took his leave, "I've been watching for you. How did your Bonanza hillside claim pan out?"

"Oh, haven't you heard?" I said. Then I gave Mr. Wold a quick account of what I had been doing since I had last seen him on upper Bonanza.

"Well, I'll be darned, Ed! You're sure having more than the usual difficulty finding gold. But, man, oh, man, that trip down the Yukon must have been something! You're mighty lucky to've escaped that crazy fellow! I don't know what I would have done in your place! Hope the Mounted Police pick him up. And say, it makes me wonder if there aren't quite a few other fellows off their rockers. Guess it's easy for some to go nuts over gold!"

"By the way, Ed, where are you camping now?" he asked.

"Down on the sand bar," I answered, "with about fifty other fellows. You know, the Mounted Police recently ordered all stampeders off the government reservation. And, man, was it cold down there last night! Why, this morning I

(Courtesy of University of Alaska)

A late boat makes it up the Yukon to Dawson, a great joy to those frozen in

Stampeders sledding water through the snow at Dawson

Famous frontiersman Charlie "Arizona" Meadows at a Fourth-of-July celebration in Dawson in 1899. Meadows owned interests in thirty of some of the richest Klondike Mines

Stampeders' consultation

found the water I left in my gold pan frozen an inch thick!"

"Yes, I'm afraid winter is coming early," said Wold, shivering, "and I certainly do want to get 'Outside' if I possibly can. I'm fortunate though, I just sold my claim number twenty-six Above, on upper Bonanza, to Dinsmore, former manager of the Juneau mines. I have the papers right here in my pocket. Ed, I got forty-eight thousand dollars for it! Of course, it was worth more, but I'm pretty darned anxious to clear out of here and get home."

Then he continued, "I should have gone out on the little *Bella.*"

"The *Bella!*" I exclaimed, startled. "When did she come in?"

"Well, a few days ago she came steaming into Dawson quite unexpectedly. And Ed, you should have heard the wild excitement! But guess what her cargo was?"

"Food?" I asked eagerly.

"No!" answered Wold vehemently, getting red in the face with anger. "Barroom fixtures and whisky! Think of it, Ed! Just barroom fixtures and whisky—when Dawson so desperately needs food!"

"Good Lord," I said, "no wonder the miners are ready to tear things loose!"

"Yes," replied Wold seriously, "and what makes the situation worse, they say the Juneau trading companies are cleaned out, and many had expected to be outfitted there before crossing over the passes."

"Great guns!" I said. "What a bad pickle we're all in at Dawson! And not only us, but the thousands who will get caught in Yukon country for the winter."

"You're right!" said Wold. "I should have gone out on the little *Bella,* but my claim wasn't sold yet. Anyway, the steamer was loaded to the guards. We all shouted to the captain when he pulled away, 'Your next cargo had better be food!' But he shouted right back that he couldn't bring food if there wasn't any in the warehouses at St. Michael, I swear, Ed, it may be foolish, but the next tub that floats, leaving Dawson, is going to find me aboard, even if I get stalled down the Yukon for the winter!"

Suddenly there was a great commotion along the waterfront, men running toward the river.

"Look!" cried someone. "A barge is coming down the Yukon! A barge loaded with men and cattle!"

"Why, it must be Dalton!" someone shouted excitedly.

Wold and I joined the crowd and rushed to the river's edge, watching breathlessly.

As the barge came closer, someone in the crowd yelled, "That isn't Dalton. It's Archie Burns, the fellow who's been freighting on Chilkoot."

"Well, I'll eat my hat!" one of the miners exclaimed. "If that fellow next to him ain't Slavin, the lightweight pugilist! Wonder why he's comin' up here?"

"For gold, of course! Gonna knock a few nuggets out of some of the big shots here! Ha! Ha! Ha!" said a fellow with raucous laughter.

"Hello, Slavey, hello!" called out a miner.

Slavin heard. He took off his hat and waved energetically, jovially calling back, "Hello! Hello, there, fellows of Dawson! It's great country you have up here!"

"Say, I've got a bright idea!" said one of the miners in the crowd. "Doyle, the Australian pugilist, is here in Dawson. Came in just the other day. How about a big fight? Kind of get our minds off our stomachs!"

"That's a great idea!" chorused the crowd. We're all in favor! Hi, Slavey, did you bring your boxing gloves along?"

"You bet I did!" he called back, throwing a few imaginary punches into the air.

"Say," said someone near by, "isn't that fellow with the big cowboy hat and leather jacket Joaquin Miller, the famous poet-reporter from California?"

"Sure thing!" said another fellow. "Haven't you heard? He's being sent in by Hearst, the big newspaper publisher, to report on the gold rush for the San Francisco *Examiner*. And, say, those are Miller's two grown sons standing near him."

"Man, oh, man! What a story Joaquin Miller will have to tell the world!"

"Say, but how in tarnation d'you suppose Archie Burns ever got them cattle over the Scales of Chilkoot Pass?" asked someone incredulously.

"I dunno, it's beyond me!" answered a fellow. "But I do know one thing—nine head o' cattle ain't gonna go far in this here hungry town. I gotta see Burns the minute he lands and tell 'im to put my name on one of them steaks. Man! I can hardly wait to sink my teeth into a nice, juicy piece of rare beef!"

It was now the 3rd day of September, 1897, and I wrote in my diary, "What will this day bring?"

Of course, I was in a blue mood when I wrote that sentence in my diary. It was my thirtieth birthday and, naturally, I thought of my loved ones far away, and felt very homesick. And, like hundreds of others in the Klondike, I had been thwarted in my search for that illusive metal . . . gold! And, like hundreds of others, I was extremely worried about the prospects for the coming winter!

But the more I thought about it, the more thankful I was just to be alive and that my leg was almost healed now, although I could see that I would carry an ugly scar as long as I lived.

Each day now, in September, the weather grew colder. Heavy frost covered the ground. It was the glistening, white, chilling, ominous calling card of winter!

I had made one more painful trip up to the Eldorado and the Bonanza, but I found there wasn't much doing there. Mining was definitely slowed up, as most of the miners were in town watching for the boats. I spent a few hours with Stacey and Captain Ellis on their Eldorado "lay." When I found them, they were down in their mine, blue with the cold, digging like mad, trying to reach bedrock before winter set in. But, it seemed, the real pay streak was eluding them and they were very discouraged. Stacey was rather quiet when I talked to him and he looked haggard and half sick. After a short visit, I went down to Euly Gaisford's claim and found that Gaisford and Breeze had gone to Dawson with the others. However, Brooks, the fellow from Orting, Washington, was there, and so we shared Breeze's cabin together. It was a bitterly cold night, the coldest so far, and I began to realize more than ever what a winter in the North would be like!

I decided to go back to Dawson the next day, as it was only a "thorn in the side" to be there—a reminder of my worthless claim on the hillside above Breese's.

It was now the early morning of the 8th of September. We had had several days of heavy frost. But now great flurries of snow swirled and drifted through the air. This was the real beginning of winter!

My tent on the sand bar was all bowed in from the weight of the snow, and I huddled close to my little Klondike stove, trying to keep warm.

Suddenly, I heard excited, muffled voices in the tent next to mine. "Hurry, Bill, grab your things! There's a big stampede on. Hurry! Let's go up there and stake!"

"Hey, fellow," I called as I dashed out of my tent into the snow, "what did you say? I overheard you say something about a big stampede!"

"Yes, there's an exciting stampede going on at Big Skookum Gulch! Grab your things, Ed, if you want to go with us. There isn't a moment to lose. In a few minutes, there'll be hundreds of fellows on the Bonanza Trail racing towards Skookum Gulch! We want to stake as close as possible to Kresgy and Peterson, the discoverers who struck it rich."

"Big Skookum Gulch . . . by the Grand Forks?" I asked incredulously. "Good Lord! I can't stake up there! I've already staked a hillside claim in that same district of the Bonanza. . . . Great Scott!" I groaned as the men hurried away. "I've sacrificed my rights in the Bonanza district! I can't stake in Big Skookum Gulch! Oh, my God!"

The snow was falling thicker, and I stood for a long time watching the figures of excited men running along the waterfront through the snow towards the Klondike River, others racing up over the hill back of Dawson to the Bonanza Trail, some crossing the Klondike to take the high ridge trail—All racing fifteen miles to Big Skookum Gulch!

I just stood there motionless in the snow, numbed with the cold and shock. A big stampede! Skookum Gulch! What a fool I was to have staked that hillside claim!

In McPhee's Saloon later, I joined a group of miners standing around the stove to keep warm. One old-timer was saying: "Who would have thought gold was there? Why, we've walked up that gulch many times. Damn the luck! And to think, Nathan Kresge and Nels Peterson, two Cheechakos, made that big discovery! The news just leaked out a few hours ago. . . . Lord! What a stampede!"

Chapter XIV

Ten Thousand Frenzied Men

By the fall of 1897, there were between eight and ten thousand men in the Klondike, not to mention those at Fort Selkirk, Circle City, Fort Yukon, Fort Hamilton and other settlements of whites and Indians along the Yukon; and although we had been rationing our food, what made us doubly apprehensive in Dawson was persistent news from the upper Yukon that a new wave of men from the States was rushing towards the Klondike. I had written in my diary as early as August 15th:

August 15, 1897 (Dawson)
All sorts of stories are afloat, but none reliable, as no one knows definitely. Reported 1,200 men are on the Dyea Trail (Chilkoot), 2,000 men on boats from Frisco, and 500 men are leaving Seattle. Governor McGraw and Judge Osbourne of Seattle are on their way, as reported. Some parties are getting frightened. Stores are closed and are not selling a thing! And nothing is known of the boats way overdue!

Now, by fall, we men in Dawson knew that thousands of gold-hungry stampeders were on their way to the Klondike, coming through the gateways of Alaska and Canada. White Pass was now open. It was gold they would all get —when they finally reached the fabulous Klondike!

The Indians had predicted an early winter, and, by August 26th, ice an inch thick had formed in our gold pans.

It was now September 19 in Dawson. How truly ironic the situation was! Winter coming on, thousands of stampeders coming into the country, threatened famine; the greatest gold discovery since the Bonanza and Eldorado—the Big Skookum Gulch stampede of September 8th—but now, something else was rapidly becoming more precious than nuggets and gold here in the Klondike: Food!

It seemed the relentless North was at last forcing all of

us to grudgingly acknowledge that gold—that hard, yellow, metal stuff—could not keep a man alive. Now it was food, food . . . and more food we all craved. How eloquently each one of us was being reminded that, after all, we were made of that pathetically destructable stuff—flesh and blood!

How desperately far from civilization we were, here in Dawson, cut off entirely from the outside world, cooped up like rats in a hole, constantly being reminded that help was thousands of miles away through an almost trackless wilderness or through a hell of freezing water and fast-gathering ice!

Flour, bacon and beans could not be bought at any price. The doors of the trading companies had now been closed for many days. With grave forebodings, we had watched the shelves of the stores grow rapidly bare before the trading companies finally closed their doors. Toward the end, all a fellow could buy were spices, sugar and a little dried fruit. The very last flour had sold for $2 a pound! In terrible contrast, the safes of the three trading companies literally groaned and bulged with gold!

A cell of the Mounted Police barracks was piled high to the ceiling with bags and boxes of nuggets and gold dust for safekeeping for the miners.

The struggle for survival was taking a fierce turn, but the cells of the Mounted Police barracks were strangely empty of prisoners. Criminals were not locked up, for there was no extra food. They were ruthlessly run out of town and driven down river to whatever fate awaited them at the hands of the Arctic.

"White man must listen! White man, listen! No more river boats come with food!" the Indian scouts persistently warned along the Yukon.

"No more river boats! No more river boats come with food!" the words echoed and passed from mouth to mouth through the streets of Dawson, sweeping back into the snow-covered gold fields.

But temporarily, at least, it seemed that the full impact of the bad news could not be fully comprehended. Perhaps it was because not one of us really wished to face reality, perhaps it was, too, because we had been haunted all summer with the apparition of threatened famine.

Many were saying optimistically, "Even though anchor ice is running heavily now in the Yukon, as long as the river is not completely closed in, there is still the possibility a river boat may get up to Dawson."

How we hoped these men were right! Oddly, and not too strangely, the gold camp was still aglow with wild enthusiasm over the recent startling Big Skookum Gulch stampede which had happened so unexpectedly. Large nuggets and hundreds of ounces of gold dust from the big stampede were being already jubilantly shown in Dawson, spilled out from thick pokes of the newly rich stampeders for all of us to see!

"What a fool I've been!" I kept repeating to myself over and over. And to think that, only a short time previously, I had stood on the top of that very hill at the Grand Forks. Well, such was my luck! Dame Fortune smiled on some, turned her back on others. Our frantic search for that illusive gold was simply a big game of timing and chance!

It seemed incredible to think of it! Four hundred bench claims, each claim, 100 x 100 ft., now marked off the steep side of Big Skookum Gulch facing downstream, right limit. Miners' stakes from all the new Skookum Gulch claims now bristled along the side of the gulch, four stakes to a claim. Sticking up out of the snow, they looked like a young forest.

"Yea," said a tired old miner talking to a group of us in Dawson, "I tell ya, fellers, some is lucky and some is not! Now ya take me, fer instance, I've nothin' much to show fer all o' my work. But, ya take Nathan Kresge and his partner, Nels Peterson, well, they is definitely lucky! This is the story of Big Skookum Gulch stampede hot off the griddle as I heerd it.

"Ya see, them two fellers, Kresge and Peterson, had been in the Klondike about four months. They see they was jest out o' luck fer a claim on the Bonanza and Eldorado, 'cause everythin' was staked plum solid. But they happens to be scoutin' up Big Skookum Gulch a coupl'a weeks ago and spied what looked to be an abandoned claim. Thar was one o' them prospectin' holes sunk down fourteen feet in the bottom of the gulch and filled with water. Well, since thar didn't seem to be nary a soul around workin' that there claim, and since the name and number was cut clean off them four stakes, Kresge and Peterson begins diggin' around, tryin' this spot and that on the deserted claim, which was really claim # 6. But findin' nothin', they starts diggin' like fools up a little way on the hillside near rim-rock above # 6. They tore off the thick moss . . . and what d'ya think they saw? Well, sir, clingin' to the roots of that there moss an' starin' them right in the face was a great, big, shiny nugget! At first, they thought a miner must'a dropped it. But they scratched around in the gravel and found, to their amazement, some more o' them big, yellow nuggets!

"Gosh, by this time they was gittin' mighty excited, diggin' like mad, scoopin' up the sand 'n gravel into their gold pans and runnin' like crazy down the hill to a rocker they'd set up by the water hole. Thar, they pans the small gravel 'n black sand . . . and how much d'ya think they got? Eight hundred dollars! Jest think of it—eight hundred dollars of shiny, yeller gold!

"Then, by golly, them fellers Kresge and Peterson realize with a bang they'd made a whoppin' big discovery! Naturally, they tried to keep it quiet. But now, I asks ya, how in creation could fellers just burstin' with news like that keep it quiet? Then, by the eighth of September, as ya all know, the news leaked out, and bang—the big stampede was on! Golly Moses! Ya never saw such a wild scramble in all yur life. Why, they come runnin' through the snow by the hundreds to Big Skookum Gulch even after dark, stakin' by lantern light!"

"Yes," broke in another old Yukoner, "the mining experts are mighty puzzled over this new discovery. They say for the first time, gold has been discovered on a hillside. And man, oh, man, are the old-timers confused. Say they just can't account for it, and don't know how in tarnation gold ever got up there on that hillside. Yep, they is all mighty puzzled! Why, even big Alex McDonald, the Klondike King, is astonished. But says it just goes to prove the old saying: 'Gold is where you find it!' Goes to prove too that water through that gulch musta been pretty high at one time!"

"Yes," said another old miner, "the experts are calling

attention to the fact that the nuggets on Big Skookum Gulch rim-rock are very rough and close to the surface, which indicates their real source couldn't have been too far away."

"Yeah," chimed in another fellow, "and have you heard that just below in the gulch some rich specimens of 'float' have been found? Some think that very rich beds of quartz, heavily impregnated with gold, lie concealed somewhere beneath the surface. Now they're asking, 'Where are those rich beds of quartz which probably fed Skookum Gulch? Are they buried deep in the head of the gulch, or hidden some place not too far back in the hills towards the Indian River?"

"Gosh!" said a young miner who was listening excitedly. "It must be the Mother Lode you're talking about!"

"Yes," the miner broke in quickly with a gleam in his eyes, "you guessed it, young fellow, that's just what I mean—the Mother Lode! But where in tarnation is it?"

Like hundreds of other anxious fellows whose food was running dangerously low, I waited in Dawson, hoping that a boat would get through with supplies. While waiting in the gold camp, however, with several others, including Abe, the Jew, I was cutting and piling wood for the A.C. Company, as they needed quantities of fuel for their big stoves when they would officially be opened for business again. But we fellows who were working for the A.C. Company were no better off than anyone else. It didn't net us any food, as some would think, because they didn't have any! However, we were getting $8 a day in gold dust. But it was hard work and the weather was horribly cold. Our hands almost froze to the logs. Finally, work had to be suspended because of the weather.

It was now Sept. 22, and I wrote in my diary from Dawson:

> A miners' meeting was held at the Opera House to protest the 10% and 20% tax levied against the Yukon miners. Capt. Morgan was chairman and Livernash, a reporter from the S.F. *Examiner,* was secretary. Over three hundred irate men were present. Food shortage

is critical. I may have to pole up the river to get "Outside" unless a boat comes in!

(Livernash was one of Randolph Hearst's reporters, who arrived in the Klondike soon after Joaquin Miller.)

The following day, I wrote again in my diary with much distress:

Sept. 23, 1897

I went to work for Palace Restaurant, as I am out of grub! Will work a day or so. Wheeler was on a tearing drunk last night. Tried to get him back to camp but could not, as he was so crazy drunk!

About two weeks previously, off and on, I had taken care of Wheeler, the man I wrote about in my diary. He came from a good family in San Francisco.

I had been apprehensive about my fast-diminishing food supplies and wondered desperately what I would do when they were gone. But, it seemed, luck was with me in the form of another's misfortune! Wheeler's tent happened to be pitched near mine on the sand bar, not far from the Mounted Police barracks. One night I had been listening for hours with much distress to his fits of coughing. At last, I could stand it no longer. I went to his tent and found he was quite sick. He had a heavy cold on his chest and had developed pleurisy. Poor fellow, he was in bad shape. A frozen tent was certainly not a good place for a sick man. Immediately, I set about to see what I could do for him.

For several days and nights I doctored Wheeler, often getting up in the cold to help him; and for this he was mighty grateful and richly repaid me by sharing his grub with me! When he'd get to coughing too hard, I'd grab the St. Jacob's Oil and rub his chest hard and give him a big dose of pain killer. But several times the pleurisy pains were so severe that I said in desperation, "Wheeler, I'm going to fix you up!" And I proceeded to make him a mustard plaster—three tablespoonfuls of mustard to a cup and a half of flour, mixed with a little hot water. I spread the thick, hot, gooey stuff on a cloth and slapped it on his chest.

"Say, Ed," Wheeler would groan as the plaster would begin to burn like fire, "you're sure a horse doctor . . . just burning the hide off me!" Then he'd reach for his favorite internal remedy, a bottle of whisky, and take a big swig. "May as well sizzle inside, too, as well as out!" he would laugh ruefully.

But as I mixed those mustard plasters, how I hated to use that good flour. Why, a cup and a half of flour would keep a fellow alive for several days. But, after all, it was Wheeler's flour and Wheeler's pleurisy!

By the 23rd of September, fortunately for Wheeler, his pleurisy was better and he didn't need me to doctor him any more; but it was unfortunate for me, because, by this time, I was completely out of food, as I wrote in my diary on that date. But luckily, I had managed to get a job cutting firewood for the Palace Restaurant after I stopped working for the A.C. Company. The weather had turned a little milder, and as long as I had to be working outside, I was mighty thankful for the change in temperature. For the moment, at least, I had food and work at the restaurant, but I wrote again in my diary:

September 24, 1897 (Dawson)

Worked until 1 P.M. for the Palace Restaurant. A party is going down river and wishes me to go. I fear I will have to winter at St. Michael if we wait here any longer for boats. Not only that, no one has grub, and the restaurants are using spoiled flour. Tomorrow may bring boats. If not, a truly serious matter with us here in Dawson!

Yes, the restaurants were using spoiled flour by late September, making horrible-tasting stuff. And we, who had no food, were obliged to eat it or go hungry! The vile, musty flour had been brought down the Yukon by a stampeder who saw his chance to make a small fortune. He got it cheap at Skagway—paid $2.50 a sack—and then freighted it over Chilkoot and down the Yukon. Of course, he had heard of the threatened famine . . . and when he reached Dawson he sold the flour to the restaurants for $35 a sack!

As a result of eating this horribly vile stuff, most of us

fellows became violently sick . . . and I wrote again in my diary the morning of the 25th:

> Woke up at 4 A.M. Have diarrhea very bad. At 6:30, I heard Wheeler up in next tent. Went over and got some hot ginger. Am now feeling some better!

In spite of winter coming on and the threatened famine, stampeders were constantly coming in droves down the river. But now, with the ice running, they were having increasing difficulty landing. Many fellows were swept past Dawson, caught in among the chunks of ice, and we never knew what became of them.

There had been no mail brought into Dawson for many weeks, except by parties coming down the Yukon, and we were all hungry for mail from home and news from papers, no matter how old. One stampeder who landed safely had a Seattle newspaper dated August 11, 1897, which contained vital news of the Klondike. We all read it eagerly. The following warning, issued by the U.S. Secretary of the Interior, C. N. Bliss, called attention of prospective stampeders to the hazards of getting into the country and the seriousness of conditions in the Klondike. It made us realize more than ever the gravity of our situation here in Dawson.

(When the following article was written, August 11, 1897, White Pass Trail was, in places, still under construction, although the stampeders were beginning to use it the last of July.)

> To whom it may concern:
>
> In view of information received at this department that 3000 persons with 2000 tons of baggage and freight are now waiting at the entrance to White Pass in Alaska for an opportunity to cross the mountains to the Yukon River, and that many more are preparing to join them, I deem it proper to call attention to all who contemplate making that trip to the exposure, privation, suffering and danger incident thereto at this advanced period of the season, even if they should succeed in crossing the mountains. To reach Dawson City when over the pass, 700 miles of difficult navigation on the Yukon River

without adequate means of transportation will still be before them, and it is doubtful if the journey can be completed before the river is closed by ice. I am moved to draw public notice to these conditions by the gravity of the possible consequences to people detained in a mountainous wilderness during five or six months of Arctic winter, where no relief can reach them, however great the need.

(signed) C. N. Bliss
Secretary of the Interior

The Canadian Government had also published dire warnings to stop stampeders from starting into the Klondike at this time, due to the serious conditions; also, it published warnings to all stampeders who were running short on food to get out of the country; warned that it would be absolutely hazardous to build hopes that any more river boats could get up the Yukon from St. Michael before the spring of '98.

Each day as winter advanced, the weather grew more severe in Dawson and our apprehension was approaching panic. The wind from the north kept coming at us like knives, cutting us to the bone, and all who could, crowded into the saloons and dance halls to get out of the penetrating cold. A few fellows hopefully gathered in shivering little groups in front of the doors of the trading companies, doggedly hoping that, in some miraculous way, the doors might be opened and, by some miracle, food would appear on the shelves again.

By late September, the Yukon was frozen out thirty feet from shore. Now it was a common sight to see a number of fellows fishing through holes cut in the ice, Eskimo fashion. Usually, these men were blue with the cold. Very few had any luck. Other hungry fellows took their rifles and went back over the hills with much determination. Some returned with a few jack rabbits; most of them came back empty-handed. A party of hunters was hurriedly being organized to go back into the Rockies for big game, but it would be a long, hazardous trip. They tried to get Indian guides, but the Indians didn't want to go with them.

With the days growing shorter and colder, we began to

feel more desperate. Darkness fell early. And with more darkness, more robberies took place. Two men were shot for stealing from caches, caught in the very act; one was killed outright, the other died later. These robberies stirred the owners to a wild fury of vengeance and they threatened sure death to other thieves. Secretly, a vigilante party of miners was organized to keep a sharp lookout for cache robbers. Their motto was: "Shoot first . . . talk afterwards!" When shots rang out after dark, we all looked at each other and shuddered. Another cache had been robbed; another man shot! We knew the Mounted Police would have to turn a deaf ear. It was evident the law of the frontier was speaking. It was every man for himself!

Rumors were flying around Dawson, however, that before anyone would actually starve, food would be confiscated and redistributed by the Mounted Police. They'd start first with the "sure thing" men, the gamblers, and the dance-hall girls. Next, would come the surplus of the miners themselves. Naturally, everybody was riled and in a frenzy of uncertainty—those with food, and those without it.

I was particularly fortunate, however, to have several good friends, like Wheeler, the fellow with pleurisy, and Paul Hebb, whom I had met six weeks before on the Bonanza Trail.

A number of times, Hebb invited me to his Dawson cabin with a few other fellows, and somehow he always managed to give us enough to eat. Good old scout, Paul Hebb! It was at Hebb's cabin that I first met the six men who were going to play a big part in my life before long. They were: Billy Moore, Captain Tibbetts, N. H. Bertram, George Hill, T. W. Calhoun and Shelley Graves.

Right away, the seven of us began talking over our serious predicament and to formulate plans to escape the North if relief ships did not arrive soon. The situation looked so grave now that we thought it wise to secretly get a boat and keep it in readiness. (Paul Hebb was very fortunate, however. He had adequate food in his Dawson cache and planned to remain in the Klondike.)

A couple of days after I had met the six men in Hebb's cabin, I ran into ex-Councilman Coates from Tacoma. "Ed, I'm really frightened!" he began telling me. "You know I'm too old a man to battle the North at my age. It's true, I've made a good clean up on the Berry claim, but this famine is a catastrophe I never counted on. If no more river boats arrive, I don't know what I'll do. Some fellows are starting down the Yukon; others poling up the river in open boats; some even waiting until winter to walk out over the ice. But it seems I just can't face either alternative; and I can't get enough food to stay here in Dawson this winter. What are you going to do, Ed?" he asked anxiously.

"Coates," I said, "there're seven of us who've made tentative plans. We'll know what to do just as soon as Captain Hanson and his two Indian guides return from their scouting trip downriver at Fort Yukon. If Captain Hanson says there is positively no hope of relief ships getting through to Dawson, the seven of us are going to make a dash downriver in an open boat. We hope to make it to St. Michael. There, we might be lucky enough to catch a late steamer back to the States before the ice closes in. We know it's a desperate chance to take; but, if necessary, we'll risk it!"

"Ed, you men are crazy! Why, it's fifteen hundred miles to St. Michael," said Coates, aghast. "You can't possibly make it this late in the season. Why, you'll all be crushed in the ice floes on the river or freeze to death on the way! And don't you know, Ed, there are hundreds of miners who've been stranded at St. Michael since the last of August? Even if you reach there, you'll be no better off than right here at Dawson. Reports have it that the men are rioting, threatening violence and vengeance on the North American Transportation and Trading Company for being stalled there at St. Michael. Some still want to get up to Dawson in river boats; others want to get 'Outside.'"

"And I can tell you more," said Mr. Estridge, a mutual friend of Coates and mine, who had been listening. "Sam Wall and McGillvra, newspaper man, just poled up the river from Fort Yukon and brought news that the *Hamilton* did fight her way up the river as far as Fort Yukon two weeks ago. She brought passengers and provisions, but in her effort to get over the shallow sand bars so that she could reach Dawson, she unloaded her entire cargo and all of her passengers, but failed to make it . . . even though she drew only two feet of water! She finally started back down river toward St. Michael."

"Yes," said another fellow by the name of Fisher, who had joined us, "the two newspaper men also said that the *Hamilton* brought very tragic news up the Yukon from St. Michael. They said the *Cutter Bear* pulled into St. Michael with news that the *Nevak*, a stern-wheeler, was caught in the ice pack in Bering Sea. Had lost her way. Forty-two of her passengers were crushed to death in the ice jam. Only Captain Whitehead and his wife and several seamen escaped . . . saved by the *Cutter Bear*."

"What a horrible tragedy!" I said with a shudder.

"Now, Ed, do you see what I mean?" said Coates with a shiver.

"Yes, I see what you mean, Coates!" I said thoughtfully. Then, turning to Estridge, I said, "From the reports you give us, Fort Yukon seems to be the logical place for us to go."

"Yes," replied Estridge, "it would seem so, but with all those passengers who've been dumped there among the miners and Indians who live at Fort Yukon, the supplies from the *Hamilton* might be just a drop in the bucket!"

"Well," I said, "if we have to leave Dawson, it's worth a try! But I still hope to make it all the way to St. Michael!"

"Well, Ed," said Coates, "you and your party of men are young and strong and might get through. But I have no way of going. Besides, I am too old to take such a chance!"

"Coates," I said, "I know how you feel. We are all in a very precarious position. Our families can't possibly know the predicament we're in here. And it's a good thing they don't! I know how much you want to get home, Coates, and I've got an idea which might help you. You know the little *Koekuk* that came down river the other day from the Pelly Indian village trading post? I've heard she's going to attempt to make it up the Yukon as far as Fort Selkirk. Now, why don't you try to get on her?"

"The *Koekuk!*" exclaimed Coates. "Ed, surely you're not suggesting I go on that little old derelict? Why, she's a rotting, floating coffin! Has been on the Yukon for years and years, used by the traders and Indians. Everybody knows she ought to be condemned. She can hardly stay afloat in calm water. Her engines break down every few miles. But in spite of all that, do you know, Ed, since she came in the other day, at least two hundred desperate fellows have tried to get passage on her? Just think, they were eager and willing to trust their lives on that little old moth-eaten wreck. And, do you know, she can only take twelve or fifteen passengers at the very most! Besides, Ed, I've heard that a party of fellows have just bought her, so that settles it. I couldn't get on that little boat if I wanted to!"

"I know what you say is true, Coates, that a party of about twelve men, including Thomas McGee, the San Francisco capitalist, and his son, have bought the *Koekuk*. But I thought they might squeeze you in. I've heard they plan to try to make it up the Yukon to Fort Selkirk and from there will attempt the Dalton Trail, which comes out at the Chilcat Indian village on Lynn Canal."

"But the Dalton Trail! Why Ed, that trail is at least three hundred and fifty miles long!" wailed Coates. "Don't you know, it leads through blizzardy country where there's apt to be very deep snow through the mountains, even in September? No," he said mournfully, shaking his head, "at my age, I could never make it over the Dalton Trail, even if it were possible to get up the river on the *Koekuk*. And I don't see how McGee will ever make it as he isn't young. But, oh, I do so desperately want to get home to my family!" he ended sorrowfully.

When I left Coates, he was almost weeping. I pitied him, a frightened, broken old man. But I couldn't ask him to join my party of men. After all, seven in a small, open boat would be far too many for safety; and the outcome would be very doubtful. When we parted, I told Coates hopefully that a river boat might yet come steaming around the bend from the north. I sincerely hoped so from the bottom of my heart!

Immediately after leaving Coates, I started packing my small supplies in a tight, compact bundle in readiness to leave at a moment's notice. I tied the long rope more securely that held the boat we seven men had managed to get. It was pulled up on the ice in front of my camp, tightly covered with canvas.

All available boats which had not previously been dismantled for shacks or firewood had been grabbed by the stampeders, who now stood guard over them. These few, small boats were now our only means of escape!

The seven of us held a hurried consultation and decided to pool all our resources. I had medical supplies for the party, but no food. Fortunately, everything each one had seemed to fit in with the general need. We were now a party of men—one for all, and all for one! We allotted hours for each to guard over the boat and supplies. However, our eyes still kept watching anxiously to the north, hoping against hope for the heart-warming sight of a river boat coming around the snow-covered bend from St. Michael.

In this tense atmosphere, it was natural that many wild and false alarm cries of "A boat! A boat!" went up along the waterfront from time to time. And, every time, our hopes zoomed high . . . and then hit rock bottom!

The ice had been slowly closing in for days along the river. Then, quite suddenly and unexpectedly, a warm Chinook began blowing from the south. The freeze halted and the ice started to break off and disintegrate a little in the river. Old Yukoners watched in amazement, as this was a very unusual happening. A thrill of excitement surged through Dawson! Maybe a boat could yet get through! Perhaps fate had turned a beneficent eye on us, after all. We all relaxed a little, waited, tightened our belts and hoped.

The little *Koekuk* with her party of men was not waiting, however. On September 25th, hundreds of fellows lined the waterfront to see her off and wish the men good luck and Godspeed. There was much last-minute advice and many verbal messages for friends and relatives on the "Outside" if the men should make it safely. The little *Koekuk* finally pulled away amid much excitement and shouts from the crowd. Her rickety little frame trembled, her old motors wheezed and coughed as she turned her prow slowly and started unsteadily upstream. Fascinated, we all watched dubiously as she bravely fought her way against the heavy current, trying to dodge the oncoming chunks of ice, until she finally disappeared around the big bend of the Yukon to the south. Truly, she was like a brave little old lady making her last, gallant stand!

"She'll never make it to Fort Selkirk, I tell you!" said an old sea captain who had been watching apprehensively. "Those men are just throwing their money and maybe their lives away!"

"Better do that than to stay in this black hole and die of starvation and despair!" said one man bitterly. "If I could have got passage, believe me, I would have gone on her!"

Little did we know when the *Koekuk* pulled away that she would live up to the adverse predictions sooner than we thought and that her passengers would spend seven perilous days on her, during which time she constantly fought the river and only made 35 miles altogether. Her machinery broke down at least a dozen times. And once something went wrong with her steering apparatus and she ran full speed ahead into a rocky shore where her bottom was scraped and part of her bow violently torn away. Finally, after a frightful week, the party of men, with nerves shattered, managed to get her back to Dawson, coming down with a terrific ice floe and mighty glad to be alive!

It was later recounted how Thomas McGee and his party, after their perilous trip on the *Koekuk,* finally started back up the Yukon in Indian canoes. Many times they were nearly capsized or crushed against the ice; and once they were caught in such a dangerous place in the ice floes that their Indian guide broke down and wept—a thing almost unheard of for an Indian. He was sure their canoes and they themselves would be crushed to death. But, at long last, they arrived at Fort Selkirk, and from there began the heartbreaking trek overland on the Dalton Trail, which, by late October, was covered with two feet of snow. It was said, if it hadn't been for Dalton, the trader, and his party of Indians, whom they met about 75 miles out from Fort Selkirk, they would have perished from exposure and lack of food. Dalton tried to get them to return to Fort Selkirk for the winter, but McGee and his party refused, because, they said, there was hardly any food there. When Dalton saw he could not persuade them to turn back, he mapped out the rest of their course to Chilcat and told them where there were several shelters and hidden caches of food along the trail.

Later, elderly Sam McGee became so ill that his friends

strapped him to a sled and pulled him painfully over the snow. It was about 20 degrees below zero. All in the party suffered from exposure and frostbite. Even with Dalton's valuable instructions, several times they lost their way and missed one of the hidden food caches and nearly starved to death. Many times the men despaired and thought they would never get McGee to the coast alive. But, somehow, after forty days of almost unbelievable suffering and overwhelming hardships, the disheartened little band of men finally reached the Chilkat Indian village on Lynn Canal. From there, some Indians took them to Skagway, where they boarded the steamer, *City of Seattle*, for home!

And so ended the eventful expedition which began with the little *Koekuk* at Dawson. But many more tales could be told, some of which did not have as happy an ending!

On the afternoon of September 27th, a cry went up in Dawson, "A boat! A boat is coming from the north! . . . The Indians from the mountains have signaled they've spotted a boat coming up the Yukon!"

All Dawson, wild with excitement, rushed to the river, waiting jubilantly, eagerly, hopefully.

And then, it came around the bend—a tiny little boat! Like a sighing of the wind, hundreds of men sucked in their breath in bitter disappointment and waited. After a long watch, during which time we could see the men struggling against the current and the ice, we saw there were only three in the boat—a white man and two Indians.

"It's Captain Hanson! Captain Hanson and his two Indian scouts!" shouted the men who recognized him along the shore. "He's come to tell us the news!"

A deadly calm settled over the crowd as we watched the three men land in an opening of the ice. Then, in a great wave of questioning, we rushed to the spot, shouting, "What's the news, Captain Hanson? What's the news?"

Captain Hanson leaped onto the ice and raised his hands for silence. He was a tall, commanding figure. His face was haggard and blue with the cold and he looked almost ill.

"Men of Dawson," he called in a loud, shaking voice, "there will be no more river boats up here until next spring! My Indians and I have poled three hundred and fifty miles up the river from Circle City to tell you this. We've been nearly two weeks on the way. I advise all of you who are out of provisions or who haven't enough to carry you through the winter to make a dash for the 'Outside.' There's no time to lose! There are some supplies left at Fort Yukon by the *Hamilton*. Whichever way you go—up the river or down the river—it's hazardous! But you must make the try!"

For a few seconds, we all stood in dumb, stunned silence. Nothing was heard but the crackling and grinding of the ice in the river. Then, suddenly, great consternation swept through the crowd. Pandemonium broke loose. The few women in the crowd screamed and some fainted. There was a frenzied rush to tents and shacks and to boats, frantic trading and bartering of food and supplies. All the restaurants closed! There was panicky, hysterical talk! There were angry words, shouts, curses, quarreling and fist fights! Within a short time, several hundred men hurriedly shoved off, some going downstream, but most of them poling frantically up the river. The great "starvation exodus" from Dawson had begun!

Within the hour, warning signs were posted all over Dawson by the Mounted Police: "Men, flee for your lives. All who remain in Dawson without adequate food do so at their own risk!"

It was late in the day and the seven of us hastily made last-minute preparations to leave, but decided not to pull away from Dawson until morning. That night, two of us at a time took turns standing guard over our boat with guns!

That night, no one slept. The town was in a wild uproar! It was the blackest, the most brutish night in the history of the gold camp! The cold, nerve-splitting air jangled with the discordant sounds of thousands of men in a mad frenzy. Wildness, drunkenness, stalked the streets. Caches were robbed. Shots rang out. Grim-faced men with guns defiantly stood guard over their precious food supplies. The worst in man raged unchecked. It seemed all hell broke loose that night in Dawson!

The Mounted Police had to turn their backs, deafen their ears. They could not cope with the situation and they didn't try.

And, as if to add to the great commotion of man, suddenly the Northern Lights began to play furiously across the sky in fast-moving shafts of multicolored lights, darting here and there crazily, at all angles, as if the universe, too, had suddenly gone on a mad, wild rampage!

And all through the night, the malemutes strained at their leashes and howled to the wolves over the hills, which seemed to have sensed our great distress in Dawson!

The next morning, on September 28th, the seven of us shoved off and started on our momentous trip down the Yukon. As we pulled away from Dawson, we noticed there were very few boats left along the waterfront. Most of them had gone the day before in the frenzied exodus. We knew there were still hundreds of fellows stuck in Dawson who wanted desperately to leave but could not—there were not enough boats!

As the current swung us rapidly toward the bend of the river, I gave one last look at Dawson, which, in July, had seemed like a glittering City of Promise, but which now had become a City of Despair! I had come into the Klondike full of eagerness and hope, with what had seemed like a good grubstake to Fortune; but now I was leaving practically empty-handed!

With mixed emotions, my thoughts raced back over my activities of the last three months of summer, and my futile search for gold . . . and to that worthless Bonanza hillside claim of mine! Damn that claim! It was in sharp contrast to the exciting Big Skookum Gulch stampede in which I could have no part!

With a sigh, I turned away . . . and grimly faced down river.

The wind had suddenly changed to the north and a raw, piercing gale whipped up the Yukon, chilling us to the very marrow. The temperature was dropping fast. Large chunks of ice were flowing savagely in the river, churning and grinding at each other like clawing, wild beasts. And the cold, chilling waters swirled around our boat as the winds from the opposite direction lashed at us like stinging scorpions. For a man to fall into that icy hell of water would mean certain death. He couldn't last five minutes!

We were riding with the current, dodging the ice floes, taking turns steering the boat while the other fellows huddled under canvas to keep warm, with only their heads sticking out. Most of us had grown beards. And now small icicles, formed from our warm breath, hung from our chins.

About twenty-five miles below Dawson, suddenly, to our utter amazement, we saw a river boat fighting her way upstream. We rubbed our eyes in astonishment and watched her as she gallantly fought her way against the heavy ice floes. When she finally came closer, we could see the name on her bow.

"What do you know?" said Captain Tibbetts. "It's the *Weaver* bravely making her way to Dawson!"

Swinging closer, we could see the deck hands. Frantically, joyfully, we all waved and shouted, and the captain blasted his whistle in grand salute.

"Hurrah! Hurrah for the *Weaver!*" we all shouted exultantly. "Say, are you bringing any food?"

"*Say, are you bringing any food?*" our echoes shouted back at us from the high hills along the Yukon.

We waited expectantly for the echo to die; and then it came—the reply from the *Weaver*. "Not much food," called a deck hand. "Gonna try to get to Dawson to pick up passengers."

And as the echo chanted again the reply, we all looked at each in dread.

"My God!" said Calhoun. "What joy . . . and what bitter disappointment the *Weaver* will bring to Dawson—if she does get through!"

We all fell silent, each with his own thoughts . . . I thought of the fellows back there whom I knew. And I wondered what would become of Coates, the tired, broken old man; and Linc Davis and Patton from Tacoma; I thought of Wheeler, the fellow with pleurisy; poor Wheezy, the fellow with asthma; I thought of Euly Gaisford; Captain Breeze; Captain Ellis; and, of course, good old Stacey . . . all of Tacoma. What would become of them? And, too, I thought of Mrs. Ryan, the plucky little woman who had come into the country with her husband and party at the same time Stacey, Jourgensen, Crawford and I had come into the Klondike. And I thought of the many other fine fellows I had met in Dawson. What would become of all these people? Would I ever see them again?

But, what was ahead of us on the river? And would we ever reach home?

We spent a long, bitterly cold day on the river. Our boat was almost like an egg shell against the strength of the ice . . . and it was necessary for us to keep going with the current in the center of the river, constantly alert, constantly fighting being hemmed in by ice floes.

"Aren't we almost to Forty Mile?" asked Bertram anxiously through chattering teeth. "We're almost frozen stiff. It must be at least seven degrees below zero!"

"Probably is!" replied Captain Tibbetts, pulling the hood of his parka closer around his face. "It's mighty cold. Fellows, we've got to pull in at Forty Mile for sure, got to get out of these dangerous ice floes before dark; got to build a fire and get warm, or we'll be in bad shape from the cold!"

A little later, Shelley Graves, who was in the bow of the boat, suddenly screamed, "My God, we're being hemmed in by the ice! We'll be crushed to death!"

Chapter XV

Stowaways Under the Northern Lights

What could be more terrifying to a party of men than to find themselves suddenly caught among crushing, fast-moving ice floes in a small, open boat? Such was our hazardous predicament on that fateful day of September 28th, 1897!

But even though Fortune had turned her back on all seven of us in the Klondike, Providence seemed to hold a protecting hand over us in the dangerous places on the river. It seemed inevitable that we would be crushed to death. But all at once, the great, menacing chunks of ice began moving slowly away from our boat as though propelled by an unseen force, and, to our utter amazement, we were unhurt and free again to continue down the

Yukon. From this terrifying experience, we shivered from fright, and also from the bitter, penetrating cold.

All that day since leaving Dawson, we had been riding downriver through a silent wilderness of floating ice, snow and high mountains. Strange as it may seem, we had not caught sight of a soul since passing the steamer *Weaver* fighting her way so unexpectedly up to Dawson. Now, as it grew much later in the afternoon, we viewed those high, snow-covered mountains bordering the Yukon with great alarm. There seemed to be no good place to land. And as the light began rapidly to fade, these mountains loomed up higher against the cold, graying skies like sinister, crouching monsters.

In mounting apprehension, we watched for Forty Mile, the old gold camp on the left bank. Just a little bit before 6 P.M. the bulky, mountainous shoreline receded to the left and, in the failing light, we spotted quite a large river of dark, gun-metal color coming into the Yukon through a U-shaped cut in the high mountains which stood back perhaps three quarters of a mile from the Yukon. We knew this was the Forty Mile River and that the old gold camp must be right there at its mouth, and as we drew closer to the left shore, we could spot dozens of log cabins along both banks of the Forty Mile River on a low flat, silhouetted against the snow.

Fiercely, we fought our way out of the rapid, ice-laden current of the Yukon River and up the murky, almost closed channel of the Forty Mile River for about a hundred feet, where we made a quick landing against the almost solid shore ice at the left bank just as darkness fell. Quickly, we leaped ashore and tied up our boat. How thankful we were to have our feet safe on shore!

But it gave us an eerie feeling to see how dark and desolate the place was. Not a single light glimmered in any of the cabins, and although we had heard that the gold camp had been practically abandoned, we were not prepared to find it so utterly deserted.

Hurriedly, we pushed open the nearest cabin door and lit a candle and looked inquiringly inside. There, to our great joy and relief, we saw a Klondike stove, two beds with real bedsteads, a table and some chairs. There was even a pile of wood by the stove. In no time, we were warming ourselves by a crackling fire. We blessed the last occupant, whoever he was, for observing the etiquette of the North, thoughtfully leaving wood in readiness for the next fellow. We were truly grateful! Countless times it had been the means of saving the lives of freezing men. And this particular night, we were frozen to the bone, having spent eight long hours out on the river!

After becoming thoroughly warmed and eating ravenously a carefully rationed supper from our slim supply of food, we fellows spread out in the cabin and relaxed a little, smoked our pipes and talked of Dawson. Fate had certainly dealt us some bad cards, we all agreed, forcing us out of the Klondike, away from our hearts' desire . . . gold! But, after all, we agreed again, it was much better to be taking our chances on the river, no matter how dangerous, than to 've stayed in Dawson to starve.

Now, for the first time since we seven fellows had been thrown together by circumstances, we began visiting, talking of home and ourselves.

Captain Tibbetts, I discovered, had been a real sea captain, once master of a small ship running between Juneau and the States; N. H. Bertram had been manager of a general store in Juneau; George Hill was a middle-aged writer and former newspaper man from Seattle, out to get his fortune; Billy Moore was a building contractor from San Francisco who said he'd like to get into politics if he ever reached home again. T. W. Calhoun didn't say what he was, nor did Shelley Graves; but Shelley was about twenty, and I surmised that he had probably skipped the last years of college for adventure in the gold rush. Being the youngest of the party, he was vibrant with strength and enthusiasm. Captain Tibbetts was the eldest of the crowd; Bertram, Calhoun and I were about the same age, around thirty.

"What a fine group of men!" I thought as I looked at them. It seemed we couldn't have been better suited if we had taken weeks to form our party. In the danger spots on the river, every man had kept his head. This was a mighty good sign, I thought.

"What do you men think our next move should be, now that we've reached Forty Mile safely?" I asked.

"It's a cinch we don't want to be frozen in at this deserted, Godforsaken spot!" said Shelley Graves with a shiver.

"Great Scott, no!" agreed Captain Tibbetts, "even though tonight this place is a welcome haven of refuge. But, men, today has certainly given us a foretaste of what fifteen hundred miles of river to St. Michael will be like!"

We all fell silent for a little, while the cold northwind whined outside the cabin, reminding us what a lonely, isolated spot we were in. And in the long, eloquent pause which followed, our imaginations ran rampant. Mentally, we began taking serious stock of our situation. Here we were, several thousand miles from home, with only about a week's or ten days' supply of food left. Winter was closing in, the ice slowly locking the river to boat travel! There was uncertainty as to the fate of the *Weaver,* which was surely the last boat of the season! Yes, it was truly a frightening prospect for any group of men!

"Well," said Tibbetts, glancing around the circle of tense faces as he pulled out his small poke of gold dust and laid it on the table, "I know I haven't enough gold to pay passage all the way home. But I'd give all this gold if only I could go down the river on the *Weaver.* Once at St. Michael, we might catch a late steamer or whaler headed for the States. Believe me, I'd take my chances on any ship . . . and would even be mighty glad to work for my passage."

"You said it, Tibbetts. Those are exactly my sentiments, too," agreed Calhoun. "And I think we're all about in the same fix as for gold. Look! Here's my poke. And it's mighty slim, too!"

"Yes, and here's mine," said Bertram as he put his small poke of gold on the table. "What wouldn't I give to set foot in Seattle again!"

"Me, too," said Moore. "And this is all I've got to get me back to the States."

"And here's mine," said Shelley Graves, flinging his down.

"And mine, too," George Hill and I both said as we laid

our small pokes with the others.

"Well, fellows," I said, eying the seven small pokes of gold in the center of the table, "it's plain to be seen . . . none of us are Klondike Kings! By all indications, we should continue downriver in our open boat. And, as Tibbetts suggests, once at St. Michael maybe we could work our way back to the States. I, for one, would like to save what little gold I have. I'd hate to arrive home flat broke!"

"Me, too," said Calhoun. "But how about trying to work for our passage downriver on the *Weaver* if she comes back? At Forty Mile she's sure to stop to take on wood at the big woodpile!"

"Ha! you're right," agreed Shelley Graves.

"Yes," said Moore, "but you can bet your last ounce of gold that the *Weaver* will be loaded to the guards with fellows trying to escape the famine."

"It's almost certain, then," said Bertram seriously, "that they will not have room for us on the *Weaver*, in any case."

"Well," broke in Shelley Graves, "if they won't take us even to work our way, then I, for one, will try to sneak aboard. And if I succeed, you fellows could do the same!"

"As stowaways!" we all exclaimed, aghast.

"Yes, you bet, that's just what I mean—as stowaways!" he replied with a determined gleam in his eyes.

"But how in creation could a party of seven get themselves aboard without being seen?" I asked incredulously.

"Ha! I think I know just how," said Captain Tibbetts. "I haven't been a sea captain for nothing! Men, we're in a mighty tough spot here. I certainly don't relish the idea of continuing downriver in our open boat."

We all nodded tensely, realizing that our plans, and perhaps our very lives, hinged on the fate of the *Weaver*.

Being very exhausted and with thoughts full of misgivings for the future, we rolled wearily in our sleeping bags and slept fitfully. But all during the night we took turns stoking the fire while the temperature outside dropped lower and lower; and before morning it had hit 10 degrees below zero.

At daybreak, we awakened to a magnificent, but cold and frightening scene of more ice and snow surrounding us; and, to our consternation, found our little boat frozen in solidly in the Forty Mile River. But, fortunately, there was still a free-moving channel at the very mouth of the Forty Mile, and also in the center of the Yukon. However, both channels had grown alarmingly narrower during the night, with more and more large chunks of anchor ice clogging the river, some caught in between clutching fingers of ice reaching out from both shores.

"Good Lord," cried Captain Tibbetts, grabbing an axe. "We've got to chop our boat out of the solid ice . . . and quick! She's still our only means of escape:"

We all grabbed axes and frantically chopped the boat loose, then pulled her up on the shore ice and held a council.

"Great guns!" exclaimed Moore. "If this weather continues, the river could close in most any minute. I think we should pull out of here immediately."

"But, fellows," said Tibbetts, "I figure that if the *Weaver* did reach Dawson last night and started back down the river this morning, she should reach here this afternoon, and she'll most certainly stop for wood. It'll be worth the risk to wait right here."

"But how long can we risk waiting?" asked Calhoun anxiously.

"Not more than just today, at the very most," replied Tibbetts. "After that, we'll certainly have to start out again in our boat and make a dash for Circle City or Fort Yukon, where we might be able to wangle enough food to help us get down the Yukon. Or, who knows? we might even be able to get on a boat that we don't know of, making a run for it to St. Michael," he added hopefully.

"Yeah, but Circle City and Fort Yukon are from three hundred to four hundred miles away," said Calhoun dubiously, "and from there we'll still have over a thousand miles through a gauntlet of ice to reach the coast. And don't forget, fellows, then it'll be Bering Sea!"

"Good Lord!" said Tibbetts, "I know, the odds seem to be terribly against us. But are you willing to trust my judgment and wait for the *Weaver*?"

"We'll wait, Tibbetts," we all answered earnestly.

While waiting impatiently and uneasily for the *Weaver*, we began poking around among the deserted cabins, all the time keeping an eye on the river. But time seemed to drag intolerably heavy on our hands.

"Great guns!" exclaimed George Hill. "What wouldn't Dawson give for these snug cabins! Why, the miners would pay a pretty fortune for them, perhaps five or six thousand apiece. It would be a veritable Bonanza in real estate. Seems a crime for them to be empty when hundreds of poor fellows are shivering in tents in Dawson right now. Here these cabins sit, furniture, stoves and all, with only the mice to enjoy them!"

"Yes, this place is sure a ghost town!" said Shelley Graves. "Kind of gives me the willies. Just looks like everybody picked up and left in a powerful hurry."

"It surely does," said Tibbetts. "Guess it was just a little over a year ago—August seventeenth, to be exact—when George Carmack made that exciting, big discovery up there on Bonanza Creek. That was the news that rocked the world a few months later. And just think how that discovery has changed the destiny and lives of thousands of fellows, including ourselves. It certainly was the death blow to Forty Mile! They say when Carmack and his two Indians tore down here to Forty Mile to register their newly discovered claims, they had nuggets that set this town agog, and soon the place was roaring with the gold fever, although for ten years or more they'd been finding gold in good-paying quantities here along the Forty Mile. However, they say it was just about all worked out, yet the claims are still held by the old-timers."

"Jumpin' Jupiter!" exclaimed Shelley Graves. "I'll bet it was a wild-eyed stampede out o' here! Golly, how I'd like to 've been here! Just looks like they grabbed food, blankets and gold pans and took off on the run for those millions in the Klondike!"

"Guess that's about right," said George Hill. "And that's how those lucky fellows like the Berry brothers, Antone Standar, Frank Phiscator, Knutson, Cobb, Thomas Lippy, Alexander McDonald, and some of the rest, got the choicest claims and became real Klondike Kings!"

"And, yes," said Captain Tibbetts, "I've heard it said the little steamer *Ellis* happened to come plowing up the Yukon just about that time, and one hundred and fifty miners jumped aboard from here and went along, steaming up the Yukon towards the place that is now Dawson. All landed at the mouth of the Klondike River, getting there only a few days after the big strike. Of course, in no time flat, all of those lucky miners were tearing along the Bonanza and Eldorado, staking like mad. Holy mackerel! What a stampede it turned out to be!"

"Yes," I said, "and don't forget the fellows from Circle City, too, how they poled over three hundred and fifty miles up the Yukon to the Klondike River. McPhee told me some of the fellows in Circle City were dead drunk when the news struck, but their buddies just piled them into boats and took them along anyway. Those drunks were the possessors of what later proved to be some of the richest claims. By George! Just think how close all those men really were to the most fabulous gold deposits the world has ever seen. Fortune was surely smiling on them! Why, those men at Forty Mile and Circle City were only a stone's throw away from the Klondike, in comparison to the great distances we stampeders had to come."

While discussing the beginning of the exciting Klondike gold rush, we all walked across a little foot bridge spanning the Forty Mile River to the other side, where there were a number of rather large log buildings and more cabins.

"This must be the Fort Cudahy side I've heard so much about," I said as we looked around. "And there are the old warehouses of the N.A.T. Company by the river. And there's the old trading post itself. Yes, and that must be the Mounted Police barracks," I said, indicating a log house with bars at the windows and a flagpole still standing in front.

"Gosh, everything looks awfully deserted around here; but if these buildings could only talk," said Shelley Graves, "what wouldn't they tell?"

"Yes," agreed Bertram, "I'll bet they could tell many an exciting tale!"

"I used to hear some of the tales," said Captain Tibbetts. "Some of the passengers who got on at Juneau used to say that Fort Cudahy was quite a lively place a few years ago. Said it was originally the biggest trading center for trappers, miners and Indians in this region. They said that John Cudahy, of the wealthy Cudahys of the Chicago meat packers, was one of the big trading company's founders. Yes, sir, a syndicate of Eastern capitalists established the North American Transportation and Trading Company."

"By the way, fellows," I said, "did you know that the Canadian-American boundary line passes only about twenty-five miles from Forty Mile? They say if you were to draw a straight line from Mount Saint Elias, near the Gulf of Alaska to a place called Demarcation Point, near Icy Reef in the Arctic Ocean, you would have the Canadian-American boundary line. Just think, it took William Ogilvie and his surveyors ten years to survey it. They finally got it straightened out shortly before the Klondike gold rush. Lucky thing, too, because people up in this area half the time didn't know whether they were on American or Canadian soil after Alaska was purchased from Russia. In fact, it was definitely determined, when Ogilvie surveyed the boundary line, that old Fort Yukon, which had been established by the Canadian Hudson Bay Company years ago, was really on American soil. They say, also, that George Carmack came over Chilkoot Pass with the famous Ogilvie surveying party over ten years ago. But, of course, Carmack didn't stay with them. Got sidetracked at the Tagish Indian village. Married Kate, one of their beautiful Indian squaws. They say she was with him when he discovered the gold, as were Tagish Charlie and Skookum Jim."

"Well, that's fate for you!" said Moore.

"But to get back to the vital subject of food," said Shelley Graves, "this cold weather has increased my appetite. Golly! I'm hungry as a wolf! D'you suppose there could possibly be any food in those warehouses? Man, oh, man, I could sink my teeth into some good old canned beef!"

"Well, couldn't we all," I said as we walked rapidly towards the buildings. But after peering carefully into all of the darkened, partly boarded windows, it was quite evident that the shelves were absolutely empty.

"Gosh, what a forlorn hope that was!" said Calhoun in disappointment. "Cleaned out, slick as a whistle . . . and me with a gnawing ache in my stomach!"

"Yes," I said as I pulled my little diary from an inner

pocket to make some important notations and to get my mind off our disappointment, "but isn't it strange how a gold camp like this can become absolutely deserted and almost forgotten! It makes me wonder if Dawson could some day have a similar fate."

"Great Scott, no!" said Shelley Graves vehemently. "That could never happen, not in a hundred years! Why, Dawson is practically sitting on the biggest pile of gold in the world!"

"I hope you're right, Shelley," I said fervently, "because I want to come back some day to try for my share of that illusive gold! Fellows. I've bucked misfortune ever since I came into the Klondike . . . like the rest of you. Seems I've miscalculated every move. But such bad luck surely can't pursue a fellow forever!"

"Hell, no!" said Shelley Graves explosively. "Believe me, Ed, I'm going back to Dawson too, some day!"

The pale winter sun was sinking behind the mountains when we returned over the foot bridge to our cabin on the Forty Mile side of the old gold camp. Before entering, we scanned the Yukon anxiously for the *Weaver;* but, as yet, there was no sign of her. Naturally, we wondered if she had slipped by unnoticed. The very thought of it gave us the chills.

Back in the cabin, we built the fire up to get warm, as the weather had turned much colder. One of the fellows found a deck of cards and so, to pass the time, we played a few games of whist. Often, however, we put down our cards nervously, paced up and down like caged lions and looked anxiously through the small window facing the Yukon. But still, no sign of the *Weaver!*

"Where in tarnation is that blasted boat?" roared Tibbetts, pounding his clenched fist on the table. "She'd better show up. Why, we could have been fifty miles down the Yukon by this time!"

About 4:30 in the afternoon, suddenly there came a loud knock on the cabin door. We all jumped to our feet in astonishment and Shelley Graves leaped to open the door.

"Well, well!" said a grizzled old miner, eyeing us from the doorway, "if it ain't a party o' men. I saw smoke comin' out o' this here chimney, so thought I'd better come over t' investigate. I jest got in from up the creek a short time ago."

"Come on in," we all called. "We thought we were the only inhabitants of Forty Mile."

"No, ya ain't," said the miner, eyeing us carefully. "Ya see, I'm here as sort o' caretaker for the A.C. Trading Company on this side of the river, and also for the N.A.T. Company on the Fort Cudahy side—that is, when I'm not minin' up in the hills. Now 'n then, a few strays come in from the creeks, but, aside from that, I'm jest about the only one what lives around here any more. Jack McQuesten, that trader they call the 'Father of the Yukon,' was one of the last ta leave Forty Mile. He was manager of the A.C. Company. He went 'Outside' this summer. Said he guessed he might as well go a-visitin' in the States, since there was nothin' much doin' at Forty Mile no more. Guess ya saw them big, empty warehouses?"

"We surely did," I said. "And judging from their size, this must have been quite a gold camp."

"Yep, it shore was. But it ain't like it used ta be," said the old miner a little sadly as he came in and sat down. "No, sir, it ain't like it used ta be. Why, I've seed this place when it was jest plumb full o' people. Why, there used ta be a coupla hundred fellas here. We used to have shows 'n dance-hall girls 'n everythin' . . . 'n gold galore—jest like they're havin' at Dawson right now. Yea, sir, it's shore strange what a year kin do ta a fella and a town like this! Yep, it shore is strange . . . jest nothin' here any more," he said dolefully.

Then the old man went on to say that Forty Mile had had its lean years, too, years when the boats hadn't made it up the Yukon. But he said it had never looked as bad as it did now for Dawson and the entire Yukon country for the coming winter.

After a short while, the miner got up to leave, telling us he was going back into the hills for a day or two. But he warned us, saying, "Fellers, take it from me, there ain't a scrap o' food here in Forty Mile fer ya. If the *Weaver* comes down from Dawson 'n stops here for wood, I'm tellin' ya, ya'd better be on her when she leaves. Don't try ta go down that there river in yer open boat. I'm warnin' ya. It's too dangerous with them big chunks o' ice runnin' so heavy in the river. I don't think ya'd have a ghost of a chance. I know, 'cause I've seed boatloads of fellers crushed in the ice, right out there in the river in plain sight, and there wasn't a goldarned thing I could do ta help 'em. Yep, fellers, take it from me. Git out o' here while the gittin's good!"

After the old fellow had gone, a gloom fell over us, and silently we began eating a very skimpy supper, measuring every mouthful.

Suddenly, about five o'clock, Shelley Graves looked out of the cabin window and almost dropped his precious cup of coffee. "Hey, fellows, here comes the *Weaver!*" he yelled excitedly. "Here she comes, I tell you, and she's heading in to Forty Mile for a landing. She's coming in for wood!"

In wild excitement, we grabbed our parkas, pulling them on as we dashed out into the snow and onto the ice along shore and stood watching eagerly as the steamer struggled to point her prow into the mouth of the Forty Mile River. It was evident she was making for the big woodpile. But from her slow progress, we could see she was having a hard battle coming in against the terrific ice floes.

"Holy smoke!" exclaimed Tibbetts, "this boat doesn't look like the *Weaver*. She's much smaller and is pulling in from the direction of Circle City."

Breathlessly, we watched as the steamer's lights suddenly blazed on, as it was now getting dusk. After a frantic struggle, she finally reached the mouth of the Forty Mile and slid in against the shore ice almost directly in front of us.

"Great guns!" exclaimed Calhoun, "You're right, it's not the *Weaver*."

We all pressed closer as the captain came out of the pilot house and, leaning over the rail, gave crisp orders to the deck hands.

"Why, it's the little *Bella!*" I said, recognizing Captain Ball.

"Yes, it's the *Bella*, all right," said the captain. "But we've had a hell of a trip all the way up the Yukon. At Circle City while we were taking on wood, about two hundred miners swarmed aboard and ordered us at the point of guns to give up nearly all the cargo of food we had. I tell you, it was damnable and outrageous! And, to think, I had pledged to get that food to Dawson! It was rank piracy—nothing but rank piracy—forcing me at the point of guns, even though they brought gold dust to pay for the cargo they took!"

"Great Scott!" I said. "Those men must have been pretty desperate. But, Captain Ball, are you still going to try to make it up to Dawson?"

"You bet I am!" he replied fiercely. "There's only one thing to do now. Get up the river as fast as I can. Pick up as many hungry men at Dawson as possible and take them down to Circle City or Fort Yukon. I'm pulling out of here just as soon as those deck hands can get enough wood aboard."

"Captain, will you pick us up on your way back?" begged Tibbetts urgently.

"Sorry, fellows, I couldn't promise that. But if the *Weaver* comes down, better try to get on her. Of course, she'll probably be loaded, too. But I wish you luck, men—the best of luck!"

As we watched the little *Bella* pull away from Forty Mile and saw her struggling against the ice floes with searchlights blazing, George Hill commented, "That captain is a fool to try to make it to Dawson tonight!"

"Ah, no, he's a very brave man!" exclaimed Captain Tibbetts with great admiration.

When the lights of the gallant little ship had at last faded out of sight, we seven men felt more desolate than ever.

About 6 P.M., Shelley Graves, who had taken his turn at watching along the riverfront, burst into the cabin shouting excitedly, "Fellows, here comes the *Weaver!* This time I know it's the *Weaver*. See, she's headed in for a landing from the direction of Dawson. And Lord, let's hope she makes it!"

Again, as when the *Bella* had come in only an hour earlier, we raced out onto the ice and watched the captain blaze his lights along shore, searching for a place to land. Several times his lights flashed on us and we waved frantically, trying to guide her to the spot near the woodpile. At last, she found the almost identical place where the *Bella* had come in, and in a few minutes had made an expert landing alongside the shore ice.

But our great joy quickly turned to consternation when we saw she was riding very low in the water and that her decks were black with men!

Hurriedly, a gangplank was pushed ashore and immediately a crew of deck hands with wheelbarrows went scurrying over the ice to the woodpile and started loading the boat amidst a clanging of bells and a grand commotion on deck.

The captain, the purser and several others came out onto the ice with lanterns, inspecting the boat and sternwheel paddles for any possible damage from the ice.

"Captain, how're chances of getting aboard?" asked Tibbetts, stepping forward eagerly.

"Sorry," the captain replied sternly, "but we positively can't take on another passenger. Can't you see? We're already loaded to the guards, way beyond capacity!"

"I am sorry, though," he added, softening a bit, "but we took on all we possibly could at Dawson. Had to pull away leaving hundreds of men still begging to get aboard . . . men who would have paid anything to've been on their way 'Outside.' By the way," he added, "we passed the *Bella* about a half hour ago. If she makes it back down the river, you men better try to get on her, because, as I said before, we can't possibly take you."

We all looked at each other. Well, that was it! No need to stand here any longer shivering on the ice. No need to argue. There was no doubt about the finality of Captain Geiger's voice.

Just as we turned to go back to the cabin, we overheard the captain say to a passenger, "No, we're not leaving Forty Mile till morning. It's too dangerous. There's a bad stretch ahead. We'll pull out of here at daybreak and make a dash for it!"

Back in the cabin, we seven men grabbed our things and began rolling them into tight, compact bundles to strap on our backs.

Then, for nearly four hours, we kept a close vigil, tensely

watching the *Weaver* from our cabin window as, one by one, her lights went out along the decks. By eleven o'clock, all was silent and there seemed to be only two lights left burning—a dim light in the captain's cabin and another on a lower deck, probably in the men's washroom.

Now we were ready to try our scheme.

"It's very dark, and that's in our favor," said Captain Tibbetts. "Here's the plan, fellows: After we blow out the candle, each man, at fifteen-minute intervals, will quietly leave the cabin and walk stealthily down onto the ice towards the rear of the *Weaver*. She's firmly anchored tight against the shore ice, so no need to worry. Each one, when he reaches the rear of the boat, should swing himself up cautiously from the ice onto the deck, where there's an open space. He should be very careful not to make any noise, and, once aboard, should immediately lose himself on the boat in the darkness."

"Yes," said Shelley Graves. "I want to go first. But I must warn you—the deck hand said there will be men sleeping all over the boat. Says there just aren't enough sleeping spaces. So watch your step, fellows, and don't stumble over anyone. Believe me, I'm going to be careful!"

"Do you think they'll see us?" asked George Hill nervously.

"No," laughed Captain Tibbetts softly, "I don't think they'll see us. But, fellows, if we should get caught, promise me you won't tell Captain Gieger that I'm a former sea captain. Naturally, it would be quiet embarassing."

"No, we won't," we all promised.

"Another thing," said Captain Tibbetts, "try to bed down near the engine room, if possible. But, of course, I know it'll be the most popular place on the boat. It's going to be mighty cold on deck!"

By 1:00 P.M. all was well with us. Our entire party of men had slipped aboard the *Weaver* according to plan and were scattered in various parts of the boat. And by the pale light of a lantern in the men's wash room, I took the time to add a few hasty lines to my diary of my impressions of Forty Mile.

Sept. 29, 1897 (Forty Mile—Cold!)
The steamer *Bella* passed at 5 P.M. and landed at the Forty Mile side. The steamer *Weaver* came down at 6 P.M. We all scrambled aboard. It was so dark they couldn't see us!

After adding this brief entry in my diary, I flipped the pages back to the entry I had made only two days previously to see what I had written under stress and in the wild excitement of that last momentous day in Dawson.

Sept. 27, 1897 (Dawson—Cold)
Captain Hanson came back from Circle City. Poled all the way . . . over 350 miles. Two Indians brought him. Says no more boats will be up this fall. Consternation reigns supreme! Men out of grub and will have to leave the country. I am in a pretty pickle! I think it's really too late to go up the river, and our only chance is to go down to Fort Yukon and stand chance of getting steamer to take us to St. Michael. Mr. Coates is almost crying. We will start tomorrow in an open boat for Fort Yukon. There are seven of us. Everyone is ore-eyed. More excitement here. Some men are brutes!

What a hectic twenty-four hours that had been! Long would I remember it!

As I looked through a porthole of the *Weaver* out onto the dark, icy Yukon, I wondered: Where were those hundreds of men who had started from Dawson in that freezing weather in open boats? How fortunate we were to be aboard the *Weaver!*

Suddenly, I turned and caught sight of myself in the little mirror in the men's room and said with a sheepish grin, "Why, Ed Lung, who'd have thought you would ever be a stowaway?"

Chapter XVI

Gold Rush Reporter—Joaquin Miller

It was now late morning of October 1st, 1897.

Like phantom ships, huge chunks of snow-covered ice slid past the *Weaver.* Our ship was making good speed, considering the heavy ice, and we were now about seventy-five miles below the old gold camp of Forty Mile. All of us knew it would be a miracle if the ship got through the ice floes and up past the Arctic Circle.

"Holy mackerel! It's cold as hell out here on deck!" said Captain Tibbetts as he braced himself against the cutting, tearing, snow-filled wind sweeping across the Yukon from the north. "Ed, I haven't talked to you since we all slipped aboard last night. Man, oh, man! Am I glad we waited for the *Weaver!* A mighty good thing, too, it was so dark when we scrambled aboard and no one noticed us!"

"Yes, luck certainly was with us," I said. "But it makes me feel bad when I see those wrecked boats sticking up out of the ice. We've passed at least a dozen already."

"Yes," said Tibbetts, "poor devils! . . . I'm wondering if they were any of our friends?"

"We'll probably never know," I said: "but, Tibbetts, where are all of the fellows in our crowd?"

"Well," he said, "so far all is well with us. I've just been checking on the boys in our party. Shelley Graves seems to be having the time of his life. Saw him in a couple of crap games. The other fellows are talking to the miners. Man, oh, man! This little ship is sure loaded to the guards. And I'm telling you, some of the fellows on board are loaded with gold. Most say they're mighty darned glad to be getting out of the Klondike. Say they're never coming back!"

"Yes," I said, "I've been talking to some of them also. Have been mixing with the crowds all over the ship, as you suggested last night. But, Tibbetts, I haven't seen a soul I really know. However, I just had a talk with Joaquin Miller, the famous gold-rush reporter. I was certainly surprised to see him aboard. Had heard he was going 'Outside' over the Dalton Trail with Dalton himself. But Joaquin said, when the steamer *Weaver* arrived in Dawson so unexpectedly, he just grabbed his things and got on board . . . and considered himself mighty lucky. He also considers himself mighty lucky not to have had to walk hundreds of miles through deep snows over the Dalton Trail. Says he still feels the effects of that long, hard trek over Chilkoot Pass, which was less than two months ago. Tibbetts, I was surprised when Joaquin Miller told me he was in his middle fifties. He doesn't look it! Carried an eighty-pound pack over Chilkoot! Packed in just like the other miners."

"Great Scott!" said Tibbetts. "Imagine a poet, a fellow who probably hasn't done a lick of work in his life, packing over Chilkoot Pass!"

"Yes, but Joaquin Miller is not just an ordinary poet," I explained. "He has lived in the out-of-doors most of his life and has tremendous vitality. He doesn't look a day over forty."

"Sounds like quite an interesting character," said Tibbetts.

"Yes," I said, "and we talked of many things to pass the time. Naturally, in the course of our conversation, I told him of my own hazardous trip into the Klondike, and he spontaneously said, 'Then, Ed Lung, you, too, banged at the Chilkoot—that rock-locked gate to the golden door. And didn't it seem God didn't care and that God wasn't there?' Of course, Tibbetts, Joaquin Miller was waxing poetic, but his words certainly described the hellish Chilkoot, which most of us have cause to remember. I agreed with him, too, that in this vast wilderness, when a fellow finds himself alone, it seems the deadly silence thunders from the mountaintops.

"He showed me a handful of big nuggets he had acquired in the Klondike, saying, 'This is a majestic country, a marvelous country, but you can have it all and all of its gold! As for me—give me California and its brown-gold hills. And let me stand on the "Heights," my home overlooking the sun-kissed bay of San Francisco. But if I were a younger man,' he added, 'I would then say: Yes, give me this great country for a few years, and let me wrestle with it and let me try to conquer it for a while!'

"As we were talking, it began to snow and Joaquin said eloquently, 'Ah, cold, white petals from heaven!' Then he invited me into his stateroom. Said, 'Come on in, Ed, where it's warm.' So I, not having a stateroom of my own, was eager to get inside, and once there, was reluctant to leave, so I stayed on. We smoked our pipes and talked for several hours and discovered we had mutual friends in Dawson and in the East. One in particular—Walt Whitman—though he's been dead the past five years. You see, Tibbetts, I was glad to talk of Walt Whitman, the famous poet, because he used to be a neighbor of ours. Lived 'catercorner' across the street from us in Camden, New Jersey. He used to come often to our parsonage to hear my father preach on Sundays at the Baptist church. Used to bring his manuscripts to read to us, too. I mentioned to Joaquin Miller that my father used to say, 'Walt, you are a great poet. Someday, America will really appreciate you, but it may not come in your lifetime.'

"Then Joaquin Miller said, 'How right your father was, Ed! Walt Whitman was a truly great man, and is growing greater since his death. I knew him well. How I admired him! Truly, he had his fingers on the pulse of America . . . understood and wrote about the rugged qualities which have helped build our great country. I wonder what he would have written about this country and the big stampedes? I wonder what his rhythm of the North would have been . . . with the beat of gold?'

"When I remarked to Joaquin that he reminded me very much of Walt Whitman in appearance, he seemed greatly pleased and said, 'Why, Ed, I've been told that many times before.' Then he grinned and said, 'People often used to say that both our figures and figures of speech were quite similar. They say that, in our poetry, we both sing the Songs of the Soul and hear the Sylvan Voices of Nature . . . and —love the women! God bless the women!' he ended with a twinkle in his blue eyes.

"I was just thinking, Tibbetts, when you found me here on deck, what a small world this is. Wasn't it strange that I should have come to the top of the world to meet America's other great pioneer poet? And that I should be a stowaway?"

"Sure is, Ed. Are you making a note of Joaquin Miller in your diary?"

"You bet I am!" I replied. "Hope he doesn't find out about me, though."

"Don't worry!" said Tibbetts. "But say, Ed, is he the fellow with the long, graying blond hair and blue eyes . . . and wears big whiskers which cover about two thirds of his face? Is he tall and lean, sticks close to the captain? Heard him say he has some valuable documents he must get 'Outside' at all costs. Heard him say millions of people were waiting anxiously to read his stories of the gold rush."

"Yes, that's Joaquin Miller," I said, "and anything he writes and signs his name to has the magic touch."

"Yep, he shore is quite a feller, all right," broke in a miner who had been listening. "He's had plenty of adventure in his lifetime, too. Heard ya talkin' about that Miller. I was mighty surprised when he told a crowd of us gathered around him last night that he was only fourteen when he ran away from home in Eugene, Oregon. Said he made fer Mount Shasty where he got a job as cook fer a lot o' miners. But, one day, he said he seen a visitor ta camp a-fillin' his shoes wi' gold dust as he was gittin' ready ta leave. Well, that fella Miller says he ran fast as he could ta tell tha miners they was a-being robbed. An' what d'ya know? Them miners grabbed that thief jest as he was gonna make his gitaway, and they was gonna hang him on the spot. But finally decides they was gonna make him dig his own grave first.

"But that made Joaquin Miller awful sick. Said he never counted on seein' a feller hanged right in front o' his eyes. He said he got sicker n' sicker as he watched that thief feller a-diggin' his grave; and jest about as the grave was finished and them miners was gittin' the rope ready, Miller ups 'n tells the miners he just couldn't cook fer 'em any more if they went on wi' that hangin'! Well, the miners saw right away they was in a tight spot fer a cook; and the thief, he saw he was in a tighter spot, so right quick-like he tells 'em he has a sweetheart over on that Oregon coast, and he was right sure if they spared his life, she'd come a-runnin' ta cook fer 'em . . . and that she was a helluva good cook, too!"

"What happened then?" we all asked breathlessly.

"Well, ta make a long story short, that gal sweetheart o' his come a-runnin' post-haste ta save her sweetie's neck n' starts cookin' fer tha miners like mad. And, by golly, what d'ya know! Soon there was ta be a weddin' and all o' tha miners was invited. Yes, sir, and Joaquin Miller was feelin' so relieved an' good about the whole thing that he set right down and writ a poem ta be read at the weddin'. They didn't have no preacher, so one o' tha miners read the weddin' cerimony and tha others, led by Miller hisself, kinda chanted the poem that he had writ fer the grand occasion.

"Joaquin Miller recited that there poem fer us last night. Can't remember jest how it went, 'cause it must a had a dozen verses. But the gist o' it was all about love 'n gittin hitched . . . with a lot o' religion 'n nature all mixed up in it somehow. It ended by tellin' what a feller was gittin' into . . . 'n what he was a-losin' by gittin' hitched. Anyway, fellas, it was a mighty important poem, that was, 'cause it helped them two git married up . . . 'n it was the first poem Joaquin Miller ever writ!"

"By Jiminy!" said Tibbetts. "It sure sounds like Joaquin Miller has had a colorful life, chuck-full of adventures, all right. Must be a fascinating talker."

"You bet he is!" replied the miner with enthusiasm. "And it takes an awful lot ta hold me spellbound. But that Miller fella sure has a way o' tellin' things. It ain't no wonder they sent him up here from that there newspaper in San Friscky to write up the gold rush. Guess he'll have plenty ta tell 'em when he gits back!"

"Yeah," said another miner, "that Miller fella's quite a pioneer, all right. Last night he said he was from old Indiany, practically born 'n raised in a covered wagon, 'n as a boy came rollin' west across the plains, over that ol' Oregon Trail. Said they was really headed fer Californy, 'cause his father had been bitten bad by the gold fever when he heard about that big discovery at Sutter's Creek in forty-nine. But when they lands up near Eugene, Oregon, his father decides sudden-like that Oregon is the best place fer 'em, after all. Miller says, in no time flat, they staked fer a homestead 'n there they set fer quite a spell. Yes, sir, that Miller fella says it was while he was a-livin' in the wilds that he larned a lot o' lessons not taught in books. Now, I tell ya, fellas, thar's a man after me own heart! 'Cause I never was much fer them lessons taught in books!"

"Yep," broke in another miner, "Joaquin Miller sure entertained us last night and helped to push our spirits up, real tremendous-like. Told us lots of excitin' things about his life. Reminded us we was all livin' through a mighty excitin' time ourselves. Yep, he told us lots of excitin' stories. And we was mighty grateful, too, 'cause it sort o' helped ta keep our minds off our troubles. He went on ta tell us that he got his edication sort o' on the run. Says his father was a country schoolteacher and tried ta edicate his sons proper-like, but Joaquin got the wanderlust so bad that one day he jest picked up 'n left home. Yep, that Miller fella must'a been a mighty smart one . . . 'cause he jest picked up most o' his larnin' here 'n there, sometimes a-settin' around the campfire near Mount Shasty, sometimes down in Mexico, 'n sometimes down in Arizony. O' course, he did finally end up at that little college in Eugene, Oregon, and then taught school fere a spell. But he was so plumb full o' the love o' nature an' excitin' adventure that one day he jest up an' went a-minin' fer gold in Montany with his brothers."

"Yep," said another miner, "by that time, he had picked up enough larnin' to be a county jedge an' a lawyer. What d'ya think o' that? He even ran a small country newspaper in Oregon fer a spell. But he said he craved action an' adventure so bad, he jest couldn't set still. Finally got a job ridin' the Pony Express from Millersburg, Idaho, to Walla Walla, Washington, jest fer the wild excitement of it all. Said he was sometimes chased by bandits and Indians who was after that gold dust he was a-carryin' out fer them placer miners along the Salmon River there in Idaho.

"Yeah, and d'ya know that all the time he was a-chasin' around the Northwest a-doin' all these excitin' things, he was a-gatherin' stuff 'n writin' some o' them there poems about the great outdoors, like the *Songs of the Sierras* he told us about what made him so famous an' what them there nobility in England went so wild about when he took a trip over ta meet all o' them fancy dukes 'n duchesses? That was quite a spell ago, when he was much younger. Think he said it was about twenty-seven years ago. He told us that them Englishmen said he was the true spirit of America, of the rugged, pioneer West. Joaquin Miller said he sure put on a show fer 'em an' dressed the part, too. Wore a bright red shirt, a leather jacket, a big cowboy hat an' his pants tucked inta high-topped boots an' all. He said them ladies and duchesses sure went fer 'im, 'n liked the way he dressed, And d'ya know, fellas, he said it kinda helped ta sell his poetry, too."

"Yes, Joaquin Miller is a mighty colorful personality," I said with a laugh. "And we're mighty lucky to have him aboard. But, seriously, fellows, do you know that he's using all of his powers of persuasion to try to get Captain Geiger to make a daring dash downriver to St. Michael, even though the river on ahead might not look too promising? But he's hit a snag that maybe the rest of you don't know about. The captain has told Joaquin that if it looks at all doubtful he can make it to the coast after reaching Fort Yukon, rather than take a chance of being stalled and frozen in at some isolated spot down the river, he'll dump us all off at Fort Yukon and gather together all the food he can scrape up, then make a run for it back upriver to starving Dawson."

"Holy mackerel!" exclaimed Tibbetts, looking at the threatening chunks of ice grinding close to the steamer and the snow now pelting us hard from all angles. "The way things look at present, we might not even make it as far as Circle City! But if we should go to Fort Yukon and there is a ghost of a chance of reaching St. Michael from there, I hope the captain listens to Joaquin Miller and takes that chance. We must all stand back of Joaquin!"

Chapter XVI

Men Against the Ice

How beastly hot it was here in the engine room! It was late in the afternoon of our first day out from Forty Mile, but I didn't complain, although my face was scorched and swollen and my hands blistered and bleeding from handling the rough, heavy chunks of wood which I was heaving into the furnace every few

(Courtesy of Juanita Miller, his daughter)

Joaquin Miller in Klondike costume. Gold nuggets form the buttons

Chief "Schwatka" was the oldest Indian guide in Alaska

The North West Mounted Police Station at Gold Bottom, Yukon Territory

minutes. The very lives of all on board depended on keeping that greedy furnace stuffed and fed and the engine running smoothly. How deafening the roar! How hissing the steam. And how nauseating the smell of oil on hot machinery! But nothing must stop those two long rods moving back and forth, back and forth, along the floor of the engine room to the pivots that turned the big stern-wheel at the rear of the boat.

And Lord, how we prayed that the captain would be able to dodge all those big chunks of floating ice in the river! A broken paddle on the stern-wheel could be fatal in our dash down the Yukon. Yes, we stowaways had been assigned a very important job to do, and we were working like galleys slaves to do it well.

"Say there, Ed Lung," called a deck hand, poking his head into the engine room. "The captain says you're to come off duty now and let one of the other fellows in your crowd stoke awhile. Says Shelley Graves will take your place. The captain says, when you leave here, you're to go to Joaquin Miller's stateroom. Miller wants to see you."

"Thanks, fellow," I said, wiping my forehead. "I'll be mighty glad to leave this fiery hole in Hades!"

In a few minutes, I was knocking at Joaquin Miller's stateroom door.

"Ah, come right in, Ed. I've been waiting for you," he said, extending his hand cordially. "So you're a stowaway!" he said, laughing heartily. "Why didn't you tell me, Ed, when I was talking to you earlier today? You know I wouldn't have given you away."

"Well, I suppose not," I said with a sheepish grin, "but, you see, I'm not very proud of being a stowaway. In fact, I'm mighty embarrassed about the whole thing."

"Oh, come now. Don't feel too badly about it, Ed. That's nothing to be embarrassed over. Why, once I was accused of being a horse thief—was even put in jail!"

"Well, that makes me feel a little better," I said with a laugh. "But yours sounds like a pretty good story!"

"You bet it is!" he answered with a smile. "Sometime I'll tell you about it. But right now, sit down and have a glass of rye. Guess you need it after what you've been through."

"Thanks, Joaquin, I don't drink, but I'd surely like a cigar."

"Of course, Ed," he said. "Here, have one."

Eagerly, I took the cigar he offered me, bit off the end, lit it and leaned back in the chair, puffing contentedly while Joaquin Miller continued.

"As you know, Ed, I'm not only a poet, but also a reporter for the Hearst newspapers and I came into the Klondike to gather firsthand all the exciting material I can scoop up on the gold rush. And, of course, after being up here over two months, I have a great deal to show for my trip. In my valise I've already got reports on Chilkoot, the trip down the Yukon, Dawson City, the fabulous gold fields, the amazing riches of the Bonanza and Eldorado and other creeks, the newly rich Klondike Kings. And now, this terrible famine . . . and our flight downriver from Dawson on the *Weaver* to reach the 'Outside.' And as you know, I'm counting tremendously on getting these stories back to the States, hot off the griddle for publication . . . for all the world to read! But, Ed, this story about you seven men slipping on board the *Weaver* as stowaways intrigues me. It's a new angle. Think it'll make a mighty interesting story. And how I like true adventure! And how I like to write about it!" he said with great relish and an excited gleam in his blue eyes.

"You've already told me this afternoon about your trip into the Klondike in the early summer and your fruitless search for gold. Now come on, Ed, finish the story to date," he urged.

"Well," I said, "like hundreds of others who were almost out of food, I left Dawson with a party of men on that fateful day of September twenty-eighth after Captain Hanson arrived from Circle City with news that there would be no more boats until the spring of ninety-eight. As you so well know, Captain Hanson's announcement was like a bombshell to most of us in Dawson."

Joaquin nodded. Then I went on to tell him about our harrowing day on the river in freezing weather; of fighting the ice for our very lives in our small open boat; of our landing at Forty Mile, the ghost town of the Yukon; of our waiting for the return of the *Weaver;* of our consternation at seeing the ice gradually narrowing in the river, of our apprehension over food, with only ten days' supply left; of the *Bella's* sudden appearance and the *Weaver's* arrival an hour later from Dawson; of the captain's refusal to take us on as passengers because the boat was already loaded to the guards. And then I told him how we sneaked on board the *Weaver* after dark and scattered all over the boat; how I bedded down near the engine room, and how hard the floor was before morning.

"Ed, I can surely sympathize with you men," Joaquin said as he made quick notes on a pad. You surely had a harrowing experience. I would certainly have hated to've been in your shoes. But tell me exactly how you were discovered as stowaways and how you felt?"

"Well, as I said before, I don't feel very good about it. I blush to think of it, but it was like this: While we seven men were eating our lunch in the dining room today, I thought I saw the purser's eyes fastened on us suspiciously. He looked puzzled and was probably trying to place us as having gotten on at Dawson. Even though we were worried, we ate a hearty meal, throwing all caution to the wind, just as we had at breakfast time—only at breakfast time we had been careful not to sit together!

"However, I felt quite relieved when I saw the purser disappear. But Great Scott! when I thought all was well, and we were about to leave the table, the purser returned, walked straight up to us and said sternly, 'Men, Captain Geiger wants to see you immediately.' "

"Good Lord, what did you do then?" asked Miller, making notes rapidly on his pad in his broad, scrawling handwriting.

"Well," I said, "there we were, caught red-handed, and in the dining room, too. Of course, we all felt like criminals as the purser marched us off to the captain. I kept thinking, 'And I, a minister's son!"

"Tibbetts kept whispering, 'Boys, look pleasant and don't tell who I am!"

"Ha, ha, what a walloping situation!" said Miller. "But what then?"

"Well, believe me," I said, "we were all as meek as Moses when we faced the captain. There we stood grinning in a sickly fashion with bad cases of indigestion."

"It'll make a good story all right," roared Joaquin Miller. "Wish I could have been there to witness it! But tell me, what did Captain Geiger say?"

"You can bet your boots he was plenty angry," I said. "Got red in the face and shouted he'd put us ashore if he could, but said it was impossible because of the ice. Got more upset as he talked. Said the boat was riding dangerously low in the river. Said we might get shipwrecked or stalled in the ice, or frozen in some place. Said he shouldn't have seven blankety-blank extra-men to worry about, and that if we did get frozen in, he'd have to feed his passengers first, and that we might have to go hungry."

"Yes, what then?" asked Joaquin Miller, still smiling, but beginning to look serious at mention of food and of being frozen in.

"Well, to appease the captain," I said, "we offered to give him all the gold we had to pay for our passage, but he refused to take it, saying that as long as we had sneaked on as stowaways, we'd have to work for passage. And that, Joaquin Miller, is how I happen to be down in the engine room stoking the furnaces."

I continued talking to Joaquin Miller, elaborating on the situation, answering a few specific questions of interest to him, when suddenly, there was a brisk knock on the stateroom door and a deck hand poked his head inside and said brusquely, "Ed, Captain Geiger says he wants to see you. Guess he's anxious to know all the news you can give him about the miners confiscating that cargo of food from the steamer *Bella* at Circle City."

Early the following morning, October 1st, the furious elements of the North were in a vengeful mood. A blizzardy wind from the Arctic whipped hard against the boat as we plowed our way downstream, running a terrific gauntlet of ice. We shivered as we listened to the wind shrieking along the decks of the *Weaver*, howling like a dozen banshees while the snow piled higher and higher along the decks, enshrouding the boat in a blanket of white. We gave fervent thanks that we were aboard the *Weaver* and not out on the river in our small open boat in that kind of weather.

We passed more broken boats and saw forlorn little groups of men huddled on the icy shores around flickering bonfires behind huge chunks of ice, trying to keep out of the furious wind.

"Passengers, men, we're going to try to pull into Circle City on the left bank of the Yukon and wait for the storm to pass," was the word passed along from Captain Geiger to the passengers and crew.

"Keep the steam up, fellows," called the engineer to Tibbetts and me as we worked like Trojans to feed the roaring furnace.

"Gosh, nothing must stop us now," said Tibbetts a little later as he eyed our diminishing wood supply with apprehension. "We certainly must pull into Circle City. Only got enough wood to last an hour or two more."

Being very curious to see where we were going on the river, at intervals we opened the ice-covered portholes and looked anxiously out onto the Yukon. In these brief glimpses when the heavy curtains of snow would sweep momentarily clear, we could see that the river had widened considerably and that the high, snow-covered mountains had gradually receded away from the Yukon on either side. Now the country was fast changing into a very wide plateau.

"We've got just about eight miles more to go to reach Circle City," said the engineer, "and Lord, let's hope nothing stops us."

A short time later, about 10:15 A.M., we heard scurrying feet on the upper deck.

"Wonder what's all the commotion?" I asked.

"Circle City!" yelled Shelley Graves, bursting into the engine room. "It's Circle City, fellows. Come and see for yourselves. Looks like quite a crowd of miners and Indians on shore, with a few women, all waving and shouting to us. And, by George, Ed, it's quite a place! Dozens of log cabins! What a sight for sore eyes it is!"

All who could, rushed up on deck and we ran to the portholes to see the heart-warming sight of this log-cabin town, reported to be almost on the Arctic Circle.

It was exactly 10:30 A.M. as we pulled into Circle City and made a hazardous but safe landing against the shore ice. And although we were truly thankful to be there, most of us had a desperate urge to continue down river as fast as we could toward St. Michael. We knew that every hour might count in our race with the river. The view ahead, as far as we could see, was anything but encouraging. A sea of frightening ice seemed to loom before us, blocking our way below Circle City.

Immediately, we stowaways, with the help of the deck hands, began loading wood in the event Captain Geiger should make the daring dash downriver in spite of the ice. But after a few hours, the captain announced to the passengers that he simply couldn't risk it. Said we would have to lay over until the following day and hope for a change in the weather and possible shifting of the ice.

However, the next day, October 2nd, found the *Weaver* and all of us still at Circle City, and although the storm had ceased toward the evening of that second day after our arrival, the captain still wouldn't budge in his decision to remain at Circle City. To pass the time, I put my pencil to work and wrote in my diary that morning of the 2nd day of October:

> (Circle City—Clear and Cold)
>
> Beautiful Northern Lights last night. My cold is very bad. Captain Geiger says he thinks we're laid up for the winter. Tough prospect! Ice is very much thicker in the river. The steamer *Bella* has not shown up from Dawson. The ice has been running all day and it has been steadily growing colder. The grub on the steamer *Weaver* is all gone, so the purser says. Joaquin Miller says he hasn't given up hope yet. But I see we are bound up for the winter. A very unpleasant prospect! We moved ashore and are now in Captain Morgan's cabin. (Captain Morgan stayed in Dawson.)

Not only had we moved ashore, but all of the passengers had done the same, except Joaquin Miller, who seemed stubbornly determined to stay with the ship in spite of the danger of the ice. We felt little doubt now that we would be frozen in at Circle City. All of the passengers from the *Weaver* were in a frantic uproar about the food situation. It was rumored that the N.A.T. Co. had a secret cache of food stowed away somewhere at Circle City. Captain Ray, a U.S. military man who had come down on the *Weaver*, was backing the passengers in their demand that they be fed by the trading company in the event that they were frozen in for the winter. However, our party of seven men, being stowaways, could lay no claim to these demands. Again, our situation seemed truly desperate. Here we were, a little farther down the Yukon, but with hope waning for reaching the "Outside."

As we stood on the bank of the river in front of Circle City looking anxiously down the Yukon, it seemed that the icy jaws of the North were rapidly closing in on us. There was now only a very, very narrow channel of free-running water, hardly enough room for our boat to slip through in the center of the two-mile-wide Yukon. And there was ice and more ice piling up on the horizon along the Yukon Flats, the beginning of the great frozen barrier of the Arctic Circle. How could we ever get through this perilous stretch and reach home?

Now it seemed the great door of the Yukon had snapped shut on its icy hinges. All of us would have given half the gold in the Klondike if we could have transported ourselves in some miraculous way across that barrier to St. Michael and then home.

Truly, an ominous, frightening prospect—winter lay ahead!

Chapter XVII

Prisoners of the North

It was now October 7, 1897, and for a day or so after our steamer *Weaver* had come into Circle City against the ice, bringing 150 of us from Dawson, this place had seemed like a real haven of refuge from the early winter snowstorms and formidable river.

But now, after being here a week, it took on the aspect of an ugly prison spot.

I suppose we all should have been grateful to 've reached this spot safely, but now the cold, vibrant atmosphere seemed permeated with the overwhelmingly bitter disappointment of all of us when we realized we were probably stranded here at Circle, and it seemed that we could not continue downriver to escape the North. We were like prisoners, hardly consoled at having reached this gold camp on American territory.

In looking over the town, we discovered that this Arctic gold camp, which sprawled along the Yukon on the left bank (facing downstream for perhaps a mile and a half), was made up of several hundred log cabins. A dense forest of stunted spruce and tamaracks fringed the rear of the town. Of course, the most important spot in Circle City was the two-story log house of the American Commercial Trading Company located in the south end of town. There was also another smaller trading post called "Healey's." The town boasted an "opera house," several dance halls, a missionary school for Indians, a military barracks and a very dark cubbyhole of a jail. We discovered that the town was governed by several U. S. Army officers, and immediately noticed the less severe atmosphere of the place in contrast to the stern rule of the famous Canadian Northwest Mounted Police in Dawson.

But if this part of the country was under a different regime, so also was there a great difference in the character of the country. There were no mountains crowding the place, as around Dawson and Forty Mile. They appeared rather far in the distance, lofty and white. To the east, across the Yukon, they seemed about ten miles away; to the west about thirty miles; to the northwest about fifty miles; and to the south only about seven or eight miles away.

This unusually low, open area where Circle City stood was the very beginning of the famous Yukon Flats, stretching like a great, white frozen plain due north, with no mountains in sight in that direction.

The contour of the riverbank at Circle City was a rather shallow half-moon, with the deepest bend to the south toward Dawson. Here the great Yukon River widened at Circle to nearly a mile across. But we were told that a short distance downriver to the north, it spread out in places, reaching a width of two or three miles where there were many false channels, islands and treacherous sand bars.

It had been reported by the Indians that, in ages past, the Yukon had many times flooded the great Yukon Flats for hundreds of square miles, mostly to the northwest, leaving thousands of small lakes behind. Of course, now the whole area was rapidly freezing over and would soon look like a great white desert of icy wasteland.

Circle City was the most northerly gold camp of any size on the Yukon. We discovered it had about 125 inhabitants, including 50 Indians who had their cabins in the north end of town on the riverfront. Their leader was Chief Ezias Joseph, chief of about 300 Yukon Indians, some of whom had small villages in the close vicinity of Circle City and Birch Creek. Circle City had been, and still was, the supply headquarters for the placer mines along Birch Creek and its many small tributaries, which included the colorfully named creeks: Gold Dust, Discovery, Bedrock, Mastodon, Squaw, Preacher and others. (Birch Creek ran along parallel with the Yukon to the west for perhaps 150 miles. It was eight miles from Circle to the closest point of portage on Birch Creek where the placer mines began.)

Naturally, there was still somewhat of a golden aura yet surrounding Circle City, which had grown into prominence around 1893, although by now interest had waned. Circle City was in a decline because of the glittering Klondike.

Now with great apprehension we viewed the steamer *Weaver* partly covered with snow and frozen tightly in the ice about 150 feet off shore. Then we glanced out fearfully to that narrowing center channel of the river, which was still free-running, open water, but which threatened closure almost any hour. In the almost icebound river our boat seemed like an utterly helpless thing, leaning at a precarious angle, its big reddish-colored stern-wheel heavy with icicles. Trapped and completely deserted now, of passengers and crew, it presented a forlorn, helpless picture—a broken link to our homes in the States!

I knew that my wife Velma in Tacoma would be half wild with anxiety and heartbroken if she received no word from me. It seemed intolerable that I should cause her so much grief. I knew, too, that the newspapers "Outside" were sure to print frightening stories of starvation and tragedies on the Yukon, along with glowing reports of gold mining. These accounts would come from miners who had fled the North in the late summer or early September.

Our most famous passenger stalled with us at Circle City, Joaquin Miller, was almost crying to get out of the country with his brilliant gold-rush reports. As we waited in Circle City, there was a mounting tension among us. We all knew the food was gone on the *Weaver* and there wasn't much in evidence on the scantily stocked shelves of the two trading posts, certainly not enough to feed all of us hungry men now crowded in at Circle City. It was impossible to reconcile ourselves to our frightening predicament, and most of us were even beginning to wonder if we'd ever reach home again.

Twice now since the first of October, the crew of the *Weaver,* with the help of some of the passengers and us stowaways, had succeeded in chopping the steamer free from the ice which held it; and then we had tried desperately to cut a clear passageway to the open, free-moving channel in the center of the Yukon. But the weather was so bitterly cold now that the water, which was exposed to the air, froze almost as soon as the surface was cut away.

Captain Geiger told us he couldn't see much hope of freeing the steamer, and it seemed that he, for one, was now resigned to the fact that his ship was bound up for the winter.

But if our boat was under heavy pressure from the ice, so also was our captain under heavy pressure, too. One hundred and fifty disgruntled, desperate men can exert a tremendous pressure! Joaquin Miller, who was perhaps one of the most impatient and determined of all of us, kept after the captain night and day until he finally promised that if, by some miracle, we were yet able to get the *Weaver* out into the open channel, he would be willing to try to make the hazardous dash down the Yukon. This possibility had kept us all in a jitter of suspense for nearly a week while we worked like demons on the ice. But when the temperature dropped lower and lower, and our vessel became more and more icebound, panic and despair seized us.

In desperation, we all began talking excitedly of other means of escape. Captain Tibbetts, the former sea captain of our party of men, urged that we might yet escape through the ice channel and go downriver in a small open boat. Right away, we bought one from the Indians.

However, as is usually the case when there's a vital and desperate question to settle in a group of high-strung men, we fellows couldn't agree on exactly what we should do. Some of us were for starting out at once, and the others were for waiting at Circle for a short while.

Captain Tibbetts, Shelley Graves and I argued that we should strike out downriver immediately, since we had a few days' supply of grub left among us. We argued we'd have a better chance to survive the winter if we could get down to Fort Yukon, where we had heard the steamer *Marguerite* had left her cargo of flour in late September.

"But why leave Circle City and tackle that hellish river right now, unless it's absolutely necessary?" asked Bertram in alarm.

"You're right," agreed Hill. "At least we're safe here from the ice, and we could make our grub stretch further if we tighten our belts a little more!"

"Yes, and who knows? something unforseen may yet help the grub situation," said Moore, looking hopefully downriver.

"Well, I don't know exactly what we should do," said Calhoun, shaking his head dubiously. "But I tell you, fellows, we've got to face it. The blunt truth is—we're all in a tight spot here! Not only our party, but every last man in Circle City!"

"You're right, Calhoun," said Moore. "It's not going to be pleasant when three hundred or four hundred men become hungry as wolves this winter! Nope, it's not going to be pleasant!"

For a while we walked on in silence. We had been scouting along the river, walking gingerly on the shore ice for a short distance toward the Yukon Flats, when suddenly Tibbetts pointed to the north and shouted, "Look!"

We stopped dead in our tracks and saw a mirage-like vessel in the distance through the cold, frosty air, looking almost like a spirit ship coming upriver out of the mists from the north. And as we looked in amazement, suddenly a great cry rose up behind us at Circle City, exultant, full of hope. Someone on the bank had caught sight of the steamer, too, and had passed the word along. All of Circle City was rushing to the riverfront.

Joyously, we retraced our steps, turning often to watch the steamer as slowly she fought her way upstream, coming closer and closer to Circle City against the terrific, churning, oncoming ice floes of the open channel.

"Oh, pray God she makes it!" screamed one of the few white women of Circle City. "We're almost out of food!"

"Oh, I'm so glad to see that boat, I could just cry," wept another woman hysterically.

In tense, concentrated silence, with eyes focused only on the steamer, we watched for a long time as the ship painfully struggled closer and closer and finally maneuvered and wedged herself into a small opening off the center channel.

"It's the steamer *Victoria!*" shouted someone in the crowd. "Golly, she's a sturdy little ship, and she's got a wonderful captain and crew!"

Then the crowd went wild; and many of us rushed out onto the ice. "Did you bring any food? Say, did you bring any food? Tell us! Tell us, quick!" we all shouted eagerly.

"Wait and see!" the deck hands sang out half-tantalizingly. "Just you wait and see!"

And to our great joy, they began unloading cargo. Hurriedly, they rolled out crates of foodstuff and a few sacks of flour onto the ice and began loading them in wheelbarrows and on small sleds to haul to the trading companies, while we hungry men hovered near, mentally taking inventory of everything. Immediately, we could see that the stocks were disappointingly small.

While the crew hauled this precious cargo over the ice, we followed along, eagerly pelting them with questions: "Was there food in any quantity at Fort Yukon?" "Did they think it would be possible to get downriver in a small open boat?"

And as the deck hands pushed and hauled the freight along, they answered: "Fellows, we advise you not to try to get downriver in a small boat. They've been just pulling the wrecks out in front of Fort Yukon. You'd probably be crushed in the ice, too. Believe us, we just barely made it here on the *Victoria!* . . . No, there certainly isn't a lot of food at Fort Yukon, only a moderate supply. And everyone there is being put on ten-day rations, with warnings to make it stretch farther, if notified. . . . Down the Yukon below the American fort, the grub situation is very acute. Some Indians seemed starving."

While we were mighty thankful for the coming of the *Victoria* and her supplies, no matter how small, still, this news struck like a death knell to our glimmering hopes of getting downriver.

But if we were hard pressed for food at Circle, Dawson was in a much tighter situation. Men in small open boats were still daring the river to escape starvation there. They kept coming, and coming down the channel. Most of these frantic men made safe landings on the ice in front of Circle City, but some were swept on. Many empty boats floated past, some jammed in among cakes of ice, some sticking up out of the water at all angles—prows, sterns or sides up.

Grimly we viewed these wrecks. Only occasionally were we able to capture an empty boat and pull it up on the ice. One boat, in particular, came down minus occupants, but loaded with camping equipment intact. Captain Tibbetts and I and several others were able to pull it out of the channel and up onto the ice. Then we waited to see if anyone would show up to claim it. If not, the prize would be ours. But, later in the day, two white-faced men came walking along the rim ice from the south. They were from Dawson, half-frozen and covered with frost, scared to death and almost ready to collapse from exhaustion and exposure.

Yes, it was their boat! They had lost it about six miles up the Yukon. They said it had broken loose from its moorings when they had gone ashore for wood. Left without any equipment and not knowing how far they were from Circle City; they were absolutely terrified, but had started out walking on the rim ice. They said they couldn't have gone on another mile!

This was a happier ending than for most fellows. More often the story was merely those forlorn, broken boats—and we just had to stand helplessly by and watch the savage river in action!

That night, I wrote with trembling hand in my diary: "Many a sad tale will be told before winter is over; and many a poor fellow will never return to his home and friends, having met with sudden death on this river!"

With all of these wrecks coming down from Dawson, we began wondering what had become of the little *Bella*. However, a boatload of stampeders landed at Circle City, bringing news that the little *Bella* had reached Dawson safely. They said it had been immediately commandeered by the Mounted Police, who gave free passage to the most hard pressed of the miners. Also, the Mounties had rounded up a group of dance-hall girls and ordered them to leave on the *Bella*. Now the distressing news was that the little *Bella* had gotten downriver as far as Forty Mile and there she had been caught in the ice, loaded to the guards with frightened passengers.

The unhappy plight of the *Bella* was very bad news for us at Circle; especially so for my party of men and Joaquin Miller, because we had talked about this boat as a last hope of going down the Yukon by steamer before the ice would completely close in. We had hoped that if, somehow, the little *Bella* could get through the ice as far as Circle City, her captain might decide to continue the dash downriver toward St. Michael. We had figured that this small steamer might be able to skim through the ice floes.

But now, this possibility of escape seemed utterly blasted. Foolishly, perhaps, we had pictured ourselves going out on the ice to meet the *Bella* when she came by Circle City and persuading her amiable young Captain Ball to haul us aboard, as we had previously talked to him about passage on his steamer at Forty Mile.

"Well, that chance is gone!" Joaquin Miller swore in disgust as he came to our cabin to talk things over. He threw off his parka, began warming his hands by the Klondike stove, and continued, "Men, it surely looks bad for us! Looks like we're destined to stay in this frozen hell hole for the winter! I tell you, fellows, it makes me feel like starting out right now in a small boat, in spite of the grave dangers; or else, perhaps, walking on the rim ice close to shore. In a week or two, the Yukon will be completely frozen over and then I could travel on to St. Michael on the Bering Sea."

"Great Scott!" said Hill. "Do you realize, Joaquin, that that little hike you're considering is at least twelve hundred miles and would take you until spring? Maybe even summer! If you're going to hike in any direction, I'd say you'd better start back toward Dawson and from there to the coast. But from Circle City, I figure it's just about a one-thousand-mile trek to Dyea. And, brother! That, too, would probably take you until spring. By then, the steamers will all be running again!"

"How ironic!" I said.

"I know it sounds like a foolish idea," said Joaquin, looking half sick, "but I'm disappointed like Hades at being stuck here . . . maybe to starve; especially so, since I've got these newspaper dispatches. Don't you realize what that means? Unless, I can get 'Outside,' or send these stories some way, the news will be old stuff . . . and you know what that means to newspapers! Of course, you know I'm under contract with Hearst!"

"Yes, I know that," I said, "and I know how you must feel, Joaquin, but we're all burning to get out of this blasted place, too. And what makes it doubly bad, Joe the mail-carrier is frozen in here with us!"

"Yes, it's a devilish predicament we're all in!" said Joaquin vehemently. "Well, I won't stand it much longer, I tell you, not even if I die in the attempt! I've made up my mind that, just as soon as the Yukon is frozen over, I'm starting out, probably toward Dawson. And don't try to stop me!"

"Without food?" asked Tibbetts incredulously.

"No, I'll not be without food. Think I can make a deal with the trading company and perhaps wangle some frozen fish from the Indians. You see, I've made some good friends with the Indians, and Chief Joseph is my special friend."

"And how about dogs to pull your sled?" asked Captain Tibbetts anxiously.

"Well," exclaimed Joaquin, "I'll attempt it without dogs,

if necessary, But, of course, I'll try to get malemutes, if possible."

"You won't have any luck!" broke in Calhoun. "We've tried. And every fellow in town has tried. There are just no malemutes or huskies to be had! Only a few old sourdoughs have any, but try to buy them! Why, those oldtimers would just as soon part with their grub! And you know, Joaquin, they say that starting out over the ice for that long a trek without dogs is almost like committing suicide. It's almost impossible for a man to drag a sled loaded with all of the necessary equipment he'll need for such a long and hazardous journey!"

"Well, I'll risk it anyway," said Joaquin in stubborn desperation. "Yes, even if I perish in the attempt! Haven't I lived in the wilds all my life? I'm a good hiker. Besides, I won't be alone. Canovan, the French-Canadian, has promised to go with me. He's a good frontiersman, too."

"But, Joaquin," I said. "It would tax you to the very last ounce of energy. I guess none of us Cheechakos can fully realize how perilous it would be in forty degrees and fifty degrees below zero! Too many have already been lost on that river. I'd surely hate to see you waste your life so unnecessarily!"

While Joaquin Miller and Canovan and all of us waited impatiently at Circle (for we knew not what), we paced the snow-covered banks of the hateful river like caged lions, watching the ice on the Yukon gathering . . . gathering . . . piling up thicker and thicker in the center of the river, seeming to make this icy, prison-like camp more formidable, more heartbreaking! And we all tightened our belts to destroy that persistent, gnawing, hungry feeling.

As time dragged on at Circle City, almost any other place on earth would have seemed more desirable! The town literally seethed with unrest and belligerent, arguing men. It seemed like an Arctic Devil's Isle, from which there appeared to be no escape—except, perhaps, in our little open boat in that narrowing channel. But, as yet, we had not quite reached that extreme stage of desperation—especially after seeing all of those broken, wrecked boats floating down from Dawson. We knew full well, if we were foolish enough to try it that way, that the savage river was waiting for us, too.

There certainly wasn't much doing at Circle City to help pass the time. The "Opera House" was boarded up, as all the show girls had cleared out of town in early September. And there wasn't much use attending the dances, either, as there were only about twelve white women left in Circle and it was more like a free-for-all! However, there was a small lending library, but as yet we had been too upset to settle down to any sort of reading.

We did make a trip up to the nearest "diggings" on Birch Creek, about eight miles away. However, after being in the Klondike and seeing the Bonanza and Eldorado, these mines seemed tame and unexciting, and there was no incentive to go gold hunting, as all auriferous ground in the near vicinity of Circle had been staked three or four years earlier.

About the 9th of October, the thermometer began hitting new lows and the Yukon was freezing tighter. The old-timers were saying, "The river will soon be completely frozen over!" It was an ominous warning that we would have to start rustling food for the winter, and as fast as we could from every source possible! We knew full well we couldn't depend on the small portions of very closely guarded and rationed food being doled out so begrudgingly at the two trading companies. So we held a serious council in the cabin and decided immediately to divide our group into food-rustling parties, to go hunting, to go fishing in the air holes in the ice, and to go bartering with the Indans. I volunteered for the latter job.

After much scouting and visiting with the Indians in and around Circle City and out toward Birch Creek, I triumphantly returned with a little dried fish and a small slab of frozen caribou. I was able to get these precious food items by putting in an order for a reindeer parka, fur-lined moccasins and gloves with several Indian squaws. Jubilantly, I burst into the cabin to show the fellows my contributions. I found the hunting party just as elated, having brought in a couple of grouse and several rabbits. But the fishing party had nothing to show for their efforts except frostbitten hands and feet.

"Well, fellows," said Tibbetts as he eyed our somewhat replenished larder, "at least we won't starve for a while, but we'll have to continue our food-rustling parties regularly if we're going to survive the winter."

Chapter XVIII

The Pirates and Outcasts

Now it was an extremely galling sight to see the crew of the *Weaver* so fat and well fed, apparently doing nothing for their good fortune other than being just the lucky crew of the *Weaver*. These men had installed themselves in the log-house restaurant which had closed before our arrival at Circle, but which evidently had a pretty good supply of food yet cached away. We stowaways sarcastically named these men the "pirates," as they were now sleeping and eating in what we enviously considered absolute luxury. The "pirates" seemed not the slightest concerned about us, the stowaways, who had worked with them stoking the boilers and doing other various jobs coming downriver. Nor did they worry at all about the passengers, who now were foraging around Circle and vicinity for their grub. Truly, it seemed the "pirates" were living up to the old saying of the North, "Every man for himself!" One of the fellows seemed to like the title of "pirate" so much he fixed himself up to look the part. We called him "Red."

Seven high-strung, impatient, chronically hungry men living on short rations and nursing bitter disappointment are a lot to be crowded into one small cabin! Besides, Joaquin Miller and Canovan were steady visitors. When they would come to our cabin, Joaquin always held the center of the stage. And how he loved to talk and talk and tell us stories of his adventures—and enlarge upon them!

Whenever we could, we snatched the opportunity to tell some of our own adventures too. Soon, it got to be a race to see who could grab the center of the stage first and hold it longest. Consequently, some pretty raw tales were told. The old saying surely was true, "If you really want to know a fellow, just go on an extended camping trip with him."

Of course, this was no ordinary camping trip, and it

was inevitable that, after a while, we would all begin to grate and jangle on each other's nerves more than a little! Finally, even Joaquin's eloquent flow of stories and flowery poetry became "just so much 'crow talk,'" as one fellow expressed it sourly.

We found that music, more than anything, tended to ease the tension among us. A fellow by the name of Bates often brought his guitar over to our cabin and we'd blow off steam, singing old songs at the top of our lungs, at times nearly raising the roof. At these song fests, our cabin would be pack-jammed with a crowd of fellows. When Joaquin would come, he'd grab the stage, as usual, and sometimes quote poetry while Bates would accompany him with musical chords. How Joaquin loved the limelight. We all thought he should have been an actor. One of his verses he often chanted to Bates' strumming accompaniment, and which seemed to be on his mind, was:

> Forgotten? . . . No! We never do forget.
> We let the years go . . . wash them clean with tears,
> Leave them to bleach out in the open day,
> Or lock them carefully away like dead funeral flowers
> Till we dare unfold them without pain.
> But, we forget not, no, never can forget!

I could never learn whom Joaquin had in mind, but the words were rather beautiful and haunting, and I wrote them down in the back of my diary.

"Look at Joaquin," Tibbetts whispered one evening when Joaquin was chanting these wistful lines, "I'll swear he's thinking of some sad love affair. You know, they say he was mighty popular with the women."

There were now eight in our party. A man by the name of S. M. Graff, a young Canadian lawyer, had attached himself to our group and finally crowded into the cabin with us. He was a fine fellow and we liked him a lot.

We stowaways of the *Weaver* were now known all over Circle City as the "Outcast Club" and had tacked up our shingle over the cabin door with the names of the eight members. Canovan and Joaquin were associate members.

OUTCAST CLUB OF CIRCLE CITY

C. E. Tibbetts
H. S. Graves
N. H. Bertram
W. L. Moore
R. H. I. Hill
T. W. Calhoun
S. M. Graff
E. B. Lung

It was now the middle of October.

Although winter had begun unusually early in the North, this year the Yukon country was due for another big surprise: A warm, almost balmy Chinook wind began blowing down the Yukon from the south. It was a very strange phenomenon for this time of year and soon the water in the center channel began to rise from the melting snows and ice and sweep over the surface of the frozen river.

There was great excitement at Circle City. Our hopes zoomed high! We began picturing the *Weaver* freed from the ice. Captain Geiger seemed hopeful, too, and said the prospects looked much brighter. Said that we might yet make it 1,000 miles downriver as far as Anvic; said there was a portage there which would save us about 300 miles of dangerous boat travel. He said that this portage overland would bring us out on Bering Sea at Fort Get-There, just about a mile south of St. Michael, where the steamers left for the States. Captain Geiger told us that if we could make it there, there was a bare possibility we might yet catch a very late steamer home. However, he reminded us that the whole trip hinged on the warm Chinook and the volume of water and ice it produced in the river. He didn't go into any detailed explanation, though, or just how ominous the river could be under a too-prolonged, unseasonable warm spell, and at the moment wasn't telling us all. However, he assured us he would give us several hours' notice if he thought that we could make the trip. Naturally, this news put us in a ferment of expectation!

The warm weather continued. The water rose more and

more, flooding the ice higher and higher. To us Cheechakos, it seemed like the heaven-sent answer to our prayers! Soon the *Weaver* would be freed. Now she was standing in several feet of water, although she was still held firmly by the ice underneath.

Each hour we waited, eagerly watching the river day and night, and constantly besieging the captain with questions. But the old Yukoners kept assuring us that, any time now, the Chinook might cease and blasts from the North would follow, then winter would be upon us again! But the warm Chinook kept blowing, getting warmer by the hour.

The old-timers scratched their heads and looked in wonder, then looked very apprehensively at the river. The rapidly melting ice and snow was gathering more and more volume and the surface was now flooded four feet deep, with masses of ice thundering and running wild in the center river like huge battering rams gone wild.

"No, men," said Captain Geiger on the bank of the river to a crowd of us, "I would never attempt to take the *Weaver* out into that caldron! Looks as if all of the ice of the upper Yukon has torn loose and is running out! When the warm weather ceases, that ice will get caught and pile up and freeze some place downriver, and there will be frightening consequences. It's the ice coming from upriver and jamming of the river below that we captains fear the most!

"Men," he added regretfully, "I'm sorry to disappoint you, but if we attempted it now, probably none of us would ever reach home again!"

Well, that was it! Once more our hopes were blasted. You could almost hear the terrible letdown of all of us as silently we trudged away from the river toward our cabins.

All during this time the sun was shining unusually warm. It was almost like late spring. Suddenly, on October 12th, the little *Bella* made a spectacular and dramatic appearance. She rounded the bend of the river about one quarter of a mile away. We could hear her, whistles blowing, passengers screaming, as she came racing with the terrific ice floes.

"Great Scott! It's the *Bella!* Something's terribly wrong with her!" yelled Tibbetts excitedly. "The passengers are scared to death! Listen to 'em!"

We could see she was leaning at a dangerous angle. Then, as we watched, she turned completely sideways, getting the full impact of the wild current, with its battering rams of ice! Several times the little ship seemed to shudder. We feared she would capsize in front of our eyes, but, miraculously, she kept afloat. We knew she couldn't take that beating many minutes and we couldn't go to her rescue. Fearfully, we watched while she slowly and painfully inched her way sideways to safety into the slough.

We all gave a shout of relief and rushed to the river bank. Immediately, several small flat-bottomed boats cautiously put out from shore.

One of the white-faced passengers exclaimed as he came ashore, "Holy mackerel! What a helluva ride! Twenty miles back, something went wrong with the steering gear, and then, to cap the climax, we broke a couple of paddles on the stern-wheel. Lord! We knew we were in for plenty of trouble . . . and didn't know where we'd pile up. Fellows, I tell you it was just like riding in a crazy floating coffin over Niagara!"

"You bet! That Captain Ball is a great captain! I'd trust my life with him anywhere after this," said another fellow gratefully.

"Ooh! My, my!" wailed a painted dance-hall girl hysterically, "I thought I'd never see my grandmother again!"

"Say, I could just kiss the banks of Circle City!" cried another daughter of joy fervently.

When Joaquin dropped into our cabin that night, he said gravely, "I can see now why Captain Geiger refused to take the *Weaver* downriver! And, fellow, I've been talking to some of the passengers who came on the *Bella*. They tell me the food situation is still very bad at Dawson. They say, however, that a raft with a few sacks of flour did get through from the upper Yukon. They say this flour was like gold to the miners and was snapped up immediately for one hundred dollars and more a sack . . . and that the men would have gladly paid a bigger price. They said there was a terrible scramble for it. They also told me that some stampeders came into Dawson with a few crates of candles and were selling them for one dollar apiece! Yes, and they told me that stampeders were still arriving, but that they themselves were glad to clear out! However, they hadn't counted on being dumped at Circle City. They expected to get to Fort Yukon."

"Yes," said Tibbetts, looking very serious, "and do you realize what this added number of people from the *Bella* will mean to us here at Circle City and our already meager supplies? I think some of us should pull out of here and fast, in spite of the river! We'd better go while the going is good and the Yukon is still open!"

We talked long and earnestly that night, facing the situation squarely. We knew that, if everyone stayed in Circle, the already skimpy rations would be cut to the bone. We realized there was just one small chance left of getting downriver . . . at least to Fort Yukon, where those few extra supplies were, and it would have to be in our open boat. So, in spite of the overwhelming odds against us, our party decided to leave the following morning. When Joaquin Miller bade us good night, he said he was going to talk to Canovan about going that way, too.

But the next morning, we were all due for a terrible shock. It was while some of us were eating a hurried breakfast that Tibbetts came racing back into the cabin, followed by Shelley Graves.

"Men," he cried excitedly, "our boat has been stolen! And not only that, nearly all of the other small boats along the riverfront have been taken! They say our boats were stolen early this morning by some of the men who came down on the *Bella*."

"Yeah, and they say most of the 'pirates' cleared out and all of the dance-hall girls went with them!" cried Shelley angrily.

"Well, I'll be a son of a gun!" exclaimed Moore. "Those dirty 'pirates'! Who would have guessed they'd pull a dirty trick like this?"

"Yeah," said Calhoun, "but what beats me is why they'd leave the luxury of that restaurant!"

"Well, I guess it's quite obvious they wanted to help get those dance-hall girls to Fort Yukon," said Moore.

"Gosh," said Shelley, slightly recovering from his anger, "some of those gals weren't hard to look at, either."

"Well, I don't wish them any bad luck, but I hope they all get stuck in the ice—for a while, at least, to cool their heels!" said Tibbetts grimly.

"Well, fellows," I said, "there goes our last chance of getting down the river."

"Yes," said Tibbetts, "and that leaves us much worse off than we were before the *Bella* came in."

"I tell you, Ed, we're caught like rats in a trap here at Circle City!" said Joaquin rather hopelessly when I met him on the bank of the river a little later. He was pacing nervously up and down with clenched fists, looking angrily downriver. "Ye gods! Who would have thought those 'pirates' would play such a scurvy trick on us!"

"Yeah," said his companion, Canovan, with a hard laugh, "but I'd say since they've gone, it's mighty good riddance, after all. And, of course, there will be a little more grub for the rest of us here."

(Later, we learned that the men who had stolen our particular boat were trapped in the ice only thirty miles downriver.)

"Many a sad tale will be told before the winter is over and many a poor fellow will never return to his home," kept beating at my mind after I heard this news." (I wrote these words in my diary.) Well, Fate, it seemed, had taken the trip downriver completely out of our hands. Maybe it was all for the best! At least we were still alive at Circle . . . and kicking!

That night of October 23rd the temperature took a sudden nose dive, dropping to fourteen degrees below zero. We all knew that the flooded Yukon, which by now had risen ten feet, having become jammed with ice somewhere below on the Yukon Flats, as Captain Geiger predicted, would now begin to freeze over in real earnest. (We were mighty glad that the riverbank was fairly high at Circle City; but even so, if the river had continued to rise so rapidly and the freeze hadn't started there might have been danger of its flooding the bank at Circle.)

I slept fitfully on my hard, homemade cot that night, shivering from the cold, and had frightful nightmares. Several times I imagined I heard faint cries for help out on the river, but being very keyed up, I thought I only imagined it.

The following morning when I looked out on the Yukon, I saw a heartrending sight. There, about a half mile up the river, were three men caught in the ice in their small open boat. They must have come down sometime in the night, and there they were now, helplessly trapped in the newly formed ice.

All day we watched these poor men as the temperature grew colder and colder and as they struggled pitifully to try to free themselves from the ice. All day they called for help and several rescue parties attempted to reach them, but it was absolutely futile! The rescue parties themselves broke through the ice just off shore and we had a hard time saving them. The old-timers shook their heads and said sadly that it would probably be twenty-four hours or more before the new ice would be solid enough to hold the weight of a man.

All of Circle City was shocked over the terrible plight of the three men. We knew that no human being could survive the extreme cold for that long a period, stalled in an open boat with no fire to keep warm. Utterly helpless to give aid, all day we watched these ill-fated men. And all day they called for help while we paced the banks and shouted encouraging words, which seemed to echo back with hollow despair. But at last, darkness fell over that awful, heartrending scene. None of us slept that night. All of us suffered mental torture and offered prayers for their deliverance, while over the cold, brittle ice their faint, pitiful, agonized cries still reached us. Then, finally . . . all was silent.

The next morning, early, as the gray, morbid dawn broke, we looked fearfully out onto the river. There was the boat, dark and silent, caught in the cruel ice, and it appeared absolutely deserted. Immediately, of course, we surmised that the men were dead in the boat, and we waited, thinking that, when the ice had hardened enough, we would go out to bring in their bodies. But in a short time, a young fellow came racing along the waterfront with the startling news that he had just discovered the corpses of three men near the bend of the river. Evidently, during the night they had tried to escape from the boat over the thin ice; but must have fallen through. Somehow, they must have managed to pull themselves up onto firmer ice and had struggled on . . . only to literally freeze in their tracks near the riverbank.

When these unfortunate men were hauled on sleds through the streets of Circle, we all looked in horror, then turned away, sick at heart. A death pall seemed to settle over the gold camp and all activity stopped. This horrible tragedy taking place before our very eyes was too gruesome and shocking to contemplate. I, for one, knew that I would be haunted by their contorted, frozen bodies and horror-stricken, marble-white faces for the rest of my life!

The next day, while Moore and I were gathering firewood, he said, "Ed, seeing this terrible tragedy has had a very bad affect on me. I'm a coward, completely unnerved! And here, Graff and I were secretly thinking of clearing out over the ice within the next few days!"

"I can't blame you for wanting to leave," I said in surprise, "but, brother! after what happened yesterday, you fellows had better be doubly sure the ice will hold!"

During the next twenty-four hours, while the Yukon was still in the relentless process of completely freezing over, other heartbreaking, grim reports reached us at Circle. The worst news of all was that fifteen men had been caught in their boat and frozen to death upriver not far from Circle City. Again everyone in Circle City was shocked. Truly, it seemed that tragedy and death were stalking the Yukon!

When we heard this last frightening news of the fate of the fifteen men, we at Circle huddled in cabins and talked almost in whispers. Moore and Graff suddenly changed their minds about tackling the river and were mighty glad to remain in Circle with the rest of us!

Now it was October 28th, four days after the three men had been frozen to death at Circle. Joaquin Miller and Canovan were determined to start out for Dawson in spite of the fact that the ice was still very new, and in spite of the fact, too, that they had no dogs.

This particular, momentous day dawned clear and crisp,

with a cold winter sun. Every man in Circle knew it was the day Miller and Canovan had chosen for their departure. Many shook their heads dubiously as they began gathering in little groups at the river to see them off.

"Fellows, why don't you grab your things and come along with us?" urged Joaquin as he and Canovan pulled up at our cabin, dragging their heavily loaded sleds. They were both bundled to the ears in thick clothing: big parkas, fur caps, fur-lined gloves and Indian moccasins.

"Joaquin, you surely make it sound like a short, easy jaunt," I said, "and I wish we could go with you, but we can't possibly get ready."

"Ah, come on," said Joaquin. "With the equipment we all have put together, we could get by. You know, it'll be a great adventure! And you may be very sure I'll write this trip up for the newspapers . . . and you'll all be famous some day!"

"No, Joaquin," said Tibbetts firmly, but with a little laugh, "we'll pass up the fame! We're going to stay alive here in Circle and try to assemble an outfit; also, we hope to get a few dogs. Maybe we'll catch up with you—who knows?"

"Joaquin," I said anxiously, "why don't you wait here longer?"

Joaquin looked at me with a friendly smile. "No, Ed, I can't contain myself another day at Circle! I'm a strong believer in Fate . . . and I feel an urgent call to get out on the ice and be on my way. Perhaps there's a reason—who knows? Maybe we'll be able to help some poor devil out there on the ice . . . and, at the same time, I'll be making my way back towards civilization with my long-delayed stories. Yes, and think of the experiences I'll have to write about afterwards! You know, there's a certain excitement in daring the elements! I'm willing to risk it . . . and bet on it! And don't worry about us, fellows, we'll make it. Canovan knows the country."

The crowd was gathering on the riverbank. A few cameras clicked as Joaquin turned to us and said: "Men, it's certainly been good to know you. Thanks for all the extra meals and interesting evenings which I've enjoyed with you in your cabin. I shall never forget you jolly men of the Outcast Club of Circle City. Goodbye, all, and thanks. . . . Hope sometime we meet again."

We all shook hands warmly. Somehow, we hated to tell Joaquin Miller goodbye. He certainly had helped brighten our stay at Circle City. This brilliant, colorful fellow would leave an empty place in our group of men when we sat around evenings in our cabin on broken-down chairs and boxes, sipping weak coffee or smoking our pipes, trying to pass the time. Yes, we would miss him—that was certain. There could never be another Joaquin Miller!

Now the crowd was milling closer for last farewells.

"Say, Joaquin, you and Canovan aren't really going without dogs, are you?" suddenly asked Weymouth, a newly arrived fellow at Circle, as incredulously he eyed the two sleds stacked high with miscellaneous equipment.

"Sure," said Joaquin.

"Good Lord. You fellows don't realize what's ahead of you! I'd never start out like that. I don't think the devil himself would, either!"

"Ah, come now," laughed Joaquin a little uneasily. "You make it sound pretty grim, but the trip probably won't be nearly as bad as you anticipate. Don't worry, we'll be all right. We're counting on good traveling weather and Indian shelters along the Yukon. I'm sure we'll be in Dawson before you know it. Once there, we'll get malemutes and more food, then strike out for the coast . . . and I'll wager we'll be in California basking in the sun while you poor fellows still shiver in your boots up here!"

"Well, if self-assurance does it, then you'll make it!" said Weymouth. "But I'm warning you, it won't be any California picnic!"

Now there were many last-minute messages and warnings—mostly warnings. Joaquin and Canovan suddenly looked a little ill and turned away quickly toward the river, letting their sleds gingerly down the steep embankment to the river. They seemed nervous and anxious to get started. Once on the ice, they adjusted their sled straps tightly over their shoulders; then, with a wave of their hands, they turned resolutely up the river, staying close to shore.

A fresh blanket of hard, coarse snow had fallen during

the night, and under the heatless winter sun it sparkled like rock salt. The two men started out with a good, brisk gait, but we could see that their sleds pulled heavily. As they walked along, they passed close to our ship, the *Weaver,* still held in the steel-like grip of the ice. Two of the remaining "pirate" deck hands, who had climbed aboard for some forgotten items, came out near the big stern-wheel and waved and shouted a boisterous farewell. Joaquin and Canovan returned the salute without stopping.

Soon, the men passed the *Victoria* and the little *Bella* and also another ship, the *St. Michael,* which had been caught in the slough since summer. As we watched, the men changed their course and zigzagged around several broken, splintered, submerged boats caught in the ice. Then, on and on, the two men went toward the center of the river, while Joaquin's tall, lean figure diminished in height, and Canovan's stockier figure became more squatty.

As their sled marks lengthened out across the ice, the old Yukoners shook their heads and began talking among themselves. "Why, the crazy fools, going off half-cocked like that without dogs! And I don't think they even had a stove or tent." "Well, I'm afraid it'll be the finish of that poet-fellow, Joaquin Miller, and Canovan!" "Yep, it sure will be a miracle if they ever reach Dawson alive!" "The only hope I can see for 'em are the Yukon Indians along the way! . . ."

While the crowd talked on, we kept a close eye on the river and the departing men, who were now growing smaller and smaller in the distance. At last, they reached the bend of the river—two small, dark figures silhouetted against the ice and snow. Now they had stopped and were waving a last farewell. Their voices came faintly: "Goodbye, men of Circle! Goodbye! . . ."

Then, in response, a great cry went up from all of us on the bank: "Goodbye, Joaquin and Canovan! Goodbye! Good luck!"

And as we watched, their forlorn, lonely figures disappeared quickly around the bend into the silent, bleak wilderness of ice and snow.

"Fellows, I'm fearful for Joaquin and Canovan," I said. "And I believe Canovan was fearful, too. He seemed nervous and apprehensive this past week. I regret now that we didn't try harder to dissuade Joaquin."

"Yes, perhaps we should have tried harder," said Tibbetts, "but I don't think it would have done much good. You know Joaquin's mind was completely made up, and he had exacted a promise from Canovan to make the trip with him. He even promised him immortal fame!"

That night, as our party of men walked along the riverfront viewing the silent Yukon and the four steamers frozen in the ice, we glanced up at the wond'rous Arctic heavens, brilliantly scintillating with millions of stars. There was the North Star and the Big Dipper almost beneath, tipped as though spilling out Arctic gold. There was the Milky Way, like nebulous snow across the heavens. There, too, far to the southeast, was the head of Orion appearing on the horizon. Far to the northwest, sunk low in the heavens, was Job's Coffin. And, high over all, in infinite space, hung the Northern Cross!

Wistfully, I looked at the stars and thought of the great distance we were from home. And then I thought anxiously of our friends, the intrepid Joaquin Miller and Canovan, who were somewhere out there on the frozen river. How were they faring? I wondered.

But how could we know, though we feared it, that Joaquin and Canovan were destined for great hardships ahead; that they would be caught in blizzards; at times wander lost in storms on the ice; that Joaquin would suffer from snow blindness; that they would have to chop their way through mountainous ice blocking their path; that, once, Canovan would fall through a thin spot in the ice and be rescued by Joaquin; finally, that they would have to discard some of their supplies to lighten their loads. And if it had not been for friendly Chief Lewis and his people and several white packers, they might have disappeared from the face of the Arctic!

How could we know as we looked at the stars that night of October 28th, 1897?

Chapter XIX

Footprints in the Snow

It was the bitterly cold morning of November 9th, 1897. Snow was falling fast, like large, white polka dots coming down through a thick, hazy curtain from grayish, leaden skies.

I trudged along through the heavy blanket of snow on the icy surface of the Yukon River. It was awkward business, this—breaking trail on snowshoes, dragging my heavily loaded sled behind me and trying to avoid those half-concealed chunks of jagged ice blocks sticking up from the frozen surface of the icy river beneath me.

I paused and raised my hand to wipe the snow from my eyes. I could just barely make out the course of the river through the driving snow. It was necessary that I keep to the left side of the river, headed north. How easy it would be, in this kind of weather, to become lost and completely turned around and unknowingly be headed in the wrong direction. Surely, Circle City, at the most, couldn't be more than seven miles away to the north; but what a strenuous, long, weary seven miles they would be, judging from the half mile which had taken at least two heartbreaking hours to cover since leaving Fish Camp early in the morning.

I strained my eyes harder so as to see through the driving snow. Naturally, the visibility was very poor. Only a small portion of the great wilderness of ice and snow showed close at hand, but the cold desolation from thousands of square miles of Arctic wilderness seemed to scream at me.

To the north, no living thing appeared in sight. Only occasionally the ghostly shape of rocks or trees indistinctly loomed up along the shoreline as I trudged closer to the bank of the river.

Anxiously I glanced up at the grayish, monotoned sky. It was certain there would be no sun today. I knew that the heatless winter sun was sulking somewhere to the east, low on the Arctic horizon. At the very most, a fellow could only count on about six more hours of this opaque daylight.

Then that awful Arctic night would swoop down over the Yukon country!

Yes, I must try to break trail faster, or it would mean another miserable night out on the Yukon in this stormy, bitterly cold weather.

Now, as I trudged wearily along, my thoughts began keeping rhythm with each labored beat of my straining heart. It certainly was fortunate that my party of men had all crowded into my tent at Fish Camp last night and held that serious council to consider our slim chances of making it to the "Outside." Yes, I thought with great relief, it was very wise that we had immediately decided to make tracks back to Circle City. How utterly foolish we had been, thinking we could pit our strength against the relentless North to try to make that 1,000-mile trek to Juneau without dogs! I chastened myself, blamed myself severely, for having been a persuasive factor in this foolhardy attempt.

But how I had chafed, and how desperately anxious and restless I had been, to tackle the trail—yes, anything to get away from Circle City and be moving on the Yukon in the direction of home and family in Tacoma. Of course, now it was a bitter pill to admit defeat, but it was far better to see the mistake before it was too late! Well, anyway, we were returning to Circle City. I speculated that the fellows there would give us the horselaugh when they saw us again.

I was more than humble—I was glad to be leading my party of men back toward Circle, from where we had so hopefully set out just two days before. But how unusually unwieldy my snowshoes were becoming! How increasingly tired I felt, and how numb and cold my feet were! It seemed like the runners of my homemade sled were pulling heavier and heavier each moment. It seemed as if it were loaded with lead, pressed hard over coarse desert sands. Yes, I knew it now, it was certainly too dangerous to attempt a long trip to the "Outside" without dogs, even though several intrepid souls like Joaquin Miller and Canovan had started out. But where were they now? Well, they had been gone for nearly two weeks and no words had come of them!

Frantically, my thoughts returned to Circle City. Yes, it was truly a place of refuge there; but it was a tragic place, too. Already the frozen bodies of a number of unfortunate, hapless fellows had been brought into Circle for burial.

There was the pitiful case of poor Ryan—such a fine fellow!—who had come North for gold. Well, they had brought him into Circle City only a few hours before our departure. His feet were badly frozen—already his toes and feet were turning dark—gangrene had set in!

"Poor Ryan's gone too long with those frozen feet," said a miner. "A week is too long! I'm afraid we'll have to amputate both his feet above the ankles."

"How?" I had asked in utter horror.

"Well, damn it all, they'll have to be sawed off," the miner had said grimly, "and the job will have to be done by one of the toughest miners in town—one of us with the strongest guts and the sharpest saw! No, sir, there isn't a doctor here among us. It's a damn shame, too!"

Now I shuddered at the thought of poor Ryan. A fellow losing both feet! How helpless he would be up here in the Arctic. But it could happen to any of us out here on the Yukon! It was too horrible to contemplate. All for the eager desire for that hard, yellow, metal stuff—gold! And had Ryan found any gold? No! And even if he had, was it worth the loss of both feet?

I tried to put these horrible, unpleasant thoughts from my mind, but they refused to take flight. Then I thought of another pathetic fellow recently brought into Circle City. But this poor fellow was dead! A miner had found him miles out from Circle slumped over in the snow, bent almost double, near his heavily loaded sled. The poor fellow was frozen as hard as marble. At first glance, it had looked to the miner who found him as if the poor fellow had just sat down too long to rest and had frozen to death there. But on closer inspection, the miner had discovered that he had had a terribly mangled and very badly broken leg. What had caused it? No one knew, nor did anyone know his identity.

"It's plain," said the miner who had brought the unknown fellow into Circle City, where we gathered around him, "that that poor devil shot himself. He was all alone, you know, and realized he was too helpless to go on. He thought he would die anyway, so he quickly ended it all with a bullet through his head. I found the revolver sunk deep in the snow almost under his body!"

"Ah, yes," said an old-timer in Circle shaking his head grimly, "and these early winter tragedies are just the beginning! Men, I'm afraid, when spring comes, we'll have a number of corpses to thaw out and bury—a very unpleasant job! We can't put 'em in pine coffins all doubled up in sitting positions. Those poor frozen devils will have to be stored down in the empty log house near the cemetery in the south end of town. The corpses will just have to wait until spring for decent burial."

"Holy mackerel! And Caesar's ghost!" a white-faced miner shudderingly exclaimed. "It gives me the willies to think of it! Frozen men sitting down there in that log storehouse all winter . . . waiting for spring to thaw out! From that end of town, believe me, I'm steering clear!"

"Yes, how terrible it would be to be a victim of the ice!" I muttered to myself with a shudder. It seemed as if I could see the faces of those pitiful victims all over again. I reached under my coat to my hip pocket to see if I still had my precious little book—my diary. It told the whole story from my first day going North in the gold rush. It told of my fruitless struggles and search for gold in the Klondike, on the Bonanza, the Eldorado, and of the hardships and the heartaches. If anything should happen to me here in the Arctic, well, I knew my wife would eventually know the full story. I had written my name and address in big letters inside the cover before I had started out on the ice.

I paused a moment and glanced back over my shoulder. Coming single-file through the fast-falling snow, my party of men moved silently not far behind me. How comforting it was to know I was not alone on the frozen river! Wearily, my party of men followed in my footsteps in the trail I was so painfully breaking.

In the lead, and directly behind me, was Captain Tibbetts, bent almost double, straining hard, dragging his heavily loaded sled behind him; a few feet back of him came Shelley Graves, struggling with his sled; then came Calhoun, Bertram, Moore, Hill and Graff with their sleds And though I couldn't see them clearly in the mist of falling snow, in the rear came the snow-covered, shadowy figures of Henry Pinkus, the Jew, and Tom Fisher, the Englishman—two strangers who had joined our party just a mile out from

Circle City, two days ago. Pinkus had told me, immediately upon joining our party, that he was headed toward Dawson with a sledful of candles, which he was eager to sell for a dollar apiece. He had rubbed his fur-gloved hands expectantly as he announced with relish, "I'll make lots of money on those candles in Dawson! There's lots of money to be made by a good merchant up here! Yes, I'm glad to travel with you men. Let's hurry and reach Dawson!"

Well, now, it seemed that Pinkus wasn't going to get those precious candles to Dawson and make that small fortune—at least not for a long while! I struggled on; my thoughts continued.

All at once, I felt a little ill and wobbly. I staggered a little and stopped. Well, what could a fellow expect anyway? Surely, a thin strip of bacon and a skimpy portion of rice hurriedy washed down with weak black coffee wasn't enough for such grueling, strenuous exercise, especially in such bitterly cold weather. It would take every last ounce of my reserve energy to continue.

"Say, Ed," called Shelley Graves, taking long strides to catch up when he saw me hesitate, "let me break trail for a while. Give me the snowshoes."

"All right, Shelley," I said gratefully as I wearily unfastened the snowshoes. "I'll drop behind for a while. But keep a sharp eye out for the left riverbank. Always try to keep it in sight. We mustn't get turned around for a minute. Almost any time a blizzard could whip up the Yukon. We've got a long, hard tug of war ahead of us yet!"

"Don't worry, Ed," said Shelley. "I think I know my way on the river by instinct. Think I know the direction of Circle City blindfolded!"

"Perhaps," I said, "but we can't take any chances. How are your feet holding out? I mean those horrible sores on your heels?"

"Oh, those," laughed Shelley ruefully, with forced nonchalance, but in apparent pain. "Well, they're hurting me more than yesterday. But I'm determined I'm not stopping for anything, even if I have to walk on bleeding stumps! So it's forward—charge!—up the Yukon! on to Circle City!

"But frankly, Ed," he added, lowering his voice to a worried whisper, "I'm really concerned about Tibbetts. He's much older than any of us. You know, yesterday he petered out several times, just barely made it to Fish Camp last night. And say, did you know his feet were wet that last half mile?"

"Yes, I found out," I said with a shiver. "It was a mighty lucky thing we made it to that deserted camp last night. When we got there, I discovered my feet were wet, too. I'll say it was a miracle that none of us had frozen feet! But it must have been a trifle warmer yesterday and the strenuous exercise, no doubt, saved us from frostbite. To-day, I don't think we would be so lucky. I haven't seen any good place a fellow could build a fire in this driving snow. Let's hope it isn't necessary to stop!" I concluded.

"Gosh, let's hope it isn't necessary!" said Shelley Graves with a serious tone. "Let's hope we can all keep going and make it around that last bend to Circle City before darkness falls."

All day my party of men and I stumbled on through the snow. At intervals, all except Tibbetts took turns breaking trail. But because I had been the most determined and the most persuasive in our party to attempt this unsuccessful trip, naturally I felt the most responsible. Therefore, I wanted to bear the brunt of the trail-breaking.

Late in the afternoon, the snow ceased, and this helped greatly; but it was already dark as we finally stumbled around the last big bend of the river—and there was Circle City! Tiny glints of candlelights twinkled out across the new-fallen snow from cabin windows. What a welcoming sight it truly was to us weary, footsore, half-frozen men! Those lights gleamed like little friendly beacons.

Once again, as on October first, the gold camp was a wonderful place of refuge! As fast as our unsteady legs would carry us, we made for Captain Morgan's old cabin and pushed open the door to find it exactly as we had left it. Soon, we had a crackling fire going, then a little hot food, and we rolled thankfully into our sleeping bags and soon were snoring our great fatigue away.

The following morning, Joe Lamour, Circle City's stranded and very popular mail carrier, came by our cabin and banged on the door.

"Hey, who's in there?" he shouted as I hurried to open the door. "Well, I'll be darned!" he said in pleased surprise when he saw all of us. "If it ain't the stowaways and outcasts! Golly be, if I'm not glad ter see you back here. You know, I was pretty doggone worried about you all starting out the way you did, half-cocked, without dogs!"

"Well, sir," said Tibbetts, limping across the cabin, "That Indian village, Fish Camp, was far enough for me, and I admit I nearly collapsed before getting there. And I thought I'd never make it back to Circle today, and wouldn't have if it had not been for the boys helping with my sled several times."

"Jumpin' Jupiter!" exclaimed Moore, "Are we glad to be back! I'm telling you, those last four miles were almost as bad as crossing Chilkoot, and I believe my feet were colder and hurt more!"

"Yeah," said Joe, "now will you Cheechakos believe us old sourdoughs when we tell you not to start out over the ice unless you're properly equipped? I guess you fellows realize now the hazards of traveling on the river in bad weather, pulling a hundred and fifty pounds of dead weight on homemade, wooden-runner sleds. And say, that reminds me—that poet-fellow, Joaquin Miller, and Canovan are having a pretty tough time!"

"Where are they?" I asked anxiously.

"Well, Atwood, the packer, came in. Said he saw 'em out on the ice only twenty-five miles south of Circle City. Said the wolves had been following 'em too. Think of it! They'd been on their way over a week and had only made twenty-five miles! Of course, it's because they haven't got dogs to help them with their sleds. For the same reason, I'm staying right here in Circle. The mail can wait!"

"How can Joaquin and Canovan survive?" I asked apprehensively, thinking of our own recent hardships.

"They won't!" said Joe emphatically. "That is, unless they meet up with men traveling with dogs going their way up the Yukon. Atwood urged Miller and Canovan to return to Circle, but do you suppose those stubborn idiots would come back? No, sir! Said it was too far, too terrible, to walk back to Circle those twenty-five miles!"

"Humph! How about that heartbreaking trek ahead of

them to reach Dawson?" asked Tibbetts gravely.

"That's just the point," said Joe, "they have over three hundred miles of torturous ice ahead of them; but you can't convince some fellows—not that poet-fellow, when he's made up his mind! What do you think he said?"

"What?" I asked.

"Well, Joaquin said, 'When a fellow sets his hand to the plow, he should never turn back!'

"You men were wise to come back," continued Joe. "You'll be darned fools if you stir from Circle without malemutes. We old Yukoners know the dangers. Now, you take poor Ryan, that fellow who had both feet so badly frozen over a week ago. Well, they sawed off his feet just above the ankles. It was gruesome. I tell you they had turned almost as black as ink! Well, the poor devil didn't feel the pain too much at first, 'cause they was frozen so bad—just like an anesthetic—but he cried when they was cutting 'em off. How sorry we all felt! Lord! Today, he's suffering terribly, though. Keeps hollering and hollering for something to deaden the pain in those stumps. Gosh, it's horrible! And all the miners have got to give him is whisky! But it ain't enough. Just makes you cringe to hear him moanin' and sufferin' so!

"Yes," added Joe sadly, "there've been too many frozen hands and feet. We all know that if frostbite is treated immediately it can be cured. The common way, of course, is to rub the frozen parts with snow or ice. Oddly enough, it seems to pull out the frostbite and gets the blood circulating. But lots of times the miners aren't aware of it when they are frostbitten. Many's the time I've had some fellow grab up a handful of snow and begin rubbing my nose like mad. Seems like that's one of the most vulnerable spots. We're all worried about two young miners who came in from Birch Creek with frozen hands. They may have to be amputated, too. Oh, I'm telling you it's been an evil winter up here—the worst I can remember on the Yukon. There hasn't been enough food to go around, and too many green Cheechakos are wildly roaming the North looking for gold!"

"Joe," I asked anxiously, "do you think we are stuck here for the winter? Do you think there is any possible way of procuring dogs?"

"Sure, Ed, you can get dogs, all right," said Joe sarcastically. "There's a fellow here at Circle named Ellinger whose got nine dogs for sale. He wants ten thousand dollars for 'em. Just think of it! Ten thousand dollars for nine dogs!"

"Great Scott!" I said, "Why, that's over a thousand dollars apiece!"

"Yep, and those animals of his wouldn't bring more than fifty cents apiece in the States!"

"Why, it's incredible—just highway robbery for cur dogs," I said. "Why, none of us have that kind of money!"

"Well, I predict anarchy and black violence in most of the settlements along the Yukon in the next few months," said Joe. "You just can't coop up hundreds of hungry men without serious trouble. I hear already there's been plenty of trouble up at Fort Yukon. A fellow brought down news that the 'pirates' of the *Weaver* had been in terrible rows and fist fights over the dance-hall girls, love and food rationing. I'm thinking the pirates should have stayed at Circle City. Anyway, one of them is reported to have shot a man. He's been arrested. The man isn't dead yet, but they'll surely hang the pirate if that fellow dies.

"Yes, continued Joe, "another story reached us this morning. Remember Captain Ray, who several weeks ago went to Fort Yukon to guard the N. A. Trading Company's gold? Well, he was robbed. Someone took almost ten thousand dollars in gold dust at the point of a gun. Captain Ray thinks it was one of the men from the steamer *Bella*, though the face was covered with a mask."

"The news is terribly distressing," I said, "especially since we know all of these men."

"Yes, the Yukon is certainly in bad shape," said Joe. "Guess Mr. Prevo, the Episcopal missionary of Circle, should try to get up to Fort Yukon to help tame those wild, unruly hyenas. A little religion might help! Some think those 'pirates' are really going to the bad, for sure. Why, it's being rumored they might even return to Circle City and begin looting the camp. Men, if I were in your place, I'd never leave your cabin unguarded. Everybody in Circle is watching his grub like a hawk.

"And say," continued Joe, "that reminds me. Prevo is

having church services down at the schoolhouse tomorrow night. I'm delegated to invite all fellows to come and hear the sermon. They'll be serving something light to eat. Of course, you know it's an inducement to get the miners to come out. But, by golly, a fellow would be crazy not to, especially if he's getting a free handout! Besides, the singing's fun! You know, Ed, Prevo has some good hymnbooks, and when the fellows sing, they always speed up the tempo of these hymns so they turn out to be real peppy songs, sort of happy-like!"

"Is there any more exciting news you can think of before you go?" asked Bertram eagerly.

"Well, that's about all I can think of right now," answered Joe. "You know, I'm the walking, talking newspaper of Circle City. But listen, fellows, there is something else I could tell you. There's been an interesting rumor afoot. I can't put my finger on it right now. But it's a vague whispering of great quantities of gold . . . maybe somewhere in the Arctic Circle, possibly not too far away."

"Where could it be?" we asked excitedly.

"Oh, I dunno," answered Joe rather evasively. "Perhaps there's nothing to it. Maybe it's only fools' gold someone's seen! But if I find out, I'll give you a tip," added Joe as he fastened his parka and prepared to leave to go to the next cabin to invite the men to church services.

"Yep." Joe said as he closed the door, "I'm sure mighty glad you fellows decided to return to Circle City!"

Chapter XX

Circle of Gold

After our foolhardy attempt to get out of the North over the ice on November 19th, 1897, without sled dogs, my party of men and I settled down in Circle City, trying to reconcile ourselves to a frugal, monotonous existence. Now we realized full well that we were trapped for the winter and that we would be utterly foolish to attempt that 1,000-mile trip to Juneau without sled dogs. In the bitterly cold, bleak days which followed, when it seemed the endless nights intruded into daylight hours, darkening them more and more, and when sometimes the dead, blue-faced moon put in an early appearance and seemed reluctant to leave, casting her pale shafts of light down over the frozen Yukon, causing those weird, boat-shaped shadows (from our trapped steamer) to move along the ice in the direction of St. Michael, yes; on these dreary days when the wolves stalked the Yukon and howled their hunger to the elements, we would huddle in our cabin talking . . . talking of home and gold.

Home was uppermost in our thoughts and conversation. The very thought of it brought a terrific yearning and longing, like a burning, gnawing pain tearing at our very beings. And coupled with that great longing for home was that fateful, unsatisfied, feverish desire for gold.

Near Dawson, about 350 miles to the south in the Klondike, were the great claims on the Bonanza, the fabulous Eldorado and dozens of smaller gold-bearing creeks, pouring out the 200 tons of gold predicted for that winter of '97 and '98. The thought of it was quite maddening, though it was being said by the old sourdoughs that there must be other vast treasures of gold somewhere in the Arctic Circle in quantities, equaling or surpassing the Klondike. However, it seemed that all eyes were turned toward Dawson. Only half a million was expected from the Birch Creek area near Circle City on American territory, in comparison to those 200 tons of gold predicted from the Klondike!

But some of the lucky Klondike mine owners whom we knew in Dawson had not been so lucky, after all. Many had been forced to leave their claims to go in search of food, and many a poor fellow had already fallen ill of the scurvy, that dreaded disease. In its last stages, the flesh grows spotted, dark-green and ugly black, the victim hemorrhages and spits out his teeth like popcorn from gums that can no longer hold them in place. Yes . . . all this for gold!

We had heard of two fellows who had prospected for a whole year. Then, suddenly, Dame Fortune smiled sardonically on them. Yes, they had struck it rich! But, only a few days later, both died of scurvy in their lonely cabin not far from their "pot of gold"! They had been too weak to go in search of help. How ironic! Their fortunes and lives forfeited for lack of proper food! News had reached us that Stacey, my former partner, was ill again in Dawson. Good old Stacey! Earnestly, I hoped that Captain Ellis would look after him and that he would soon recover.

As the days wore on in Circle City, my party of men grew more high-strung and at times very quarrelsome. Some bad fist fights occurred in our cabin, fired by two quarts of whisky which several in the party had acquired and were drinking too freely. These quarrels, which we called "teapot-tempests," we tried to pass over lightly, but they were very distressing and temporarily put the interior of our one-room cabin in shambles!

Now it was very evident that our party of men, like dozens of others frozen in at Circle City, were ready to fight at the drop of the hat—"just like a pack of malemutes, snarling and snapping at each other," as one of the fellows put it. Even the mildest among us was becoming combative. Consequently, I spent no more time than was absolutely necessary in the cabin. I realized with a terrible jolt that being frozen in like this was spirit-killing, bringing out the worst in all of us, although I realized, too, that my party of men were good fellows, as good as any stuck at Circle City.

I was very glad, however, to get temporary jobs of freighting and hauling firewood. For this, I could use my homemade sledge; and, I discovered, by pouring water on the edges of the wooden runners and letting them freeze, repeating this several times (a trick I had learned from the old Yukoners), I would have slick sledding for a number of hours. For every cord of wood I hauled from the woodpile two miles away, I collected $10 in gold dust. Little by little, my small poke was growing heavier.

Sometimes, Shelley Graves, Moore and Graff would take their sleds and go with me, making a caravan. Often, on these hauling expeditions, we would scramble out of bed early, leaving Bertram, Hill, Calhoun and Tibbetts still snoring in their bunks. Sometimes, of course, they took a few turns, too. We'd grab a cup of coffee and a couple of small sourdough pancakes, then be on our way while the stars were still shining; and, if the day remained clear, usually those same big golden stars would be blinking down on us before we could get our last load back over the snow into Circle. Gradually, we began calling ourselves the "Golden Starlight Express." Naturally, because we were very nearly broke, we were most eager to collect all of the gold dust we could from this enterprise, though the jobs proved heavy and the work grueling. Many times we would have frostbitten fingers and toes, as the temperature usually ranged from 40 to 50 degrees below zero. How we longed for sled dogs to help us with this temporary work! And, also, how we longed for dogs with which to make the trip "Outside"!

It was now the 21st of November, and I was alone this day, coming back with a heavy load of wood. I struggled along the trail, pulling my sled, wishing more than ever for a dog team. It was then I met two miners coming from the direction of Circle City. They stopped and we had a little visit. I had seen these men once before in town and barely knew them by sight. They proved to be friendly fellows from remote Mastodon Creek and we talked about gold in the Arctic Circle. They said they had great faith in the region, that they thought there were many gold discoveries yet to be made in the Circle . . . but, for some reason, the gold deposits were not as concentrated as they were in the Klondike area. In other words, prospectors would have to go far out to prospect. Then, in the course of the conversation, they asked if I had had any luck prospecting, to which I rather shamefacedly said, "No, not yet!" Then they asked if I wouldn't like to have some dogs to pull my freight sled and go places.

"Great Scott!" I said, "I'd consider it a big favor if you'd tell me where I could procure dogs at a reasonable price. Ellinger is asking over a thousand apiece for his dogs!"

"An outrage!" exclaimed the miners. "Now, listen, Ed Lung, if you'll haul our eight hundred pounds of freight up to Twelve Mile House Station on Birch Creek, we'll try to see that you get some malemutes. And we'll gladly pay you twenty cents a pound for freighting, more than we usually pay the Indians. They have been packing for years, but they're getting so independent lately it seems we can't depend on them. Now, if you'll get our supplies up to Twelve Mile House for us, we'll have two of our miners pick the load up there and relay it on to us at our mines on Mastodon Creek. Naturally, we wouldn't expect you to freight over the Mastodon Trail. Often, snowstorms whip up and completely obliterate the trail. There are two routes a man can take to get to Mastodon Creek. The shortest is about seventy miles long and follows mostly along Crooked Creek. That's the way we go. But just let a fellow take the wrong fork of the river, and he'll find himself way over there on the other side of Mastodon Dome in very wild and hard-to-get-out-of wilderness . . . maybe even wandering in those Tanana Mountains."

While the miners were talking, mentally the accountant in me was quickly summing up the deal. At twenty cents a pound for eight hundred pounds, it would be $160 they were offering. Why, I'd have to deliver sixteen cords of wood to earn that much, making forty-eight trips, walking four miles round trip for each one-third cord, amounting to 192 miles of walking! Great Scott! If I contracted to haul this freight, I thought eagerly, I'd most likely get dogs to pull the sled and if I got dogs, my party of men and I would be the luckiest Cheechakos in Circle City!

"Men," I said excitedly, "tell me how can I make this deal?"

"Fine, Ed," said the miners. "We're expecting two freighters, Carrol and Martin, to come into Circle City by dog team tomorrow from Fort Yukon with our freight. As we explained to you, we're looking for a reliable packer who will deliver this freight to Twelve Mile House for us. Now here's your chance, Ed. Carroll and Martin usually bring a couple of extra dogs to sell. We believe you can get these at quite a reasonable price if you'll go out on the trail to meet them. We think it would be wise if you start out about noon tomorrow. And, for the love o' Mike, don't tell any of the other fellows in Circle City except your own party, or you'll probably have a wild stampede out there on the ice ahead of you. If that should happen, the freighters' price would probably double or triple, because, as you know, dogs are almost worth their weight in gold here!"

"Don't I know it!" I said fervently. "I believe every Cheechako in Circle has been trying to buy dogs!"

Before I parted from the miners, we had made all necessary arrangements and I had a note of introduction hastily scribbled on a scrap of paper. Jubilantly, I returned to town. Meeting the miners and getting that note was the best thing that had happened for many days. Truly, the future looked much brighter now. As I walked along, I began whistling a merry tune. Even the heavy logs seemed to pull easier.

It was still early in the day when I dumped my load of wood at the cabin of Mrs. Zabrisky, wife of one of the steamer pilots (she was half Indian and half white). I collected my gold dust from her, then decided to make one more trip for wood; but this time it would be for our own cabin and I would go to the gulch, a little closer to town.

I had just entered the shallow gulch to the south of Circle City and had begun cutting wood when, suddenly, I heard a dog bark. Quickly, I looked up and saw Bertram coming down the trail toward me pulling a load of wood. I was very surprised to see a big black malemute running along behind him.

"Great Scott, Bertram!" I called, "Where in blazes did you find that dog?"

"Right here in the gulch," yelled Bertram excitedly, "and Ed, I'm sure he's lost! He's been following me for the last half hour and there hasn't been another soul here during that time. Take a look at him. See, he's got a broken harness, Ed, have you ever seen this dog in Circle City or on the Birch Creek Trail before?"

"No, Bertram, I'm quite sure I haven't," I said as he drew up and I leaned over to pet the friendly dog. "But I'm sure some poor devil is missing him. It's evident he's broken away, maybe from some stampeder who needs him desperately out there on the Yukon. You know, a valuable dog like this just doesn't drop out of the blue!"

"He sure looks like a fine dog, Ed," said Bertram. "And man! what a great find if no one turns up to claim him!"

"Well, if they do," I said, "you'll have something with which to identify him."

"What?" he asked.

"Why, his broken harness, of course," I said. "And looks like it has an 'S' cut into the leather."

"So it does," said Bertram; and as he spoke, he reached

down and unclasped the broken harness, hurriedly tucking it under a large chunk of wood on his sled. "There, it's out of sight," he said. "Now, just let 'em try to get this dog!"

As we walked back to Circle a little later—Bertram, I and Rover (Bertram had begun calling him "Rover")—I recounted my good fortune of meeting the miners and the prospects of getting a dog team.

"Glory be!" said Bertram. "It's certainly been a lucky day for us, hasn't it? I've noticed when luck changes, it surely comes suddenly. Why, Ed, it means maybe we can go prospecting for gold!"

"Prospecting for gold?" I asked curiously. "But where? You know everything's staked on Birch Creek and others around here."

"Oh, I dunno, maybe over there in those mountains to the west, beyond Mastodon Dome," he answered rather vaguely. "Some fellows call it the unknown country of the Tanana Indians. You see, Ed, I've been looking over at those snow-capped mountains lately, getting awfully curious, hankering to go like everything. I've a good hunch there's lots of gold over there and I've been hearing the fellows talk a lot about it too! They say there've only been five or six explorers who've poked their faces into that wild country that they know of. Trouble is, they say the Indians over there are pretty hostile, not at all like the mild Yukon Indians. But everybody claims there must be gold in there. It's an exciting speculation when you know full well that all of this big country is auriferous territory."

"But, Bertram," I said, "you're not really serious? Why, that country is a vast wilderness with absolutely no trails beyond Mastodon Creek. And think of all of the deep snows in the mountains this time of year!"

"Yea, I know all the hazards," said Bertram, "and I know what else you're going to say, too. You're going to remind me that we don't have enough grub to leave Circle City for any prospecting trip. But I've been figuring since you told me about those freighters, Carrol and Martin, that they must have extra grub. Say, now, I'm wondering if we couldn't buy some from them? Then maybe we could start out for the Tanana. Ed, wouldn't it be exciting to be heading into that back country right now, probably toward a million dollars for each one of us?"

"Yes, maybe," I replied. "But, Bertram, it isn't as easy as all that. And don't forget my business deal. It comes first. I've contracted to get that eight hundred pounds of freight up to those miners so that we can get dogs. I'm telling you, if there was a stampede out of here today . . . well, no matter how exciting it would prove to be, I'd have to fulfill my obligation first!"

"Of course," said Bertram solemnly, "but don't forget, Ed, we all came up here for gold, too. And as yet, we haven't had a chance to strike it rich. This may be our last big opportunity!"

That night, the boys in our cabin were in very good humor. Rover was heartily welcomed into the inner circle of the "Outcast Club." The men petted the big dog and fed him morsels of food from their frugal supper. He seemed happy to be with us and we were overjoyed to have him, and also happy over the prospects of getting a dog team.

"Ed, I'd say you and Bert had a banner day!" said Tibbetts, approvingly slapping us on the backs, "but we'll have to keep our fingers crossed about Rover."

The next day, November 22nd, at noon, Moore and I prepared to go out on the Yukon to meet Carrol and Martin.

"Wish us luck," we called as we told the gang goodbye at the cabin.

"Wish me luck, too," said Bertram. "I'm going to tack up a sign at the trading company announcing that the 'Outcast Club' has found a dog. Think of the excitement that will create. Probably be a big stampede to our cabin. Well, we'll keep 'em busy here while you fellows go out to buy the dogs!"

As Moore and I walked briskly over the rather well-packed trail, he said thoughtfully, "I've a feeling, Ed, that Rover is going to belong to us. He'll be worth his weight in gold to us, especially if we are lucky enough to get those other dogs and can work him into the team."

Moore and I walked briskly for about two miles and were getting a little discouraged, thinking that, perhaps, the miners had sent us on a wild-goose chase, when all at once we saw two very long dog teams racing towards us over the ice from the north. The dark forms of dogs, sleds and drivers were silhouetted against the white of the snow as they moved rapidly in our direction. Moore and I walked quickly on to meet them.

When we came together a few minutes later, the drivers called "Whoa!" to their teams. It was the custom for travelers always to stop on the ice when meeting strangers to ask about the news and weather and everything in general; but Moore and I skipped the salutations and went right to the point.

The two men answered: "Yes, we are Carrol and Martin. Yes, we have dogs to sell, but we wanted to sell them to packers or freighters, not to Cheechakos."

"Well, men," I said, handing them the note, "I'm Ed Lung and this is Billy Moore. We're new freighters, and here is a message for you."

"All right," said Carrol after he'd read the note, "I'll sell you three dogs from my team. As they stand, they are Chattel, Caution and Pointer. You can have them for three hundred dollars apiece, including harnesses."

"Good Lord!" I said. "That's wonderful!"

"Yeah, it's mighty reasonable, too," said Martin. "It's because you're going to haul that freight for those miners up on Mastodon."

"You won't change your minds when you get to Circle, will you?" asked Moore uneasily. "Because we'll have to pay you in gold dust at our cabin."

"Of course not," replied Carrol. "The deal is made. You have our word for it."

"But say, have you fellows ever driven a dog team before?" asked Martin curiously.

"Well, I haven't," I said as I reached down and petted the furry head of Chattel.

"Well, then," said Martin, "all you have to remember is when you yell 'Gee!' the dogs go to the right; 'Haw!' to the left; and 'Mush on!' means go like hell straight ahead. And, of course, 'Whoa!' means stop, just like when you're driving a team of horses."

"These dogs we're going to sell you are pretty smart," said Carrol, "but they don't understand much English yet. They were owned by a Frenchman up on Porcupine River.

The Frenchman gave up his claim early this fall and sold these dogs to us at Fort Yukon. Said he was getting out of the country on the last boat. Said he wasn't going to sit the winter out watching those Indians near his diggings starve to death like so many did last winter. That Frenchman made us promise if we sold the dogs we would find good owners."

"Thanks, fellows, you've found them!" I said gratefully as I reached down and petted Chattel again. He whined and strained at the harness to get closer to me. "Good boy," I said, "I know we're going to be friends!" Chattel whined a little and gave me his paw, and we sealed the pact.

"Good Chattel," I said, "I'll teach you a lot of English . . . and maybe I can learn a little French, too." Moore chuckled at that and leaned down and petted the other dogs.

We men chatted for just a little longer, then Carrol and Martin said they had to be on their way. They cracked their whips and yelled "Mush on!" calling back to us that they would stop at Captain Morgan's cabin bright and early the next morning to turn the dogs and freight over to us.

"It's no use trying to keep up with those men," said Moore as the dogs started with a jerk, quickly picking up speed. "The two packers will run along behind the sleds for a short distance, then jump on the back runners and ride. The trail is very smooth and slick here on this part of the river and they'll be in Circle City in no time!"

Moore and I reached our cabin late in the afternoon just as the sun was dropping fast behind the cold, snow-capped mountains to the west, and although we were very tired, we were in high spirits. Indeed, we were lucky men!

"Fellows," we called jubilantly as we pushed open the door, "congratulate us! We've bought three fine malemutes!"

"Hurrah!" said Bertram. "It's wonderful! And, so far, no one has been able to identify Rover, although dozens of men have tried. Fellows, you'd 'uv died laughing to 've heard them!"

"Yes," said Tibbetts, "it looks like Rover'll be ours, all right! But we can't feel sure for several days yet."

That night in the cabin we celebrated our unbelievably good fortune. We weighed and counted out the gold dust by emptying out every last fleck of gold in our pokes. By shaking the sacks, we found we had just barely enough to pay for the three dogs, with a little over for extra grub Carrol and Martin had agreed to sell us.

Who cared if we would be broke in the morning? We would have a little more grub and own three wonderful malemutes! . . . And yes, perhaps four, including Rover. Could anyone in civilization possibly know what that would mean to us fellows stranded up here on top of the world! No, how could they? Yes, my party of men knew we were in luck. We were certainly going to have a very much greater sense of security once we got those dogs promised by Carrol and Martin.

On that momentous morning of November 23rd, 1897, Rover was still with us, and the two packers kept their word and came to our cabin early. When they left, we were flat broke, but lighthearted. We owned Chattel, Caution and Pointer, plus a new supply of flour, some extra canned goods and some dog food. The 800 pounds of freight was stored in the A.C.C. Company's warehouse, waiting for us to haul up to Twelve Mile House station.

Before the freighters left, they gave us a few essential instructions concerning the care of the dogs and what to feed them, saying we should try to get dried fish from the Indians; also we should give the dogs a little bacon cooked with flour whenever we could spare it.

"Of course, fellows," remarked the freighters as they shook hands to say goodbye, "that'll be a big problem from now on. We wish you luck! If you have any trouble getting dried fish from the Indians, appeal to Chief Joseph."

As soon as the freighters had gone, Moore and I took our two sledges around to the warehouse and loaded up. We each had 400 pounds and two dogs to pull the heavily loaded sleds. We thought we could manage it, as the trail leading out of Circle looked smooth and quite well traveled. Naturally, we were anxious to get started, although we noticed the sky looked rather gray. Somehow fate was working against us, as far as this trip was concerned. We had only gone about a mile when it began to snow, coming down in thick flurries. Moore and I decided it would be very unwise to continue and hurriedly retraced our steps to the warehouse. The fellows there said we had shown good judgment, as a heavy snowstorm was in the making, which might last for days. "Better not try it again until the weather clears!" was the warning. "A good packer watches the weather."

While we were disappointed at not being able to continue our journey, still, during that short trip, Moore and I had learned a great deal about our new dogs. Chattel was very temperamental, but a good worker; Caution was a little lazy and needed coaxing; Pointer was a very nervous, high-strung animal, but with understanding could be managed. And we discovered, too, that big Rover was a powerful dog and a good worker, but could be very stubborn at times. As Moore summed it up later when we returned to the cabin, "Maybe it'll take a few times out on the trail to learn all of the peculiarities of these dogs and to know just how to manage them. But, Great Scott! How fortunate we are to own them!"

The storm raged for the next five days while the pages of late November turned slowly. During that time, on November 24th, Joe Lamour, the stranded mail carrier, came to our cabin bursting with the exciting news that he had heard that fifty men had secretly slipped out of Circle headed for the Tanana region in search of rumored gold. Six of them had been damned idiots . . . had started off half-cocked with scarcely any supplies, and worst of all, had had no sled dogs! "Who'll know where to look for them in that big country if they get lost?" raged Lamour. "Probably in the spring, vultures will be picking their bones!"

We had all shivered a little at the thought of those men leaving the comforts of their cabins and daring the elements. But who could tell? Maybe some of them would be lucky enough to stumble onto gold somewhere off in that wild, unknown region so far to the west. Yes, the thought was intriguing!

While the storm continued, we talked of gold, and we knew that dozens of others at Circle City were also discussing the same possibility.

Then, as we waited, Pinkus came to our cabin to beg us to go out on the Yukon Trail with our dog team to help him find his crates of precious candles, which he had foolishly persuaded an unwilling, heavily loaded packer to take along to Dawson. Word had just come back that his candles had been lost or dumped off the sledge somewhere on the ice twenty miles south of Circle City.

"I'm nearly broke," he wailed. "I bought those boxes of candles with almost the last cent I had, and I expected to get a dollar apiece at Dawson. Now they are being covered with snow, maybe lost forever on the ice!"

While we pitied Pinkus, we simply would not allow ourselves to be persuaded, reminding him that we had an important freighting job just as soon as the weather permitted. Besides, in that section of the river there were reported to be great blocks of frozen ice, some as big as houses piled up in the river near where the cliffs rose high and slippery.

Yes, we fellows knew, now that we had dogs, there would be many in Circle who would want to team up with us. Perhaps it was a good thing we had 800 pounds of freight to deliver at this time!

It was now the day after Thanksgiving. All we had had the previous day to remind us of the holiday was a can of plum pudding gotten from Carrol and Martin. This day of November 26th dawned clear and cold, the temperature stood at 40 degrees below zero, when Graff, Bertram and I went to the warehouse to get those 800 pounds of freight. Moore was feeling indisposed and we advised him to stay at Circle. Soon we had our two large sledges lashed together, piled high with freight and tied down securely. The dogs stood waiting expectantly in the harness.

"Let me give you a little advice," said the trader as we were about to leave. "You're very heavily loaded and you shouldn't try to make it to Twelve Mile today. The trail is very fresh after the snowstorm. Stop at Eight Mile House tonight. The innkeeper at that station serves meals to the packers and miners and has a number of bunks, too."

We thanked the trader for his advice and were soon mushing out of Circle. We were surprised at how well the dogs were working. They seemed to sense our important mission. Soon we came to the gulch through which the trail led, meeting many fellows packing freight on their shoulders. Only a few had dog teams.

"How's the trail ahead?" we asked anxiously as the snow grew deeper in places.

"Not good, fellows. With this very cold temperature, a heavy crust is forming which makes traveling difficult. But, by tomorrow, the trail should be well packed, with so many traveling on it."

Our progress became very slow, and in places we got off the trail and had to put our shoulders to the sleds and help push them along, being on the alert for concealed rocks and stumps. But when the trail finally reached the level ground again, it was easier and it wound in and out among the stunted, snow-draped trees of spruce and birch, making almost a fairyland picture. On some of the trees, great icicles clung like sparkling Christmas-tree ornaments of dazzling crystal. The sun was bright and glistened on the snow like millions of diamonds rained upon the earth. But the winter sun shed almost no heat in this frozen land, affecting little the snappy sharpness of the air, which made us tingle as we struggled along, our eyes squinting continually from the terrific glare of sun on snow and ice.

As we began encountering more and more strangers on the trail, naturally we became quite uneasy about Rover, fearful that someone would suddenly call out for us to stop, and immediately demand him. But, so far, there had been nothing but friendly words called hurriedly as we passed the others on the trail or as we stopped a moment now and then to rest and talk about our freighting problems.

We had gone perhaps three miles when, suddenly, a fellow coming down the trail stopped dead in his tracks, visibly staring at us. The fellow looked a little familiar, I thought, and yet everyone at Circle City looked familiar to me by now.

"Hey," he yelled as he rushed toward us. "Stop! Wait a minute. I've got to talk to you."

My heart sank. I was sure this was it! He had recognized Rover. When the fellow drew up, I expected him to grab Rover and then there would be a nasty scene. But, to my surprise, he rushed past Rover up to me, slapped me on the back, and exclaimed, "Why, Ed Lung, it's you!" It was then

I recognized Fitzgerald under a mop of whiskers, his furry parka pulled half down over his eyes.

"Why, Ed, it's good to see you!" he said, clapping me on the back again. We clasped hands warmly. Fitzgerald and I hadn't laid eyes on each other since Stacey, I and he had built our boats at Lake Linderman in early June, getting ready to come down the Yukon to Dawson.

I introduced him to my companions and then we had a quick, lively visit for a few minutes, putting each other up to date on all that had transpired since last we had seen each other at the lake.

"Poor Stacey," I said, "he's sick in Dawson. I don't know where the Ryans, the Kellys, the Hydes and the rest of them are now."

"Yes, it's hard telling where they might be now," he said. "Remember, Ed, how optimistic we all were at Lake Linderman? Remember how we used to sit around the campfire at night and talk about how we all were going to be millionaires once we reached the Land of Gold? Why, it seemed when I was building that boat, every time I hammered a nail into those boards, I could hear the ping of gold! Ed," laughed Fitzgerald wryly, "who would have thought we'd both end up as packers frozen in at Circle?"

"It's only temporary work," I said with a grin, "but what do you think of our dog team?"

"Well, I'd say you're lucky, you fellows owning these malemutes. . . . And that big black dog—he's a fine specimen!"

"We're not quite sure of him yet," I said. And then I told Fitzgerald hurriedly how we had acquired Rover.

"Ed, I sure wish you luck," Fitzgerald said cordially. "I'm hoping for your sake that Rover will be yours. He's a powerful dog and makes your team complete."

"Yes," I said, "I believe Rover's got the strength of two dogs when he wants to use it . . . and he's sure working hard on this trip!"

In a minute or two, we had bade Fitzgerald goodbye, he promising to look us up in Circle City. Then we were on our way again. However, we continued to meet more and more fellows on the trail coming from Birch Creek, and we anxiously watched their expressions when they saw our dog team. But, so far, all was well. We saw no spark of recognition in their eyes for Rover. They only had looks of admiration and a little envy for our team, and they marveled how our dogs could pull such a heavy load. Rover, somehow, seemed to know he was on parade and strutted his strength, helping Chattel, our lead dog, tremendously.

As we continued along the trail, all at once we began seeing strange prints in the snow, now and then accompanied by crimson bloody spots.

"Golly!" said Bertram. "They look like horses' hoof prints."

"But they can't be!" I said incredulously.

"Well, they sure are," said Graff. "Look, there are some perfect hoof marks. The trail is all caved in from the weight of the heavy animals. I'll eat my hat if they aren't horses! They seemed to 've come into the main trail from that little side trail from the southwest."

"Great Scott! Whoever heard of horses way up here on the Arctic Circle?" I exclaimed. "If it's true, they must have been brought in by steamer by way of St. Michael sometime last summer. And there they are about a quarter of a mile ahead of us—real horses!"

As we hurried along, we asked the packers coming our way, "How come horses? From where?"

"Sure, one of the few fellows who owns horses lives up here. Lives at Medicine Lake, a place about twenty-five miles from here. 'Good Medicine,' that lake, the Indians say. Hot springs . . . also 'good medicine!' we white men say. The fellow who owns those horses does packing sometimes. Too bad, though, for his animals! Sometimes they get split hoofs from the cold, and torn ankles from the rough edges of the frozen snow! He ought to know better than to subject them to such torture!"

Soon we caught up with the fellow and his horses. They pulled off the trail for us, plunging and wallowing awkwardly in the deep snow, spilling more blood which sickened us. Poor beasts of burden! (How many times we saw their sufferings in the Yukon and later in the gold rush of '98, especially on White Pass.)

"It's pathetic how really out of place horses are in this frozen country," said Graff after we got ahead of them.

"But did you know, fellows, at one time they think there was a species of wild horses in this part of the country?"

"Why, no," we said very much surprised.

"Yes," said Graff, "we all know that mastodon and mammoth roamed up here in prehistoric times, millions of years ago, but scientists also say that a species of wild horses once roamed these plains too. That was before the great climatic change."

As we walked along, trying to mush the dogs at a faster pace, the sun dropped rapidly behind those big mountains off in the direction of Mastodon and Mammoth creeks to the west. We were getting very anxious to reach Eight Mile House, but we figured we had about four miles yet to go. Anxiously, we watched the sky, hoping that the weather would remain clear.

Gradually, the sky changed from cold, winter rose, to violet . . . and then to deep purple. The much-wished-for stars appeared suddenly like golden candles, scintillating in the Arctic heavens.

"We've got lots to be thankful for," I said as we strained our eyes harder to see the trail in the changing light. "We'll make it all right to Eight Mile House by starlight, but we musn't try to go on farther tonight. That trader at the warehouse at Circle City was right. Eight miles of this in one day is enough for any group of packers and their hard-working dogs!"

Watching the trail, we continued through the woods. Luckily, the country in our vicinity was quite flat. The stars were bright and the snow reflected enough light so that we could see rather well. But, suddenly, we heard a weird, hissing, crackling sound almost behind us, and all at once the great Northern Lights came flashing through the sky, darting here and there in brilliant colors. Then, quiet suddenly, they subsided, and then came on again a few seconds later, changing form, like sweeping, waving plumes across the heavens in pastel colors, delicately hued, as though a chorus of dance-hall girls were coyly waving plumes to entice some poor fellow to give up his hard-earned gold.

It was about 8 P.M. when we finally saw real candle-lights twinkling out across the snow from a large log structure by the side of the trail. We knew this was Eight Mile House. Truly, we were glad to reach this place, as by this time, we were chilled to the bone. We'd been out on the trail for eight long grueling hours with no hot food, and we knew our dogs were very hungry and tired. What a welcome place this was for weary travelers! We knew that we must be very near to famous Birch Creek, although we couldn't see it in the dim light. This was the first portage station for the miners of Birch Creek and vicinity.

Outside, around the station, we could see a number of sleds pulled up and many dogs staked out. They set up a series of howls, which announced our coming.

"Come on in, fellows, after you've fed and tied up your dogs," said the innkeeper as he welcomed us. "No need to worry about anything, the dogs'll be safe and so will the freight. I've got a little hot food left, but I'm sorry to say there's only one bunk left. Seems everyone and his cousin stopped here tonight!"

In no time, we were seated at a rough wooden table eating ravenously food served from a big Klondike stove. As we ate, the innkeeper introduced us to the miners and packers who were there for the night. Soon, we began joking with them and among ourselves about how we three were going to sleep in that one narrow bunk.

"Ed, how do you think we're going to manage tonight?" asked Graff a little worried. "I'd sure like a good night's sleep!"

"Oh, I don't know," I said. "Maybe we can draw straws. Two can sleep at the head and one at the foot. But we're going to be packed in like sardines, no matter how we figure it!"

"Well, I'll help you settle this," said one amused miner. "Let's make it simple," he said, flipping a coin on the table (a very unusual sight, as most exchange was in gold dust in the North). "The first one who gets tails, sleeps at the foot."

"Here, Ed, you flip first," laughed the packer.

I took the coin. "Well," I said, "I'll be the goat. I'm not usually lucky, . . . but here goes." I threw the coin into the air. It came down, hit the table with a ping, whirled on its side for an eternity, then teetered and settled down flatly on the table.

It was tails! Just my luck! There followed a lot of laughter and joshing again. But after a little, the conversation lagged, and then gradually the men began turning in, "hitting the hay," as they called it. Bertram and Graff soon followed suit. But I, not being anxious to face those two pairs of steaming feet, sat by the big round-bellied stove with the innkeeper. Finally, all had gone to bed but the two of us and we talked in low tones, occasionally listening to the various pitched snores which reached us through the thin partition of the sleeping quarters.

The innkeeper was an old Yukoner, a fascinating talker, and while I was losing a little sleep, I was gaining a lot of information about this part of the country. Somehow, those men slipping out of Circle for the Tanana had made a bigger impression on me than I had wanted to admit; and so now I was eager and curious to learn all I could about the region to the west. Pathetically little was known of this territory. It was a country that belonged to the United States, yet much of it was wilderness with a very big question mark after it. Rumor had come to us at Circle City that a very great mountain, probably the highest on the North American continent, had been discovered somewhere beyond the Tanana and been named Mount McKinley in honor of our President. It had been discovered by two intrepid fellows (now in Dawson), Dickey and Monks of Seattle, the year previously, in 1896, while they were exploring and prospecting up the hazardous Shushitna River from the coast, not far from the Copper River. This great mountain had for years been known to the Indians as Bulshaia, meaning "Great Mountain."

Spellbound, I sat and listened as the old innkeeper talked.

"Yes, sir," he said, "the Russians sold us this country we call Alaska thirty years ago for just a little over seven million dollars. Think of it! They thought they were getting a lot of money for this God-forsaken country, too. And there were those in the U.S.A. who thought we were getting stung. Said there was nothing much up here but ice and snow and a few Indians and Eskimos. Scornfully called this country 'Seward's Folly,' or 'Uncle Sam's Icebox.' But Seward, our Secretary of State, who engineered the deal, didn't mind. You see, he had visions for this country, and already, I guess, it's paid for itself and then some! Well, sir, Seward is dead now, but he'll long be remembered by all of us. You know, when Russia sold Alaska to us, she didn't have any idea of the treasures frozen up in here. But many think that the Canadian Hudson Bay Company did. You see, they had a special understanding with Russia to use some of her Alaska Territory for fur trade, and they had their combined trading posts and forts established all over the North at strategic points. Fort Yukon was once one of their main trading points before we bought Alaska. Now it is known that the Hudson Bay Company knew there was gold in the North more than three decades ago, but they suppressed the news, threatening their employees and the Indians with dire punishment if they divulged the secret. Of course, they never guessed the greatness of the gold deposits then. Even when the news finally leaped out, the Hudson Bay Company made it almost impossible at first for prospectors to travel on H.B. Company river steamers which plied the large rivers and some of the remote streams, always flying the H.B. Company flag. You see, that great Hudson Bay Company regarded the entire North country as their own great fur-trade empire. It seems they had received a special charter from their British King many years ago, giving them undisputed commercial sway over Canadian territory, starting from that huge body of water called Hudson Bay near the east coast of Canada. And what a tremendous empire it proved to be; a vast network of forts, trading posts and station, with thousands of traders and Indians working for the company. And all of these posts were pretty closely guarded by Canadian soldiers and Northwest Mounted Police.

"Well, now, as you know, you can't hold back the hand of progress, even a great company can't. Soon, gold was discovered by explorers in startling amounts in southwestern Yukon Territory at Dease Lake, which started the famous Cassiar District in 1873. About the same time came exciting gold discoveries along the Stikine River, the Pelly, and at different spots down the Yukon. Gradually, the power of the Hudson Bay Empire began to wane with the coming of other trading companies wedging into the North, like the A.C. Trading companies and others. Then, suddenly gold was discovered by Canadian and American prospectors in the Sixty Mile and Forty Mile area, Forty Mile was partly on American territory, as you know. This was almost the first big gold discovery in the interior of our new American Alaska, except, perhaps, for a little gold on the Koekuk River several years before. Of course, everybody knows that the Douglas and Treadwell mines at Juneau on the Pacific Coast on U. S. Territory of Alaska, started back in 1880. Well, after gold was discovered in the interior on the Forty Mile, next came Circle City with its Mastodon Creek and its famous Birch Creek. And then, of course, as you know, gold was struck again in the latest, momentous discoveries of the amazing Klondike a little over a year ago.

"And now, Ed," said the innkeeper as he began blowing smoke rings from his freshly lighted pipe, "just as surely as the seasons change, I think some other wonderful, startling discoveries are yet to be made, probably to the west, maybe within the Arctic Circle. But it's a wild, difficult region.

"Now," continued the innkeeper, his eyes taking on a peculiar, fiery glow, "suddenly come rumors, inklings of great quantities of gold in the Tanana."

"But so far," I said, "they're only rumors, conjectures, speculations, or whatever you might want to call them. It's nothing tangible, actually. Nothing where you can say, 'So and so knows . . . he says such and such.' But what do you actually know? What do *you* say about it?"

"Well," replied the innkeeper a little cagily, "young fellow, I've been here for some time running Eight Mile Station. I've made good money, too, maybe more than if I'd been out in those hills chasing around after gold; but if I were a young fellow like you, well . . . I might set out for that country. I haven't been much beyond Mastodon Dome, but I can tell you this: It's a rugged, brutal country over there, where a fellow would be absolutely on his own in a labyrinth of mountains and more mountains as far as you can see, probably for a hundred miles or more towards the Tanana Valley from Mastodon Dome. And in the wintertime like this, those mountains are avalanche-laden with deep snows. There is something else to consider. In the great Tanana country there are said to be two kinds of Indians—the valley people and the mountain men. What makes it bad is they are reported to be very hostile; though twenty or thirty years ago, a few Russian and American explorers forced their way into the Tanana to explore and make hasty maps, but none of them are ever known to 've stayed, because of the inhospitable, suspicious attitude of these Indians."

"Great Scott!" I said, "Those explorers must have been very courageous!"

"You bet they were!" said the innkeeper, "especially when they knew that a number of years ago some of the Russians had been massacred for no apparent reason by the Indians not far from the mouth of the Tanana."

"Good Lord!" I said with a shiver. "But, say, how long do you think the Tanana River is, anyway?"

"Well, it's rumored to be about six hundred and fifty to seven hundred miles long. But no one really knows. It's thought to be second in size only to the Yukon, and its source is reported to be way over there in the area of Mount Wrangel, near the headwaters of the Copper River."

"Golly," I said, "what an immense country it truly must be! But with Indians in there who are evidently bent on keeping us white men out, I can see it's a very dangerous territory!"

"You bet it is," said the innkeeper; "but, strangely enough, occasionally a few of those wild Indians see fit to wander over here, bringing wild meat and furs which they expect to trade for tea, coffee, sugar and flour. Their wants are very simple and they let you know in a hurry what they're after by sign language. They don't speak a word of English, as far as I know. They just point. Believe me, I barter with them cautiously and see that they get what they want immediately. After that, they don't waste any time around here. They're gone before you know it! And they never go back the same way they come!"

"But have you ever seen these Indians with gold?" I asked tensely.

"Why, yes," he replied slowly, "a few times. I've seen them with good-sized nuggets and some pretty big copper nuggets, too."

"Have you ever asked where they got the gold ones—using sign language, of course?" I asked with mounting excitement.

"Of course I have, Ed," said the innkeeper, "but they always shake their heads fiercely and glare at me and make some pretty savage noises which tell me plainly to keep my nose out of their business and out of their country, too! But I've been thinking lately, Ed—one of these days those Indians are going to have to tolerate us white men over there in their country."

"When did you last see any of these Tanana Indians?" I asked.

"Oh, about a year ago," said the trader thoughtfully. "If they come at all, it seems they generally get here in the winter about in December. It's interesting to note that our Circle City Indians are quite afraid of those Tanana fellows. I've always thought there must have been bad blood between them; maybe some time in the past they've had some pretty bloody wars. Well, anyway, our Yukon Indians say, 'Tananas, bad Indians! Angry men! Bad enemies! Carry rock clubs! Have two-edged stone axes! Sometimes let fly quick! Kill fast!' So you see, Ed, those Tanana men are not to be fooled with!"

"Great guns!" I said, "Sounds like they're still in the stone age!"

"Yep, that's it," said the innkeeper. "Anyway, they're not at all like our friendly Yukon Indians around her."

"Tell me, if you were risking going into the Tanana for gold, where would you look first?" I asked eagerly.

"Well, I think I'd strike out for the upper Tanana region first," he replied, "because its upper tributaries are not too far from the gold belt which runs through the Klondike; and secondly, because the western sources of the Tanana River are very near the headwaters of the Copper and Shushitna rivers, which flow to the Gulf of Alaska. In the past, a number of Tanana Indians have been seen by miners and traders going down these two rivers to the coast to trade with the Thlinget Indians and others. An old trader named Olson at Port Valdes on Cook's Inlet, who has been there a long time, has reported seeing these Indians with big gold nuggets. Says they always seem to come through the high Mentasta Pass around the first of February, and he thinks they bring their gold from someplace in the upper Tanana region. Also, the same Indians have been reported as coming down the Shushitna River, and sometimes down the Matanooska River to the forks where the Matanooska and the Knik rivers meet and where they say there's an old trading post. All the old miners there believe that Indian gold lies in big quantities in the country several hundred miles above, in the Tanana region. They seem pretty certain it isn't on the Copper or Shushitna rivers, either, because only fine gold in rather limited quantities has been found on those rivers to date.

"Now, about twenty years ago, there were two men who pushed their way into the upper Tanana from the Yukon side from the Sixty Mile River, and, again later, from the Forty Mile area. They were not looking for gold, especially. They were traders. All old Yukoners know Arthur Harper and Bates. Somehow, these two men were allowed to go through the territory unmolested by the Indians. Guess it was because Harper had such an uncanny understanding of the natives. As you know Harper later was the one who rebuilt the trading post at Fort Selkirk after the fort had been pillaged and burned by the angry Chilkat Indians from the coast. While Harper didn't actually see much gold in the Tanana, the Indians gave him to understand there were large quantities. Now, most everything we know of value concerning the upper reaches of the Tanana is from our friends, Harper and Bates. But, as yet, the source of that gold is still a mystery."

"Well, if Arthur Harper and Bates could get along with those savages, why couldn't some of the rest of us?" I asked abruptly.

"I suppose you're right," said the proprietor, "but I'll tell you this—I wouldn't want to get very chummy with 'em. No, not even for gold! Ed, the few I've had occasion to deal with are crafty, wily, ferocious-looking fellows. I wouldn't trust 'em and I don't mind saying that I think the few Tananas who come here and occasionally go into Circle City, are the real mountain men, the fiercest of all!"

"Jumpin' Jupiter!" I said, "I'm not suggesting to get too friendly with them, but I think if those savages could be handled with a good measure of kindness and perhaps some brightly colored gifts besides, a fellow might be rewarded with some valuable information, or leads concerning gold in their country."

"Yes, Ed," said the trader, "but I've tried everything and it's got me nowhere! Others have tried, too. Why, I'll wager there've been dozens of fellows who've in one way or another tried to learn where that gold is. A few stampeders have been foolish enough to attempt to follow them back to their villages from the Yukon side or the Copper River side. It seems, too, that many prospectors on the coast this last year have been trying to push their way up through that hostile Copper River territory to reach the gold fields of the Klondike, trying to find a shorter route to Dawson. Many have reported they've been met with, and turned back by hostile Indians, some with very primitive weapons, others with old muskets, shooting crude copper bullets!"

"Great guns!" I said, "I certainly wouldn't want to be hit by copper bullets, would you?"

"No, Ed, I certainly wouldn't want to be hit by 'em, either. They could result in deadly poison," said the innkeeper. "Fortunately, they think the Indians only have a few old guns and a limited supply of gunpowder, probably stolen from traders or ill-fated prospectors!"

"How can a fellow distinguish between these wild Tananas and our numerous Indians around Circle City, if they slip in here?" I asked breathlessly.

"Well, if you look closely, you can see the difference," said the trader. "The Tananas are a little taller than our Indians here, some of them quite handsome, and they have quite a different look. It's hard to describe exactly, except to say they dress entirely in skins and have a very fierce, wild look . . . just like untamed horses right off the mesas. Listen, Ed, if you're really going to be on the lookout for Tananas, watch closely for concealed bone daggers or weapons of black polished stones, especially black basalt. If you see Indians with these, be careful! They are the Tanana mountain men who could rip you down the back with one swing of their stone axes . . . but they're the fellows who could tell you just where that gold lies hidden!"

"Here, Ed, I'll show you something," said the trader, reaching into a box and producing a small map, which he quickly spread out on the table. "Here is a crude sketch of all that is known of that great Tanana country. Take a good look at it. Whatever you do in the future, Ed, I wish you luck!"

"Thanks!" I said. Then added eagerly, "May I copy this map?"

"Sure," said the proprietor. "Here's a pencil and here's a piece of brown paper. Help yourself."

"Thanks, fellow," I said gratefully as I began copying the map. "Say, by the way, can you tell me what the trip will be like tomorrow?"

"Well, Ed, the trail should be smoother from here on. And you'll find Twelve Mile House very similar to this one. Just follow the trail for four miles. It crosses Birch Creek on the ice. Twelve Mile House is on the other side of the river. I suggest you fellows get an early start in the morning. No doubt, you'll be able to make it up there and get back to Circle City in one day, like so many of the packers do, though it'll be a trip of sixteen miles altogether. But, of course, when you start back, your sleds'll be empty and you might even ride part of the way."

"Thanks for all your good advice," I said, as quickly I began filling in lines to complete the exciting little map.

"Don't mention it," said the innkeeper, yawning a little as he locked the heavy door. "When you're through, Ed, blow out the candles. It's almost midnight. Hope nobody else comes along tonight . . . and if they do, well, they'll just have to sleep on the floor!"

After the proprietor had gone to bed, I stared at the little map for some time. It seemed I could visualize that great unknown country to the west with its hundreds of rushing rivers, deep-cut, glacier-blocked canyons, surrounded and guarded by high mountains and populated with fierce Indians carrying stone clubs, stone axes, shooting copper bullets and carrying bags of bright yellow nuggets!

Ah, yes, it was an intriguing territory, all right! Thousands of square miles of American territory! What a treasure house it must be!

About an hour later, I blew out the candles and wriggled into that narrow bunk, facing those four clammy feet of Graff and Bertram. My mind was not there at Eight Mile House.

As I went off into a troubled sleep, I thought: "A fellow might be greatly rewarded if he ventured over into the beckoning, mysterious Tanana—for centuries untold, locked hard within that tremendous, icy Circle of Gold!"

Chapter XXI

The Call of the Tanana

It was the blood-freezing day of November 28, 1897, and colder than hell outside, colder than it had been the day before when it had registered 53 below zero when I had frozen my nose and cheeks coming back to Circle City from Twelve Mile House with Bertram and Graff, where we had taken our new dog team, pulling sleds loaded to the guards with heavy freight for those two Mastodon Creek mine owners. It was a lucky thing for us that I had met those two miners. Through them, we had been able to get our sled dogs. Now, my party of men and I counted ourselves among the fortunate few who were frozen in at Circle City, as malemutes were just about worth their weight in gold!

But coming back from that strenuous freighting trip, not only had I frozen my nose and cheeks, I had hit my knee a terrible wallop, straining and bruising it badly when I ran to jump on the empty sled to catch a ride. This mishap was very unfortunate for me, as it was the same leg I had injured so badly with a pickaxe, cutting it to the bone when I had been prospecting on the Bonanza several months before. Now I knew I'd be laid up again for a while. How exasperating it was! And how a fellow needed his legs in this brutal country! But what a lucky break it was for me that Graff and Bertram had noticed that telltale marble-white look to my face just when they did. That peculiar white look was always a sign of frostbite. They had yelled to the dogs to stop, then, without saying a word, they had quickly grabbed up handfuls of snow and began rubbing my face vigorously with it. I was startled, for I hadn't realized that my face was frozen at all. More forcefully now, after yesterday, I could see that it would be very foolhardy for a fellow to travel the icy trails alone! Why, only this morning of the 28th in the early hours, Giddings, who had left Circle City alone, headed for Dawson, three weeks previously with two dogs, came staggering back over the ice of the Yukon. He was half frozen and starved and said that the wolves had eaten up all of his grub and he had been forced to turn back over that frightful, storm-swept trail.

We were all shocked at Giddings' gaunt appearance. None of us recognized him at first as he had changed so, and his dogs were in pitiful shape. He brought word that our friends, Joaquin Miller and Canovan, had been more fortunate than he. After they, too, had suffered greatly on the ice from exposure and hunger, they had been picked up by Al Thayer and his Indian packers with their string of sled dogs and had been taken on to Dawson. It was just a month to the day now since Joaquin Miller and Canovan had bid the crowd goodbye here at Circle and had bravely started out over the frozen river, headed for Dawson.

Now, with shivering chills we listened to the wail and shriek of the wind as it cut like a knife through somber, darkened Arctic skies. Surely, old King Winter was roaring down upon us here at Circle City with fiercer velocity and more determined vengeance than ever before. We were mighty thankful for the shelter of our little log cabin. There was plenty of wood piled high in one corner, and the small Klondike stove near the center of the room snorted and glowed almost red hot.

We had just eaten an early supper, and the odor of sourdough pancakes and rancid bacon grease hung heavy in the air, mixed with the pungent odor of steaming socks, which always seemed to be hanging near the stove to dry. And now there was a new odor among us, floating low, close to the floor. It was the acrid, furry smell of malemutes. Yes, we were keeping our valuable dogs in the cabin at night, as we couldn't take the chance of losing them!

I reached down and petted the shaggy, furry head of Chattel, my devoted shadow—this dog which was to play such an important part in my life later. The other three dogs, Pointer, Caution and Rover, were curled up in the corner, noses buried under their tails. It was pretty certain now that Rover, the big black dog Bertram had found in the gulch, would belong to us, as no one had shown up who could really identify him, though many had tried. Truly, it seemed these dogs gave us a new feeling of security. That dreaded thousand-mile trek back over the ice to Juneau didn't seem quite as formidable. But Giddings' return to Circle City this day, telling of his grim experiences on the ice and of the terrible sufferings of Joaquin and Canovan and others, had given us all a frightful jolt!

Now I glanced around our one-room cabin. All was peaceful, a rather unusual atmosphere for our group of high-strung men. Shelley Graves, Calhoun, Moore and Bertram were reading. They were sprawled out on bunks, straining their eyes by flickering candlelight, devouring some badly worn adventure stories which they had gotten from the miners' small lending library at 25c a copy. They could keep these books for only a few days. A fellow by the name of Henry Lewis was the librarian. Graff and Hill had finished all the books in the cabin and now sat at the table writing letters, which, in all probability, would never reach the "Outside."

Captain Tibbetts was in his chair across the table from me. I had been sitting there for some time, writing, catching up on my diary, my injured leg propped up on a box. Tibbetts had a pile of socks and moccasins he was trying to mend. Every now and then, he'd give a low grunt of pain when he'd prick his finger, and although I offered him the use of my thimble, he gruffly declined to borrow it.

His quick, staccato expressions of pain reminded me of my own troubles. Golly, how that confounded knee ached, and how my nose and cheeks burned! I could feel them getting very feverish and swollen, and I knew in a few days the skin would peel. Curses on having such tender blond skin, anyway! Or, maybe, I just hadn't kept the hood of my parka drawn closely enough around my face. But, after all, I was pretty lucky. I finally closed my diary, tucked it away carefully in my vest pocket, then I drew out a piece of folded brown paper.

"Fellows," I said, as I began spreading it out on the table, "maybe this is a poor time to mention it, but I've got something to show you."

Slowly, the men put aside what they were doing and gathered around the table. Tibbetts, however, kept right on with his mending, barely glancing up.

"Remember our talk of possible gold somewhere else in this territory?" I asked. "Yes? Well, while I was on that trip to Twelve Mile House, I talked with a few of the Birch Creek miners and also the innkeeper at Eight Mile Station. They seem to feel that there may be very rich deposits of gold some place over there in that vast Tanana region. But they all say it's a difficult country to get into!"

As I talked, I began pointing with a pencil to my little hand-drawn map on the brown paper, and I could see the men were listening to me intently.

"Here is Circle City, where we are right now," I said. "Over here, a little to the west, is Birch Creek, running parallel with the Yukon. As you can see, Birch Creek has many tributaries, some coming from those high mountains to the west and southwest. Over there is Mastodon Dome, and below, flowing to the east, is famous Mastodon Creek. And see, there's another peak a little to the northwest, almost in a line with Mastodon, marked Porcupine Dome."

"Why, Ed," said Tibbetts, who had put down his mending and was leaning forward to get a better look at the map, "that region over there reminds me a little of the Klondike, with its King and Queen Domes; but, of course, you know the Birch Creek area around Circle City could never compare with the Klondike. And I'd say that hodgepodge of moutains over there toward the Tanana are much higher and would be a damn sight easier for fellas to get lost in!"

"Well, I'm not denying that," I said, "but just think of the gold that might be beyond those mountains in the great Tanana region! Now, fellows," I said as I traced a long line running northwest beyond the mountains, "this is the practically unexplored Tanana River. Seems to stretch out for six or seven hundred miles. And look—several of the Tanana's main tributaries come from the direction of the Copper River and Mount Wrangle in the Alaska Coast Range. This map shows without a doubt that the headwaters of the Tanana River are in that great mineral belt which stretches eastward from Mount Wrangle inland across that immense upper Tanana territory, and extends all the way to the Klondike, where the amazing Bonanza and fabulous Eldorado are located."

"Well, what about it?" asked Moore with a big question in his eyes.

"Just this, fellows," I said eagerly, "there must be untold quantities of gold almost any place along the upper Tanana River. Think what it would mean to us if we could get into that big territory! We could cut through those mountains to the southwest past Mastodon Dome. Why, it might not be more than two hundred miles to the Tanana from here, and we could prospect in likely places along the way. Once we reach the Tanana, we could go upriver over the ice, or build a boat and wait for the spring breakup. Just think, we might be lucky enough to strike a real Bonanza!"

"Good Lord!" said Tibbetts, jumping to his feet in alarm. "Why, Ed, you're not really serious about going to the Tanana, are you?"

"Yes," I said, "I certainly am! But if going west over those mountains seems too hazardous, there's that longer route to the Tanana I've been hearing some of the miners talk about. Although much longer, this way might be safer in the end. We could take our dog team and go north from Circle over the frozen Yukon, way up past Fort Yukon, probably four hundred miles to a point where the Tanana comes into the Yukon River. From there, we could push our way up the Tanana. But it would be a long, cold trip of nearly a thousand miles to where we might want to go in the upper Tanana."

"Great Scott, Ed!" said Tibbetts. "I thought you were anxious to get sled dogs and get up the Yukon and out of this damn country! Now, here you are, wanting to plunge deeper into the North, where the chances are none of us would ever come out alive!"

"I know the great chances we would be taking," I said thoughtfully. "And no one is more anxious to get home alive than I! But I remember that I came up here for gold and Fate has just laughed in my face. And lately, I've been thinking a great deal about the Tanana. Maybe it's because I've been hearing so much about those Tanana Indians carrying big yellow nuggets in wild-skin bags. Now where do you suppose they find that gold? That's what fires my imagination. That's what keeps sticking in my mind. Yes, we've got dogs now, and a little more food, and we're mighty lucky, too, and probably stand a better chance of getting out of the country if we want to go now. But, suddenly, I feel a strong urge to go to the Tanana to look for gold. I'm willing to take the chance. But how about the rest of you men?"

As I spoke, I glanced around the table at the tense faces. I could tell from each fellow's expression what he was thinking. Shelley Graves, Bertram and Hill were with me. Mentally, the argument seemed to be teetering about half and half between the eight of us. But I could see Tibbett's strong displeasure mounting. This was the first time I had really come up against his tremendous will to domineer and command a situation. Heretofore, we had both seen almost eye to eye in our decisions. Suddenly, Tibbetts spoke again, as though he had firmly taken up the gavel. He pounded on the table for emphasis. "Well, I can tell you this, Ed. I'm not starting out in any direction to that God-forsaken country over there. It may be U. S. territory but we know absolutely nothing about it yet. Why, it could be a wasteland, with very little gold in there, after all. Besides, not one of us is in good enough shape to battle a wilderness like that. No, sir, Ed, I don't intend to leave my poor old carcass over there in some canyon, or frozen stiff on some icy mountaintop! No, I'm certainly not interested! I want to get back to civilization. Right now, I'm getting my stuff mended and my outfit ready for a dash up the Yukon . . . and soon! Gladly would I forget all about this blasted, fruitless search for gold, which, I've noticed, always seems to take you over the next . . . and the next . . . and, yes, the next range! It's just like following a damned mirage . . . to nothing!"

"You're right, Tibbetts!" said Graff. "I agree with you! Let's get out of this country. The sooner the better!"

"I'll be ready to start up the Yukon any time the three of you are ready to go," said Moore.

The others were silent, still looking wistfully at the map. Then Tibbetts spoke up again, this time a little more softly, persuasively, "Aw, come on, Ed, and you fellows, no need for hard feelings or parting of the ways. Let's all get our outfits together and head back up the Yukon. You know, compared to getting into that wild unexplored Tanana, going up the Yukon to the 'Outside' would be almost like a Sunday-school picnic, in spite of its hardships! If we split up now, it means dividing up the dogs and the grub, and then we all might end up like Giddings—or worse! Who knows? I tell you, fellows, we'd better stick together . . . and forget the Tanana!"

Suddenly, there was a loud knock at the cabin door and, before any of us could open it, our friend Joe Lamour, the mail carrier, swept in with the wind and banged the door shut. Surprised, we all greeted him warmly as he began peeling off his heavy parka and mittens.

"Hello, fellas! It sure is a night to be indoors! But I came over to see you men about something very important. And hello! What's this?" he asked as he glanced curiously over the table.

"Oh, I was just showing the boys a little map of the Tanana I copied while I was away," I said rather evasively.

"Well, I'll be jiggered!" said Lamour. "It's a good copy, too. But, Ed, you'd better think twice before you undertake that trip. Seems like there's dozens of Cheechakos here at Circle just like you, all fired up, rarin' to go to the Tanana! But if you go in there, it doesn't mean you'll ever find gold! Why, I'll wager a lot of the fellas who've started already will be tryin' to get back. And you can bet your boots, some will never return. Just think of wandering in those mountains in blizzardy weather like we've been having! And it's certain, from now on, we're in for some of our worst storms!

"Fellas, remember Ryan, the poor devil who had his

feet cut off here at Circle City a few weeks ago because gangrene set in after frostbite? Yes, he was out wandering around looking for gold, too. Now he's such a pathetic fella, still in bed, dead broke, and with no way of earning any money. Well, he's the reason I came here tonight. Henry Lewis, the librarian, is getting up a benefit Christmas program for him. And we've all gotta help. Lots of talented fellas stranded here at Circle City, you know. And I think we can have a fine show. Lewis wants to raise at least six hundred dollars. Wants each one to give two dollars, a good pinch of gold dust. We want your Outcast Club to put on a rousing performance of solos, chorus and dance. Bates will do the accompanying on his guitar. It's going to be a snappy, three-act minstrel show, not very Christmasy, but we won't worry too much about that. *Casey Moran, the little showman from Dawson, will have charge of the whole thing. Now, how about it, men?" asked Joe anxiously. "Will you help us?"

"Well, I surely feel terribly sorry for Ryan," I said, "but Christmas is almost a month away, and a lot could happen before then. However, if I'm still at Circle, I'll be glad to help!"

"Good!" said Joe. Then, turning to the others, "How about the rest of you men?"

"Sure," said Tibbetts, kind of speaking up for the others. "We'll all help if we're here, too. But I'm telling you, Lamour, I'm not much of a singer, and I can't do any fancy high kicking!" He laughed.

"Oh, no," grinned Joe, "it's just a shuffling step we want. Just sort of keeping time to the music. And your act will be in blackface. Don't think anyone would even recognize you!"

"Golly, it sounds like fun!" chimed in the others enthusiastically. "If we're in Circle at Christmas, you can sure count on us."

"That's the spirit, boys! Thanks. I'm going to count on you, then. Now I've got to be leaving. Got to make the

---

* Casey Moran, the showman, is not to be confused with Casey Moran the newspaper reporter from Portland who went to the Klondike with a relief expedition in the fall of 1897.

rounds," said Lamour, pulling on his parka and mittens. "But, just one more thing. Since you've been thinking about the Tanana, it might really pay you to stick around here for a while. You know, some of those Tanana Indians have been known to come into Circle near Christmastime or later in January. Now, if you could get several of those Indians as guides, well then, you'd really stand a chance of reaching Tanana. And if you get there, maybe they would guide you to that gold and you'd be the luckiest Cheechakos of all, for those Indians have never revealed the secret of where they find those nuggets to any living white man! But, men, I'm telling you right now—those Tananas are real savages. Would have to be handled carefully. Can't speak a word of English!"

After Joe had gone, we all talked excitedly about the Tanana and this new possibility of getting into that region with Indian guides who might lead us directly to that gold. Finally, we took a vote on it . . . and unanimously decided to remain at Circle until after Christmas, and maybe on into January, hoping those Tanana Indians would come. Strangely enough, even Captain Tibbetts now seemed willing and eager to remain. We talked on and on, far into the night.

"But if those Indians do turn up, just how are we gonna make ourselves understood?" asked Moore anxiously.

"Well, we could always use sign language," I said. "All Indians understand that. But what a great advantage it would be if one of us could only speak their language. Then we might really gain their confidence and help!"

"Say, now, that gives me an idea," exclaimed Tibbetts. "I just remember that I used to get along pretty well with Indians. It was when I was a sea captain and my boat used to dock at the different Alaskan ports. Yes, sir, I learned to speak a little of the Thlingit dialect."

"Golly, come to think of it, I speak a little Thlingit, too, and even a little Chinook . . . a sort of common Indian lingo," said Bertram rather excitedly. "Yes, I learned to talk a little of these two languages when those Indians from villages near by used to come to trade at the store I was running at Juneau. Now, I'm wondering if the Tananas could understand me?"

"Man, oh, man!" I said. "Now we're getting somewhere! I'll say you fellows better brush up on that Indian lingo of yours. You know, a few of those wandering, migratory Tananas have been known to go to the coast by way of the Copper or Sushitna rivers. Great Scott! now isn't it just possible those Tananas would pick up a little Thlingit or Chinook?"

"Sure, it's possible," said Tibbetts, "but it's only about one chance in a thousand that the same Indians would ever come as far northeast in this direction as Circle City."

"Yes, but it's possible," I persisted.

"You bet it's possible!" said Bertram.

Suddenly, we all looked at each other with new light in our eyes. Even Tibbetts' were lighted up with a strange, excited glow. It was quite evident that, in spite of all he had said about the Tanana, and that blasted, fruitless search, he was still secretly dreaming of gold! Now he was willing and almost eager to wait for the Tananas to go over the next . . . and the next . . . and, yes, the next range!

During the following two weeks (while we were waiting and watching for the Tananas), I was laid up with my injured leg, just as I had expected, and I couldn't get very far from the cabin. But some of the other fellows were out on the trails hauling firewood or milling about town, on the alert for the Tananas and gathering news.

Disconcerting rumors kept coming from up and down the Yukon which caused us much anxiety. It was said about 150 men were raring to leave Fort Yukon, anxious to get down as far as Circle City. At first, we were very apprehensive over this, because of the dangerous food shortage already at Circle, but it was said that, if these men came, they would actually help the situation at Circle, as each one would bring extra supplies from the Fort. Also, it was said that Captain P. H. Ray, the U.S. Army man who had come North on a mining survey for the United States Government in the early summer, had seen the critical food shortage and had taken full command of the situation. We were very thankful for this, as he had issued military orders to the trading companies, forcing them to ration the limited food supplies more fairly both at Fort Yukon and

Circle City. In fact, it was being said that Captain Ray was making reports for the United States Government, recommending the establishing of future trading posts, to be built at different points along the upper Yukon in Alaskan United States territory, to ward off future famines. He recommended locations at the mouth of Mission Creek and American Creek and others, as he predicted the greatest gold rush of history for the coming year of '98.

Another rumor, which showed much evidence of truth, was one saying a very large cargo of whisky had been caught halfway between Fort Yukon and Circle City in the early freeze, and there it was, stalled for the winter, a huge storehouse of liquor! Now, we at Circle began to see much evidence of this fact! It seemed that, around the first of December, quite suddenly the miners were in a prolonged state of celebration. There wasn't much food in the North. Well, so what! There was lots of whisky! Why not just get slap-happy and forget all about being frozen in, and the whole damned country with all its frustrating problems? Several of the fellows in our cabin finally succumbed and got roaring drunk.

This was very distressing to me, as I didn't drink. But there I was, stuck with it in the cabin. On several occasions, they whooped it up all day and all night, and in the morning the place looked as though a typhoon had torn through. But I reminded myself that these same scenes were being repeated in nearly every cabin in Circle City, and that my party of men were really no worse than any of the others.

Captain Ray tried earnestly to stop the carousing, calling upon the miners to keep up their courage and morale without relying on that false, momentary crutch, liquor. And I reminded the fellows in my cabin that they'd better stop drinking and sober up, or they wouldn't know a Tanana Indian from a mountain goat! That jerked them back to their senses.

During the two weeks I had to stay in the cabin, several friends came to see me. Gus Lindecker, a fellow from Tacoma who had been gold weigher at the Dominion Hotel at Dawson, came often to play whist with me, and once we made sourdough doughnuts and they turned out to be real

Arctic sinkers—but tasted pretty good. During several days, we took turns reading Mark Twain's *Gilded Age* aloud. Also, during the early part of December, I had begun making a parka of wolf skins which I had collected. Altogether, it cost me only $2.25, and when I was finishing it up the fellows said it looked as good as any the Indians could make. That, of course, was quite a compliment. The little silver thimble my wife had slipped into my kit just before I left Tacoma on the S.S. *Mexico* had made the work much easier.

Yes, I, too, like Tibbetts and the others, was steadily getting my outfit ready for a long trip. But I wondered which direction that trip would take me.

I hadn't heard from my wife for a long time, nor had my wife, I was afraid, heard from me, although I had tried desperately to get a letter out to her these past few months. I was sure she had no idea where I was. Whenever the nights were clear, I hobbled to the little cabin window or ventured out with Chattel at my side to locate the Big Dipper and the North Star. When I found them, I would look wistfully for a little while, then turn and gaze far to the south, wondering if she, too, were watching these same stars. Yes, before I had left Tacoma, we had agreed that they would be the link between us while I was away in the North. Somehow, I always drew strength and courage from this little ritual and I hoped and prayed that she would, too, and dear Velma would know I was safe! But how excruciatingly homesick a fellow could become way up here in the North!

On December 9th, news flashed through Circle City, brought down by several packers, that a terrific fire had swept along the waterfront of Dawson, destroying many cabins, hotels and saloons; also, the new opera house had burned to the ground. There had been almost nothing the miners could do to stop the raging fire, as Dawson's main water supply, the Yukon, was frozen over solid.

For several days, the fire at Dawson was the main topic of conversation at Circle City.

"Fellows, the only good thing I kin see about this fire," said an old-timer, "is they might put up better buildings next time."

"Yea, but golly, wouldn't I like to be in Dawson fer jest a few hours to poke around through those ashes!" said another old-timer.

"Sure thing," answered a miner, "right now, a fella could pan out plenty of nuggets and gold dust!"

"Why, yes," said a Cheechako, "jest think how much of it has fallen through the wide cracks in those wooden floors in the cabins, saloons, hotels and dance halls, spilled out by some of those rich Bonanza Kings and jest carelessly swept up. And think o' the nuggets the boys have thrown at the actresses . . . and missed! Yes, sir, I've seen it all with me own eyes. And, by golly, there's plenty o' gold in those ashes . . . and you kin bet, it's as good as new!"

"Yes, you're right," said another old sourdough, "it's true a few will gain from this terrible fire. But now, wouldn't you hate to be in the shoes of that fellow who was with Belle Mitchell, who started the Dawson fire? They say she threw a lighted lamp at him in the early morning hours in one of her fits of violent temper while they were having a quarrel."

"Yea, I sure would hate to be that fellow, all right!" said a miner, "but most of all, I'd hate to 've been in his shoes when he saw that red-hot, flaming lamp comin' at him! Yea, I tell you, she's a bad actress with a mean, vile temper! But he must've been pretty quick to 've dodged her and that lamp. Oh, isn't it a pity he couldn't have stopped the flames before they spread from that room!"

Yes, it was Belle Mitchell who, in a fit of jealous rage, started this terrifying fire. And she was the same evil woman who was to start the great conflagration of Dawson the following year in 1898 in the Green Tree Hotel, when she threw another lighted lamp at a rival prostitute in a violent early-morning quarrel over a love affair, causing a great part of Dawson to burn again for a second time in what was estimated to be almost a million-dollar fire. Yet, for some unknown reason, even after the second devastating fire, this woman was still allowed to remain in Dawson, to be a constant menace to the gold camp.

(How could I know then that I was destined to see the smoldering ruins of that second fire which started October 14th, 1898? It had looked to everyone as though all of

Dawson was doomed. This second fire occurred when the weather was 10° below zero, but, fortunately, the Yukon had not frozen over as yet, though ice was running in the river. Hundreds of men formed bucket brigades and a brand-new, unused fire engine was hooked up to the river. Many were seriously injured in this fire, but no one was killed. No one had any insurance and it was a total loss to everyone. When it was all over, Dawson seemed a hopeless, utterly burned out city!)

Now, as the days wore on in Circle City approaching the middle of December, my party of men sobered up and became more and more on the alert for the Tananas. And I was very impatient to be out on the trails again. But when I tried to go a little distance with my sled for firewood, I had warning twinges of pain which told me to take it easy a little longer. It also seemed that rheumatism was setting in, the kind so many fellows seemed to have, and I frantically exercised and rubbed my leg with St. Jacob's Oil, that patent medicine everyone was using. I was absolutely determined to get myself back in shape again to be ready to take off when the rest of the fellows did.

After the middle of December, we began practicing in earnest for the minstrel show. Bates, the guitarist, came over evenings, and we just about raised the roof with our lusty singing and the cabin rocked and shook with our rhythmic, rather awkward, heavy-booted steps. By this time, I was joining in.

But not only were we working hard on our blackface act, we were also keeping a sharper lookout in the daytime for any new Indians coming to town. But, as yet, we had not been rewarded by the sight of a single Tanana Indian!

As the time before Christmas grew shorter and shorter, we couldn't help wondering more and more what lay ahead for all of us. For the last several weeks, the daylight hours had been getting less and less, approaching the shortest day in the year. On December 21st, I wrote in my little diary: "The sun doesn't appear in the heavens at all now. Days are only three hours long."

And on the 22nd, I wrote by early candle light: "Had a good rehearsal. Will give benefit concert Saturday eve at

Circle City Opera House. The building is made of logs, 80 x 50 ft., with a small stage. Has two boxes. The boys are all very homesick here in Circle City, fighting like packs of Siwash canines!"

Now events at Circle City were speeding into a quicker, tenser tempo. There was anything but a Christmas holiday spirit in the air. Plenty of trouble was brewing, and there was an exciting episode in the making. Quite a few men had already arrived from Fort Yukon, some of these were of the *Weaver* "pirate" crowd, and there was visibly an element of great restlessness among them like a seething volcano about to erupt. With these men had come many hatreds and unsettled disputes. There had been grim happenings up there—crimes unsolved and unpunished by law, as the hundreds of men who had found themselves frozen in at Fort Yukon were not willing to bow to the authority of a few U.S. Army officers who had been stationed there to make weather reports, surveys, and to govern a few whites and Indians settled there.

I just happened to be in town about 6 P.M. the evening of the 23rd, near the A.C. Trading Co., when a miners' meeting was suddenly called. The reason, I soon discovered, was that Weymouth, who had recently come down from Fort Yukon, had been seized and locked up for the robbery of the N.A.T. Trading Co. at Fort Yukon where $9,000 in gold dust and several hundred dollars in supplies had been stolen a few weeks previously. A fellow by the name of A. M. Bolton was hastily appointed by the miners to champion Weymouth. Immediately, Bolton sent for Crane, the officer who had recently come down from Fort Yukon and was now in charge at Circle City, but Crane refused to come to the meeting.

Then the crowd yelled belligerently, "Why in hell was Weymouth arrested without a warrant, anyway? We declare he is innocent. The fellow who said Weymouth stole that gold and grub is probably the guilty one!" A heated argument ensued. Then someone shouted, "Let's demand the keys to the jail and, if Crane refuses, we'll tear the door down!"

Suddenly the excited crowd rushed in a body to the jail and I was swept along with them. When they banged on

Dawson burning in 1899. Ed Lung is on the right, with his friend, Joe Latshaw. Dawson burned three times between 1897 and 1900.

The flood at Dawson, June 1, 1898

Circle City. In its heyday it was a trading center for miners, trappers, and Indians

Stampeders' barges caught in the ice

the door, Captain Dunn appeared and tried to soothe and pacify the mob. He said Crane, the officer they despised, had fled out of town and was heading back toward Fort Yukon. The crowd shouted, "Coward! He's run out on you, Dunn. Don't be a fool. You're alone and can't stop us! Give us the keys to the jail. You haven't a warrant for Weymouth's arrest!"

But Dunn stood firm and flatly refused to turn over the keys. Then, suddenly, the crowd parted and out sprang big Red McConnell. He rushed at Captain Dunn and the two men grappled. Then, after a fierce scuffle, McConnell got the upper hand, pushed Dunn against the wall and pinned back his arms while the crowd went wild! Then, yelling like Indians, with clubs and axes they battered down the door of the cell . . . and Weymouth, white and shaken, came out a free man! A few minutes later, in front of the jail he stood in the snow under pale lantern light and spoke to the crowd. He made an impassioned speech and thanked them for his release. Vehemently, he declared his innocence.

Now, Weymouth was free to go where he pleased! But, that night, all over Circle City there were plenty of hot arguments over this episode of temporary mob rule, men declaring he was guilty, others saying he was innocent, nearly all taking sides. However, our party of men resolved to keep out of it because none of us knew all of the real facts of the case. And, as far as I could ever learn, the $9,000 theft of gold dust and valuable supplies at Fort Yukon by the masked bandit remained a mystery.

"Say, where in tarnation are those confounded Tananas, anyway?" exploded Shelley Graves in disgust. "I'm frozen to the bone. Seems to me I've been chasing Indians around Circle almost all day! Have cornered some pretty wild-looking ones, too. And fellows, what do you suppose they all turned out to be? You guessed it! Yukon Indians! Just plain Yukon Indians! I'm beginning to think now those Tananas are just a myth!"

"Don't get discouraged, Shelley," I said, "but I'm really hoping those Tananas won't turn up now until after Christmas. It'll give us a little more time to get our outfits together. Besides, we want to help with the show. . . . And how Ryan appreciates what we're trying to do for him!"

"Yea, he does," said Tibbetts. "But, Ed, I'm giving those Tananas just a few days after Christmas to get here. After that, Moore, Graff and I've decided we'll strike out. The weather's a little milder now and this is the time to head up the Yukon toward civilization. Gold or no gold, we're getting tired of being frozen in in this hell hole . . . caught like rats in a trap!"

"Yes, Tibbetts," I said, "we've certainly been like rats caught in a trap here at Circle City ever since the first of October! But let's not split up now! If those Tananas do come—and I have a feeling they will—and if they lead us to that gold, then, I'll say it's been well worth it!"

Chapter XXII

Big Nuggets and Yellow Dust

It was now the day before Christmas, 1897. Since the middle of December, my party of men and I had been on the alert for those illusive Tanana Indians (who knew the secret of the gold in their country, usually carried big yellow nuggets, and might wander into Circle City during the Christmas season). But looking for the Tananas was now becoming more difficult, because many Yukon Indians were coming in for the holidays, bringing wild meat and furs to sell at the trading company. We had been warned by a few old-timers that the Tananas were savage fellows and that they couldn't understand a word of English. But the latter was also true of many of the Yukon Indians, and a few of these rather harmless natives, at times, looked so fierce and wild that I wouldn't have cared much to 've met them in a lonely spot.

The big community Christmas tree celebration was a momentous occasion, and was to be put on this afternoon of the 24th at the Opera House at Circle City. Already it stood decorated and waiting for the date. All Indians had been invited, especially the Indian children—and how they were looking forward to it! They had been getting ready for days, rehearsing for their little program just as we fellows had been doing for the big benefit minstrel show which was to come off Christmas night.

It was now early afternoon, just about a half an hour before the Christmas tree program was to start. I decided, on the spur of the moment, to attend the big affair, so pushing through the crowd at the Opera House, I got one of the last seats. In a few minutes, the place was packed to the door with jabbering, excited Indians and a few whites.

I was surprised to see how the log-built Opera House, an 80- x 50-foot building, had taken on the atmosphere and pungent aroma and look of Christmas since our minstrel-show rehearsal of the night before. The edges of the stage and the two small boxes on either side were decorated with aromatic sprays of evergreens. The huge, candle-lighted Christmas tree stood near the front of the building, just a little to the side of the right box. It was gaily clothed and draped in brightly colored paper chains, assorted handmade ornaments, gaudy beads, strings of last year's yellowed popcorn and, most amazing of all, a few strings of wild cranberries, saved and brought in by the Indians for the occasion. Tacked along the windows on either side of the building, were sprays of spruce and fir. Near the back of the Opera House on the left side, stood the round-bellied stove, warming the place. Though they weren't lighted now, spaced along the two sides from front to back were lanterns suspended from the ceiling; also, lanterns hung above the stage, and several were half concealed near the edges of the stage among the foliage of greens.

Although the decorations around the stage were very Christmasy, the actual scene on the stage was not. There was a back drop representing summer-blue sky, a river zigzagging off to the horizon, and a Mississippi River boat pulled up to the dock.

Yes, I was most interested in this scene. I could picture my party of men and me up there on that stage in less than thirty hours in the minstrel show. As I waited for the Christmas tree program to start, mentally I began running through the words of my solo numbers—"Tell Me with Your Eyes" and "Postillion." I wondered if the fellows in the chorus would give me support and if they would keep together in the trick blackface shuffle dance. Then I broke out into a cold sweat as I thought of the new number we'd been asked to do to fill in on the show almost at the last minute—"costermongers," we'd been asked to be.

"What in hell are they?" Moore had asked our little director, Casey Moran.

"Oh, they're the fruit-and-vegetable peddlers, so well known in London. Even sometimes sell fish and furs, so that's what I'll have you fellows do from wheelbarrows. You see, costermongers cover their pants and vests and coats with hundreds of pearl buttons in certain designs as a mark of special distinction. So, fellows," he had laughed, "get busy and round up all the extra buttons you can find in Circle City; mix them up and sew them on any old way to make your costumes as funny as possible. I'm depending on you fellows to be the comedians!"

Consequently, we had spent many long hours this past week sewing on buttons of all colors, sizes and descriptions until, at last, we had exhausted the supply in Circle City and finally had resorted to making our own, cut from tin cans. What ridiculous, amusing costumes they turned out to be!

"But hardly the thing for a Christmas program," I thought. "Now if only the benefit could have been scheduled for New Year's Eve, this act would have been perfect!"

Well, to add to the fun, Hill, of our party, was going to come out dressed as a hula girl in a skimpy grass skirt which had been found in an old box of costumes, and wiggle his charms across the stage in among the group of us gaping costermongers. A lot of comedy and horseplay was to follow. Yes, it should be a good show, all right, even though most of us were only amateurs. But, as I thought of it, I knew in spite of the hilarity and humor of our act, we fellows hadn't had enough actual practice on this number. I perspired a lot when I reviewed it in my mind, and felt uneasy. I was anxious that our crowd would make a good showing.

Now I turned my attention to all of these Indians crowded into the theater. I wondered if they would be satisfied with this free Christmas tree celebration? What would happen if they all tried to crowd into the minstrel show tomorrow night? The Opera House had only a limited seating capacity, and there were scores of miners who would want to come. But we had been assured that the price to get in the show—one big nugget or a generous pinch of gold dust—should keep the Indians away.

Now I was listening to the Christmas tree program: the hymns, the carols, the reverent, tender words spoken about the birth of the little Lord Jesus. The Episcopal missionary was telling the story. The Indians listened attentively, eagerly. I wondered how many of these strange Indians understood enough English to grasp the Christmas story. The Indian children of Circle City—those being educated in the mission—took up the theme. They rocked a cradle and the Shepherds and Kings and Wise Men came with gifts. Their voices were sweet as they sang. I began feeling homesick as I thought of Clemy, my little son, so many thousands of miles away. How was he faring this Christmas? Well, I couldn't allow myself to dwell on it! I promised myself I'd be home next Christmas, for sure! But now, I had work to do—a minstrel show to help put on . . . gold to find. . . . Suddenly, I resolved to round up my crowd as soon as the children's program was over and get the fellows up there on that stage for an extra rehearsal, as the big dress rehearsal was coming off tonight! With this settled in my mind, I listened to the Christmas tree program and enjoyed it much more. I also watched the Indians in the Opera House for any possible Tananas in the place, but so far as I could tell, there were none among us.

It was now later in the afternoon after the crowd had gone home from the Christmas tree program.

"Come on, boys," I said, "we've got to do a better job as costermongers! Gotta put more punch in the chorus, more zip in the steps, more humor in the lines when we hold up the fish and furs and when Hill hulas unexpectedly across the stage. Fellows, we've gotta match the humor of his grass skirt and all his antics, and yes, those tin-can buttons on our costumes that'll be shining and flashing like big, gaudy sequins!"

As I spoke, I came to a halt in front of the rows of empty seats.

"Well, Ed," said Tibbetts, puffing, "this is an extra practice we never expected. We sure need it. But if the other two boys were only here, it would be much easier. With Shelley Graves and Bertram still out chasing Indians, well, it makes it tough, 'cause we need their support . . . and I'm kinda lost when I don't have Shelley to watch for the cues!"

"Yeah," said Moore, "we do need this extra practice, all right, with the show coming off tomorrow night. Those fellows should be here. But last I saw of Shelley and Bertram, they were headed for that deserted shack a half mile out from town. They said that Indians are camped in that cabin. Have a suspicion they may be Tananas."

"Piffle!" said Tibbetts, "I believe they're just wasting their time!"

"Ha," said Moore, "Shelley isn't one to give up, though. No, sir! Why, he pesters almost every last Indian he sees. When he corners a likely-looking Indian, he sidles up and says in English, 'You Tanana?' Then, without waiting for an answer, he continues bluntly, 'Show me where there's gold in your great Tanana country!' When Shelley says 'Tanana,' he usually waves his hands and gets awfully excited and points dramatically to the west. Yes, he sure has the gold fever bad! Once he was talking like this and gesticulating wildly to a big Yukon Indian who turned on him fiercely and said, 'Ugh! White man crazy fool! Him better get up Yukon quick to Klondike. There . . . much gold!' "

"Ha," laughed Calhoun. "It's a wonder he hasn't been scalped by now! But haven't we all had similar experiences?"

"Yeah," said Tibbetts. "Lately, I guess we've all been fooled by some of these Yukon Indians, mistaking them for Tananas. Several times my face has been pretty red, too, and pretty soon it gets so confusing, a fellow begins to wonder if he'll know a real Tanana if he sees one!"

"Well, come on, boys," I said, "we've gotta step lively with this practice. Got that benefit show to put on for Ryan, no matter what!"

We had just swung into our first steps again when Shelley Graves poked his head in the door of the Opera House, looked cautiously around, apparently to see if we were alone, then came bounding up the aisle. "Men! Men!" he cried. "They're here. They're here!"

"Who? Who's here?" we all asked.

"Why, the Tananas, of course! They're here!" cried Shelley excitedly.

"What? The Tananas?" we all yelled incredulously, stopping dead in our tracks.

"Fellas, I tell you they're here. And they're at the A. C. Trading Company right now! Yes, sir, Bertram and I followed 'em from that old shack to the store and watched and listened. Why! the poor clerk doesn't understand a word they're saying. Just doesn't know what they want. Bert got me off in a corner. Whispered he's sure, at last, these are the real Tananas. Says they have all the earmarks. They're tall, can't speak English, dress entirely in skins, and boy! they carry stone hatchets! We know, because while we were hiding behind some trees on the outskirts of town, we saw them rip the bark right off some logs for firewood. Don't know, but they must have nuggets, too. But they haven't shown any yet."

"Good Lord!" I said, "if what you say is true, won't the men at the trading company tumble to who they are?"

"Don't think so," said Shelley, "because, as you know, there are so many new Yukon Indians here in town now who can't speak English either, and who look pretty fierce, too!"

"Say, Shelley, how many Tananas are there?" I asked excitedly.

"Only four," said Shelley, "but when I left, they were talking so fierce and loud—sounded like a whole tribe of Indians on the war path. Why, you should have heard 'em! One of the new clerks came out of a storeroom and listened, then sneaked back and brought out one of those new-fangled inventions, an Edison phonograph machine. He turned it on and placed it so's to get the whole thing down on a blank recording cylinder. Of course, the Indians didn't see it. A few of the miners were standing around listening and laughing and that seemed to make the Indians as mad as a bunch o' hornets!"

"Great Scott! Of course it would!" said Tibbetts. "Come on, fellows, let's get over to the trading company."

"No," said Shelley quickly, "Bertram says, 'Be at the cabin. Get there fast as you can!' Now I've gotta dash back and help him. The plan is—we're gonna try to coax the Tananas to our cabin."

"Yes, let's cut the rehearsal!" we all cried in an uproar as we grabbed our parkas. "Tell Bertram we'll sure be there, waiting!"

In no time flat, we had run the short distance to our cabin. For a brief moment after we first got inside, we looked at each other in sudden awe. So the Tananas had actually come to Circle City, and, evidently, we were the only ones, so far, who knew it! But could we keep it secret?

Captain Tibbett's voice boomed out as he took command, "Men, we haven't much time to plan this visit. It certainly is a surprise to me! If there are only four Tananas in their party, I'd say it'd be better if there are only four of us in the cabin to meet them. Ed, I think you and I and Bertram and Shelley had better handle the Tananas. The rest of the boys'd better skip out o' here before they come. But, I'd say, don't go far, in case we need you! But, men, wait—before you leave, hunt through your things and haul out anything bright you can find to catch their eyes. We've gotta have presents to give them!"

"You bet!" we all agreed spontaneously as pandemonium broke out and we all grabbed for bundles and boxes and began rummaging through. I yanked out a bright-red wool blanket, scarcely used; Moore, red socks; Graff, a red bandanna; Hill, some long red-flannel underwear; Calhoun, more highly colored socks; Tibbetts, a red tie—his only one—his pride and joy. Hastily, I spread the blanket out on a bunk. The men piled their treasured articles on it.

All at once, we heard Shelley's voice outside warning us that we were about to have company. Without stopping to fasten their parkas, Calhoun, Moore, Graff and Hill dashed out into the snow.

Then, in no time, we heard Bertram's and Shelley's voices outside and, before we could fully compose ourselves, the cabin door swung open, and filing in ahead of Bertram and Shelley were four tall, well-built Indians, the best-looking specimens I had ever seen. They were swathed in heavy fur parkas, wearing leather trousers and moccasins of the same skins. I glanced at them keenly and thought I caught the faint outline of several hatchets and long, slender knives concealed beneath their parkas. "Tanana mountain men!" I thought with a tingling shiver.

All four Indians pushed back their parka hoods and stood near the center of the cabin, looking at Tibbetts and me, questioning half-defiance in their dark eyes. There was a certain wild handsomeness in their boldly chiseled, coppery-colored features, almost like wild, high-spirited stallions right off the range. This look I hadn't seen in the faces of any of the Yukon Indians.

The first Indian had a lofty, haughty air, as if he was used to commanding the others, and out of the corner of their eyes, they watched him for their cues.

Bertram stepped forward and said quickly to Tibbetts and me, "Fellows, this is the chief of the Tananas. Now, I'm going to speak to them in Thlingit and try to introduce you." He turned and spoke to them. We bowed solemnly, but the Indians never bowed in return or gave any sign they understood him. Then Bertram said in English to us, "Oh, well, I'll try another way." He moved four chairs to the center of the room and motioned the Indians to sit down. But they looked at Bertram and the chairs and remained standing, their eyes warily taking in every detail of the room and us, but I could see that they had noticed the prospective gifts piled on my bunk. I wondered what would be our next move. I waited breathlessly.

Suddenly, before Bertram could speak again or Tibbetts could come into the conversation and try out his Indian lingo, Shelley Graves took the situation into his young, impulsive hands. He grabbed up the armful of gifts and stepped in front of the Indians, holding them high under the nose of the chief. Then, slowly, he set them down on a chair, exhibiting them one by one, turning and letting each article be thoroughly seen and appraised—the red socks, the wonderful, long red underwear, the beautiful red tie, my treasured red blanket. . . . He waited a minute, then reached into his pocket and produced his empty poke, saying boldly in English, "I don't know how to talk Indian, but look, Chief, we know you've got gold in your country—lots of it! Come on now, Chief, be a good Indian! Show us where that gold is and we'll give you all these fine gifts!" Shelley pointed dramatically to the gifts again, then to his empty poke, and vehemently to the southwest. He was certainly working himself up into a lather.

The chief stared hard at Shelley, scowled at him, then turned to the others and there followed a fierce conversation for a little.

Captain Tibbetts touched Shelley firmly on the shoulder and said, "My Lord, man! You're making the Indians angry. They know you want something, but you should know you can't force Indians in any language. It's not the way to handle them. Let me talk to them in Thlingit. Sit down and listen."

Tibbetts grabbed up the presents and took a few paces towards the chief. He spoke haltingly, but with great solemnness and dignity. Often he paused to point eloquently to the west and southwest and to the presents. I listened but, of course, I couldn't understand a word he was saying, although I did recognize a few of the same Indian words Bertram had used. Still, with all of Tibbetts' efforts, the Indians never spoke a word or moved an inch or gave any sign that they understood or desired the bright-colored, enticing gifts.

Tibbetts was talking faster now, more nervously. He began to perspire freely. He stopped to mop his forehead. He began talking again, then stopped and glanced over at us quite helplessly. Hurriedly, he put the gifts back on the chair and leaned over to whisper to Bertram, "Bert, you see I'm not making any headway and I've exhausted my vocabulary. I don't think they understand a word of Thlingit, after all. Of course, they may be just playing dumb. I told them we wanted to go to their country and that we needed them as guides. I told them they could have all of these wonderful gifts if they would take us and show us where they find gold. As you see, they don't answer. I'm stumped. So, Bert, you'd better take over."

"All right," said Bertram, looking a little worried as he stepped forward closer to the Indians. "I'll try again, but Tibbetts, it's beginning to look pretty hopeless. You know, Indians can be very cunning or very sincere, however the mood strikes them!"

Again Bertram spoke, this time almost fluently. One

could see that he had talked Indian often in the store at Juneau. All he needed was a little practice, and he was surely getting it now! But, in spite of Bertram's speech, it seemed the Indians couldn't, or didn't want to, understand. They just stood like stone images.

I began feeling very uneasy, almost wishing the others in our party would suddenly show up. This was certainly an absurd, awkward situation.

"Bertram," I said softly, "how were you able to coax them here, anyway?"

"Well, Ed, I showed them a small flask of whisky and let 'em smell and taste it. Guess that's how I got 'em here."

"Great Scott, man!" I said. "You can't give them whisky. Why, it wouldn't be safe!"

Suddenly, I got an idea. We had left some coffee simmering on the back of the stove and it was still hot. In a jiffy I was at the stove pouring out cups of the steaming, blackish liquid. Then I motioned the Indians to take off their parkas and sit down and drink with us. To my surprise, they looked quite pleased and acquiesced by pulling off their leather jackets; then, rather awkwardly, they sat down at the table and took up the cups and drank with us. None of us spoke a word for a few minutes. There wasn't a sound but the audible inhaling of the hot liquid.

As we drank, I got another inspiration. I reached into my pocket and pulled out my little hand-drawn map of the North and spread it out in the center of the table. Almost immediately, I could see a wave of interest flash in the eyes of the Indians. The chief put down his cup, leaned forward and examined the map closely. He turned and spoke quickly to his companions. Ah! This was my big chance . . . something I hadn't expected. I grabbed up a thin piece of kindling and pointed first to Circle City on the Yukon, then to Birch Creek, then I skipped over a wide area representing mountains and pointed to the existing line of the Tanana River. Then I pointed to the chief with admiration, which I truly felt, and said, "Tanana! You great Chief Tanana!"

Instantly, the chief was tense with understanding. He looked pleased and pointed proudly to himself and then pointed eagerly to the map and nodded several times saying, "Tanana! Tanana!"

"Yes, great Chief Tanana, tell me: Is there gold, much

gold, in your country—maybe near, maybe far from Belshai?"

"Belshai! Belshai!" suddenly cried the Indians, jumping to their feet, extending their arms high and with exultant, reverent eyes looking skyward as if in worshipful salute to a great deity.

"Holy smoke!" exclaimed Tibbetts softly. "Ed, you've sure struck a chord there. Why, those Indians are stirred to the core. It was that name—Belshai!"

"Yes," I said, "it was a shot in the dark. Belshai is their great mountain—you know, the one recently discovered. Wish I knew where it is. You know, it isn't even on the maps yet. Must be a huge giant of a mountain. Tibbetts, maybe if we could see it, we'd know why the Tananas hold it in such great awe."

As I spoke, I had another inspiration. I dug deep in my vest pocket and drew out a little picture of my wife. It was the one she had given me just before I left Tacoma, and from it her big brown eyes looked out tenderly. A crown of saucy brown curls rested above her intelligent forehead. It was a beautiful picture. And how I prized it! I put the photograph down on the table in front of the chief so that he might see it. In a moment, he lowered his eyes and I could see his face light up with interest when he saw the picture. He took it up and began examining it, then showed it to his companions who passed it around. All said something quickly. While the Indians were doing this, I gathered up all the gifts and spread them out on the end of the table to show them off to good advantage.

Now I approached the chief and said slowly, in English, as I pointed to the photograph of my wife, trying to use sign language, too, "I want Tanana gold for her. She needs many things. Gold will buy food, a house, furs to keep warm . . ." As I spoke, I took the picture gently from one of the Indians and laid it in the center of the table by the map of the Tanana. Then I took my only nugget and placed it on the map. I moved the nugget along, slowly, tracing the entire length of the Tanana River with it, pausing at intervals to look searchingly into the eyes of the chief. "Show us where gold like this is located," I kept saying. "Where is it? Is it here? . . . here? . . . or here?"

Immediately, I could tell the chief understood. He seemed excited and I could see he was almost bursting with the knowledge of gold and where it was in the Tanana. It was plain, too, that he was softening. He looked at the picture of my wife, at the nugget, then turned to his men and talked rapidly. They seemed to be arguing about something almost fiercely. Then he said something firmly and they ceased abruptly. Then, turning quickly, he snatched up the picture from the table and, before I knew it, he put it under his leather tunic.

"My Lord," said Bertram in surprise. "The chief has taken your picture, Ed. But, I guess you gotta humor him. He understands what you want, all right, and Jumpin' Jiminy! he's talking now in a mixture of Thlingit and Chinook. He's saying, 'Chief wants picture of pretty squaw! Indians won't tell where Tanana gold is. But will show white man if he promises to keep knowledge secret.' "

"Bertram, tell him quick in Chinook or Thlingit, or whatever way you can, that we solemnly promise," I said eagerly.

"Holy mackerel!" exclaimed Tibbetts, coming into the conversation. "Now I understand, too. They say they leave for Tanana in three sunups. That'll make it Monday morning . . . early!"

Bertram spoke again very slowly in measured words. The chief was listening hard to understand. Bertram was reiterating what had already been said. In answer, the chief held up three fingers of his right hand, paused, then made three sunup signs (holding the thumb straight out, arching the forefinger down to the thumb, then bringing it slowly up three times, forming a sign of the rising sun).

Bertram nodded. Yes, no mistaking it—we would be leaving in three days. . . . They understood and we understood. It seemed too good to be true! Glory be! Then it would be westward, ho! in three days, bound for the Tanana . . . and gold!

Suddenly the chief stood up, pulled on his parka, and the others followed. Then, with one sweep of his powerful hands, he quickly gathered up all of our fine gifts from the end of the table, rolled them into a tight bundle in my red blanket and handed it to one of the Indians. Then, to my surprise, the chief came over and, for a brief moment, looked searchingly into my eyes and said something rapidly, then pointed to his parka where he'd put my picture. I held my breath. What was he going to do? Suddenly he put his right hand over his heart, paused a moment, then held his hand up with palm out as if taking an oath of good faith. Then, to my surprise, his hand came forward to me. Impulsively, I extended mine, too. For a few seconds we clasped hands firmly, white man's and Indian's way of expressing friendship and trust, and I was sure I felt a friendly vibration. After that, without another word, silently the chief turned and the Indians all filed out of the cabin behind him. Again, I thought I caught the faint outlines of hatchets and knives under their parkas. "Well, what of it?" I said to myself. "They must have weapons to obtain food and for protection against animals and hostile Indians in this wild country."

No one in Circle City could possibly guess the great anticipation and excitement that took place in our cabin after the Indians had gone and when the rest of the fellows returned to hear the good news. Rapidly, we began making plans. How fortunate it was, we said, that we could still be in Circle to help with the benefit show. Yes, and we were lucky to have over two full days to prepare for the trip.

"Say, it looks like you fellows are getting ready for a long trip," said the clerk at the A. C. Company as he wrapped up extra rations of food we had inveigled out of him when we rushed to the store before it closed late that same afternoon.

"Sure," said Tibbetts nonchalantly. "Who knows? Maybe we'll be heading out of Circle any day now. The weather is favorable. It's milder. And now we've got dogs. And the show will be over Christmas night. Yes, it'll be the time to leave Circle City."

"Say now," said a miner, "hear you fellows are putting on a swell minstrel show at the Opera House tomorrow night. Hope you take in a lot o' gold for poor Ryan. My whole gang's coming, for sure. Golly, how we've been wishing for some good entertainment here in Circle!"

"Yeah," said the clerk, "but did you hear? Turner, the manager of the A. C. Company, is putting on a big Christmas feed for the boys of the show. And you kin bet your boots, it'll be the best feed in town, too. The lucky dogs! Gee," he said as he turned to us, "how I envy you fellows! Yeah, Turner came in today and just about cleaned out some of the shelves here in the trading company."

"Yes," I said, "he's promised us roast duck, canned sweet potatoes, cranberry sauce and all the trimmings. Sounds too good to be true after living on those skimpy portions of beans, bacon and sourdough pancakes all winter."

It was now Christmas Night, just a few minutes before the big minstrel show was to start. We fellows in the cast had just come from Turner's Christmas banquet. My, how we had enjoyed every mouthful! We hadn't had so much good food in many months. Why, I even had to let out two notches in my belt. But I felt thankful that my solos came near the end of the program. It would give me a little more time to catch my breath.

I glanced nervously over the audience, feeling sudden pangs of stagefright. I noticed every seat in the house was taken, all except four in front of the stove. Now the audience began whistling and clapping for the show to start. Suddenly, there was a lull. Then four tall Indians, in the most gorgeous fur parkas I had ever seen, came single file into the Opera House and walked proudly down the aisle to the seats in front of the stove. Everyone watched as they took these seats.

"Jumpin' Jupiter!" said Tibbetts under his breath. "As I live and breathe, if it isn't the Tananas!"

"Well, my goodness, how in the hell d'ya suppose they ever got in here?" whispered Bertram in alarm.

"Only way I know, they must have used some of their big nuggets or gold dust," said Bertram.

"Great Scott!" I whispered, "They're the only Indians in the Opera House. I'm afraid that it may mean trouble."

Now it was eight o'clock and time to start. The opening scene began with a rousing cheer as our combined choruses of two dozen men and a half dozen women opened the show. We, on the stage, were there to meet the river boat. It had come in with clangs and whistles amid the cheers of our crowd on the dock, joined by the cheers of the audience. Everybody in the house went wild with excitement. It wasn't hard to work up great enthusiasm over such an illusion. (How we men, during the last summer, had watched for river boats which never came! And how wild we had gone when a few did come in!) As the master of ceremonies stepped down the gangplank to announce the numbers, he was greeted with roaring applause! Certainly it sounded as if Circle City were starved for entertainment. How long had it been, anyway, since we'd had any? Well, not for many months!

We on the stage could tell from their faces that the audience was completely with us 100%, eagerly waiting for every song, every joke, every dance, every move . . . anything that would happen up on that stage. So, with pleasure and abandon, we romped through the first act. Our costermonger song went over with a bang, way over our expectations. Some of the fellows forgot their lines, but ad-libbed, making it even funnier, and brought down the house.

The audience roared with laughter when Hill wiggled his wicked hips and oogled his big eyes at us costermongers and the audience. His humorous cavortings in the skimpy grass skirt brought a rain of nuggets, which were promptly gathered up by a Negro boy for Ryan.

But now it was getting pretty stuffy in the Opera House. Occasionally, I caught a whiff of perspiring Indians. No one had paid any attention to them during the show, as they had been so quiet. But now they were receiving dirty looks. At last there was an intermission. Our master of ceremonies came out and mysteriously announced a special treat.

Suddenly, a man came from the back of the building carrying a gramaphone under his arm with a big horn. Without saying a word, he walked to the center of the stage and placed the box on a small table. He wound up the thing and carefully set the needle over a black, shiny cylinder. Then he clicked the machine on and left the stage. Everyone watched, spellbound. Some of the old-timers had never heard of, or seen, this new invention, the phonograph. What would it be like? I knew it hadn't originally been scheduled for the program.

The needle scratched a little, then, all at once, there

were many weird sounds coming out of the horn. Strange, fierce, wild noises were all scrambled together like a cat-and-dog fight; then the voices tapered off and there was a static pause. Now they were going at it again and, mixed in, we could distinguish a white man's voice strongly arguing, remonstrating. Indians' voices coming in again—hostile, angry, threatening; then again, a white man's voice breaking in at intervals, calling for order; Indians' again, shouting vehemently, distraught; now white man's again, and vague, distant and much mocking laughter.

"Great guns!" exclaimed Bertram. "Why, that's the record the new clerk from Dawson made of the Indians in the trading company yesterday. But the crazy fool! He just can't know what he's doing."

With great apprehension, we all glanced at the Tananas by the stove. The audience was looking, too, some snickering. The Indians appeared frightened. They stood up, staring wildly at the box and horn on the stage. Again, the record blared out. The Indians looked panicky. They scrambled to the aisle and stood a moment fascinated, listening to their own voices. How could this be? What terrible magic had the white man found that he could bring their voices from a box? They backed toward the door, terror written on their faces. Then, with a rush, they stampeded like wild horses for the door, fought it open, and bolted out into the night.

Now everyone in the Opera House was laughing loudly. It was a grand finale to the episode. There was a burst of wild, spontaneous applause. The clerk laughingly mounted the stage and said, "As you may all have guessed, those were the Indians . . . and they're probably still running!"

Then he explained how he had obtained the record the day before in the trading company. He ended up by saying that, as yet, the Indians hadn't gotten what they wanted and he doubted if they ever would now. There was another big round of applause and the practical joker bowed and took his phonograph and left the stage, looking very much pleased with himself. The show proceeded, with the audience in a more hilarious mood than ever. High humor continued clear through to the very end of the last act and every number was received with extremely great enthusiasm.

They were all in such a jovial mood, I wondered if they would care for a sentimental number when my turn came. But the audience listened attentively to my solo, "Tell Me with Your Eyes." However, on the rousing "Postillion" number, the fellows in my crowd came in with a bang and cracked some whips as they sang, "The phantom horseman you will see! He'll crack his whip and shout; Ho-la! Ho-la! Ho-la!" And the audience joined in with me when I repeated, "Then one glass more where the ale is fine . . . A toast, sweet ladies fair . . . To each man's home, good masters mine . . . An' may he soon be there! . . ." And then, we all ended with a rousing cheer as we sang, "The sparks shall flash as on we dash—Ho-la! Ho-la! Ho-la!"

By this time, the audience were all on their feet singing with almost frenzied enthusiasm. Never had there been such a show at Circle or such an appreciative audience! Everyone in the cast and those connected with it were herded out onto the stage to take a bow. Turner, manager of the A. C. Company, came to the platform and gratefully thanked all of us and the audience for helping to make the minstrel show a success. He announced that $700 in nuggets and gold dust had been taken in from the show, with more donations still coming in. He said all of the gold would be given to Ryan so that he could buy crutches and take the first boat "Outside" in the spring, with a little left over as a homestake. Turner wished us all a very Merry Christmas and said he knew this night we had certainly made one man that much happier in Circle City! And he conveyed Ryan's great thanks to us.

After the speech, there were cheers again and little Casey Moran invited everyone to remain for the Christmas ball.

"Golly, am I glad that's over!" said Moore as we left the stage and began moving benches and folding up chairs.

"Yeah, what a relief!" agreed Bertram. "But, for amateurs, I guess we did all right!"

"Yes," said Tibbetts, "but say, fellows, speaking of that gramaphone. It sure is a wonderful invention. But, confound it, anyway, why did that clerk have to try it out on the Indians tonight, of all times!"

"And did you see the wild look on their faces?" said Calhoun with a laugh. "I'd sure like to've had a picture of those Indians when they heard their own voices comin' out of that horn!"

"Well, golly! Guess I would have been scared, too, if I hadn't known what it was," said Shelley.

"But I'm afraid they were terrified half out of their wits!" I said dubiously.

"And, just as the clerk said, they probably ran all the way back to their cabin," laughed Tibbetts.

"But seriously, fellows, don't you think we should skip the dance and find those Indians and try somehow to explain to them?" I asked a little uneasily.

"Aw, no," laughed Tibbetts, still amused. "Give 'em time to cool off! By Monday, if they're still scared . . . well, then we'll try to explain it someway. But say, for the life of me, Ed, I don't see how we're gonna explain that talking machine to savages."

"I think it was a dirty, mean trick to play on them," said Hill. "But yet it could be to our advantage in the end if those Indians think we white men have supernatural powers."

"But do you realize," I said in a low whisper, "that if the Tananas hadn't been so terribly frightened and in such a wild hurry to get away, they might have become quite hostile and might even have thrown their stone hatchets at the box and horn and smashed the whole thing to pieces! . . . Then, by Jiminy! it wouldn't have been nearly so funny!"

"Guess you're right," whispered Bertram. "And, believe me, if that had happened, all hell might have broken loose in here tonight. Those Indians might have suddenly gone berserk and wrecked the place."

"Well, then, guess we should be thankful they just got out o' here!" said Moore in a low tone.

In spite of Tibbetts' advice to keep away from the Tananas, I still halfway felt we ought to go see them this night. But all were flushed with excitement over our success in the show and, after all, it was Christmas night and the holiday spirit strongly prevailed. So, for the moment, we forgot the Tananas and, as we changed our costumes, we even teased Hill about keeping his grass skirt on to be number thirteen lady, as there were only twelve white women in the crowd.

Well, all in all, it was an unusual Christmas Night, long to be remembered—a sumptuous banquet! a bang-up minstrel show! a new talking machine! four wild Tanana Indians! twelve sparkling, smiling women! one hundred and fifty homesick men!—all crowded into the 80- x 50-foot Opera House. And, at the box office, bags of big nuggets and yellow gold dust!

Yes, all of this because a poor fellow named Ryan had met with misfortune in the North!

Chapter XXIII

Twelve Moons and a Warning Arrow

It was now the 26th of December, 1897. And now that the Christmas Benefit Show was over, excitement among my party of men and me was mounting at the thought of leaving Circle City the following morning with the Tanana Indians (who were going to act as guides to take us to their country to find gold). During the last few weeks, we had heard some rather frightening stories about the Tanana Indians. Tales repeated from the early explorers seemed to indicate that there were two kinds of Indians in the Tanana—the valley Indians, and the mountain men. It was said that the mountain men were the fiercest kind of all in the region, although it was reported that both had cannibalistic tendencies and sometimes used the carved skulls of humans in their savage rituals. But we were so anxious and eager to get into the great Tanana, that we were willing to take the risk.

While we were eating a hurried breakfast that morning of the 26th, I suggested that, before we start packing, we check on the Tananas to see if they were still in that shack at the edge of town. But Tibbetts remonstrated again, saying, "Oh, let's leave the Tananas alone. Why bother them? Remember, this is Sunday, our last day here in

Circle City, and we surely need this time to get our outfits ready and with a little time left over to relax, to rest up after our big show last night. After all, fellows, I'll kinda hate to leave this snug cabin. Only the devil himself knows what's ahead of us when we start out tomorrow with those savages for the Tanana!"

"Say, fellows," I said as I studied my little map. "I've been wondering. Which route will those Tananas take us—southwest to the headwaters of the Tanana, west over the mountains to the middle Tanana, or on that long trip north over the ice of the Yukon to the mouth of the Tanana and on up the river?"

"Well, Ed," said Moore, "there's still another way I've been hearing about lately. It's through that big lake area northwest of here. But the Yukon Indians speak of it almost in fear. It's a very low, flat, wide area of maybe fifty square miles or more. They say thousands of lakes lay in there almost thicker than peas in a pod. They say each lake is deeply fringed with an almost impenetrable, jungle-like forest. Guess the Indians know how to get through there, but only a few have ever tackled it. They say in winter those lakes are frozen solid and are covered with deep snow. And in summer, it's like a huge, subdivided swamp, a hell hole of stagnant water and mosquitoes!"

"Yes, but what's beyond that lake area?" I asked in alarm.

"Well, the Indians say beyond that there are many mountains rising like barriers, guarding and blocking off the Tanana. And they think the mysterious range almost to the north is inhabited by spirits."

"Why?" I asked curiously.

"Well, fellows, it's strange; they say those mountains seem to glow and move a little, and that they hardly ever appear the same way twice."

"Humph!" said Tibbetts. "Just pure superstition! Pure bunk, I tell you. But, just the same, I don't think I'd care to get lost in there!"

We all fell silent. I was wondering if any stampeders had gone in that direction looking for gold.

By early afternoon, we were all packed and ready for

our big adventure to the Tanana. Some of the fellows began nervously playing cards to pass the time, but I was too restless to settle down to anything.

"Shelley," I said quietly, "let's go out for a breath of fresh air and a little walk about town."

"Sure," said Shelley.

Quickly we pulled on our parkas and made ready to go. The fellows in the cabin paid little attention when we announced we were going out for a stroll. A fresh blanket of snow had fallen Christmas Night. As we tramped along, it seemed our steps turned as though drawn by a magnet toward the shack of the Tananas. About a half mile out, we spotted the cabin in a lonely clump of stunted spruce. A thin curl of smoke rose from the chimney. To us, it was an assurance that the Indians were still there. But, as we approached closer, our steps began to lag.

"Shelley," I said, "after all, perhaps it was foolhardy for us to come here. You know, it might be awkward business to meet those Indians suddenly. They might think we're snooping or spying on them. What would we say without Bertram and Tibbetts as interpreters, especially if they're still afraid over that phonograph, like they were last night? I guess maybe Tibbetts was right, after all. Maybe we'd better steer clear of the Tananas today. Let's make tracks out o' here and get back to the cabin. We just can't take the risk of spoiling our chances of getting into the Tanana now!"

"Hell's bells, no!" said Shelley. "Let's get away from here quick, before they see us!"

Hurriedly, we retraced our steps through the snow. When we entered the cabin, the fellows put down their cards and Tibbetts said rather sarcastically, "Well, Ed, did you and Shelley have a good 'powwow' with the Indians? And did you explain the 'magic box' to their satisfaction?"

Shelley and I looked sheepish and shook our heads and I replied, "Well, no, but Shelley and I are glad to report that the Indians were very much at home this afternoon. We saw smoke coming from their chimney."

"Well, now, that's just fine and dandy!" said Tibbetts. "We'll see them bright and early tomorrow morning. . . . and that's soon enough to suit me!"

Now, I guess, it was natural that all of us should be a little edgy and uneasy about our trip. In the late afternoon, all of us settled down to write long last letters to the "Outside." We knew it would probably be summer before they would be delivered, but when would we again be in contact with civilization? In the letter to my wife, I mentioned where I was going and of my great hopes for gold, but told her not to worry, that we were going into the Tanana with the best guide in the world—the chief of the Tanana Indians himself! The tone of my letter was very optimistic, and although I myself felt some qualms of apprehension, I never mentioned it.

As far as keeping our promise to the chief was concerned, we hadn't told anyone at Circle City. But what would the fellows think when news would get around that our whole party of men had disappeared without saying a word? Sure, they might guess where we had gone. Yet they couldn't be sure, and in a day or two we would be completely swallowed up by the wilderness. And, yes, my party of men and I would be very much at the mercy of the Tananas if they should turn on us. Although two or three of the fellows in the crowd had guns, I had none and had never carried one. But what good would they really do us against the cunning of savages? Well, the die was cast! We had decided to risk it! And, more than likely, the Indians would act in good faith. They had taken our gifts and seemed sincere enough in the cabin. Surely, they would lead us to a new Bonanza or Eldorado in the Tanana!

Sunday night, the weather turned very cold and it began snowing a little. But, in spite of it, I got Shelley Graves and several of the others to go to the Episcopal church services with me. There weren't many there, as everyone seemed exhausted from the Christmas benefit celebration. It was good hearing the well-loved Christmas hymns again. But the minister had to cut his sermon short because the building was so poorly heated. However, we fellows all had a good, satisfied feeling when we got back to the cabin. After all, we had gone to church . . . and when would we have this opportunity again?

It seemed Monday morning came before we knew it.

We got up at 5 A.M. It was dark and cold, but it had stopped snowing. We ate a quick breakfast, then packed our last-minute things. Truly, it seemed, high adventure was in the air! Harnessing the dogs, who seemed eager to go, we closed the cabin and away we sped over the snow toward the shack of the Tananas. The light was just turning gray as we mushed silently along.

"We've gotta hurry," said Tibbetts. "Mustn't keep those Indians waiting."

We urged the dogs to a faster pace and soon we could see the cabin in the distance in a clump of trees. But we were surprised to see that no smoke was coming from the chimney. We hurried faster and, in a few minutes, drew up and stopped at the cabin door. Tibbetts knocked briskly while we all waited anxiously. The cabin had a strange, silent look and I had noticed in the pale light that the snow was badly ruffled up and disturbed for a number of yards, extending out into the forest to the west.

Tibbetts knocked again, but there was no answer. Then he pounded on the door. Still no answer . . . all was dead silent inside.

"Well, I'll be damned!" said Tibbetts. "What are those Indians up to, anyway? I'm going in there if they don't come out pretty quick." He yelled something in Thlingit and, hardly waiting for an answer he laid his shoulder to the door and almost fell in as the door suddenly gave way.

In a few seconds, we were all inside the cabin with Tibbetts. We could tell immediately that the place was completely deserted, although it was almost pitch black inside.

"Well, I'll be damned!" said Tibbetts again.

Quickly, I lighted a candle and began looking around. The shack showed signs of having been recently abandoned. A few fresh scraps of venison and bones lay on the greasy, rickety table and on the floor. The stove still felt warm, with a few hot coals left in the grate.

"The dirty, blasted Indians! They've gone for sure. They've run out on us!" exploded Moore. "Well, we might've known they'd play a scurvy trick on us like this!"

"Look," I said. "Here's something!" As I spoke, I held the candle closer and there, on a small table near the window, the candlelight caught the gleam of at least a dozen nuggets. I was startled! And there, propped up against the wall, was the picture of my wife which the chief had taken. The offering of nuggets by the picture spoke eloquently.

"Well, I'll be!" I said as, gratefully, I picked up the cherished photograph and the gleaming nuggets. "Am I glad to get this photograph back! And look at the big Tanana nuggets he's left as presents for her!"

"Yeah," said Tibbetts a little sarcastically, eyeing the nuggets. "The meaning is very clear, all right. The chief has left them for her . . . but I still say those Indians are dirty savages, running out on us like this!"

"Gosh, fellows. Look here!" called Shelley, who had lighted another candle and was examining the rest of the room. "Come here, quick!"

"Yea!" exclaimed Hill with a low whistle as he looked over Shelley's shoulder. "We've found a lot of Indian symbols scratched here in charcoal on the wall."

In a jiffy, all of us had rushed over and held up the candles closer. Sure enough, there on the north wall were a number of Indian symbols which had been hastily scrawled on the flatly hewn logs. First, there were several long, swooping lines forming a symbol resembling a comet, with a downward swirl at the tail; following it was a large circle with a heavy dot in the center; next, came a black square with a horn-like thing suspended almost directly above it; then, from right to left on the next log below, were four pair of moccasins headed west, and an arrow pointing the same way to a symbol which looked like a large, jagged "M"; and beyond this was drawn a long, snake-like symbol; on the third log below were twelve half moons in a row; then came another arrow, this time pointing east to a jagged "M"; four pair of moccasins followed the arrow, and a crude picture of eight men terminated the whole thing.

"What on earth does it all mean?" we asked in puzzled amazement.

"Well, it must be a message for us," said Tibbetts.

"It sure is," said Bertram. "By Jove! I think I'm beginning to get it. Look, fellows. That third symbol isn't Indian at all. Why, it's a crude drawing of a box with a horn!"

"A gramaphone!" we all exclaimed.

"Great guns! Now, it's all beginning to make sense," said Bertram excitedly. "It's saying: 'Indians greatly fear spirit-filled box that talks to white man with big horn. Indians must return quickly over mountains to own country. Will return in twelve moons. Take white men to Tanana then.'"

"Why, the dirty, thieving redskins!" exploded Tibbetts. "They skinned out o' here with my red tie and all those other valuable presents and they know full well we won't be here next year!"

"By gum! We'll not let 'em get away with it!" said Shelley vehemently. "What d'you say, men? Let's follow 'em! They can't be more than two hours ahead of us . . . and their tracks will be easy to follow in this fresh snow."

"Sure, let's go after them," everyone cried excitedly, eager for the chase—that is, everyone except Tibbetts.

We all looked at him questioningly as he hesitated and held back. Then he said, "All right, boys, I'll go, too. You know, I'm not one to give up, but I don't think it's wise. Seems like we'll be taking an awful chance."

"Of course," I said, "but, after all, the Indians weren't hostile to us—only terrified at the phonograph in the minstrel show, which they naturally thought had evil spirits. And, after all, it's our own fault. We saw how frightened they were Christmas Night. We should have gone to see them. Let's go after them now . . . and try to explain. Maybe we can still get to the Tanana."

"Yes, you're right, Ed," agreed Bertram. "I believe, in their own primitive way, the Indians are trying to be fair. Otherwise, they wouldn't have bothered to give back the photograph and leave the gift of nuggets or write a message on the cabin wall."

"Well, you win, fellows," said Tibbetts. "Let's hit the trail fast!"

"Look!" cried Shelley, who had bounded out of the cabin ahead of us and was examining the snow. "See, it's all stirred up here, like it's been beaten with branches and sticks in front of the cabin. And see those dozens of moccasin footprints leading off into the forest and dozens more coming back."

"What are those Indians up to, anyway?" said Moore. "Must be a trick to throw us off the trail."

"Sure it is," said Bertram. "Let's all fan out quick. Whoever picks up the real trail, whistle three times."

In a few seconds, we were like bloodhounds, all looking sharply, eagerly following every footprint to its conclusion back in front of the cabin. The moccasin tracks took off in all directions, leading crazily in and out among the trees and then returning back to the mess of jumbled snow in front of the cabin. But, in a few minutes, I found some tracks which led out about a thousand feet to a tree which had at one time been hit by lightning. It was broken and split at the middle, and a large limb still hung from the tree, caught at the end and held up by a big rock. From this there was a jumble of large boulders stretching out for some distance. The tracks I had been scouting suddenly ended at this tree. I was puzzled, because I saw no tracks leading away from the tree. Suddenly, as I looked up at the broken limb, I could see where the snow had been skinned off in places. I climbed up a little and looked . . . and there, to my joy, I saw a number of footprints on top of the big rock. Ah, this was it! The Indians had climbed the tree, shinnyed down the limb to the rock, and then had jumped from boulder to boulder, which acted as stepping stones in the snow. By the last one I found four distinct pair of footprints hurrying off into the forest.

I whistled quickly and, in a few minutes, dogs and men joined me and away we went in eager pursuit of the Indians. And I, who had been humorously dubbed "Chief of Scouts" on our packing trips around Circle City, took the lead. The clearly defined trail pointed out almost due west. It led straight into a country where I had never been before. Once we crossed a small frozen stream. We saw no cabins, no miners and no living thing. All was a white, flat, snow-covered wilderness with forests of spruce and birch trees.

We followed this trail for several hours and then we came into a hodgepodge of beaten snow and many tracks leading out and back from this, very similar to those by the cabin. Here we wasted about a quarter of an hour following trails which went nowhere. Some went ahead, circled crazily and backtracked. But, finally, we discovered the real trail and away we went again, in hot pursuit.

The weak winter sun was at its best now about noon, and we tried to go faster. We ate from our knapsacks anything we could find as we traveled along. How far we had gone, we had no idea.

"Hey," said Shelley, who was now in the lead and who had suddenly stopped, "fellows, look! Here's a wide area of stirred-up snow and dozens of tracks entering the spot, but none going out!"

Quickly, we all pulled up and stared incredulously at the tracks, then held a serious council. How could we account for all of those footprints coming into the center and apparently none going away? Why, it looked as though a whole tribe of Indians had walked into this spot and then disappeared. But surely Indians couldn't vanish into thin air or be completely swallowed up by the snow!

"The cunning Injuns," said Moore, laughing softly. "It's still the four of them, all right, who've stirred up all this snow. But this time they've tried to fool us by walking backwards in different directions into the forest and then have run back to the hodgepodge of snow here and jumped up and down like crazy. Can you beat that? They've repeated this ruse many times."

"Well, fellows," said Tibbetts, "if we want to catch them, we've gotta follow all of those tracks again until we find the ones that turn and go towards the Tanana. Great Scott! though, I wonder how long they're going to keep this sort o' thing up!"

"Well, by Jiminy!" said Shelley, "it's sure they can't walk backwards for very far and make any headway. No, not even Tananas! Those Indians have sure wasted a lot o' time today trying to throw us off the track!"

Once again, we all fanned out and scouted the tracks. Tibbetts soon called out that he had found a single pair of moccasin tracks that extended out beyond all of the others; also that they seemed to be coming from the west and, like the others, were headed toward the area of stirred-up snow.

"Look," said Moore, examining the trail closely, "this pair of moccasin tracks are much deeper than all the rest. Shows three pair of feet have carefully stepped backwards in the tracks made by their chief. Well, I'll be jiggered!

Imagine four Indians walking backwards in the same foot tracks!"

"Come on," said Bertram. "Let's follow this trail. It's a sure thing those footprints have got to right-about-face toward the Tanana pretty soon! As Shelley says, even Indians can't walk backwards for very long!"

"Yes," said Tibbetts, "but it's very evident those Indians are using every trick and ruse to discourage us and keep us from following them. Maybe we should turn back."

But we all shook our heads decidedly and didn't follow his advice. Truly, we were like bloodhounds, reluctant to give up the chase. We continued to follow this peculiar trail for perhaps several hundred feet to a place where the snow was slightly rumpled. But, to our disappointment, only a single pair of moccasin prints emerged and pointed west. It was exasperating.

"Here again those Indians are stepping in the footprints of their chief," said Moore. "But this time, at least, they're going straight ahead for a change!"

Now we hurried faster and about a quarter of a mile farther on, to our joy, the tracks seemed to hesitate, then suddenly four distinct pairs of moccasin prints appeared and pointed the trail. Now they went on boldly, and there was no more back-tracking, circling or subterfuge. It was a straight, clear trail . . . and it seemed to speak: Hurry! Perhaps the Indians suspected we were close on their heels, or maybe it was something else which was causing them to throw all caution to the winds.

It was now getting late in the afternoon, and the light was fading fast. The sun had disappeared and the sky had turned a dull gray. Soon, a few flurries of snow fell lightly, but still we pressed on desperately, hoping yet to catch sight of those illusive Indians before dark. Anxiously, we strained our eyes now to see their fading footprints, which, to our dismay, were beginning to gradually lose form, slowly being obliterated by large, feathery snowflakes.

"Great Scott!" I said to myself as I struggled along in the lead, "if we could only catch up with those Indians! Surely, we're not going to lose them now after we've come so far! But I guess we'll soon have to make camp. Visibility's getting worse and worse, and we're all dog-tired!"

I was about to suggest that we make camp when, suddenly, out of the stillness, I heard the distant call of voices. They seemed to come through the trees from almost directly behind us. Anxiously, I looked back to see if any of our party were in distress. But the men and dogs seemed to be all right. However, they had pulled up and stopped, and seemed to be listening, too. Again the calls came, and this time a little closer. It certainly couldn't be the Indians. But who else could be in this God-forsaken country? Now, as I listened, it sounded as though someone was calling for help. I ran back to our caravan, and all of us looked at each other in astonishment as we stood dead still in the snow. Then we all cupped our hands and shouted, "Hello! Hello! Who are you?"

In a moment, the tall figure of a man came struggling through the snow; then came another, and another following closely behind. All three were bent under the weight of heavy packs.

"Caesar's ghost!" exclaimed Tibbetts. "Why, they're white men! And they look like they're ready to drop!"

"We sure are, pardners!" said the tall man in the lead as he staggered up to us and stopped to catch his breath. "Thank God, we've caught up with you, at last. Couldn't 've gone on much longer. Yes, you look surprised as hell to see us! But we're mighty glad to see you! And we happen to know that you've been hot on the trail of those Tanana Indians. And what a devil of a merry chase they've led us all on today!"

"Well, I'll be jiggered!" said Moore, "Looks like a stampede in the making!"

"Yeah, it's a stampede, all right," laughed one of the men a little ironically. "And there's a whole flock of fellows comin' behind us . . . maybe twenty of 'em. They've been hot on our tails all day. And we know those fellows are having an awful struggle, too. Why, they're carrying even heavier loads than we are. But they're lucky to have one dog in the crowd."

"Well, how far back are they?" I asked.

"They're only a few minutes behind us. Caught sight of 'em just a little while ago . . . just before it began to snow," said the stranger.

"Good Lord!" we all said as we sucked in our breaths and stared at the three men incredulously. "A stampede to the Tanana! Why, this is something we never dreamed of!"

"What d'ya know about that!" exclaimed Moore. "A whole regiment of gold-crazy men following us to the Tanana! Well, now, maybe those Indians guessed it. And, say, do you suppose they think we've double-crossed them?"

"Yes, maybe," said Tibbetts, and I noticed that his face looked a little drawn and white. "Fellows, I haven't said anything, but I've been noticing the last half hour, before it began to snow, that the trail seems to be leading us in the direction of the northwest."

"Do you mean to say that you think those Indians are deliberately leading us into that hazardous lake area?" asked Shelley in alarm.

"It certainly seems that way," said Tibbetts. "And look, fellows, here's something I found sticking in the snow back aways on the trail. It's a bone arrow. . . . Might have been dropped by mistake—or left as a grim warning!"

The sight of that arrow gave us all a spine-tingling sensation. But before anyone could speak, Tibbetts continued. "I'm telling you, men, we'd better consider this very seriously before we follow those Indians any farther . . . before they lead us into that labyrinth of frozen lakes and forests where we might never find our way out!"

"You're right," agreed Moore with a shiver. "I wouldn't follow those savages into that hell hole for all the gold in the Tanana!"

"Nor would I," said Bertram. "Besides, by morning their trail will be completely obliterated by snow!"

"It'll be covered, all right . . . and then some!" said the tall stranger. "Fellows, don't you know there's a heavy blizzard in the making? See how the snow's coming down faster now, and feel the wind from the northwest beginning to cut us like knives? Men, I'm telling you, we haven't any time to waste. Gotta make camp and dig in fast!—Tananas or no Tananas!"

Almost before he had finished speaking, sharp, icy, snow-filled winds tore at us viciously and the snow began coming down in thick, heavy sheets. Yes, Old King Blizzard had swooped upon us with almost no warning, or perhaps we had been too intent on following those cunning, puzzling moccasin prints to see the ominous signs.

Suddenly it became almost impossible to see each other through the driving snow, even a few feet away. And while we hurriedly scrambled and pulled out our tents, sleeping bags and equipment, the other men on the stampede behind us staggered into camp, guided by our shouts and calls.

Soon we were a bedlam of supplies, men and dogs, all pulling, hauling and fighting to get under cover from the biting storm. There was absolutely no time for order, no time to talk, no time to ask questions. It was a fight for survival! And, as we lay shivering and huddled in our sleeping bags, wondering what lay ahead of us, we listened almost with fear to the snow-filled wind as it shrieked and howled its vengeance from that treacherous lake area straight off the icy peaks of those mysterious mountains far away to the northwest, which, the Indians said, sometimes glowed and moved a little.

What a cruel trick the North had played on us! What great help the elements were giving the Tananas to shake us from their trail! Could it be that taking this northwesterly direction was only a ruse, only another one of the Indians' cunning tricks?

How thankful we were to be back in Circle City after those exhausting three days of wandering in a frozen wilderness! And how gratefully my party of men and I warmed ourselves around the little Klondike stove while our friend, good old Joe the mail carrier, served us hot coffee and sourdough pancakes. Yes, good old Joe would have our story firsthand for all of Circle City.

"Suff'rin' cats! Ed, go on—finish telling me what happened that night in the blizzard!" he urged eagerly as he handed me a second cup of steaming black coffee.

"Well, Joe," I said, "it was like this: That wind blew so hard in the blizzard we couldn't even pitch our tents, so all thirty-one of us crawled into our sleeping bags just as we were, clothes, parkas and all, pulled the tents over our heads and held on for dear life! By this time, the storm was tearing and clawing at us like ten thousand demons and the snow was coming down in buckets. All we had to eat were the crumbs we could find in our knapsacks. I tell you, Joe, it was so beastly cold we nearly froze to death. And all night we worried about our dogs, which we'd turned loose. We were afraid they'd been swept away in the storm. All night we kept listening anxiously for their barks, but there wasn't a sound—only that confounded, shrieking howl of the blizzard. Why, I don't think any of us slept a wink that night. We had to constantly keep shaking the snow off the tents because it kept piling up so thick and heavy it almost suffocated us. It was a ghastly night, I'll tell you! And I remember saying to Tibbetts who was huddled next to me, 'Guess you were right, old fellow, about following those blasted Indians. Look at the predicament it's got us in! I'm terribly worried. What if we've lost our dogs? . . . And what if we can't find our way back? By morning, it's certain that all tracks, including our own, will be completely gone . . . will be buried deep under the snow.'

" 'Well, morning will tell!' Tibbetts had groaned. 'But don't worry about it now, Ed. We'll find our way back, somehow, if we survive the night!' "

"Great Scott!" And how did you get back?" asked Joe anxiously.

"I'll tell you," said Tibbetts, setting down his third cup of coffee. "In the morning we were mighty thankful to find that the blizzard had passed. Without a doubt, it was the worst storm of this winter. First thing when we piled out of our sleeping bags, we called for the dogs, but they were nowhere in sight. Why, everything was covered with another two feet of snow! Man, talk about a wilderness! It was a terrifying sight! And absolutely no trace of those dogs! We all threw back our heads and called long and loud . . . and, to our great joy, the dogs appeared. And where do you think they were? Completely buried under the snow, covered up by the storm! Why, we could have stepped on them, they were so close. If we'd looked sharper, we might have seen the air holes that kept them alive and breathing. In a minute, they were shaking themselves free of the snow and came crawling to us, wagging their tails and whining. And were we relieved and glad to see them!

"By this time, all the other fellows in camp had wiggled

out of their sleeping bags. It surely was a sight to see them come to life out from under the snow-piled tents, or anything that covered them. And you can bet your boots, there was quite a commotion around camp! What a dejected, sorry-looking crowd we really were! But, right then and there, we all held a council. Of course, our first concern was to get our bearings. But all thirty-one of us admitted that we had no idea where we were, or how far from Circle City we had come. When the storm had struck us the night before, we happened to be in a rather wide, open space, completely surrounded by dense forest. Whether there was a frozen lake under us, we couldn't tell. Anxiously, we waited for the sun to show its face so that we could get our directions, but it didn't oblige us. Every thought or hope of going to the Tanana, of course, had been wiped out by that storm. Now, our only thought was to find our way back to Circle City.

"For hours we floundered through the deep snow and wandered aimlessly, getting nowhere fast. But, finally, Ed put Chattel in the lead. And good old Chattel led the whole outfit slowly and painfully back through the snow. Late in the afternoon of the second day, we came to a frozen creek . . . and there, to our amazement, was Twelve Mile House, big as you please! We went wild with excitement. It was too good to be true! Needless to say, we stayed at Twelve Mile that night. Some slept in bunks and some on the floor, but you can bet your boots, we all slept like logs!

"Well, Joe, as you know, it's a well-defined packing trail from Twelve Mile House back to Circle. And so, here we are! And you'll never know how glad we all were to see the streets and cabins of town again and all of you men in Circle City. Why, we even didn't mind it too much when the fellows along the riverfront ribbed us with hoots and catcalls when they saw us coming into town almost dragging our tails behind us!"

"And, I suppose, looking pretty hang-dog, too," laughed Joe.

"Yeah, I suppose so," said Tibbetts. "Yes, when some of the fellows saw us, they yelled, 'Well, boys, how's the weather over in the Tanana, anyway. And, say, did those Indians send you all home just loaded down with bags of gold?' "

"Yes, I'll bet they ribbed you plenty!" said Joe. "But don't let that bother you. You're all very lucky to get back alive. But, say, tell me, how did the rest of those fellows who followed you get wise to the Tananas?"

"Well, after all," I said, taking up the story again, "I guess that was fairly easy. It seems those men had been secretly watching for the Tanana Indians for weeks, too, just like we had. So, when they saw them at the benefit show Christmas Night and heard that record played on the phonograph, they pricked up their ears and eyes and guessed who they were. It only took a little sleuth-footing Sunday afternoon to find out where the Tananas were staying. Yes, and secretly, they'd been keeping track of our party of men and watching our cabin too, because they'd heard us dickering at the trading company, heard us say we needed supplies . . . maybe for a long trip! and so they just put two and two together!"

"Yes," said Tibbets wryly, "they saw us leave our cabin early that morning and they got to the shack of the Tananas just a little after our party had started out following the Indians. They also discovered the Indian signs in the cabin and guessed what they meant. Then from the cabin, it was quite easy to follow our well-defined trail."

"Well," sighed Joe, "all of you men certainly had an exciting adventure . . . and maybe a mighty close call, too! But who knows? If that crazy fool with the gramaphone hadn't come in Christmas Night the way he did, and if just your party of men could have gone along with the Indians as you planned, why, who knows? They might have kept faith and led you to great treasures of gold!"

"Great treasures of gold!" I sighed wistfully as I pulled out a few big shiny nuggets, a fair sample of Tanana gold that the chief had left as a present for my wife.*

* How could any of us know that it would be almost a year and a half more before gold would finally be discovered by white men on several small tributaries of the Tanana River, way up by its headwaters, and about 200 miles from its mouth? And that it would be almost four years before gold would be discovered near the Chena Slough in the great Tanana Valley by an Italian immigrant, Felix Pedro, on July 22, 1902? And that Fairbanks, the largest U.S. city that far north in the Arctic Circle, would be born in that same year . . . and that it would be only a short distance from the colossal Belshai, or Mount McKinley?

"Well, fellows," continued Joe Lamour, "are you gonna stick around here until maybe the Tanana Indians come back next year?"

"Hell's bells, no!" exploded Tibbetts. "We're clearing out o' here by the first of the year! Heading back up the Yukon!"

"Jumpin' Jupiter!" said Joe suddenly, "D'you fellows realize that in three days it'll be the beginning of eighteen ninety-eight! And I still have that mail that's been piling up for months to take 'Outside' by dog team!"

"Well, it's about time you got going!" said Tibbetts with a laugh. "Because you've got a lot of our letters to deliver, too!"

As I poked up the fire, I said thoughtfully, "Eighteen ninety-eight! I wonder what that year will hold for all of us stampeders on the Yukon?"

Chapter XXIV

The Ancient Channel

It was now early morning of March 26, 1898. I bounded up a steep stairway towards an ugly, square-shaped boardinghouse overlooking Puget Sound, Tacoma, Washington. Trembling with excitement, I put down my shabby, grease-stained canvas bag and eagerly rang the doorbell. Were my wife and little son Clemy still living at this address? I hadn't heard from Velma for months, almost a year. Dear God! How would I find things? Had they received any of my letters from Dawson or Circle City while I had been frozen in?

My heart flipped and pounded violently. Impatiently, I rang a second time, and, as I waited, I glanced down at my worn trousers tucked into heavy boots and looked at my faded mackinaw. For the first time in many months, I became fully aware of my hardened, weather-beaten hands nervously holding an old, battered felt hat. I turned and suddenly caught a glimpse of my reflection in one of the plate-glass windows.

Holy mackerel! What a shaggy, lean, gaunt fellow I truly was! Regretfully, I wished I'd taken time to have my heavy beard shaved off. Wished, too, I had stopped long enough in town to buy new clothes with some of the nuggets and gold dust from the poke I carried in my hip pocket. But I had been consumed with eagerness to reach home without delay. Ah! home in Tacoma at last! What magic in that word—home! How could those always living in civilization fully appreciate all that it meant? How many times during the past year in the great, lonely wilderness, had I almost despaired of ever seeing my loved ones again? And walking that thousand miles over the ice of the Yukon from Circle City to reach the coast hadn't been easy. How many times had I and the men I traveled with been caught in blizzards, suffered from untold hardships, hunger and cold? How many times, too, had we nearly fallen through the hidden air holes in the frozen river? Yes, almost three months of traveling through an icy hell to reach Skagway to catch a steamer home!

Impatiently I rang the doorbell again for a third time. Suddenly the door opened and a tall, good-looking blond fellow in his early thirties asked crisply, "Hello, what is it?"

"Does Mrs. Ed Lung live here?" I stammered uncertainly, a little taken aback.

"Why, yes," answered the man, eyeing me critically. "Wait a minute . . . I'll call her."

I pushed my way behind him into the parlor as the man called loudly, "Velma, a man to see you."

My heart skipped some beats as I waited, hat in hand. Then I heard the rustle of skirts . . . and Velma entered the room. She stood looking at me quizzically, a big question in her lovely brown eyes. But I could see there wasn't the slightest recognition of me in her expression. She probably thought I was just a poor fellow looking for work or lodging.

"Yes," she said politely, "what may I do for you?"

I was dumb and speechless. I could feel blinding tears welling in my eyes. Then I cried out. "Velma, oh, Velma, you don't know me!"

She ran to me. . . . In a moment, she was in my arms, sobbing hysterically. "Oh, Edward! Truly, I didn't know you—not until I heard your voice. Can you blame me? I haven't heard from you for so long . . . I thought you were dead! So many reports have come. Hundreds of stampeders have perished in the North. Oh! It's too good to be true! You've really come back to me. Thank God! Oh, thank God!"

Then Velma pulled away and looked at me closely. "Yes, Edward, you've changed a great deal . . . and that beard! You appear much older and look so very tired and, oh, so terribly thin! Are you ill?"

"No, my dear." I laughed happily. "There's nothing ails me that just seeing you and Clemy and being home won't cure. But who the devil was that handsome young brute who opened the door? For a moment, he had me worried."

"Oh, him!" laughed Velma as the stranger entered the room, extending his hand. "Edward, meet my country cousin, Charles Davis, from Oregon." And before he and I could cordially acknowledge the introduction, there was a bustle and big clatter in the hall and two women and a small boy burst into the room, eagerly surrounding me and exclaiming, "It's Edward! Edward!" and "Oh, Daddy! Daddy!" They were Mrs. Clement, my auburn-haired, rather beautiful mother-in-law, and pretty, blue-eyed Ena, a young sister-in-law, and my dear little son Clemy. Naturally, a grand commotion followed . . . all talking and laughing and crying tears of joy at once. Never did a man have a happier homecoming than I on that glorious, memorable morning of March 26th, 1898!

And it seemed that, in no time, the whole neighborhood was astir and knew that Edward B. Lung was back from the North, for little Clemy lost no time running his legs off to give the neighbors his own small-boy variation of the exciting details. Yes, his daddy had returned from the faraway land of ice and snow, malemutes and gold, and had brought some shiny, big yellow "nuddets," a whole sackful for him and his dear mummy. And now he could have a toy train and big red wagon, and his mummy lots of pretty things!

Yes, I had brought a sackful of glistening gold home from the North—about $800 worth. $140 of it was in nuggets; some for freighting at Circle City; and some as gifts from the Tanana chief. But $660 of it was in gold dust I

Ed Lung joined a party of men who had dogs and trekked to Skagway, 1000 miles over the ice, Ed Lung second from left

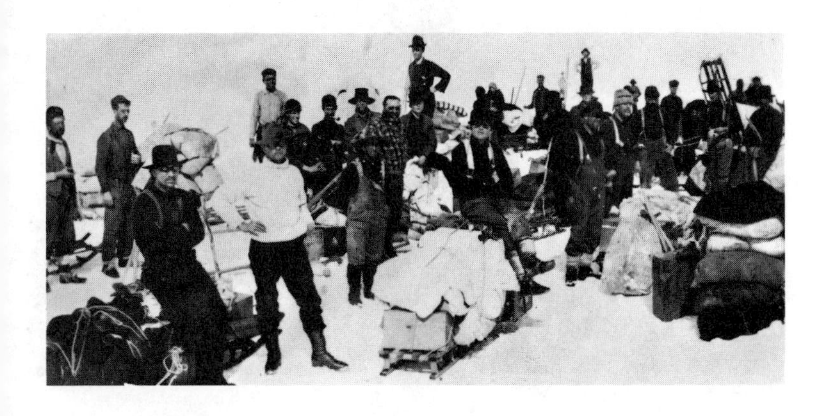

Stampeders on the trail without the aid of dogs

Chilkoot Pass in 1898. Note the Aerial Tram at the upper left

Ben Atwater, famous mail carrier of the Yukon, made runs of up to 1,500 miles over ice

had gotten for selling Chattel, my faithful sled dog. However, a fellow doesn't relish that kind of gold. Every time I looked at it, I thought of good old Chattel. Why, selling him was like selling a friend! How many times he had nearly lost his life to save mine! How hard he had worked to pull my heavily loaded sled over the dangerous ice in all kinds of blizzardy weather!

Surely, God, when He had created the animal we call dog, realized man's great need, especially in the North, and put a great big measure of His own unfailing love in the make-up of this useful, humble and devoted creature. I hoped Chattel's new master, Hamilton, would be good to him. An old miner had startled me one day when he had said, suddenly, "Ed, have you ever thought of something? Spell d-o-g backwards—what do you get?"

Not only everyone in the neighborhood knew I was back from the north, but soon the whole town. The newspaper carried an article about Edward B. Lung's adventures in the North that touched off many personal calls. What attention I drew overnight! Old friends, new friends, acquaintances, even strangers hurried to our home. The doorbell jangled constantly. Everyone wanted to ask questions about the much-talked-of Land of Gold and wanted to check on the confused, conflicting reports of the famine and conditions in the Klondike during the past winter. Many inquired anxiously if I had news of relatives and friends who had gone North the year before in the first gold rush.

In many cases, I did have news—especially of Stacey, my former partner. But it was rather bad news for his family. I had to tell them that the last time I had seen Stacey he had been confined to a narrow cot in the crowded little Catholic hospital in Dawson, where twelve much-needed nuns had just arrived over the ice from Circle City to help take care of the patients. Though Stacey was very ill, he had seemed quite optimistic about recovering, and hoped, even yet, to strike it rich! He had sent greetings to his family—even managed to write a little note to his wife, which gave her new hope.

But I was quite troubled and worried about Stacey, because he was just a shadow of his former self. And even though he was very ill and had appeared glad to see me,

I thought there was still a note of strain in his manner toward me—something of the same manner I had noticed the day we had parted on the Eldorado the summer before. Now, as I thought of Stacey, I was still puzzled and bothered about this. Nevertheless, it had been hard to say goodbye to him in Dawson. If it had been at all possible for him to make the trip "Outside" I would have brought him home to his family.

"Now that you're back in Tacoma, Ed, what are you planning to do?" I was asked by a friend who stopped me on the street.

"Oh," I said, "I'm not exactly sure yet, but I can see that hard times are still with the country."

"They sure are!" said my friend. "The gold rush has helped somewhat by thinning the ranks of men looking for jobs. Naturally, the stampeders coming through Tacoma and outfitting here have been of some help, too. But, so far, the wheels of industry haven't speeded up enough to suit any of us, and you have no idea how tough it's been. Hundreds of men in Tacoma are still out of work . . . as they are all over the country."

"Yes," I said anxiously. "It makes it bad when a man has to provide for a family. I can see it's been tough sledding down here trying to make a living. Of course, that's what I'm faced with now. The gold I brought from the North, naturally, won't last very long."

"We're sorry, young man, there are not enough jobs here," said one businessman. "We'd like to put you on, but we just can't! You say you're Ed Lung, just come from the North? Yes, we've heard about you. Now, wait a minute, let's talk. What chance would you say there'd be for me and my partner if we decided to close this blasted business and strike out for the Klondike?"

"Well, sir," I said, "the chances of getting gold are hardly worth the hazards. I'd say it's paying too big a price for the whistle! Just to pack your goods over Chilkoot or White Pass is a tremendous ordeal. You'll need an iron constitution and the strength of an ox! Soon, the ice will go out . . . and it means you'd have to build your own boat at

Lake Linderman or Bennett and try to get through the treacherous Canyon and White Horse Rapids, and then on down the Yukon to Dawson. Yes, there's gold up there all right! But to find it! It'll probably take a hundred years or more to fully prospect that great country. Yes, there are some lucky ones who struck it really rich. But at least seventy-five percent of the stampeders will never find much gold. I am one of them! Yes, you admire these nuggets and gold dust. Gold is fascinating, beautiful, isn't it? But you can't know the hardships back of each fleck of gold. To go after it, you must be willing to risk your life, run the gauntlet of a thousand dangers, endure every imaginable hardship. Even then, there's no assurance you'll find gold. Perhaps it is well that so many stampeders turn back when they've only gone a little way along the gold trail."

It seemed that everywhere I went, people cornered me, stopped me on the streets and talked eagerly of gold.

"Is there room for you up there, you ask? Sure, fellows. And brother, how there's room in that wilderness; and how easy it is to get lost! You ask if it's true about the enormous quantities of gold on the Eldorado and Bonanza. Of course, it's all true! There's never been so much gold found in all the world concentrated in one area as in the Klondike, Bonanza and Eldorado. The gold coming from those rich mines is fabulous . . . fabulous beyond words! Why, I've seen washpans of gold . . . and gallon oil cans filled and brimming over with nuggets just carelessly dumped in, almost as if the hard, metal stuff were like ordinary kernels of yellow corn set in the sun to dry!

"But I can tell you, all of this gold came from the rich mines of the wealthy Klondike Kings, including a few from our town—like Euly Gaisford, the little Tacoma barber; Jimmy McMahon, the diver from Old Town; and Michael Knutson, who is now probably many times a millionaire and has the distinction of discovering the largest nugget to date on the Eldorado. Ah, yes, the excitement and lure of gold surely gets into your blood up there, all right! But, in spite of it all, I'd say: Don't go! Unless you're willing to go through hell! You might as well know, the Bonanza and Eldorado are already staked solid! And so are all of the other good streams."

Now it seemed during the first few weeks I was home that interest in the Klondike was reaching a feverish pitch. Every paper carried dazzling accounts of the great fortunes won in the North. These exciting tales were on the lips of every young schoolchild . . . and almost overshadowed and eclipsed news of the Spanish-American War.

"Say, Ed," said a friend eagerly, "will you act as guide for a group of us fellows going into the Klondike? We want to leave in a few days."

"Thanks," I replied, "but I couldn't take that responsibility. Besides, I've only been back a few weeks and I'm undecided what to do."

"Well, then, Ed, if you're looking for a job in Tacoma, why don't you try the Pacific National Bank? They might need a good accountant."

I followed the friend's suggestion and called on Mr. L. J. Pentecost, the bank president. "Come around tomorrow at ten," he told me cordially.

"Oh, Edward, I hope and pray it means a position for you!" said Velma earnestly that evening when I got home. "Having the bank president give you an appointment is very encouraging. How wonderful it would be if you receive a position in the Pacific National Bank!"

Enthusiastically, I agreed with her. But later on in the evening, I became very restless and finally said, "Velma, we musn't be too disappointed if there isn't a job in this for me. So far, as you know, there hasn't seemed to be anything for me here in Tacoma. You know how hard I've been searching for work. But perhaps you've noticed, too, how restless I've been growing lately, though I've been trying to keep it from you. Velma, I have a confession to make. There's something tormenting me. I have the awful feeling I've missed the opportunity of a lifetime!"

"Why, what on earth do you mean?" asked Velma, her eyes wide and troubled.

"Yes, Velma," I said with a heavy sigh, "I'm afraid I've missed the biggest opportunity of my life—in the Klondike. I haven't told you, or anyone, this before . . . but after my boat, the *Packshan,* which I took from Skagway, docked at Vancouver, B. C., I happened to talk to an old California miner while waiting that night to catch the train home. When he learned I had just come from the Klondike, he asked me a very startling question."

"What was it?" asked Velma breathlessly.

"Well, it was this: 'Have the miners in the Klondike ever searched for, or discovered any of the ancient channels which some of those rich, gold-bearing streams are apt to have?'

"Great Scott, Velma, how I was startled! I had never heard any miner talk like this before, and I told him I was sure they hadn't been discovered, if such existed. But suddenly, I was staggered by this momentous thought: 'What if there might be an ancient channel of the Eldorado some place?' I asked many questions of the miner and listened eagerly as he described where an ancient channel might be located. He said sometimes old riverbeds were concealed up on high bluffs, maybe miles away from, or just above, a present stream. Said sometimes could even be on mountain-tops—that is, if the country had changed contour enough during the centuries.

"Jiminy Christopher! Like a flash, all at once, that strange sugar-loaf-shaped hill in the Klondike was before me. Again, I could see it as plain as day. It's the large hill on the left side of the valley, facing downstream, which juts out and ends right at the Forks of the Eldorado and Bonanza, with Big Skookum Gulch at the steep, lower end of the hill cutting into the forks. All of the north side of this hill flanks the Eldorado River. I began remembering how, one day last summer when I was scouting for a claim, I had climbed that particular hill going up from the Eldorado side. I remember, too, how strongly I had been attracted to it, as though drawn to a magnet, and once on this hill, how I was held as though by an invisible hand, though why, I couldn't tell. All I could see as I climbed were scrubby trees, rocks and deep moss. But once at the top of the hill, I had thoughtfully pondered and looked off in the distance toward King and Queen Domes, the hub of the Klondike. And then I looked down on the Forks at the two amazing rivers of gold, the Eldorado and the Bonanza. What a thrilling, magnificent sight it was! Like many others who had, no doubt, climbed that hill, I began wondering where in creation the mother lode was hidden. Wistfully, I wished that that hill could have been flattened out in the ages past so as to spread out the gold more evenly, to make more pay dirt available to hundreds of us poor stampeders who had searched in vain.

"Then, Velma, as the old California miner talked on enthusiastically, almost obsessed with his theory of ancient channels, I became excited as I recalled a very significant thing about that hill, which now took on a special meaning. Last summer, I had noticed, while looking up at it from the Eldorado side, a very peculiar stratum resembling an old trail, high up near the top of the hill, running parallel to the river. But, I discovered, after climbing the hill, that this peculiar-looking trail seemed to break off and disappear in places by a rock or tree and was heavily overgrown with thick, spongy moss.

"Velma, as I listened further to the miner, it flashed through my mind with terrific force that this strange, phantom-like trail with its peculiar outcropping of rock must be the ancient channel of the Eldorado! But I kept a poker face and didn't let on. When I said goodbye to the miner, suddenly I was impelled by a wild impulse to get back to the Klondike as fast as possible and search that hill with all the strength that was in me. But, Velma, I was so near home that the thought of returning to the Klondike over all those miles, without seeing you and Clemy, was unbearable! So, after walking around Vancouver and battling it out, pro and con, I finally fought down the terrific impulse and took the train home. But now, I must confess, I am still torn by that same wild urge to rush back to the Klondike. And, lately, it's become almost overpowering. How I wish I could have talked to that old miner a year ago before going North! What a difference it would have made in my search for gold!"

"But, Edward," said Velma, "maybe that old miner was just joking, spinning yarns, thinking you were only a green Cheechako."

"No, Velma, he wasn't joking. He was in dead earnest. But what haunts me is that he may talk to others, or it may not be long before someone else in the Klondike will begin thinking along these same lines or stumble on it by accident. Why, only last fall, large quantities of unexplainable gold were found way above rim-rock on the Big Skookum Gulch side of that hill. This discovery put the entire Klondike in an uproar. It was the first time gold had ever been discovered on a hillside that high up! The experts just couldn't explain how gold got there on the side of the big gulch. Now, Velma, that old miner's ancient-channel theory fits in perfectly and must be the only real explanation. Since talking to him, I believe I've solved the mystery of Big Skookum Gulch, and, at the same time, the puzzle of the phantom trail around on the other side of the hill above the Eldorado. I'm sure they are both the same, part of the ancient channel of the Eldorado, though on the gulch side there were no visible, distinct signs. And how this came about, it would be pretty hard to say!

"Maybe I wasn't such a fool, after all, last summer, before the Big Skookum Gulch discovery, when, in desperation for a claim, I dug for gold like a fool Cheechako and staked that miserable ground on the side hill above Euly Gaisford's, even though the old-timers laughed and poked fun at me. It might have been only on the wrong side of the valley, about a thousand feet below the Forks, and on the wrong hill to find fortune!

"Oh, Velma," I said excitedly, "just think what it would mean if I could go back up there and discover the ancient channel of the Eldorado! Why, the wealth that could be ours simply staggers the imagination! And now that I've seen you and Clemy, I'm so in earnest about wanting to return North, I'd be willing to run all the risks and hardships to get back to the Klondike to find that fortune!"

"But, Edward," said Velma in alarm, "it would mean leaving us again . . . and I don't think I could bear the long separation and anxiety a second time! I know how you must feel, but if you go North again, you might never come back. Gold isn't worth that terrible price, is it? Oh, promise, promise you won't ever leave Clemy and me again!" In a moment she was in my arms, sobbing bitterly.

Oh, that cruel, cold, yellow metal stuff, so illusive, so hard to get! Suddenly, the lure of it all vanished completely, washed away in the wild torrent of my wife's tears, and I found myself promising . . . assuring her I'd never leave them again. Why, yes, of course I was terribly happy and grateful to be home! Yes, of course she was right. No, never would I leave them again and cause her so much mental anguish.

"But, Velma," I told her later, "I positively believe there are millions in gold on that hill above the Eldorado, just waiting to be discovered!"

The following evening found me very discouraged. I had gone to the bank to keep my appointment at ten o'clock that morning. To my surprise, I was ushered into an inner office where the bank's officials were all gathered to greet me. Almost right away, they regretfully told me there was no job in the offing. But, while blowing clouds of smoke from expensive cigars and studying a map of the North spread out on the table before them, they quizzed and pelted me with numerous questions about the Klondike—general conditions up there; chances of capital investment for those who had money, like themselves, but who couldn't go. With glistening eyes, they talked of gold and asked to see my samples of nuggets and gold dust. With fascinated, soft, clutching fingers, they examined and fondled the hard metal stuff. Were the creeks all staked in the Klondike? How about gold in American territory—American Creek, Chicken Creek, the American side of Forty Mile? And, yes, how about that great, unexplored Tanana region?

All of their questions I answered as best I could to give them the true picture, but, somehow, in their eagerness to hear more and more of very great quantities of gold, they always returned in their quest to the phenomenal, dramatic Klondike and its famous rivers of gold . . .

"Come now, Mr. Lung," one official said eagerly, "you certainly must be planning to return North. Without a job—and hard times here—with your valuable knowledge of the Klondike, you'd be very foolish not to. We gathered here this morning to talk this thing over with you and make you a business proposition. Now, how about letting us buy in on the claim we've heard you staked near Euly Gaisford's on the Bonanza? And surely you must have other good prospects in mind. Yes, you must have others you're not talking about. Mr. Lung, we'll stake you with capital on

Lynn Canal at Skagway

(Courtesy of the University of Washington)

Female stampeders at Sheep Camp on Chilkoot Pass

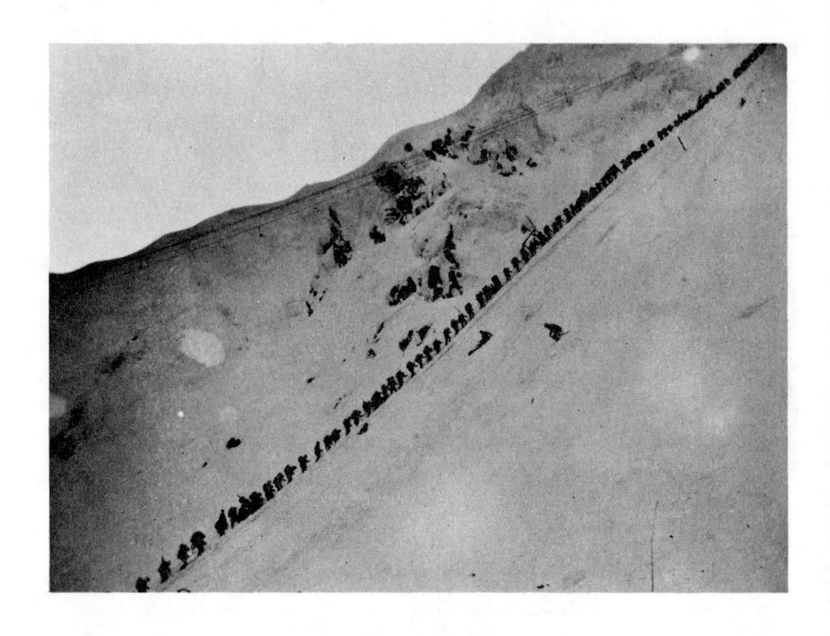

High over the struggling men we see the Aerial Tramway up Chilkoot Pass, 1898

Men looking for mail from home – sometimes delayed a whole year

a percentage basis. You pay us fifty percent when you strike it, above a certain sum which we will all agree upon. You see, Mr. Lung, we are anxious to invest with someone like you whom we can really trust. Since the gold rush has reached such a peak, there are hundreds of men floating around the country selling stock in mines and companies, probably phony ones which do not even exist. For us bankers, this is very bad business, very risky, and we have no real way of checking. Now we've picked you—you furnish the know-how and muscle, and we'll furnish the capital. And, too, if you'll consent to take him, there's one of our tellers just dying to go North with you."

"Think it over, Mr. Lung," said the bank president as he slapped me genially on the back. "We'll be more than happy to talk this proposition over further if you agree and go North. But let us know as soon as possible."

"Thank you, gentlemen," I said. "I can give you my decision immediately, I've promised my wife not to return to the Klondike. But, for your information, that barren, rocky claim on the Bonanza near Gaisford's—well, it proved to be only a dud! A solid, heavy rockslide settled that for me centuries ago . . . before anyone ever thought of gold in the Klondike. Yes, it's true, I did join a stampede on my way out over the ice from Circle City and staked some ground that was left on American Creek. But it only amounted to a few cents to the pan, and I signed that claim over to a packer named Goodwin when I reached Dawson. In this way, I paid the fee to travel with him and his party over the ice to the coast and Skagway. By doing this, I was able to save what little gold I had to bring 'Outside.' No, gentlemen, I'm sorry, you must look to some other source for your investments. I thank you, anyway."

After the surprising bank interview, days went by and still I had not obtained a job. With growing apprehension, I watched my gold gradually disappear for bills and many family expenses. Yes, it was all very discouraging. At this rate, my wife and I would never own that little home we had dreamed so much about.

Although Tacoma was now calling herself "The Gateway to the Klondike" and "The City of Destiny" breadlines were still much in evidence, just as they had been the year before when I had gone North to seek fortune. How ironic, I thought—Tacoma, "The Gateway to the Klondike!" Tacoma, "The City of Destiny!" and here I was . . . walking the streets looking for a job!

Money was very tight. Without it, a fellow was certainly handicapped. Surely, self-respect would not allow a man to live indefinitely with his wife's relatives, no matter how congenial. I began to feel very frustrated and desperate, and my thoughts naturally turned to the Klondike, to that beckoning hillside above the Eldorado. But I had given that promise to Velma!

From our front window we had a sweeping view of the waterfront of Puget Sound. Every day I could see departing steamers, packed to the guards with stampeders, as they plowed up Puget Sound and disappeared around Brown's Point, headed north for Dyea and Skagway, a thousand miles away. Wistfully now, with ever-increasing longing, I watched them go . . . these hundreds of men rushing from Tacoma to join the thousands of stampeders from all over the country on the coast of Alaska and, eventually, the Klondike would be swarming with hordes of them. Yes, and here I was—chained by a promise to loved ones! What did it avail me if I had the exciting knowledge of where to find a fabulous fortune if I could not go back to the Klondike to look for it?

"Edward," said Velma a few weeks later in May, "I can't hold you any longer. I've seen that faraway look in your eyes when you come home after seeing the boats off from the docks. Go back to the Klondike. Look for gold on that hill. I know you will never be satisfied unless you do. We still have part of the gold you brought from the North, and I've spoken to Mother, and she says she'll lend you the rest to make up the $500 you'll need to make the trip. And Edward, don't worry," she said gently, "we'll tell no one of this exciting, secret mission to the Eldorado. And our prayers go with you."

And so, on that bright, memorable day of May 15, 1898, with great anticipation I packed my outfit and travel-worn canvas bag, put on heavy, rough clothing and hustled to the docks and excitedly joined the sweating, eager, gold-

(Courtesy Emery F. Tobin)

The White Pass where the stampeders struggled in 1898. Any available animal was used as a beast of burden

Archie McLean Hawks, chief engineer on Chilkoot Pass, who put through the famous Aerial Tramway

Rescue party at scene of an avalanche at Chilkoot Pass in 1898 in which seventy persons were killed

(Courtesy of Mary Kopanski of Skagway)

Soapy Smith, gangster, confidence man, and crooked politician, whose gangs terrorized Skagway and White Pass hungry stampeders heading North in the greatest stampede of all time—the gold rush of '98!

From the crowded deck of the S.S. *Cottage City,* I waved a long farewell, just as I had done the year before almost to the day. Yes, I hated to leave all of my loved ones; but it would be for a time only, I thought. So it was goodbye again to dear, brave Velma and my little son Clemy, goodbye to Mother Clement and Ena and a few other relatives.

Velma stood with her arm around little Clemy and waved a long, long farewell with fluttering handkerchief, and I knew great tears were hidden behind that brave smile! Yes, we would be parted for a time. . . . But now I set my face North, my hopes high! I was headed for sure toward a great fortune in the Klondike—the ancient channel of the Eldorado, the richest, most fabulous stream in all the world!

Chapter XXV

Perilous Pass and Secret Hopes

It was now May 20th, 1898. Faster and faster our steamer, the *Cottage City*, churned and plowed her way up the spectacular mountain-lined, narrowing channel of Lynn Canal. It was the last day of our thousand-mile salt-water voyage from Tacoma and Seattle, and only a matter of hours now before we would plant our feet on the intriguing shores of Alaska at the new boom town of Skagway, or at the nearby Indian village of Dyea. Then we would be on our own, and it would be up to us to hit the trail, choose which pass we'd go over—White Pass back of Skagway, or Chilkoot from Dyea. To transport our supplies over those big mountains and get down the Yukon was a stupendous undertaking.

The last hour aboard ship as we approached closer and closer to our destination, animated talk flew from mouth to mouth—many reports, prospecting advice, best routes to follow, best camping spots, best outfits, warning to take in enough food, warnings—dire warnings—about Skagway and Soapy Smith with his gang of robbers, confidence men, gamblers, harlots and cutthroats. . . . These, they warned, infested the area of White Pass and Skagway and were watching like savage beetle-eyed vultures the mountain trails, the taverns, saloons, meeting the boats, even posing as businessmen, travel agents or miners.

"Say, this Soapy Smith fellow must be a regular Doctor Jekyll and Mister Hyde!" exclaimed an irate stampeder. "And I hear a few silly women of Skagway a few months ago were calling him the 'dashing, colorful Robin Hood of the North!'—just on account of a few good deeds he did, generally with ulterior motives. One of his so-called 'good deeds,' which he never expected to be discovered, was a villainous act! Seems he gave the new preacher a good-size sum of money to help build a church . . . but all the time, his men lay in wait to rob the minister on his way home. Think of it! Not only did they take Soapy Smith's generous donation, but they took all other donations as well! And to think, this slick soap salesman, this sleight-of-hand performer whose hand is quicker than the eye is the real power behind this evil ring! Now, they tell me Soapy dresses as a captain of the U. S. militia, drills several hundred of his gang in uniform. Sometimes he rides a beautiful white horse through town. Many call him the 'Shah of Skagway!' They say his big ambition, though, is to be chief of police. Imagine! It's a damned outrage, I tell you! Why, with his trained men armed to the teeth, Soapy Smith has the sinister power to declare martial law, and I understand has already threatened to do so. There's no doubt about it, Skagway is a fever-stricken, crime hole of Hades! And my advice to you is, keep a sharp eye on your money, your hand on your gun; and don't take up with strangers and, above all, don't go over White Pass unless you're armed!"

"Say, Ed, would you risk going over White Pass now?" asked one of the stampeders timidly.

"You bet your life I wouldn't!" I said emphatically. "Though at Skagway, they try to route you over White Pass. But I'm traveling alone and I'm not armed! I know what they say is true about Soapy Smith because I met one of his gang when I came over White Pass two months ago on my way 'Outside.' Believe me, I've had enough of

White Pass—or Black Pass, as some are now calling it! And I can't forget the stench of those hundreds of pitiful dead horses I saw that had pulled freight for the stampeders and died by the side of the trail. Yes, it'll be Chilkoot Pass for me. It's far healthier! Besides, I hear the big aerial tramway is supposed to be completed from Sheep Camp to the summit. If I could get my goods on it, well, I'd count myself pretty darned lucky."

"Hey, mister," said a deck hand, "just heard what you said. If you're in a big hurry, don't pin your hopes to that tramway. Thousands of fellows ahead of you are waiting at Dyea for it to be completed. But I'm afraid they're gonna have to wait a long time! They say the tramway isn't finished yet. Work was slowed up by the big avalanche that came down about six weeks ago. About seventy people were buried alive, including one of the Chilkoot tramway workers. Gosh, it was awful!"

"Exactly how did it happen?" we all asked, shivering a little, instinctively glancing up at the darkening silhouettes of cold, gray mountains to the north.

"Well, it was a Sunday morning very early, on April third," said the purser, who had stepped up to our group at the rail, sad lines etching his face. "Yes, I remember it well because I knew the tramway worker who was killed, a fine young fellow he was, too. He expected to be married in Tacoma in a few weeks. Well, to go on with the story, it had been snowing very hard for almost a week, turning into a real blizzard the day before the big avalanche. Naturally, the peaks and glaciers were top-heavy with thick, moist snow. You know the Indians have an uncanny way of foretelling events. A tramway worker told me that the Dyea Indians grew quite hostile and excited when asked to go up on the mountain several days before the avalanche, and stubbornly refused to pack anything. Said over and over, 'Me no pack on Chilkoot. Him very angry! Me no pack. You see . . . big snowslide come!' Well, the Indians had good reason to be frightened. A few of their tribesmen had been caught in small slides and killed during the winter.

"Yes," the Indians were right! Chilkoot was in a devilish mood! Well, you've heard what happened. It was the worst avalanche in Alaskan history! Even Jack Cavanaugh and Sam Heron, two old-time guides had issued the same warnings, but the stampeders were too hell-bent to get over the pass. It's almost too horrible to think of it—men, women, and animals caught on the trail! The slide covered a wide area. Some were buried sleeping in tents, others cooking and eating, as it was just an hour before noon. I've talked to some of the rescue workers. It was sure a grim job for them!"

"Yes, it surely was," said the head steward, who had also joined our group on the upper deck, "but I think what happened to Mr. Joppe and his partner, Mueller, the two fellows running a small restaurant at The Scales, was the most amazing and dramatic of all."

"What happened?" we all asked tensely.

"Well, as the purser was saying, Chilkoot was in a devilish mood that fateful Sunday morning of April third, and it all began very early, exactly at 3 A.M., when an old man came running down the mountainside to Joppe's place at The Scales. That's a place just about a quarter of a mile below the summit. The old man pounded on the door and yelled 'For God's sake, Joppe, come quick! Help dig out Mrs. Maxon and several others. A slide just came down a minute ago, and they're buried alive in their tent!' Well, it was like this that Mr. Joppe and his partner were jerked from their peaceful sleep that fateful morning, but this wasn't the big avalanche. Oh no, not yet! Just listen while I tell you the rest of it.

"Quickly, a dozen fellows rushed with Joppe and Mueller and dug out Mrs. Maxon and the others. Their tent was compeltely buried under ten feet of loose snow. Luckily, they got them out . . . and just in time! They were still alive, but badly frightened and, of course, half frozen! Like lightning, word flashed along The Scales that everyone there was in grave danger of avalanche and should flee down the mountain to Sheep Camp, two miles below. Some heeded the warning and left immediately, but Mrs. Maxon and her party were among those who didn't leave. She was suffering from severe shock. Joppe and a good many others remained at The Scales, too. Several times during that morning as they huddled close to their stoves, they could hear distant rumbling, like thunder, and they knew there were slides occurring at different spots along the mountain. But they hoped old Chilkoot would tip the avalanches away from them in another direction!

"About 10:30 A.M. a party of white-faced tramway workers came down from the summit. They were in a mad rush to get off the mountain. Said there were terrific amounts of snow piled high on the peaks and, in places, they could see it slipping a little along the glaciers. Said if all that snow should ever start coming down in a mass, it could wipe out the stampede trail, The Scales and anything else it would hit below. The men weren't fooling! They were hurrying for their lives, and as they tore through camp, they called for the remaining stampeders to 'Get the hell out of there and run for your lives! Make for Sheep Camp!'* As they ran, they threw out a long rope for the stampeders to hang onto. By this time, Mr. Joppe and all the others, including Mrs. Maxon, were in warm clothes and ready to start. The crowd hurried as fast as possible through the deep snow, all staying close together, single file, hanging onto the ropes . . . and had only gone about a thousand feet down Long Hill, reaching a place just above Stone House, where nearby is located the O. I. Powerhouse at the side of a deep ravine. Here they were slowed up, probably by Mrs. Maxon. All at once, there was a low rumbling; the whole mountain trembled and someone screamed, 'Avalanche!' There was a quick howl of icy wind and, suddenly, before they could go another step, a great wave of thick, loose snow struck them from the left and buried them to their hips. Then, before they could budge an inch, came another loud rumbling roar, more terrifying than the first, and down came a mighty avalanche, completely burying them under tons and tons of snow. That avalanche came with such terrific force that some of it immediately solidified into pure ice . . . and in places it was over thirty feet deep! All those poor people were trapped underneath! There were ten acres of it! That avalanche had torn down from the peaks two thousand five hundred feet above the trail. Just think of it! Over seventy people buried alive!"

---

* In the fall of '97, due to a sudden warm thaw, an avalanche had hit Sheep Camp, killing seventeen people.

"My God!" exclaimed a stampeder, listening in quivering awe. "Did anyone survive to tell the story?"

"Yes," said the purser, nodding his head gravely. "A few did survive, but it was only because over a thousand stampeders, including tramway workers, rushed to the scene. Got there within fifteen or twenty minutes after it happened and worked like demons digging out the victims. Said they dug fastest where they could hear faint, muffled cries, and where small, pinpoint air holes gradually appeared. These were caused by the warm breath of those trapped nearest the surface. After that, they dug long trenches to locate the victims. Some of the bodies were horribly contorted and badly mangled. Well, the first wild report that came down to Dyea said that three hundred were caught in the avalanche. But, gradually, the number boiled down to seventy—which was still horrible enough.

"Those rescue workers dug frantically, racing against time! Mr. Mueller, Joppe's partner, was the first to be dug out and, fortunately, he was still alive. But as the rescue workers dug out more and more victims, it became apparent that very few would ever be found alive! As they found the bodies, they were hauled to the O. I. Powerhouse and laid out on the floor for identification. Poor old Joppe was among them. He had been buried under six feet of snow for nearly three hours!

"Well, it so happened that Miss Vernie Woodward, a young lady who had been packing on Chilkoot for a year, was one of the first to reach the awful scene of the tragedy. She helped dig with the men. Then she went to the powerhouse to help there. To her horror, she discovered poor Joppe laid out cold with the others, his body badly bruised. It was a terrible shock! Being his sweetheart, she became hysterical. In frenzied grief, she cried and begged him to come back to her. Then, in desperation, she ripped off his shirt, pulled him up and began rubbing him, working his arms and legs and breathing her warm breath into his lungs. All who saw shook their heads and pitied her. There was no sign of life in Joppe! It looked so utterly hopeless. But it was a lucky thing for him that Miss Vernie wouldn't be reconciled to his death. She kept crying and praying and calling his name and begging him to come back to her, kept moving his arms and legs and breathing her warm breath into his body. She worked over him like this for three solid hours! Then a miraculous thing happened. Joppe opened his eyes and said, 'Vernie!' Everyone in the powerhouse wept for joy!

"Well," continued the purser sadly, "just think of it! Only eight were saved out of all those people, including Joppe and Mueller. But out of the eight, three died later. When Joppe had recovered enough to tell what had happened, he said he was terrified when he first realized he had been buried alive under the slide. As he lay there, his whole life flashed before him in a few seconds. Said he couldn't move an inch, was held as fast as if he had been sealed in a block of ice. Said he didn't call for help because he knew he would have to conserve his energy. Silently, he prayed for deliverance, and he could hear fellows moaning and praying all around him. His arm rested on a body. He was sure it was Mrs. Maxon. 'How awful!' he thought. 'We rescued her from the little avalanche only a few hours ago . . . only to die in a more terrible one!' Many disjointed thoughts rushed through his mind. Before he lost consciousness, Joppe said he heard one man near by cursing, blaspheming God as he died; others crying and calling goodbye to loved ones thousands of miles away. Said he could even hear dogs barking and whining, buried deep in the snow.

"When Joppe awakened and found himself on the floor of the powerhouse with Vernie bending over him, he said he felt oddly refreshed. He said, at first he thought he had just had a very bad nightmare! Those in the powerhouse were sure he had come back from the dead!

"Many bodies are still missing," continued the purser. "Maybe it will never be known just how many died in that awful tragedy, because no one really knows how many stampeders were on the trail that morning."

"Speaking of bodies," said a merchant returning to Skagway, "this one about Soapy Smith proves what a snake in the grass he really is! When news of the avalanche reached Skagway, he immediately sent up some of his gang posing as rescue workers, but their real motive was to rob the dead! Of all the low, despicable acts! What did it matter to him if, after being stripped of all their valuable belongings, there was no way to identify those poor victims? I guess it will never be known how many thousands of dollars Soapy Smith's gang got away with. I'm telling you, it was a sad procession of victims hauled down on sleds to Dyea and to Skagway for identification. Those that couldn't be identified were finally put en masse in common graves. Yes, there will be many wives and sweethearts waiting, I'm afraid, who will never hear and who will always wonder what happened to their men."

It was now almost 7:30 P.M. when our boat, the *Cottage City,* began whistling to land at Skagway as it rounded the big bend of Lynn Canal and headed toward the long dock which projected out into the water for several blocks. Dusk, now. The lights began coming on all over the city. A cold wind whipped down from the dark, giant mountains which rose sharply directly behind the city. That high "V" cut in the mountains was dreaded White Pass.

This was Skagway, wicked Skagway, where lawless Soapy Smith reigned as "Shah." Beckoning Canadian-Yukon Territory was over those rugged mountains to the north only about 35 miles away. And over there to the left, or northwest, somewhere along that dark, giant ridge less than a dozen miles away, was vengeful Chilkoot Pass where all of those people had died so tragically.

From the boat, under lamplight I could see great activity on shore. Hundreds of men were moving along with freight sleds drawn by horses and dogs. Several steamers were moored to the long pier and the harbor was cluttered with small boats of all descriptions and many good-sized barges. I rubbed my eyes in amazement. How the place had grown by leaps and bounds! It was simply unbelievable! Why, Skagway was now a real city in size. But it still had all the earmarks of a frontier town. Many "rough-and-ready" characters were out on the pier to meet our boat, some accompanied by malemutes and huskies.

Immediately, I inquired where the little steamer, *Lady of the Lake,* was moored, as my supplies were to be put on a barge and towed around the point to Dyea. Soon I located the captain of the *Lady of the Lake,* who told me I had several hours to kill in Skagway. He said they would be loading freight 'til midnight. He suggested that I spread my bedroll on the floor in a corner of the barge and sleep there until morning. He said that, once at Dyea, they would wait 'til sunup to unload.

I thanked the friendly captain and said, "While waiting, guess I'll go uptown and call on Sylvester, a friend of mine. Will be back before you shove off before midnight."

After I had left the captain I thought I'd have a look around. Yes, the growth of Skagway was simply phenomenal! Why, in two months' time, those hundreds of tents and lean-tos had been replaced by frame buildings. There was a flourishing business section, and I couldn't see any outward evidence of crime.

Now I was walking along a dimly lighted, crooked street. All at once, I found myself in a knot of men. One on either side grasped me firmly by the elbows.

"Say, pardner," one of them said in a low tone, "saw you come in on the *Cottage City*. Now, wouldn't you like to join us in a little fun tonight? Meet the boys, play some games—and the girls—oh, la! la! they're dolls! You know, it's a long, hard trip to Dawson," said the other fellow persuasively, "and it'll be your last chance to really enjoy life for a while. Come on with us to Clancey's Saloon. The drink's on us!"

While they talked, I was being expertly propelled down the street toward the saloon. In less than a minute, if I didn't do something quick, they'd have me inside, and, once there, it would be difficult to deal with them. So, with a sudden double twist of the elbows and a quick jerk, I freed myself and stopped short. "No, thanks," I said in a steely voice. " I don't drink or gamble and I have a fine wife at home. Besides, I know who you are. You're Soapy Smith's gang. You see, I'm not a green Cheechako like you think! I've been here before! And yes," I said as I leaned forward, scrutinizing one of the fellows closely, "remember me? Two months ago on White Pass? Yes, by golly! It was you who gave me that letter to deliver to Clancey's Saloon. And it wasn't your fault I wasn't robbed of every speck of gold I was carrying! You dirty dog, you were sending me into a den of cutthroats and thieves . . . and I've wanted to punch you in the nose ever since. . . . So, here goes!" and as I spoke, I jammed my fist into his face and he went down in a surprised heap. (I confess, quite unexpectedly!)

Then I whirled on my heel, leaped out of the crowd before anyone could grab me and took off on a fast dog trot down the street toward Sylvester's General Store. With great relief, I saw the lights still on and found the door unlocked. I darted inside and bolted the door. I found Sylvester bending over some bookkeeping in the rear of his store.

He looked up, startled, recognized me and said in surprise, "Well, Ed Lung, I'll be darned! When did you get back to Skagway?"

"Tonight, on the *Cottage City,*" I said, a little out of breath.

"Say, old man," said Sylvester, eyeing me closely, "looks like you've been doing some strenuous exercise since you arrived. Face is pretty red. What's up? No, don't tell me—I can guess," he said with a low whistle. "It's Soapy Smith's gang, isn't it?"

"You're right!" I exploded. "How in thunderation do you people of Skagway tolerate it? Here I just got in only thirty minutes ago and they've already tried to fleece me!"

"We know that people in the States call it 'lawless Skagway,' " said Sylvester, "but they musn't blame the citizens here. "Yes," he sighed, looking very worried, "we all know Soapy Smith's a dirty rat! But our hands have been tied. Guess you've heard we've had some mighty bad times around here lately. Just about two months ago that skunk, Faye, the bartender, one of Soapy Smith's henchmen, murdered our U. S. deputy constable and another fellow in cold blood. Now we've got a new marshal who is one of Soapy Smith's own men. You bet, Soapy saw to that! They've been running the town wide open. But, Ed, there's a queer quirk about Soapy, he doesn't as a rule rob the citizenry of Skagway . . . just you outsiders. That's why I can be fairly sure of doing business without being robbed. But mark my word, Ed, when you come through here again, we'll be rid of Soapy and his gang!"

"I'll avoid Skagway like poison next time!"

"Some weeks ago," sighed Sylvester, "the vigilantes would

have lynched Faye, but Soapy Smith saved him at the last minute. For days now, we've been having secret meetings. The temper of the people is not to be controlled much longer. Soapy doesn't know it, but he's sitting on dynamite. Yes, his days are surely numbered![*] The last straw was when one of his gang threw red pepper in the face of a young Cheechako, blinding him. Then the gang robbed him of all his gold. Yes, I'm afraid there's going to be a lot of bloodshed before long! And would you believe it, Ed, when I tell you that Soapy Smith comes from a good family? Yes, they tell me he's got a brother who's editor of a newspaper, the *Evening Star*. And something else that's startling—they say Soapy was educated for the priesthood! It's a good thing his mother never knew what a villain he turned out to be. So, you see, Ed, the kind of man we've got to cope with—a sly, cunning man with no conscience. On first meeting, he would impress you as a polished, affable Southern gentleman—which makes him all the more dangerous!"

A little before midnight after my visit with Sylvester, I climbed aboard the scow and spread my sleeping bag on the hard, rough boards behind a huge pile of freight. I confess, I was relieved and glad when the *Lady of the Lake* finally pulled anchor and the lights of Skagway disappeared behind the peninsula. From my hard bed on the barge, I watched the changing shoreline and the dark ridge of high mountains.

Though there always was danger of avalanches on Chilkoot, I was now eager to tackle it. I was growing tense, excited to be on my way down the Yukon, headed towards my own secret mission—searching for that fabulous ancient channel of the Eldorado!

But two days later found me still at Dyea, waiting to get my freight on the new tramway that was about to open. It happened to be my good fortune to run into some Tacoma men. One of them had a great deal to do with the tram and, as a result, hurrah! my freight was to be sent up the mountain to the summit! What a tremendous lift that would be!

---

[*] On July 8, 1898, Soapy Smith was shot and killed by Frank Reid, the city engineer.

During those two days in Dyea, I had a good chance to take in the town. Like Skagway, Dyea had grown by leaps and bounds. It was now a city of about eight thousand. From that primitive Indian village of the year before, the place now had everything—hotels, eating places, banks, stores, a newspaper, even though many of them were housed in very crude frame buildings. I stayed one night at the Olympic Hotel and the other at the Woodlawn. The last evening, I walked along the Midway toward the first bridge. I was surprised to see there was scarcely a vacant lot left in town on that broad U-shaped flat between the high mountains. At Dyea, there was plenty of entertainment. Dance halls and saloons were going full blast! I stopped to see a show to kill time and saw the Cashey Sisters. Sewell of Dawson was there, too. Yes, Dyea was a typical gold-rush town. There was no doubt about it—even to its prostitutes, gamblers, and "sure thing" men! But it didn't have the sinister atmosphere of Skagway. It was mighty good to know that Soapy Smith did not hold sway here! And for good reason—they had a very firm-fisted constable in Dyea.

I was hoping for a restful sleep that night of the 23rd, as I was leaving the following morning to tackle the big climb up Chilkoot. But, great Scott! It did not turn out that way! There was too much commotion going on in the next room and the thin partitions were like sounding boards. How many visitors that "daughter of joy" had during the night, I lost count! But, at close intervals, the squeaky door would open, there would be stealthy footsteps going down the hall and, in a moment, more stealthy footsteps creaking up the hall and a woman's hoarse, grating voice called, "next!"

It was now early morning of May 24th as I started up the Chilkoot Trail from Dyea, joining that steady procession of sweating stampeders. Many were carrying very heavy packs, others traveling light, like myself, with only a knapsack. Yes, I was among the lucky ones, all right. Certainly, this new aerial tramway was a wonderful godsend!

I hurried along the crowded trail passing over the thousand-foot Kinny toll bridge which led from the west, or main bank, of the Dyea River and passed over to an island of about sixty acres timbered with cottonwoods. From this island, the trail crossed to the opposite bank and then took us along the river toward Canyon City in the direction of Chilkoot. Five miles from Dyea, we came to Finegan's Point and deep rapids in the river. It was here our canoe had tipped over the year before and we had nearly lost everything. How well I remembered good Indian Joe Whiskers, who had helped us!

A toll road had been built to the head of navigation from where it was now "zigzag, go-as-you-please" to Canyon City, a new settlement squeezed between canyon walls 200 feet apart. And here at the foot of towering, spectacular canyon walls of breath-taking grandeur, thousands of feet high, was the new, mammoth powerhouse of the Chilkoot Tramway Company. Everything here had been constructed since Stacey and I passed this way in 1897. I marveled at the great ingenuity of man. Inside the powerhouse, I watched the machinery and the huge drum, a spool-like wheel slowly winding thirty miles of heavy cable. They said they were trying it out today, and that this cable was pulling loaded freight buckets, starting from Sheep Camp, several miles above Canyon City, up to the summit of Chilkoot Pass, and bringing them back empty to Sheep Camp again for reloading.

After watching with fascinated interest the huge wheel turn for a little, I left the powerhouse and climbed the steep trail to Pleasant Camp, a rather good stopping place among the cottonwood trees. Here, I rested and ate hungrily from my knapsack. Had I been packing, as so many others were, I probably would have camped here.

In a few minutes I again joined that sweating, plodding procession of weary stampeders mushing their dogs and prodding their horses upward, always upwards along the snowy, slippery trail. (It was fifteen miles by trail to the summit.) Sheep Camp was about as far as a horse could possibly go on the steep trail.

"Say, Ed, wait a minute, I've been trying to overtake you," called a familiar, cheery voice from behind. I turned and saw Edward Orr, former mayor of Tacoma, hurrying to catch up with me, He was now in the freighting business on Chilkoot; owned a string of horses and was working in conjunction with the Tramway Company. It was he who had arranged to get my freight on the aerial tramway from Sheep Camp. Yes, I certainly had him to thank for my good fortune!

Back in Dyea, Orr had said, "Ed, if you packed everything on your back over Chilkoot in ninety-seven, by golly! I'll see that you don't have to do it again!"

Now, as Orr caught up with me on the trail, puffing a little, he said, "Whew! This sure is a climb! And it gets much steeper above Sheep Camp to the summit, as you well know! But, say, Ed, aren't you glad you don't have to worry about your freight? As I promised, I sent your stuff on up to Sheep Camp by pack horse early this morning. The tram picked it up hours ago. By now, it's probably waiting for you at the Canadian customs at the summit! And it'll only cost you fifteen cents a pound—much cheaper than what the Indians charge!"

"Well, it's a big relief to hear this!" I said, "and I'm mighty grateful to you."

"But, say, Ed," Orr suddenly lowered his voice so that others on the crowded trail couldn't overhear, "I've kinda got the idea you're in a helluva hurry, more so than the average, wild-eyed stampeder . . . if that's possible! Now, how would you like to ride to the summit in one of our big, new freight buckets? That way, you'd get over the pass in double-quick time ahead of a lot of the others."

"Great Scott! Do you really mean it?" I asked incredulously. "Because, if you do . . . you bet I would!"

"Of course, I mean it," said Orr, "but it'll take quite a little pull. You know, the buckets are supposed to be for freight only, but this is the first day and I might be able to arrange it."

"That would be wonderful!" I exclaimed. "Because, to tell you the truth, Orr, I *am* in a helluva hurry and I've surely been dreading that last steep climb. Yes, Orr, I think I have something good waiting for me in the Klondike—something mighty good—and I'd like to get ahead of all this mob if I can."

"Well, I hope you strike it, Ed," said Orr generously, "but as for me, I think I'll just stay right here in the freighting business. I'm not doing so badly. Better pay than being mayor of Tacoma, by a long shot!"

In a short time, we arrived at the tramway platform at Sheep Camp and, after a little argument, Edward Orr arranged the ride for me. But, he reminded me, as we stood watching them finish loading supplies into the bucket which was to go ahead, it was against their policy to let a man ride. He said that, once I got on, there'd be absolutely no getting off until I reached the summit. Being anxious to get the lift, I thanked him profusely and eagerly agreed it would be O.K. and in a few minutes waved a lighthearted farewell.

Now I was seated in one of the big, iron, open buckets which could hold five hundred pounds of supplies. Tons and tons of freight were waiting here at Sheep Camp to be shipped to the summit. Among them were several Peterboro canoes.

The whistle blew, the buckets started, and I could feel myself being hoisted up fifty feet into the air by a heavy cable attached to a trolley-like affair which stretched up and rode on a long main aerial cable overhead. This stationary cable stretched clear to the summit and acted as a sort of rail. A second sliding cable ran parallel, close beneath the main one. The individual bucket cables were attached to this sliding cable, which was being wound on the giant cable drum down in the mammoth powerhouse at Canyon City.

At intervals, there were high, tripod-like towers stationed along the mountainside with huge cross arms to sustain these cables. The towers, together with the snakelike cables, could be seen for miles on the mountainside going into a high gap to Stone House, to The Scales, and on to the summit of Chilkoot. Each bucket was spaced about 150 feet apart and jam-packed with freight. But, as they had said, I was absolutely the only human cargo.

My stomach began to feel a little squeamish as my bucket jerked and began to move along a little unevenly, gradually picking up speed. No, there certainly was no getting off now! I gripped the sides of the bucket and looked down on Sheep Camp as the tram began passing over it. What a big change a year had made here!

There were tents everywhere, even in the most rugged

spots of the small plateau. Numerous shacks, small stores, restaurants, saloons and a few bath houses filled every available nook. And, of course, there were hundreds of men wallowing through the muddy-colored snow along the narrow trail-like streets with their sleds, dogs, horses and outfits. The whole place had the lively appearance of a swarm of bees about to take off for a new field of honey. Almost any last-minute item could be purchased here, but at skyrocket prices.

In Sheep Camp, I had left Orr to dash away long enough to buy a good-sized can of maple syrup while he was wangling the ride for me. It was now deposited in the bottom of the bucket, together with my knapsack. Yes, there was no doubt about it, I certainly was riding in grand style this trip —I and my knapsack and my precious can of maple syrup. How good it would taste on those sourdough pancakes! And how lucky I was that I bought it!

With great interest, I watched the unfolding panorama of country below. The bucket glided more evenly now and I relaxed, beginning really to enjoy the ride. In several places, the tram passed very close above the stampede trail and I leaned over and called out, "Hello!" to the men below. They looked up in amazement and called back enviously, 'You lucky, lucky dog!"

Yes, I was lucky, all right! Truly the tramway was a wonderful thing. And what a gigantic, glorious country I was seeing from my high, moving perch! Lynn Canal was in the distance, the blue Pacific, great snow-peaked mountains to the northeast, northwest and south. I glanced in the direction of Skagway, but, of course, it was hidden behind a mountainous wall of rock and ice. Then I looked up in the direction of White Pass, but, from this angle, I wasn't quite sure through which gap it went. I pictured how the White Pass Trail must look at this very moment. Of course, it, too, was swarming with gold-hungry men. I recalled when I had come over White Pass to Skagway just eight weeks before; how I had sat on my sled to rest by the side of the steep, crowded trail on the Devil's Slide and had made a quick entry in my diary: "March 18, 1898—Rode part of way down on sled. Trail full of oxen, horses, dogs, goats, men, women and children . . . all pushing toward Dawson and fortune! But I wonder how many will ever make it?"

I vividly recalled how cold, pinched and blue their faces looked; how tired they were as they struggled up the White Pass Trail; and how the children lagged behind and had to run to catch up! I recalled an old sourdough telling me an amusing incident in direct contrast to all of the hardships. He told of a certain young woman who was traveling alone over the White Pass.

The old-timer laughingly said, "By gum, she was dressed in a mighty peculiar outfit. Would ya believe it? She was dressed like a man in a tweedy suit, wearin' a large sombrera hat, 'n with those heavy pants tucked in high, rubber hip boots. Why, from a distance, by golly, there was a lotta' speculatin' among us fellows as ta whether she was a man or a woman, but when she drew up . . . I'm tellin' ya, she was every inch a woman . . . and then some! And would ya believe it? All she was packin' was a fancy, hand mirror tucked under one arm . . . and a banjo case under the other! By Jiminy! She looked chipper as could be, fresh as a daisy! No blankets! no food! no nothin' else! When us fellows questioned her as ta how in tarnation she expected ta get by with such meager belongin's, she jest laughed 'n said, 'There's no need ta worry. Since I started over White Pass I've had several horseback rides already, and I can always count on the hospitality of lonely stampeders. Sure, I kin always share their tent, use their blankets 'n eat their food . . . so why should I travel heavy? Yes, the dear boys are very generous and mighty grateful fer a smile 'n a song around the campfire'!

"Yes," ended the old-timer with a sly laugh, "I don't doubt but what that gal will get to Dawson and be mighty popular, too!"

Now my freight bucket glided slowly, following the contour of the mountainside, climbing, climbing. . . . The cables made a humming, metallic, clicking sound. Ah, yes, this Chilkoot scenery was grand and glorious—the peaks high, the ravine deep and bluish. I inhaled deeply of the crystal-clear, pure mountain air and felt exhilarated. The sun sparkled on the snow and I shaded my eyes from the glare. Soon it began to grow a little warm in the bucket.

We passed near Stone House, that huge pile of rock resembling a house which had tumbled down the mountain at some early date. There was the I.O. Powerhouse on the edge of the ravine; and there, the remaining parts of the avalanche still filled a portion of the draw between the mountains. With grim fascination I looked down at it and then up at the high peaks above. Yes, I could see where that awful mass of snow had torn itself loose and swept down the mountainside. With a shiver, I wondered if any of the fellows I knew coming out from Dawson by way of Chilkoot had been caught in it. And, too, I thought of how I had debated about returning to the North about seven weeks ago. Why, I figured, I might have been at this very spot if I had returned right away after talking to that old California miner in Vancouver!

As I looked down on the scene, I could visualize Joppe's party and all those people trying desperately to reach safety. And poor Mrs. Maxon—how pathetic for her! Seemed I could almost feel the impact and icy grip of that avalanche and hear the pitiful cries for help. Yes, as they had said, it was almost too terrible to think of it!

Now my bucket gradually moved a little away from the new trail, passing over a ravine six or seven hundred feet deep, where there was a rushing river below from melting snows. I caught my breath and held tight to the bucket, as here I could feel the swipe and push of the north wind as it swooped down from the glaciers and peaks. I looked cautiously over the edge of the bucket into the yawning chasm. Caesar's ghost! At this point, I knew why the buckets were for freight only!

What a tremendous relief it was when I finally swung back to the mountainside, again following its contour. My bucket was now about one hundred feet above the ground, fast approaching The Scales. I could see Joppe's restaurant ahead near the trail and men clustered around waiting to get in. Steadily, across this small, shallow, bowl-shaped spot at the base of the steepest part of Chilkoot, my bucket glided smoothly along. From here, I could see packers weighing freight on the huge scales. And there, close by, was a boat packed to this point by the Indians months before and left because it had been too heavy to carry up over the summit.

I marveled how so many stampeders could cram themselves into this one small spot on the mountains. But this was the last resting place before tackling those "icy steps to hell," and those who were packing needed to rest in order to get up steam to get over the pass.

Since the time Stacey and I had struggled up those icy steps which had been chiseled out by the Indian packers, a sturdy rope had been strung along for the stampeders to hang onto for safety. Now the trail to the summit was black with struggling humanity, almost an uninterrupted line of climbing men bent double under their heavy loads, each clinging to the rope with iron grip.

Ah, yes, I could appreciate all their struggles down there. But what a ride I was getting up here! And, certainly, the view was becoming more and more magnificent as we went higher and higher. Surely, I was a lucky fellow, getting this ride!

The tram was heading away from the trail again, perhaps fifty feet. I looked up to the summit and thought how Stacey would have enjoyed this lift! I remembered, too, how he had saved my life on the summit of Chilkoot. Good old Stacey! I wondered how he was faring in Dawson. I hoped to see him now in about three weeks. He certainly had had his share of bad luck! I pictured how surprised he'd be when I turned up again in Dawson.

All at once, my attention was drawn to the bucket ahead of me. Great Scott! It was acting queerly, lurching crazily. And my bucket was behaving badly, too. Good Lord! Something terrible was happening! The bucket ahead had jumped the trolley! As I looked in horror, it dangled crazily and swung like a pendulum, then suddenly tore itself loose from the moving cable, at the same time giving me a terrific jolt. It pitched sideways and plunged wildly to the ground 100 feet below dumping and spilling out hundreds of pounds of equipment and canned goods all over the mountainside!

In terror, I glanced at the main cable, the moving one above me and the trolley that held my own bucket in place. But, thank God! everything seemed to be intact. Only the separate cable and trolley holding the bucket ahead of me had snapped. But I shuddered and broke out in a cold sweat when I thought that I might have been riding in that very bucket. Yes, just a delay of minutes had saved me —buying that can of maple syrup at Sheep Camp!

From here on, I forgot to admire the scenery, just prayed to reach the summit safely! I grasped the sides of the bucket and hung on for dear life. As we continued upward along the steepest part of the mountain, one stampeder called out, "Hey, fellow, don't you know you're taking a hell of a chance, riding up there in that bucket?"

I didn't answer. I surely knew it and didn't want to be reminded.

When, at long last, my bucket finally reached the summit and I stepped out onto solid earth, I stamped my feet and breathed a mighty prayer of thanks and said, "Old Chilkoot, you nearly got me that time!"

The engineer at the summit looked at me in astonishment and exclaimed, "My God, man! Where in hell did you come from?"

"Guess I just came from there," I laughed wryly, "and here's a message for Ed Orr. . . . Tell him that Ed Lung had the most novel, the most thrilling and the most hair-raising ride of his entire life!"

(Later, when I met Archie McLean Hawks, Civil Engineer of the Chilkoot Tramway, and told him of my wild ride in the freight bucket, he said seriously, "Ed, I wouldn't have ridden in one of those buckets for a thousand dollars! And I can't understand how they ever let you on. It was against all regulations!")

The tramway company helped me get through the Canadian customs in double-quick time and all I had to do was to pay a duty of $26.12 on my supplies. Then, at last, I was free to be on my way. But I didn't envy those customs officers their job on that high, stormy pass.

With a thrill, I realized I was now in Yukon territory again . . . just a little closer to my goal. In a few minutes, I had reached the other side of the summit and, in no time, had wrapped myself in a piece of canvas I carried for the purpose, sat down, and pushed myself off on the toboggan-like trail, headed down toward Crater Lake a half mile below. How glad I was that I was traveling light! Orr's freighters had promised to get my stuff to Lake Bennett the next day.

As I started down the steep mountain slope, which was almost like the side of a roof, I vividly recalled how Stacey and I had slid down here after dark behind our loaded sleds, belly-flop! Yes, we certainly had taken an awful chance. I could see the hazards in broad daylight!

Now I was picking up speed, sliding faster and faster. Crater Lake down there was getting bigger and nearer by the second. Suddenly, just ahead of me, two sleds collided and over and over they all rolled—sleds, dogs and men, tumbling, gathering momentum like a huge, kicking, cursing, yelping snowball! I dug my heels in the snow to slow up.

Luckily, they landed at a good spot in a soft snowbank near the edge of Crater Lake and were digging themselves out as I landed just a few feet away. Well, it was a mishap, but luckily for all of us no one was seriously hurt—just a few bruises, lost tempers and some broken equipment.

Down the trail the stampeders' procession went, crossing over the still-firm ice of Long Lake. Hundreds of feet and scores of sleds had passed this way recently. As I crossed, I remembered the precarious trek the year before—the rotten ice, and what a nerve-racking experience it had been! And how very plucky little Mrs. Ryan had proved to be!

Late that day, the stampede procession reached frozen Lake Linderman, where Stacey and I had built our boat the year before. Again I was surprised at the great number of people here. Hundreds were crowded along the lake, building their boats. Now, almost immediately, it was my immense good fortune to run into a group of Tacoma people encamped there. Among them were Brockenbough, a former real-estate man, and Mr. Leadbetter. There was also Mr. Myers, a brother-in-law of Sam Wall, the San Francisco newspaper reporter for the *Times,* whom I had met in Dawson during the famine.

Myers very cordially said, "Ed Lung, glad to see you! I see you're traveling light. You're welcome to camp with me tonight. In the morning, another fellow and I are going over to Lake Bennett through a narrow channel opening in the ice. We're going in an Indian canoe. It'll be a ride for you, Ed, if you want it. And, if we can find them, I'll introduce you to Mr. Lapham and his son from San Francisco. They're building a boat over there at Bennett, and, I hear, they want someone who knows the country to ride with them to Dawson to sort of act as guide. Why don't you see them? It would be a wonderful chance for you to get to Dawson in a hurry."

The next day, I wrote in my diary at Lake Bennett, after a rather harrowing canoe ride through ice floes down Lake Linderman and through the low, mile-long canyon to Bennett with Myers and his friend.

> May 26, 1898.
>
> Am camped next to Pickerel and Palmer. Hundreds of tents scattered in all directions. Must be 10,000 people here, and fully that many back at L. Linderman. Will be an awful jam when they all start for Dawson. Saw Ferguson. He came over Summer Trail. Paid 1c per lb. to have stuff taken to foot of Linderman and ¼ cent to have it hauled over portage to L. Bennett.

Next day I wrote again in my diary:

> Just got straightened around here. Stove works like a charm. Ice seems to be jammed about 10 miles below us. Hear two boats were lost with outfits and men drowned. Did not see Ferguson today.

While I was hunting along Lake Bennett for Lapham and his son, a fellow called, "Why, hello, Ed." I turned and recognized Ben Atwater, a packer and mail carrier with a loaded sled and dogs from Dawson. "It's a mighty good thing I ran into you. I've got a letter for you from Stacey." Atwater hunted through his pack, pulled out a letter and handed it to me. Eagerly, I ripped it open and read:

> Dear Ed:
>
> Since you left Dawson, my illness has taken a turn for the worse. Maybe I'll never see you again. But if I don't, I want you to know something for which I humbly ask your forgiveness.
>
> Last year when food was so scarce here at Dawson,

and after we split up, I couldn't find five pounds of precious dried prunes which I was sure I had. I was positive I had them among my supplies. Remember when we sorted everything over before going to the Eldorado? Well, it was right after that that I missed them.

I'm terribly sorry to say, Ed, I thought you had taken them, and I've held it against you all these months, though I should have known you'd never do a thing like that! Now, I've received a letter from my wife in Tacoma saying that the outfitting company there charged me for 5 lbs. of dried prunes which, by some mix-up, the clerk had neglected to put in with my order. They apologized and refunded the money.

Ed, old man, you'll never know how glad I was to have this cleared up! I hope you didn't notice my attitude, but I'm afraid I wasn't good at concealing it. I want to beg your forgiveness. It's a cussed land when 5 lbs. of prunes can stand between good friends like us! I know now we should have stuck together as partners. If we had, everything might have been different for both of us.

Always the very best for you, Ed.
Stacey.

Stunned, I read the message over several times with mixed feelings . . . shocked at its contents. A feeling of hurt pride jabbed me. Stacey had thought me a thief—a thief for 5 lbs. of prunes! So that accounted for his strange, peculiar manner towards me. Well, at last I was glad to know what had ailed him. But why would he think I would steal? Hadn't I worked for the restaurant in Dawson cutting wood? Hadn't I even eaten spoiled flour when I was out of grub during that awful famine?

But, good God, Stacey must have been in bad shape to have written such a letter. . . . Sounded like he didn't think he would live very long. But it couldn't be—he would recover! I must hurry as fast as possible to Dawson—see what I could do for Stacey and assure him all was O.K., certainly no hard feelings.

Then I would tell him quietly my secret: why I had

returned to the North. Yes, Stacey and I would be partners again; together we'd set out in search of the ancient channel of the Eldorado. You bet! That's what we'd do. We'd comb every inch of that hill above the Eldorado. And, as we had so often dreamed, maybe we would both be Klondike Kings!

Of course we would!

Chapter XXVI

The Amazing Bonanza and Eldorado

For over two anxious weeks now, ever since I had watched the ice go out at Lake Bennett with thousands of other stampeders and then had started down the Yukon with Lapham and son, acting as guide, one secret, dynamic thought gripped me: an ancient channel hidden high on a hill above the Eldorado, concealing great ledges of gold! I knew I hadn't a moment to lose—not with at least 10,000 men on the river and as many more back at the lakes feverishly building boats, and still others swarming over the passes, all headed for Dawson.

Now as we three men fought our way down the Yukon in the midst of the crazy-with-haste armada of stampeders, it seemed that that beckoning ancient channel continuously moved before me like a golden, shimmering mirage. Ah, yes! My hopes were very high, higher than they'd ever been. I certainly wasn't telling my traveling companions or anyone else of my stupendous secret. Only my wife and her mother back home knew why I was returning North with such high expectations.

Why, that hill at the Forks of the Bonanza and Eldorado could be richer than anything yet discovered! The more I thought of it, the more I dreamed of wealth, and I shivered with excitement and anticipation.

But, suddenly, I wondered how many thousands of fellows were already ahead of us in the Klondike, swarming over the country like gold-hungry wolves, fairly licking their lips for yellow nuggets. And, too, how about those hundreds of men who had remained in the North for the winter? The thought of all those caused me to break out in a cold sweat, made me send the boat scurrying swifter through the water, made me determined to travel late and be up early on the river.

Each hour as we progressed down the Yukon, I kept watching the shore line anxiously for familiar landmarks. Now, I estimated we had gone at least four-fifths of the way. I kept planning just what I'd do when I reached Dawson. I'd find good old Stacey and together we'd race up to the Forks of the Bonanza and Eldorado and search every inch of that hill . . . if it took all winter! If we hit a big, rich pay streak it would be time enough then to tip off our friends to stake. Yes, Stacey and I would be very rich men. We would be Klondike Kings! I was sure of it!

When I had enough gold, I'd rush "Outside" to my family and buy a fine home and all the other things they needed. Then, the hardships, uncertainties and my wife's tears would all be forgotten on that great day! Dear Velma! How she had sacrificed to make this second trip into the North possible. I must not fail her!

It was now July 11, 1898. I bent heavily on the oars and then glanced down at Joe and Al Lapham, at this particular time both taking naps in the bottom of the boat. Yes, they were the unskilled builders of this leaky, unseaworthy little craft in which we had nearly foundered a dozen times since we had started down the Yukon. Before reaching various danger points, which I knew so well, we had had to land, build a fire and stuff fresh oakum and hot pitch into the boat's spreading seams to save us from the swirling waters. But the place where we had our closest shave with death was back at frightening, raging, Miles Canyon, riding down in the flood of water and melting ice. It was there we had hit a big rock between the high canyon walls and stove a gaping hole in the bow of our boat. Only quick action, stuffing it with a sweater and bailing like mad, and the good Lord Himself had saved us from drowning. Between Mile's Canyon and White Horse, we had seen Lippy's scow smash into a rock and crack up in the rapids. Thousands of pounds of precious food were spilled out in the river. What a terrible loss to Dawson! Also, a few horses had been on that scow. Not only had we seen this tragic wreck, but we had encountered scores of others all along the way. Below Lake LaBarge, in dangerous, rapid-infested Thirty Mile River alone, we counted six boats smashed to pieces among the rocks.

Well, I flattered myself a little, that if I had not been along to take charge of the situation through Miles Canyon, White Horse Rapids and Thirty Mile River, Lapham and son might never have made it. They certainly were not cut out for this rugged, pioneer life. Quite helpless in emergencies they had made the trip doubly difficult. But now, I told myself consolingly, once at Dawson I would be free of my charges. However, until then, I was their guide. . . . They were the greenest of the green Cheechakos. I wondered what they would do when they would finally be on their own. It was every man for himself in the North! Of course, I would try to help them as much as possible.

Joe Lapham stirred, stretched and opened his eyes and asked in a plaintive, peevish voice, "Ed, where are we now? Confound it! Aren't we at Dawson yet?"

"No," I replied, "but I figure we should be there sometime tomorrow. Just passed the mouth of the Indian River."

"Well, we can't get to Dawson too soon to suit me!" said Joe impatiently.

"I'm just as anxious as you and maybe more so!" I said. "But, Joe, in spite of our boat, we've made very good time."

"I don't think I'm going to like this God-forsaken country!" said Al, Joe's nineteen-year-old son, who had also awakened and was watching the river sullenly. "It'll sure have to repay us with a lot of gold to make this trip worth while! Man, am I anxious to get back to San Francisco!"

"Ed," said Joe, "now that we're getting close to Dawson, we want to talk to you about mining. We don't want to waste time running off on wild-goose chases. Have heard the miners are awfully close-mouthed. Won't give new fellows like us tips where the stampedes are taking place. We're anxious to make a fortune quick and clear out of the North before the snow flies!"

"You want to make a fortune quick and get out before the snow flies!" I said in half-amused surprise. "It seems like a lot of Cheechakos expect to do that! Why, Joe, that only gives you about two and a half months. You wouldn't have time to go fifty or a hundred miles out from Dawson into unexplored territory and get anything and work it before winter. I know from being up there last summer. And, of course, you've heard that all the good ground near Dawson is already staked."

"Sure, we've heard," said Joe, "but we've thought we might get a 'lay' on some rich claim . . . maybe on the Bonanza or Eldorado. They say 'lay' men always get half the gold."

"Yes," I said, " but try to find a good 'lay' like that! They're scarcer than hens' teeth . . . nearly always given to friends or relatives of the owners."

"Well then, Ed, how about it? Have you got any good leads, or do you know anyone who has a claim in the Klondike we could work on a 'lay' basis? And, too, how about that claim of yours on the Bonanza you were telling us about? You know, we're kinda depending on you to help us, Ed."

"Well, don't depend on me," I said quickly. "I might have something good to offer you later—that is, if it pans out all right and, if you are still around," I added evasively, hesitating a little. "But, I can't promise you anything right now. I'll just have to see what happens. In the meantime, however, I'll give you a note to Captain Breeze, who has a rich share of Euly Gaisford's Number seven claim on the Bonanza, just below that rocky hillside claim of mine . . . which certainly is a millstone around my neck, I'm afraid. And, by the way, Lapham, if you do go on a stampede and stake a claim, remember it's a big gamble. And you'd better know right now that the Canadian laws are very strict. For instance, any main stream, like the Klondike River with its tributaries emptying into the Yukon, forms a division, or district, in which a miner can stake only one claim. My problem is, I'm stuck with that apparently worthless claim on the Bonanza. But I expect to get rid of it soon. In other words, if I don't renew my lease, I forfeit it, and then I'll be a free miner again . . . free to stake another claim in the same vicinity. That is," I laughed a little nervously, trying to hide my excitement, "if anything is available." As I said this, secretly I was thinking of that hill at the Forks not far from my claim, which seemed to be growing more dazzling and glittering the closer we approached the Klondike.

Lapham and son looked a little puzzled and bewildered, but I didn't try to explain it further because I would be giving my great secret away.

Lapham finally said, blinking his eyes a little, "But, Ed, we just want a 'lay.' Guess we'll strike right out for the Bonanza the minute we land and try to make every hour count before winter sets in."

"All right, fellows," I said, "let's press hard today! Every last stampeder who's ahead of us may alter our chances for the future! And one more thing," I added. "Before you start on that long hike to the gold fields, better check your boots. Be certain they fit and won't raise hell with your feet! Up here, it's one of the most important things in the world to have comfortable walking shoes. Your own two feet must take you wherever you go. I know this from bitter experience. Last summer my boots were loose and ill-fitting. I couldn't buy any in Dawson and, consequently, I wore bad sores on my feet, fell several times, sprained my ankle once, and, as a result, was laid up and lost many opportunities. Had to pass up exciting stampedes where I might have struck it rich. Yes, fellows, so you see . . . fortune or poverty can actually hinge on a fellow's boots!"

"Golly, you're right!" said Joe, "But, Ed, that's one thing we made certain of before we left San Francisco. Yes, we both have good boots!"

"Good boys," I said.

It was the next day, June 12, at 12:30, when our patched, queer-looking boat finally swung around the last bend of the Yukon . . . and there, at last, was Dawson on the right bank.

I gazed in amazement, hardly believing what I saw. Dawson had risen like a miracle from its ashes of the devastating fire of the winter before. It had enlarged and spread out like an overgrown, overfed pup. It stretched from the Moosehide Mountain at the north end of town to the mouth of the Klondike River, from the riverfront, to the near foothills. Now, it was almost a solid mass of cabins, shacks, tents, warehouses and stores. And it was almost the same story across the mouth of the Klondike at Louse Town, the dirty, grimy suburb of Dawson. They seemed to join muddy hands across the Klondike River, and both were teeming and surging with humanity. Tons and tons of supplies of all kinds were piled high along the Yukon and Klondike riverfront, and there were scores of miscellaneous crafts tied to the banks.

But truly most surprising of all were the five river steamers riding proudly at anchor in front of Dawson. I remembered how, the summer before during the famine, we had longed for the sight of these steamers. Well, here they were . . . a whole year late! It was evident they had just recently arrived. No doubt, among all of them, they had brought at least a thousand stampeders. (Two of these ships had been stalled all winter and spring at St. Michael; the others had been caught in the ice at various points along the Yukon. Yes, it had taken some of the stampeders over a year to reach the Klondike!) Certainly, it had been a very long wait to reach the land of gold! Small wonder why the majority chose to come over the passes and down the Yukon the way we had, in spite of the hazards.

"It's Dawson!" yelled Al excitedly. "We've made it, I tell you! We've made it! And we've got you to thank, Mr. Lung! Now, just direct us up the trail to Captain Breeze's and we'll be on our way."

"Say, it's sure good to see a little civilization again," said Joe. "Dawson looks like quite a city. Well, we'll see it all when we come back this way. But say, Ed, if you don't mind, maybe we'll dig around a little on your claim on the Bonanza. Who knows, we might strike gold."

"Well, you're surely welcome to try!" I laughed, "And if you do find gold, I'll be glad to give you a 'lay.'

"But, Great Scott!" I said, "judging from the looks of things, I'll bet there are between thirty thousand and forty thousand in Dawson right now! I'm anxious to know how it's affecting the gold fields. Man! I'm burning to get up there and see!"

In a matter of minutes, we pulled to the shore and landed at Louse Town. Yes, I had the terrific urge to go charging up the Bonanza with Lapham and son, but I restrained myself. I knew that if I could only catch my friends, Barr and Andy, in their cabin, I could quickly learn the mining news from them. Also, they could tell me where to find Stacey. It was a little over two months now since Stacey had written that very disconcerting letter. Well, in two months a lot could happen in a fellow's life. He could be in full strength again . . . might even be working his "lay" up on the Eldorado.

To think of it! Only about fifteen and a quarter miles yet to go! And then, that exciting hill at the Forks . . . and Fortune! I could hardly contain my excitement and eagernesss. But I was really glad I didn't have to hike these last miles in the company of Lapham and son. In their big hurry, temporarily, at least, they were taking themselves off my hands. I thought to myself as I watched them start up the valley trail, staggering under the unaccustomed load of their heavy packs, with picks and shovels dangling precariously, "Yes, if Stacey and I are successful in locating the ancient channel of the Eldorado, and if it should prove rich enough, we would be glad to let these Cheechakos in on it. For, after all, Stacey and I could not stake an entire hill!"

It was just about 1:00 P.M. when I knocked briskly at the cabin of Andy and Barr near the Klondike River.

"Well, well. I'll be damned! If it isn't Ed Lung!" exclaimed Andy in surprise as he flung open the door. "Come on in! Funny thing, a lot of us fellows were talking about you just the other day. Captain Tibbetts, Shelley Graves, and Bertram and some of the others of your Circle City crowd were back in Dawson. Canovan and Joaquin Miller were here the other night and asked about you, too. Joaquin Miller will be leaving by steamer, soon. You know, he was frozen in here all winter, and how it griped him!"

"I'd surely like to see Joaquin before he leaves. And it's mighty good to see you fellows again," I said.

"Say, for the love o' Mike," said Barr, coming over and shaking hands warmly, "sit down, Ed. You're just in time for lunch. We're having sourdough pancakes and coffee."

"Thanks, fellows," I said. "I'm in kind of a big hurry, but it sure sounds good. Just brought two new Cheechakos into the country, and I lost pounds doing it! They're on their way up the Bonanza right now."

"Well, let the green Cheechakos gape and gawk!" laughed Andy, slapping me on the back and handing me a steaming cup of hot coffee and a stack of golden-brown pancakes. "Just relax Ed. You've come a long way . . . and it must have been a tough trip!"

"It surely was," I said as I took a sip of the hot liquid and a big forkful of pancakes. Umm! How good they tasted! It took real sourdoughs, with lots of practice, to make mouth-melting pancakes like these! But even so, I couldn't hold back the eager questions tugging, trembling at my lips. But I forced my voice to be very matter-of-fact as I asked casually, "Say, fellows, have there been any new strikes lately? With these thousands of new stampeders swarming into the Klondike . . . naturally, I'm wondering."

"Great Scott! Haven't you heard?" exclaimed Andy incredulously.

"Heard what?" I asked, startled.

"Why, of the astonishing new discoveries."

"But how could I know?" I asked tensely, leaning forward, gulping hard.

Andy and Barr exchanged looks.

"Fellows, for the love of Mike! Tell me quick! Where are they?"

"Ed, weren't you the Cheechako the old-timers were laughing about and poking so much fun at for digging and looking for gold on a Bonanza hill last year?"

"Yes, I guess I am," I said. "And like a fool, I finally staked on the right limit, facing downstream, just above Captain Breeze's and Euly Gaisford's claim. But what of it?"

"Too bad, Ed. It's just too damned bad!" said Andy shaking his head.

"Why?" I asked, suddenly feeling cold and limp all over.

"Man, oh, man!" exclaimed Andy. "If you'd only crossed the Bonanza to the opposite side of the valley and driven those stakes high on Adam's Hill! By golly, Ed, you'd now be sitting pretty!"

"My God!" I cried. "On Adam's Hill!"

"Yes. In fact, Ed, if you'd staked on almost any one of those hills on the opposite side of the valley, you would be a rich man right now! By George! I'm telling you, those hills are just lousy with gold! There's coarse gold and nuggets and dust in unbelievable quantities everywhere, all over those hills. Why, it takes your breath away. And, mind you, it extends for several miles."

"Several miles!" I gasped in astonishment.

"Yes, sir, it just looks like rivers of gold had been poured out all over those hills! The experts say it's the most amazing discovery of the North. Just makes us sick. None of us ever dreamed of gold up there. Kept walking by those hills time after time . . . kept looking in the valleys. But it took green Cheechakos to stumble on it. And, damn it, Ed, it happened this spring while we were away on a wild-goose stampede. When we returned, by golly, the first thing we heard when we met some miners was the big news. They said everything was staked. Every blasted foot of it! Our only consolation was that we never would have had a chance anyway, because, as you know, we already own a claim on Bear Creek."

"Well, it just goes to show," said Barr, "even the old-timers were badly fooled when they poked fun at you and some of the others. Certainly, none of us were looking for gold on a hill. But there it was, just staring us in the face all the time. And we were all too dumb and too blind to see it! Do you remember how puzzled everyone was over the gold found on the side of Big Skookum Gulch?"

"Yes," I said as I began to slump low in my chair.

"Well, it should have told us something was mighty different and peculiar about that side of the valley then. Those nuggets from Big Skookum Gulch were very rough, showing they had not been washed far from a big Lode," said Barr almost with tears in his eyes.

"Yes," I muttered in a dead, shaky voice as I sagged lower in my chair, struggling hard to keep a poker face. "Yes, it certainly should have told us to look higher on the hills."

"Well, Ed," continued Andy, "this new Lode seems to run like a great chain of gold on a series of hills each one broken a little or separated from the other by a small gulch between. In other words, each hill stands as a separate unit, yet seems to belong to the whole. Now, there's Gold Hill! It stands right at the Forks of the Bonanza and Eldorado. Ed, they're getting four hundred dollars to five hundred dollars to the pan . . . and even more. It's the very richest."

"My God!" I groaned in agony with my head in my hands.

"And, yes," said Andy, "just above Gold Hill on the Eldorado is French Hill. It's plenty rich! Strangely, though, the big Lode is centered on Gold Hill at the Forks, and then it extends on down on the Bonanza Hill's left limit. Below Gold Hill there's Cheechako Hill. Below it is steep Adam's Hill opposite your claim, Ed. Then comes Magnet Hill, American Hill, Orifero, Monte Cristo, King Solomon, Boulder, Sherry . . . and, last of all, Sourdough Hill. The gold seems to peter out below Sourdough Hill, just about parallel with the valley claim Number Sixty-five. Ed, I'm telling you, the pay streak on those twelve hills is simply phenomenal! It runs on the sides and on the tops of those hills . . . and now it appears, in one or two cases, to run deep under the hills. Think of it! Why, they are making mining history that will astonish the world when the big news reaches the 'Outside'—which should be about now."

"Yeah," said Barr, "and now there's talk that these hills may be the lion's share of the Mother Lode, although some claim there could be part of it buried in the ridges beyond the Eldorado and Bonanza, maybe around King and Queen Domes. But just try to find it! Lately, there have been hundreds of fellows up there searching and digging like mad gophers, but none of them have yet discovered a bit of gold."

"But Gold Hill!" said Andy, "they predict that it will be the richest placer ground in the world!"

"Great Scott!" exclaimed Barr. "Ed, you've turned white as a sheet. Golly, you look kinda sick. Can't say as I blame you though. After all, you did come pretty close last summer!"

"Yes, mighty close!" I whispered, staring vacantly at my forgotten plate of cold pancakes and stagnant coffee and the greasy stains on the rough table. Suddenly, my world seemed to reel, collapse and come to an abrupt end. A great light of hope had flashed out. And I shivered as if the withering north wind had struck and blasted the core of my very existence. My whole inner being seemed trembling, disintegrating under the terrific blow.

"No, it can't be! It can't be!" my spirit cried bitterly as I steeled my voice and asked in tense, almost steady tones, "Tell me, who were the lucky ones?"

"Well, Ed, naturally, there's a babble of exciting stories, especially since gold was found on so many hills almost simultaneously. With hundreds of stampeders involved, and many vying for the honor of being the discoverers, well, it's bound to be mighty confusing. But you hear the name of Andy Nelson mentioned a lot in connection with King Solomon Hill. And then, there's a whole raft of Petersons, almost one on every hill! And, yes, a man named William Loomis figures prominently on Gold Hill. But I understand Nathan Kresge and his partner, Nels Peterson, are claiming the honor of discovering Gold Hill, because, after all, they were the first to find gold on the Skookum Gulch side of the hill.

"But to start the whole thing off it took three Swedes hauling wood and dragging logs down French Hill to tear up the moss enough so that 'Caribou Bill,' Bill Seating, who came along afterwards, could see nuggets exposed there on that hillside. When he saw those nuggets—wow! He staked a claim and high-tailed it to Dawson. Then the big news was out of the bag! You can imagine! There was a wild stampede. Newly arrived Cheechakos, old sourdoughs, and high-heeled dance-hall girls scurrying like mad for those hills."

"Yeah, it's true," said Andy. "Every one of the hills on the left limit was staked first. Then, there was a rush for your side of the valley, too. But, Ed, it appears it's mostly blank! Hard luck it had to run that way! But, that's fate for you!"

"But how do you explain it?" I asked with a sick voice.

"Well," said Barr, "if you want to know more about it, come over to Dawson with us to the Gold Commissioner's office. There we'll show you a sketch by Bielenberg, a young artist who was lucky enough to stake on Gold Hill. He shows how he thinks the country must have looked millions of years ago. It's amazing, Ed. Says at one time those particular hills on the left limit must have been an ancient channel of the Eldorado, or, possibly, of the Klondike River itself. Who knows? Bielenberg says the country was probably very different then . . . maybe a high, rather flat, plateau. He explains it this way: There must have been a great volcanic pressure which pushed up the riverbed into those high hills, and then, after millions of years more, they eroded to what we see today. He calls the Klondike area the Old Schistose Formation. That's why those hills are of such a peculiar, rounded shape. It's mighty interesting, Ed. When you see that drawing, you will understand more about it and why no one suspected gold on those hills. And, too, you will see why there isn't likely to be much gold on the hills of your side of the valley."

"Ah, yes!" I sighed, feeling like an old, old man. "Yes, sometime I'd like to see that sketch. But not now. I must try to find Stacey. Can you tell me where he is?"

Andy and Barr exchanged looks again.

"Well, Ed," said Andy slowly, "Stacey went over the Big Divide not long ago."

"Do you mean," I asked, not comprehending, "that he went over King or Queen Dome? I remember he always wanted to go over there prospecting."

"No, Ed," said Andy softly. "We mean Stacey passed away in April. He died at Saint Mary's Catholic Hospital here in Dawson. Had been very ill all winter and spring. Started out with malaria, then got pneumonia and, on top of that, typhoid fever!"

"Poor Stacey!" I said in a shocked, dazed stupor. "I knew he was ill, but I had hoped he would be well by now."

"Yes, for a time," said Andy, "Stacey actually seemed to be getting better. Then he took a bad turn for the worse. We fellows went to see him often and he surely appreciated it! Toward the last, of course, we were out of town, but they said he was delirious . . . didn't know anyone . . . kept calling for his wife and family. They said it was pathetic. And, yes, they said he mumbled something about you, Ed. And it was queer—something about dried prunes, of all things! Kept talking about five pounds of prunes every time he mentioned your name. Well, it was all very strange and jumbled. Poor Stacey certainly had a tough time . . . but his troubles are over now!"

"But he isn't the only one who has passed on since you left," said Barr sorrowfully. "Why, there have been a lot of fellows died of typhoid fever this spring. When the ice began to melt, the water from shallow privies seeped into our drinking water. That's why we were glad to leave Dawson. The little cemetery on the hill back of town is full of new graves! It was a hellish winter—near-starvation, freezing weather, and hard work! Then, this spring, the frightening epidemic! It's a wonder more of us didn't drop off!"

Andy's voice trailed on, giving the details of Stacey's funeral. It had been held in Pioneer Hall, as good as could be expected. Gold Commissioner Fawcett had given the obituary. Hymns had been sung by twelve miners and the Lord's Prayer said. A sled drawn by the best malemutes in town had hauled the pine casket to the cemetery on the hilltop back of Dawson. His grave was easily found—the new mound with the big wooden cross on the high spot overlooking Dawson.

"Poor Stacey!" I groaned. "It's hard to believe! I can't imagine him dead in the frozen ground. He was so strong—so full of zest for gold a year ago!"

"Aw, come on, Ed," said Barr with a hand on my shoulder, "don't take it so hard. We know you and Stacey were good friends and were once partners. We know, too, you missed the 'gold streak' on the Bonanza. And it's all pretty tough. But we sourdoughs have got to accept what comes—be fatalists. Some make it! Some don't! Some even die in the attempt!"

"Now, what do you say," Andy spoke in a lighter tone, "let's the three of us go over to Dawson—hit the town, forget everything! Let's buck fortune, be gay, play the roulette wheels and see the shows! They say there's a new one in town, a take-off on *Faust*. Ha! It ought to give us some laughs. Come on! Let's celebrate your return, Ed, and hope for better days!"

"Yeah, you bet!" said Andy. "Dawson's really on the map now. And boy! The food that's come in! Yes, you bet! And there are some new dance-hall queens in town, too. Some million-dollar babies! They sing and dance, and boy, can they turn your attention away from trouble! All the miners feast their eyes on them. And those who have 'em, throw nuggets at their feet . . . nuggets that'd knock your eyes out! I always say, it takes a woman to jar 'em loose! Come on, Ed, finish your lunch. Let's get started! There's going to be a hot time in the ol' town tonight!"

"No, men," I said, getting up wearily and going to the window and looking out. "No, thanks, you and Barr go

Dawson is in the rear, right. Louse Town is in the foreground.
The Klondike River separates them 1898

Rich mine owners sluicing pay dirt

Klondike Kate, actress and dance-hall queen, the toast of Dawson

ahead. Besides, I have no gold to throw away. I've got the boat to unload . . . and a cache to make. Then I want to look up several old friends, including Paul Hebb."

"Oh, sure," said Barr understandingly. "But you're welcome to stay here for several days, until you get your bearings. But how about going up to the Bonanza and Eldorado in the morning to see the exciting new diggings?"

"No, thanks," I said, "at least, not for a couple of days yet."

"Well, whatever you do, try to be on hand for the twenty-fourth of this month when the *Hamilton* leaves. You know, it'll be a big time when that boat pulls out. The whole town'll be there to see her off. Joaquin Miller and a lot of the fellows you know are going 'Outside.' "

After Barr and Andy had gone, I stayed alone in the cabin for some time. I was stunned over the sudden, tragic turn of events. Then, still in a somewhat dazed state, like a wounded thing I staggered down to the river.

Yes, I was too late . . . too late for that gold of the the ancient channel. And I was too late to help poor Stacey! What bitter irony! What ghastly ill-fate had dogged my every footstep! And what a dark star we had both been traveling under here in the Klondike!

I tried to unload the boat and unpack some of my things, but my hands refused to work. Poor Velma! How could I write and tell her that her sacrifice had all been in vain; that this second trip into the Klondike was for nothing! I sat on the edge of the boat, staring at the Yukon. I knew I wouldn't be able to write for some time. Somehow, this sorrow and bitter disappointment could not crystalize into expression. But I knew that, in spite of the sun shining brightly on the Yukon this day of June 12th, 1898, it would be one of the darkest days of my life!—a day I would want to forget . . . but could never. Yes, my spirits and hopes were crushed, I had hit rock bottom.

And, somehow, as I looked at the muddy Yukon, it seemed to swirl about my feet—ugly, leering and mocking. So did the high hills bordering the Yukon seem to mock me . . . seemed to lean back on their rocky heels and laugh tauntingly at poor fools like Stacey and me who had yearned and striven so desperately hard for that ever-illusive stuff—

gold! And now, Stacey was gone. And here was I, a tremendous fortune, unbelievable wealth almost within my grasp—but gone!

Chapter XXVII

Black Sand and Gold Hill

Several days later, as I walked up the valley of the Bonanza in the company of three men, Dr. Meizner, Zabrisky and a fellow named Cady, although I thought I had overcome the first awful shock and had steeled myself for the sight of the great discoveries, I grew more sick at heart with each step of the way as we came within view of the "hills of gold." I had dreamed only of one hill . . . and by heavens! there had proved to be a dozen. Nature had lavished her wealth here in this fabulous, double chain of gold! One in the valley—the other on the hills!

A new trail led up on that very rich side of the valley. Only a few weeks ago, it had been beaten into existence by thousands of excited feet. All kinds of little footpaths led up from it to the different new hill claims, and there were hundreds of new shafts and dumps and sluice boxes already appearing on the hills, and there were hundreds of men working like beavers, burrowing deep into the hills. The discordant, raspy sound of rockers grated and scratched the air, nearly driving a fellow crazy. And there were hundreds of new, bewildered-looking Cheechakos going up and down the valley looking frantically for gold. Up near American Hill, my genial companions left me and I went it alone from there.

About three hundred feet across the valley from my hillside claim, I stopped and, with a mixture of extreme sorrow and curiosity, surveyed Adam's Hill. Yes, as Andy and Barr had said, if I had only walked across the valley, climbed that hill, and set my stakes there. I could be sitting pretty now! As I turned and looked at my bleak hillside, in comparison, how could I know that, a few years after my lease would run out, two men would take it over and, after careful blasting, would discover a large pocket of nuggets worth over $60,000 concealed under the heavy rock ledge right under where I had dug so hard in '97, and again in '98, spurred on by the sight of gold on Adam's Hill and the others? Yes, it looked almost as if Nature had sealed that pocket of wealth away from me in her own rocky vault!

Now I looked back at Adam's Hill and was surprised to see a woman squatting near a fresh pile of dirt. Fascinated, I climbed the steep hill and watched her as she eagerly, with her bare hands, picked out and washed a whole teacupful of large, shiny nuggets in less than half an hour's time from her husband's fresh dump. Mr. and Mrs. Ferguson were the owners of this amazing piece of Adam's Hill. (It is interesting to note that Adam's Hill is the only one out of the twelve hills still being worked at the time of publishing.)

In talking to the Fergusons, I learned much that I had already heard about the discoveries. Then they mentioned having met Lapham and son, and how envious they had been of the hill-claim owners. Said they had not gotten in with Breeze, or anyone else; finally, had scratched around a little on my hillside claim for a day or two, then, in utter disgust, had thrown down their picks and shovels and started back to Dawson over the hill trail. I grinned a little as the Fergusons described Lapham and son, as I had predicted their reactions when I had learned of the situation up here.

Although my feet were aching and blistered from walking over the rough, uneven trail, I was determined to see all twelve of these fabulous hills. So I continued on up beyond Adam's, passing Cheechako Hill, where the small, half gulch known as "Little Skookum" scalloped back into the hill from the Bonanza Creek. Yes, this was the first spot where gold had been discovered in the Klondike, August 17, 1896. And although George Carmack, Skookum Jim and Tagish Charlie had thought they had the cream of the Bonanza claims, now they knew that enormous deposits of gold lay close to the surface on Cheechako Hill just up above them!

With dragging spirits and faltering footsteps, I approached the Grand Forks of the Bonanza and Eldorado, where Big Skookum Gulch cut in from the right. And I almost wept as I viewed that hill which had lured me all the way back into the North! Oh, why hadn't I immediately returned over the ice after talking to that old California miner? Or, if only . . . if only I could have stumbled and kicked up some of the moss the summer before when I climbed that hill. I might then have discovered some of the gold that lay hidden just under the surface! God help me! Never again would there be such an opportunity for me. The chance of a lifetime . . . gone!

"Say, Cheechako," a nearby miner said, "I've been a-watchin' you a-starin' up at that hill. It sure is a pretty sight, ain't it? Yep! A hill o' gold, it is! Prob'ly not another one like it in th' entire world. And d'ya know that one of the fellers got a thousand dollars to the pan jest th' other day? It's unheard of, I tell ya!"

"A thousand dollars to the pan!" I gasped.

"Yes, sir! Jest think of it! And pure gold, it was! And ya know, when they get goin' good with that tunnel Alex McDonald is puttin' under Gold Hill from the Eldorado side, it's hard tellin' how much gold they'll find. Maybe a huge vein . . . because they're now bringin' up buckets full o' the richest gold quartz I've ever seen!"

"The ancient channel!" I said bitterly. "Maybe, the Mother Lode."

"You're not kiddin', brother!" said the old-timer. "And look up there at French Hill. They say it was once prob'ly an ol' river bar. And the pay runs rich—at least, three hundred feet long by two hundred feet wide!"

I glanced wearily on up toward French Hill just beyond, the last one in the Chain of Gold. Well, as far as I was concerned, glittering Gold Hill and all the others, with their gleaming white sands and gray gravels exposed to view, were now just like heaps of black sand! I finally turned away, crossed the river at the forks and went slowly down my side of the valley toward Breeze's cabin. I knew I would be welcome there.

During the next two days, my spirits somewhat came back to normal under the warmth of comradeship. A sheltering cabin is a good place to meet friends. A lot of the fellows stopped by to see Euly Gaisford to tell him good-

Famous Gold Hill. A thousand dollars to the pan was not uncommon in 1898

Looking up the Bonanza toward Gold Hill and Big Skookum Gulch

Miners rocking gold on Gold Hill. Up the valley is the Eldorado

Arrival at Dawson of a Yukon River steamer from St. Michael at midnight in the summertime

bye, as he was leaving with a fortune for the "Outside," going out on the *Hamilton.* Yes, he was one of the lucky ones!

It was one grand reunion. Many of our mutual friends stopped by. Captain Tibbetts, Shelley Graves, Bertram and Calhoun of the Circle City crowd dropped in. Captain Tibbetts laughed ruefully when I asked him if he had made it to the "Outside" and back.

"No, Ed," he replied," just about the time I thought I'd start for the coast, the gold fever bit me hard; and just like we said in Circle City, again it was 'over the next . . . and the next range,' just like following a damn mirage! And that's what I've been doing all spring! Too bad, I didn't get in on one of those Bonanza hills. Too bad you didn't, either, Ed. Well, none of us have much to show for all our pains here in the Klondike! And I'm getting fed up with the way things are being run up here. It's been exasperating, this latest law which allowed all the fellows who staked on those hills two hundred and fifty feet parallel with the river and as high as the hills goes, if it doesn't exceed one thousand feet. It's an outrage! Look at the huge layout of rich pay dirt each man gets under such a law . . . and how many others it cuts out from staking! You can bet the miners who were left out are kicking plenty. But that's the law. Who knows what it'll be tomorrow? As you know, when the Big Skookum Gulch stampede was on last year, each miner could only stake one hundred by one hundred feet then. Yes, they're making it tougher all the time for us. Now you have to take out a license in order to stake . . . another damned trick of the Gold Commissioner's! The Dawson paper, *Klondike Nugget,* is full of bitter denunciation of Gold Commissioner Fawcett and Walsh, the slick attorney . . . and others.

"Why, it actually means you have to have a permit just to hunt for the blasted 'yellow streak'! It's like this, Ed, maybe you have a permit for one district; then you find yourself in another district and you want to stake. Then you have to traipse clear back to Dawson and wait for the district to be declared open and then stand in line for hours to get your permit. But it doesn't matter to the Gold Commissioner if you have to walk a hundred miles to get it!

Many times you find they've set a date to issue permits. You wait around . . . then get itchy feet and leave town; you come back on that particular date and find, to your disgust, that the time for issuing permits was set back in your absence. And, if there's a stampede in the making, this gives the friends of the officials the first opportunity! That's how they work it, Ed. I tell you, it's just getting to be a damn racket. The miners are up in arms. They've been holding meetings and protesting violently. Yes, they're making things too complicated and tough for us now. I'm completely fed up and I'm clearing out soon!"

"But say, Ed," broke in Calhoun, "George Hill was pretty lucky. Has a good claim over on Dominion Creek. A friend helped him get it. And would you believe it? Everything on Dominion is now staked, clear to the Indian River. Even the hills are staked, as much as they've been thrown open—that is, all of them that have been surveyed since the big spring stampede here. Yes, in fact, there's very little ground left to stake anywhere. But, man, oh, man! A fellow is lucky who has money to buy up claims of some of these departing miners, like Alex McDonald is doing . . . and a lot of others."

When Captain Breeze and I were alone, we climbed up to my hillside bench claim. "Well, Breeze, what do you think I should do with this blankety claim? Shall I forfeit it and let it go?"

"No," said Breeze, "what else could you find? Go up on Hunker, Gold Bottom, Too Much Gold, Bear Creek, All Gold, Quigly—any of them, and even along the small pups and gulches—everything is taken. Maybe they're not being worked yet, but they're staked. I'm afraid there're going to be an awful lot of disappointed stampeders! Now, after all, Ed, your bench claim is part of the great Bonanza. Last year you worked hard up there, and, with your permission, I let others try. And, yes, Lapham and son scratched around awhile. Look at all the holes! But, Ed, in spite of it all, I'd say hang onto it another year. The big syndicates are already beginning to comb the valley, trying to buy up claims. You might be able to sell it. In the meantime, put down as many shafts as you can and let anyone who wants

Gold pack train in front of the famous Green Tree dance hall and hotel in 1898.

Dawson in the winter of 1898. The gold camp grew that year until there were 40,000 people

Mathew K. Stacey
Stacey had been a policeman in Tacoma before he resigned and joined the stampeders, where he became Ed Lung's partner

Mastodon tusks from the frozen earth. Such tusks were found at Dominion and other creeks

to try, have a 'lay.' And of course, Ed, you're more than welcome to make my cabin your headquarters."

"Thanks, ol' man!" I said gratefully. "I'll take your advice, and, so help me, Moses! I'll plow up that ground to bedrock! And, too, I might try my luck buying a claim. Coming into the country with Lapham and son, I was able to save a little over a hundred dollars."

"Well, that's not much to buy a claim," said Breeze, "but, I believe there's a fellow wants to sell a bench claim up on Gay Hill, up above Number Thirty-Seven on the Eldorado. Of course, it's on the wrong side of the valley." He laughed. "Way up high—but try to buy it. You know, fellows have got to branch out in this game of chance. You might surprise everybody and hit gold!"

(As a leap ahead in my story, I did buy that claim on Gay Hill during the latter part of the summer of '98 and I worked it along with my Bonanza hillside. When I put the deed in my pocket, I said, "Well, here's a deed to Fortune . . . or nothing!" As it turned out later after a great deal of firing and melting of the frozen muck and sinking a number of shafts on Gay Hill, it was a deed to nothing! And I was a $100 poorer! It surely seemed that the Bonanza and Eldorado were not for me!)

June 24th, exactly twelve days after I had landed in Dawson, found me at the dock to say goodbye to Joaquin Miller and quite a crowd of others who I knew were leaving on the *Hamilton*. There were 250 on the passenger list. It seemed all Dawson was there to see them leave. Front Street was jammed with humanity. There was scarcely space for footing, but finally I located Joaquin and the others near the steamer.

"Ed Lung!" said Joaquin Miller, cordially shaking my hand. "Well, at last I'm leaving the North! Yes, I'm going back to civilization and into circulation again! I wouldn't take a million dollars for my experience of being 'frozen in' here for the winter. But, on the other hand, neither would I take a million dollars to stay another year! I must say, however, that being in the wilderness does help the qualities of the soul! I admire your pluck for coming back, Ed. You're not a quitter! Keep at it and I'm sure you'll be sitting on top of the heap! And, yes," he laughed as he patted his satchel, "I have a heap of manuscript to show for my time! I didn't stop writing!"

Many seasoned Klondike Kings and newly rich miners were leaving on this luxury river steamer. An aura of gold seemed to surround them. Their pockets bulged with heavy pokes. They looked important and had expansive, happy, satisfied smiles as they joked and jovially told their friends goodbye. Euly Gaisford, the Bonanza King, our little barber from Tacoma, was among them! Others with him whom I knew so well were: Bob Walker, Ed Simpson, Carter and Linc Davis.

Other little knots of men were jostled near the gangplank, waiting patiently and unobtrusively to board the steamer. They were going second-class, obviously men leaving the Klondike who were not so flush. Many had barely enough money to get home. I knew several of them. But one in particular, a fine fellow, was completely out of pocket money! And it had cost him a thousand dollars to get into the country! Yes, he had had very hard luck—was beaten, licked and in poor health. He said, "Ed, I'm so blue and down in the mouth, I could jump in the Bering Sea!"

"Oh, curse your luck if you must, but give 'em the 'glacier stare' when you get home and tell 'em you searched for gold from 'hell to breakfast'!" advised Bill McPhee with a friendly grin and a pat on the back in farewell.

After the departure of the *Hamilton,* I began slowly climbing the hill back of Dawson. My own morale was particularly low. Seeing the *Hamilton* leave, and so many of my friends going "Outside," had a depressing effect. Certainly, it seemed, I was no closer to fortune than I had ever been! In fact, it seemed I was miles further away. Never would I want to end up like that one poor fellow—a broken, disillusioned man, completely whipped by the North! And yet, here I was, chaining myself to that Bonanza hillside for another winter. Should I, after all, hop the next boat and get out of the country? But to what? I had no job or even the prospect of one in the present-day scheme of things back home. Hard times were still very acute back

The Lung family as photographed by a roving photographer in their cabin on Dominion Creek. *Left to right*: Ed Lung, Clemy, Velma D. Lung, and baby Ella (Lung Martinsen)

Early Dawson, Yukon Territory, when gold rush fever was at its peak

Two "Klondike Kings" exhibit king-sized nuggets

there. How well I knew it! A job was worth a great deal to a family man . . . and they were at a premium!

I got to the top of the hill and looked down on Dawson and the Yukon. Little puffs of smoke were still showing like faint clouds on the horizon to the north, where the *Hamilton* had disappeared around the Moosehide bend of the river. Watching, I felt a forlorn and overwhelming homesickness. In about three weeks, these men would reach the States.

Presently, I found myself by Stacey's grave. He would never leave this country—this 'cussed country' where five pounds of dried prunes could change the destiny of two partners' lives. But never again would good old Stacey have to worry about getting gold. His poor family, though —how I wished there was something I could do for them! I had learned that a small sack of gold from his "lay" on the Berry claim had been mailed out to them. But how long would that last? I should write Mrs. Stacey a letter.

Then I thought of Clemy and Velma. Suddenly, a great wave of fierce determination surged through me. I breathed deeply of the clear, exhilarating Yukon air. After all, this was a great country—a big country, surely full of opportunities yet. I decided that Nature does not easily yield her treasure to some . . . and it seemed I was one of them. Well, by heavens! Let it come harder for me if it must! I clenched my teeth, knotted my fists and resolved that never, never would I give up until the North, in some measure, had repaid me . . . and yielded a portion of her treasure!

"Ed, I've certainly been looking for you," called a familiar voice.

I turned and saw my friend, Paul Hebb, coming up the trail.

"Listen, Ed," said Hebb, "this fall I'll be going 'Outside' on business. I've got a claim on the Bonanza not far from your hillside. There's a good group of miners working it for me; but while I'm away, I want you to check over and keep account of the gold and see that it gets to the bank. Also, as you know, I'm mine appraiser for the Canadian Bank of Dawson. During the next few weeks, I'm going out to the different creeks for the bank and would like you to go along with me. It will be invaluable experience; also it won't be long until I'll need an assistant. You could earn several hundred a month. Now, for a family man, that's far better than trusting to fickle fortune. And another thing, Ed, in this kind of work, it won't hamper you too much. If you hear of a stampede some place, well, you might sandwich it in between jobs . . . and you can still work on that hillside claim of yours. Also, you'll hear of mines for sale through the bank. You know I do mining on the side, and other business. Well, how does this proposition sound to you?"

"Man! It sounds great!" I said with new hope.

"Well, then," said Hebb, "we'll head over toward Dominion Creek, pass Hunker, Gold Bottom and some of the others. We'll go down into the mines and I'll show you how to take samples of the pay dirt and estimate the approximate worth of the claims. Swiftwater Bill has a claim over on Dominion we'll visit."

"Dominion Creek!" I said enthusiastically. "You bet, I'll go with with! I've always wanted to see that part of the country. And Hebb, if I can get in with the bank as your assistant—why, man! it'll mean a lot to me!"

"Well, Ed, I can always promise you a job," said Hebb enthusiastically.

"Hebb, ol' man!" I said eagerly. "If things begin to open up for me here in the North, I could send for my wife and little son. Clemy would love it, and Velma might like it, too. Why, just yesterday, I saw Miss Anderson in Dawson. She's the daughter of the agent for John Wanamaker. Quite a few women of refinement are coming into the country now. It's rugged maybe, but some of them seem to like it . . . even those living out on the Bonanza and Eldorado in crude little cabins with their husbands. Yes, Hebb, now I know what to write to Velma."

"Fine!" said Hebb. "And do you know, Ed, they're blasting and preparing the roadbed for the White Pass Railroad? In another year, it will be less difficult for women and children to come into the country."

"Sounds wonderful!" I said with mounting enthusiasm. "Well, when do we start for Dominion?"

"In two days," said Hebb with a pleased look in his eyes.

"You'll have to get out your good walking boots, Ed. We'll be hiking maybe a hundred and twenty-five miles or more before we finish our trip! We'll go right over King Dome . . . and if we have a little extra time," he laughed, "we might dig around a little for that illusive fabulous Mother Lode. Everybody hunts for it, you know. But it's my personal opinion it'll never be found up there. I think Gold Hill is the big Lode!"

"Gold Hill!" I groaned. "Hebb, you'll never know the full signifiance that place has for me!"

"I think I can guess, ol' man," replied Paul Hebb with a warm, friendly hand on my shoulder. "But, Ed, you've just got to forget it!—And look to other sources for fortune."

"Yes, you're right!" I said thoughtfully, a little wistfully. "Perhaps Dame Fortune is, after all, beginning to smile on me in her own way. But, I confess, it is all turning out so differently from what I had ever dreamed or anticipated!"

"Life is that way," said Paul sympathetically.

As the two of us turned and started back down the trail to Dawson to prepare for the trip, I felt a warm friendship for Paul Hebb who, like an answer to prayer, had come just when I had needed him!

Already, my mind was eagerly beginning to form plans.

Yes, dear Velma and Clemy! We would have a cozy little log-cabin home of our own somewhere in the Klondike!

And this dream did come true! A year later, my wife and little son joined me in the Klondike.

The story of their lives together in the North has been told in a sequel titled Trail to North Star Gold, also published by Binford & Mort.

INDEX

6.50

TRAIL
to
NORTH STAR GOLD

Sequel to "Black Sand and Gold"

By Ella Lung Martinsen

It's a true Alaska-Klondike, gold-rush story in which the author recounts the exciting adventures of her parents, Edward B. Lung and Velma D. Lung and their rugged quest for gold while living in a primitive little log cabin on Dominion Creek, near Dawson, with their three children.

Dozens of famous and colorful characters come to life, including Soapy Smith, Alexander McDonald the Klondike King, Pat Galvin, Klondike Kate, Diamond Tooth Gertie, Swiftwater Bill, George Carmack, William Ogilvie, Joaquin Miller, Robert Service, and many others. Never before, in book form, have some of these dramatic, eye-witness stories been told.

Besides being an unusual saga of family adventure, *Trail to North Star Gold* is also a valuable historical document of those momer tous years when thousand of stampeders rushed nort as the first earth-shakin news of "Gold in the Klor dike" echoed around th globe.

When Ed Lung went nort in the 1897 Stampedes, h kept diaries, and later Velm D. Lung wrote memoirs These form the basis of *Tra to North Star Gold.* The gol fields of Alaska and th Klondike are described her in detail, including where th greatest quantities of th yellow metal were founc and the largest nuggets.

In *Trail to North Sta Gold* those who like tru adventure will live ove again the intriguing gol rush with all its excitemer and rugged pathos—and i so doing will also gain great deal of knowledge c the country and history c Alaska, "The Great Land, the land of the might Yukon!

It is certain that a grea gold-rush epic, like the on which began in 1897 afte George Carmack discovere gold on the Bonanza, wi never be repeated in all it wild, uninhibited action an color.